PRAISE FOR ROISIN MEAN̶

'Repeatedly and deservedly likened to Maeve Binchy,
she is a master of her craft and a gifted storyteller'
Irish Independent

'Highly engaging and heartwarming (...) I truly adored the book
and devoured it within a few short hours'
Melissa Hill

'Like chatting with a friend over a cup of tea ... this touching and
intricate story will give back as much as you put in'
Irish Mail on Sunday

'A warm, engaging read' *Woman's Way*

'Meaney weaves wonderful, feel-good tales of a consistently
high standard. And that standard rises with each book she writes'
Irish Examiner

'The plot will draw you in, and there is both laughter and tears along
the way. Meaney is an accomplished storyteller'
Books Ireland

'If you like Maeve Binchy, this will be a treat' *Stellar*

'It is always difficult to leave her characters behind'
Go Book Yourself

'(*Something in Common*) really blew me away ...
I would highly recommend this one'
Chicklit Club

Roisin Meaney was born in Listowel, County Kerry. She has lived in the US, Canada, Africa and Europe but is now based in Limerick city. She is the author of numerous bestselling novels, including *Love in the Making, One Summer* and *Something in Common,* and has also written several children's books, two of which have been published so far. On the first Saturday of each month, she tells stories to toddlers and their teddies in her local library.

Her motto is 'Have laptop, will travel', and she regularly packs her bags and relocates somewhere new in search of writing inspiration. She is also a fan of the random acts of kindness movement: 'they make me feel as good as the person on the receiving end'.

www.roisinmeaney.com
@roisinmeaney
www.facebook.com/roisinmeaney

ALSO BY ROISIN MEANEY

Two Fridays in April
After the Wedding
Something in Common
One Summer
The Things We Do For Love
Love in the Making
Half Seven on a Thursday
The People Next Door
The Last Week of May
Putting Out the Stars
The Daisy Picker

Children's Books
Don't Even Think About It
See If I Care

Roisin MEANEY

I'll be home for Christmas

HACHETTE
BOOKS
IRELAND

First published in Ireland in 2015 by
HACHETTE BOOKS IRELAND

1

Cataloguing in Publication Data is available from the British Library

ISBN 978 1 444 799620

Typeset in ArnoPro by Bookends Publishing Services.
Printed and bound in Great Britain by Clays Ltd, St Ives plc.

Hachette Books Ireland policy is to use papers that are natural, renewable
and recyclable products and made from wood grown in sustainable forests.
The logging and manufacturing processes are expected to conform to the
environmental regulations of the country of origin.

Hachette Books Ireland
8 Castlecourt Centre
Castleknock
Dublin 15, Ireland

A division of Hachette UK Ltd
Carmelite House, 50 Victoria Embankment, EC4Y 0DZ

www.hachette.ie

For Rose and Micheál Meaney, my two favourite parents

❄
Tuesday
22 December
❄

❋❋❋

They said it had to be Matilda. They wouldn't let her use Tilly. Nobody ever calls me Matilda, she said, but it made no difference.

It must be your official name, the woman with the shiny forehead in the passport office told her. Otherwise you run into all sorts of trouble.

What kind of trouble? Tilly asked – what was so bad about wanting to use the name everyone knew her by? – but the woman just shrugged and went on fanning herself with one of her leaflets.

Red tape, she said eventually when Tilly didn't go away, which made it no clearer. So Matilda Walker was what they put in her very first passport, beneath a small photo of a rather bewildered-looking Tilly.

Just as well her date of birth was there too: nobody would have believed she was seventeen in that photo. Just be natural, Lien had said, and don't smile, you're not allowed to smile, which suited Tilly fine – she couldn't remember when she'd last felt like smiling. Don't scowl like that either, Lien had added, you look like a terrorist – and while Tilly was doing her best to appear serene and composed and not at all threatening, the camera flashed and there she was, thirteen going on fourteen. Not nearly old enough to be travelling to Brisbane on her own, let alone Ireland.

That's quite a trek, Lien had said when Tilly told her. You'll be going literally halfway around the world. Lien had got her first passport when she was a few months old. She flew to China with her parents every January to visit the relatives who hadn't immigrated to Australia

3

with her grandparents in the 1950s. Like Tilly, Lien had been born in Australia, but they could hardly have looked more different.

Tilly was five foot eight inches tall; in her stockinged feet Lien barely made it to five foot. Tilly's skin was pale as blancmange, and sprinkled with small butterscotch-coloured freckles; Lien's was more clotted cream with a hint of hazelnut and not one single freckle, just a solitary dark mole a finger's width from the left side of her mouth.

Tilly's hair, the precise biscuity shade of Ma's shopping basket, waved and kinked its way down to the middle of her back, resisting every attempt to straighten it; Lien's glossy shoulder-length bob was the rich brown-black of a coffee bean, and impeccably behaved.

But it was the eyes that really set them apart. Tilly's were the bluish-green of an acacia leaf, slightly pink-rimmed along their almost horizontal lower edges and fringed all around with pale lashes; Lien's were bitter-chocolate lozenges set in dark-lashed creamy ovals, whose outer corners tilted deliciously upwards. Lien was exotic; Tilly was homespun.

You're more exotic than me, Lien insisted. Ireland is much further away than China. But Tilly wasn't talking distances – and even if she was, she didn't feel remotely Irish.

Up to six months ago all she'd known about Ireland was that it was famous for Guinness. She knew a lot of people with Irish connections, she had classmates whose parents had both been born there, but the country hadn't held any particular interest for her – why would it? – until she'd discovered her own connection with it.

Since June she'd been finding out more, like the fact that it was the third largest island in Europe, and it had a tomb that was older than the Pyramids, and the longest river in the British Isles, and that its currency was the euro. And that some parts of it – the Cliffs of Moher, the Giant's Causeway, the Killarney lakes – were considered pretty spectacular.

She also knew that it was going to take her roughly thirty-three hours to get to Ireland from Brisbane, via Singapore and London.

Well over a day and a half for her total journey, if you added in the three-hour bus trip from home to Brisbane airport, and however long it took – a couple of hours at least, she reckoned – to get from Kerry airport, her final touch-down, to the island of Roone, which was Ireland's most westerly point.

According to Google Maps, Roone had the wonky diamond shape of a stingray, and was all of seven miles long and four miles wide. Hard to get your head around a whole island being that small, when you lived on a landmass that covered well over three million square miles. Hard to imagine a place so tiny, when Pa's fifteen-thousand-acre farm wasn't considered particularly big by Australian standards.

And yet Roone had a year-round population of approximately three hundred, if the Internet was to be believed. She tried to imagine a whole community of people living in that minuscule place on the very edge of Europe, surrounded by the sea, locked in on all sides by water.

Tilly had been to the sea once in her life. It had happened seven years ago, when Lien's mother had piled a group of them into her station wagon and driven them to the coast for Lien's tenth birthday. The journey had taken forever – over three hours of straight-as-a-pin road, nothing to look at for most of it but miles and miles of flat scrubland, nothing to do but play endless rounds of I Spy and Twenty Questions – but the sight of the Pacific Ocean, when it finally opened up before them, instantly made up for the tedium of the trip.

The vastness of it, the rumbling music it made, its briny scent and myriad colours left Tilly speechless and spellbound as she stood on the shore stretching her stiff limbs and taking great gulps of the salty air. The wet sand, when she pulled off her sandals and ventured closer to the water's edge, sucked at her bare feet. The roll of each wave as it sped to the shore hypnotised her: each crashing, shattering climax, flinging spray onto her face, was a new marvel.

. She dipped in a foot: it was cool and wonderful. She looked out over the expanse of water, at the billions, the trillions of gallons that lay between her and the horizon. She thought of the huge ships that had been lost at sea, and the thousands of lives that had literally been swept away by tidal waves, and she felt as insignificant as a tick.

She imagined crossing the sea, sailing off in a boat and travelling across the miles and miles of water to America's west coast. She pictured a Californian girl of roughly her age, standing right at that moment on an American beach, looking out at the Pacific just like Tilly. Both of them with their eyes fixed on the same ocean, the same water. She stood ankle-deep in it, feeling the tug as it pulled away from her, waiting for it to come rushing back, swallowing her feet. She remained there until Lien's mother called her for the picnic.

Lying in bed that night she licked her arm and tasted salt. She closed her eyes and tried to remember the low, murmuring sound the ocean had made, the wet splash of its spray on her face. In the days that followed she was hungry to see it again. She pestered Ma and Pa to take her and Robbie, but Ma and Pa weren't the kind of people who drove for three hours to look at a lot of water. Anyway, Robbie was still a baby, not even one yet: the trip would have been wasted on him.

On a place the size of Roone, you'd be bound to hear the sea wherever you were. The smell of it would be in the air, day and night. It would cling to your clothes, seep into your dreams and flavour them. By day you'd round a bend in the road and there it would be, spread out before you like a carpet.

Ma and Pa didn't know she was flying to Ireland. There was an awful lot Ma and Pa didn't know, and an awful lot more Tilly had been praying they'd never find out. But they *had* found out. They'd been shocked and bewildered when the truth of what had happened, or a large part of it, had finally dumped itself at their door, and now she had to get away before they discovered the worst bit.

Bali, she'd told them. Nadia's folks have a house there, she'd said. They're spending Christmas in it and they've invited me to join them.

I think it would do me good to get away from here for a while. After everything, I mean.

Oh, she'd been despicable, playing on their sympathy. Lying to them again, knowing they still trusted her, despite everything, knowing they wouldn't check up to make sure her story was true. The blind, stupid faith they still had in her, even after she'd been exposed as a liar, and worse.

I can pay my own way, she'd told them, which was the only bit of her concoction that wasn't made up. She'd waitressed at Nadia's family's Indonesian restaurant in town all last summer, and when school had started again they'd kept her on for Friday and Saturday nights. She'd saved over two thousand dollars, enough for a return flight to Ireland with a small bit left over for pocket money.

Nadia was in Tilly's class at school. The two girls were friendly, but not nearly as friendly as Tilly had made it sound. Nowhere near as friendly as Tilly being invited to join the family for Christmas.

But it was a safe lie. The family *was* going to Bali: since the first week in December there had been a sign in the restaurant window telling everyone that it would be closed for ten days over the holiday period. Not that Ma and Pa would see it – they didn't believe in eating out: they were perfectly happy with Ma's beef pie or Pa's barbecued ribs – but on the off-chance that any of the neighbours noticed it, and then got chatting to Ma, Tilly's story would be backed up.

Bali was just about close enough, Bali she would get away with, particularly when she was footing the bill. Ireland, not a chance. No way would Ma and Pa be able to get their heads around Tilly travelling all the way to Ireland on her own, no way would they agree if she told them she wanted to go there. A short trip was one thing; halfway around the world was something else entirely.

But she was going. She'd bought her ticket, opting for the cheapest route she could find, and she'd got her passport and holiday visa. In five hours or thereabouts she would be stepping onto her first plane and travelling more than ten thousand miles, and ten hours back in time.

And the minute her cab pulled up outside, her journey would begin.

'Send a text message when you arrive. You be sure now.'

She turned from the window. Ma sat at the table, her face grey with exhaustion.

'You didn't have to get up,' Tilly told her. 'There was no need.'

It was three o'clock in the morning and pitch black outside, and the heat covered them like a wet blanket. Ma had gone to bed at half past nine like she always did, and presumably slept, and dragged herself awake to see Tilly off.

'I wanted to get up,' she said. 'First time for you to leave.'

Ma had never flown anywhere, or Pa. Never left Queensland, either of them, as far as Tilly knew. She looked at the worn, honest face that was so familiar to her, the faded flowery robe, the tightly coiled rollers in the brown hair sprinkled with white.

'You'll have a good time,' Ma went on. 'It'll be nice for you, with Nadia and her folks.'

She was forgiving Tilly. Every word offered absolution.

'No need to call,' she said, 'just a text message to say you got there in one piece is all.'

'OK.'

Strictly speaking, the mobile phone belonged to Pa. It had come as a free gift when he'd invested in the new harvester a few years back, but he'd never once gone near it, so they looked on it as Ma's. Most of the time it sat on the dresser – the idea of it being mobile seemed to have got overlooked somewhere along the line – but once in a blue moon Ma would use it to send Tilly as brief a text as she could get away with.

Get sugar, Tilly might read – and more often than not, there would be a half-full bag still in the cupboard when she got home. Ma seemed to think the phone would shrivel up and die if she didn't give it an airing every now and again. It would come in handy now though.

'My texts mightn't come through right away,' Tilly said. 'Don't worry if you're waiting a while. Sometimes that happens.'

The flight to Singapore took a little over eight hours, two hours longer than the one they thought she was getting to Bali. As soon as they touched down she'd text *Landed, all well.* She wouldn't say any more than that. It wouldn't be a lie if she didn't say any more than that.

'No need to reply,' she told Ma. With a ten-hour time difference, the less communication there was between them, the less chance of Tilly's deceit being discovered.

'I don't like you getting that bus in the middle of the night,' Ma said, not for the first time. 'Pa woulda drove you to the airport.'

'No need, the bus is fine.'

She'd told them Nadia's family had no room for her in their car, that they'd asked her to get the bus to the airport. If Pa drove her there he'd go in with her, and if he went in he'd see no Nadia and family waiting to meet her, and no flight to Bali at eight o'clock.

'Woulda drove you to the bus station, at least.'

'Taxi's fine, Ma.'

Just then she heard the double clunk of a car driving over the cattle grid, and seconds later there was her cab, pulling up outside. 'Well,' she said, reaching for the handle of her suitcase.

Ma's embrace was awkward, and over quickly. She'd never been a comfortable hugger. 'Look after yourself,' she said. 'Don't worry about us.'

They'd given her two hundred dollars. Pa had handed it over the day before. 'Tain't much, he'd said, but it'll help. The tightly folded notes smelt of tobacco, like him. The sight of them had caused a guilty dip in the pit of Tilly's stomach. They were giving her money, after what she'd done.

I don't need it, she'd told him, I have enough, but he pressed it into her palm and that was that. Two hundred dollars was around a hundred and fifty euro. She'd change it when she got to Ireland.

'Happy Christmas,' she said to Ma.

'We'll miss you now,' Ma said – but they wouldn't miss her, not really. They had their own children, who so far hadn't caused them anywhere near the trouble Tilly had.

She walked out to the car. The heat flung itself at her, it leapt in her mouth and caught in her throat. She hefted her case into the boot that the driver had popped open. She slid into the back seat and met his eyes in the rear-view mirror.

'OK,' she said, slamming the door, waving out at Ma.

Leaving all the bad stuff behind. Leaving it behind for good.

✳✳✳

It was halfway through the morning, three sleeps before Christmas. The day was damp and chilly, and had been pretty unremarkable so far. Gavin Connolly was making his way home in his small white van, having finished his Tuesday deliveries. He was trundling along the coast road that encircled Roone's twenty-eight square miles, lifting a hand to the walkers and cyclists and other motorists he encountered, as every driver did on the island.

As he drove, he hummed a tune he'd heard issuing from Maisie Kiely's radio just a few minutes earlier, the one about Mary having a little baby, all glory hallelujahs. Mary Somebody the singer was called too, English, he thought, the song washing over him as he'd handed over Maisie's usual order of seven good-sized potatoes, half a dozen carrots, three onions and two litres of apple juice, along with an extra request this week for parsnips and Brussels sprouts. 'I could set my clock by you,' Maisie said, the same thing she told him every Tuesday morning.

It was while he was passing by the second largest of the island's beaches that the day stopped being unremarkable. He glanced to his right and saw what he always saw at this time of year – grey sky, silver sea, wedge of shortbread-coloured sand with ribbons of seaweed in various shades of green and purple and brown strewn across it – but for the first time since coming to live on Roone he felt compelled to stop. No, more than that: he felt an almost overwhelming urge to get out of the van and make his way down to the beach and walk across it to the edge of the sea.

He stopped humming and pressed down on the brake pedal and tapered to a crawl. He travelled another fifty yards before pulling in by a little lane and turning off the engine. He sat in the silent van, contemplating the sea and trying to figure out why it had suddenly become irresistible to him.

It made no sense. Despite packing his bags in Dublin three years earlier and relocating to a small island on the other side of Ireland where he was surrounded by beaches, Gavin wasn't generally given to spending much time on them. To put it bluntly, he didn't much care for them, these strips of sand or pebbles, or a mix of both, that featured so prominently on Roone.

He wasn't what you'd call a swimmer. He knew how to do it, if thrashing about with arms and legs and managing not to sink could accurately be described as swimming – but he had no real interest in the exercise, and so far he had successfully evaded Nell Baker's offers to teach him properly.

To tell the truth, swimming had largely lost its appeal since he'd fallen into the sea while disembarking from lobster fisherman Willie Buckley's boat on his first trip to Roone as a holidaymaker, an incident he'd been anxious to put behind him as quickly as possible – not that Willie and his buddies were inclined to let him forget – but the memory of it insisted on returning to him on the infrequent occasions that he poked his big toe into salt water after that.

Of course, beaches were more than simply launching pads for a bout of swimming. At the height of a good summer, Roone's sandy borders were largely hidden under the oily limbs of reclining tourists, every one of whom seemed to be in search of the obligatory holiday tan – but, blessed as Gavin was with the pale, freckly complexion typically associated with the Irish native, lying in the sun for any length of time, whether slathered with factor 50 or not, was a practice he considered both unaccountably boring and vaguely dangerous. Besides, a tan was completely beyond his skin's capabilities, so he never bothered trying to acquire one.

Which left the option of a beach walk, barefoot or otherwise – but while he was an avid walker whenever he got the chance, Gavin's terrain of choice was a country road or lane where he could be sure of a relatively smooth surface underfoot, rather than a beach full of undulating rows of compacted sand, or pebbles that tended to collapse under each footfall.

All things considered, he tended to keep as much distance as he could between himself and the outer edges of Roone. Whenever Laura and the children were gathering buckets and spades for a day on the beach, Gavin made himself scarce. All the more reason, then, for him to sit in his stationary van on this particular December morning and wonder why he was feeling such a magnetic pull towards the sea.

And yet he couldn't truly claim to be altogether surprised. After three years of living full time on the island, he was familiar enough with Roone to know that things often happened there for which no logical explanation could be found.

Wasn't he harvesting apples from one of the trees in their orchard all year round, and wasn't their juice renowned throughout the island for curing insomnia and psoriasis – and, if Betty Geraghty was to be believed, corns too?

Wasn't there a sign that read *The Statue of Liberty 3,000 miles* stuck into the ground just beyond the cliff barriers and pointing towards America on the island's west side? Hadn't it been there for as long as Roone's oldest resident could remember, and nobody at all able to say who had erected it? Hadn't Kerry County Council taken it down more than once, only for it to reappear before the week was out, until they'd finally given up and left it there?

And hadn't Maisie Kiely read his wife's tea leaves last year and predicted Poppy's arrival, despite Laura's laughing protestation that two sets of twins were more than enough for any mother? A third girl, Maisie had insisted, peering into the depths of Laura's teacup, and so it had come to pass – along with the dreadful other development that Maisie hadn't foreseen, that none of them had seen coming.

But Roone was unique, no doubt about it – and, like the rest of its year-round residents, Gavin had become accustomed to, and had come to respect, the many whimsies of the island.

No breeze at all, the sea like a mirror this cold, calm morning, its surface sprinkled with the usual fishing trawlers, the last of the brightly coloured holiday craft having disappeared around the end of September. Little plashy harmless waves rolled onto the sandy shore, a hundred yards or so from where he was parked. If you wanted proper breakers you had to go to the far side of the island, where the Atlantic had full rein.

Nobody about at this hour, too early for the group of half a dozen over-sixties, the hardy souls (Maisie Kiely included) who walked the beach end to end each afternoon practically all year round, unless the weather was particularly shocking. And no sign this morning of seventy-something Con Maher, retired creamery worker, who peeled off his clothes and pulled on his ancient, bagging togs and raced into the sea for a three-minute dip every single day of the year. Con had probably been and gone by now.

Gavin wound down his window and took a few mouthfuls of the sharp, briny air – now that he *did* like, so wholesome and clean it tasted, far cry from what had been filling his lungs every day in Dublin. He closed the window and got out, banging the door shut behind him and leaving it unlocked as he ambled down the narrow lane that led to the beach.

He made his way to the water's edge, hopping over the long, curly swathes of seaweed, skirting the occasional salty puddles, leaving a series of damp prints in his wake. Only half listening – because by now it was so familiar – to the rattling suck of the sea as it drew away from him, the moment of anticipation as it paused, the rushed exhalation of its return. The elemental moon-directed never-ending movement of the tide, the background music of his past three years. Keeping to its routine, as reliable as Con Maher.

When he was within a yard of the water he stopped and dropped to a squat, puzzling again as to what impulse had led him there. It occurred to him that it might have been his own subconscious, not in any particular hurry to get home, wanting to delay it for a few minutes.

Such a tragic state of affairs, when up to a few months ago the home he'd created with Laura and their children was his favourite place in the world, the place he couldn't wait to get back to anytime he had to leave it. Now his overriding emotion each time he returned home was wariness: these days, it seemed he couldn't do or say anything right as soon as he set foot inside the place.

It wouldn't last, he kept telling himself. It would pass, this troubling time they were going through. It would pass, it would have to, and they'd be happy again.

A gull gave a sudden scream high above him: he lifted his gaze to follow its swoop across the sky, and a soft drizzle began to pat his face. First rain in over a week, if you could call it rain. He eyed the dark clouds moving in over the horizon, coming to replace the cauliflower-coloured sky that currently covered Roone. A storm on the way, according to Annie Byrnes's bones, far more accurate than the Met Office when it came to predicting the weather.

A bad one, Annie had said, here this side of Christmas. We'll be battening down the hatches, she'd told them. Hopefully it wouldn't be too bad, hopefully it would be over before Christmas as well. No sign of it yet, though, the clouds the first indication of more sinister weather, but Annie's bones were rarely wrong.

He glanced down to check his watch. Better not stay too long: Laura would be wanting her nap. He got to his feet, wondering what way he'd find her today, then catching the thought and flinging it from him, reminding himself of all she'd been through since March. Have patience, give her time.

He gave a final sweep of the beach – and there the small thing suddenly was, not half a dozen yards off to his right. Part in and part out of the water, each soft, incoming wave nudging it onto the sand, each pull back causing it to roll helplessly towards the sea again.

Here it was, the reason he'd been summoned: here was what he'd been sent to find. He knew it as surely as if someone had said it aloud.

The object was soft and floppy, no corners or angles to it. There seemed to be a broken quality about it, as if someone in a fit of rage had dashed it into the sea, wanting to put an end to it. In those first few seconds, while he was still far enough away for recognition to be uncertain, the sight of it gave Gavin a heart-flick of fright.

Everything about it – the shape and colour of it, the soggy bump of it onto the sand, the way it tumbled and rolled back – suggested to him a far more dreadful delivery from the sea than the usual offerings it threw up: driftwood, lengths of bleached bone, fragments of ragged clothing, rusted umbrella spines, remnants of burst footballs, battered rubbery flip-flops, skeletal kites, dented sun-cream bottles, tattered remains of lobster pots.

This was different. This was nothing like any of them. Gavin stepped cautiously towards the limp bundle, skin crawling with apprehension, wishing all at once that Laura was there with him – she was formidable in an emergency – but of course she was at home with the children. He looked to right and left again. He willed someone to appear but nobody did. He was completely on his own.

Up close, his fears were confirmed. No mistaking the lifeless little shape now, no chance he'd been wrong. It lay face down, small limbs splayed on the sand, out of reach finally of the receding tide. He crouched beside it, sick with dread. He forced himself to reach towards it, abdomen clenched, toes curling in their runners. He touched it: its cold clamminess made him shudder.

He turned it over.

It wasn't a baby.

Relief washed through him. He gave a grateful bark of a laugh. He picked up the sodden rag doll – the precise size of a newborn but, aside from its rubbery head, made of cloth after all. No skin or bone or blood here, no silenced little heart. Its painted mouth smiled up at him, undimmed by its time in the sea.

'Hello,' he said aloud. 'Fancy meeting you here.' Round pink cheeks, black strokes of lashes above the oval blue eyes, little brown dots of freckles dancing haphazardly across the snub nose. White hair standing up in stiff spikes. 'Thank God,' he told it. 'Thank God you're not what I thought you were.'

He squeezed it out as best he could. Salt water spilled from its padded limbs and squat little torso, from the pink knitted dress that was miraculously still in one piece. Couldn't have been that long in the water, a few days at the most, he reckoned. Fallen from a boat, maybe, or left forgotten on a rock and washed out to sea. And now washed back in again.

All the way home the doll bobbed and jumped damply from the rear-view mirror he'd draped it over. They mightn't fancy it, any of his girls – the twins had a pile of dolls already, and Poppy was practically joined at the hip to her rabbit – but he couldn't have left it there on the beach. If all else failed, they'd give it to Charlie.

He reached the house that he still thought of as Walter's, probably because they'd named it after him when they'd opened the B&B. Walter's Place, they'd called it, since everyone on Roone still referred to it as that. He turned into the driveway, whistling the tune that was back in his head. He parked in front of the shed and got out, bringing the doll with him. He walked around the side of the house and entered the way he always did, through the scullery and on into the kitchen.

His wife turned from the stove. She looked closed up, like she always did these days, and he yearned once again for the gregarious, big-hearted woman he'd fallen in love with. His two-year-old daughters, seated in front of bowls of banana chunks at the table, yelled, 'Daddy!' in perfect unison, like they did each time he reappeared, whether he'd been gone for two minutes or most of a day. Poppy, propped up with cushions in her playpen, flapped her fat little arms at him, crowing in delight. His daughters, at least, were pleased to see him.

He held the doll aloft. 'Look what I found,' he told them all.

'Where is she?' Laura asked.

He turned, waggled the doll at her. 'Right here. Found her on the beach.'

Laura gave him a scathing look. 'I'm not talking about *that*.'

It took him a second, two seconds. He lowered his arm slowly. The smile slid off his face.

'Blast,' he said.

He'd forgotten his mother.

❄❄❄

She slept on the plane, although she hadn't thought she would, so keyed up she'd felt as she'd boarded the steps and threaded her way down the narrow aisle to her window seat. When the plane had begun to move she'd been horribly fearful, not knowing what was ahead, what to expect. The sudden forward rush on the runway had her gripping the armrests – was that supposed to happen? The tilt as the plane left the ground made her squeeze her eyes closed, not daring to look out at a view gone topsy-turvy – but once they levelled off, once the cabin crew began to move around the aircraft, she forced herself to relax.

She kept her gaze fixed straight ahead, not inclined to engage with the man next to her. She had no book, and no appetite for the magazine that poked from the seat pocket in front of her. With her head so full of the trauma of the previous weeks and months, and the uncertainty of what lay ahead, reading was completely beyond her. Eventually, maybe an hour into the flight, she fell asleep.

When she woke, a stewardess was telling her to fasten her seatbelt for landing. She was stiff from the cramped space, and cold from the plane's air conditioning, which felt like it was on full blast. Goosebumps were rising on her bare arms, her toes curling in their thongs.

Her sweaters were all in her case, which was checked through to London. Her jacket was out of reach in the overhead compartment, along with her hand luggage. Easily known she was a novice traveller; probably plain as day to all the other passengers. She'd grin and bear it, and tell herself she was lucky to be out of the steam room that was Queensland in December.

The plane dipped and bucked as it descended, making her stomach lurch and her ears block unpleasantly. She shifted in the seat – why was there such little room? – and yawned the last of the sleep away as she made circles with her neck, trying to work the ache out of it.

Her eyes were still gritty with fatigue. She longed for a bed, or anywhere she could stretch out to ease her cramped muscles. Stupidly she hadn't even tried to sleep last night, thinking it hardly worth the effort when she had to be up before three in the morning. What had she been thinking, with so many travelling hours ahead?

Her heart sank at the thought of two more flights, the next nearly twice as long as this one. She reminded herself that each hour on a plane was taking her further away from Australia, further away from the man who had ripped her heart in two. She'd concentrate on that, focus on the gap between them that was widening more with each mile she travelled.

She risked a look through the window and saw skyscrapers huddled far below, hazy with smog. She thought of the passengers on the planes that had left Boston on a bright September morning in 2001. Did they know, had the hijackers told them, they were going to die, or did the horror bloom slowly as they approached New York, as they flew much too close to the twin towers of the World Trade Center?

She shuddered, trying to dislodge the thought, trying not to follow it through to its hideous conclusion.

'You OK?'

She started at the closeness of the voice, almost in her ear. She turned.

'Sorry,' he said. 'Didn't mean to give you a fright. Thought the turbulence might be bothering you.'

He was Pa's age, or maybe a bit older. Grey hair, a grizzle of white on his chin. Navy sweater, blue jeans. Face full of pores and crinkles, nose big and squashed-looking. They hadn't exchanged a word up to now.

'Soon be there,' he said. 'Ten minutes, fifteen the most. Always a bit bumpy on the way down, nothing to worry about.'

'My first flight,' she told him. Her mouth felt dry. She could have done with some water.

'Your ears popping?' he asked, and when she nodded he reached into the seat pocket in front of him and drew out a roll of mints.

'Suck it slowly,' he said. 'Keep swallowing.'

It helped a bit. The plane swooped sharply, causing a collective murmur of alarm that rippled through the cabin.

'Nothing to worry about,' her companion repeated, and she tried not to worry.

'What time is it?' she asked, to take her mind off the movements. 'In Singapore, I mean.'

'Two hours earlier than Australia,' he told her, and she sent the hands of her watch the wrong way around, back to just before two in the afternoon. It was as if they were being given a chance to live that couple of hours again. Imagine if she could turn back more time, if she could rewind the last seventeen years to the day when a woman in a Brisbane hospital had given birth to a baby she didn't want.

They hadn't told her, Ma and Pa. They'd waited until she'd asked.

We're doing a project on family trees, she said to Ma. Her twelfth birthday not long gone, year seven just begun in school. I need the names of everyone in our family, as far back as you can go.

The names, Ma said – and something different in her voice made Tilly glance up from her folder.

All the ones you can remember, she said – but instead of giving her an answer, Ma went to the door and called Pa in from the yard.

I need both sides of the family, Tilly told her, yours and Pa's. I can get his later.

Hold on, Ma said, in the same peculiar voice. Wait for Pa.

And when Pa came in, they told her together.

We really wanted you, Ma said.

We did, Pa said.

We were real happy when we got you.

That's true. Real happy.

You were a real good baby. Slept right through from three weeks, didn't she?

She did.

Hardly never cried. Only cried when you were hungry.

Tilly had tried to take it in. She wasn't their child. She didn't belong to them, she belonged to someone else. Everything shifted a little bit inside her. Everything shuffled around.

Was I called Tilly when you got me? she asked.

You were Matilda on your birth cert, Ma replied, but we reckoned you were much too small for that big name, so we changed it to Tilly.

And what happened to my real parents? she asked, but they couldn't tell her anything about them.

We got you from a place in Brisbane, Ma said. Never met your real folks.

What kind of a place?

An adoption agency.

You went all the way to Brisbane to get me? she asked. They never travelled: Pa didn't even like driving the seven miles into town.

He shook his head. A lady from the agency brung you to us on the train.

You were so tiny, Ma said. You weren't even one week old. I was scared I might let you fall, and you'd break.

She was, Pa said. Real scared. I remember.

We were so happy to get you, Ma repeated, because I was told I couldn't never have children of my own.

But Robbie is your own child, Tilly said. Robbie was three, and Tilly knew he was Ma's because she had seen Ma getting fat when he was growing inside her.

He is, Ma agreed, her face going soft. He's our little miracle. Ma had been forty-five when Robbie was born.

And two years after breaking the news of her adoption to Tilly, when Robbie was nearly five and Tilly was fourteen and Ma was three weeks off her fiftieth birthday and Pa was fifty-eight, they'd had another little miracle and called her Jemima.

They went looking for Tilly when they thought they couldn't have any of their own, and then they had two of their own.

I'm adopted, Tilly told her teacher. I don't know anything about my family tree – and the teacher just nodded and said Tilly could use her adopted family then, it didn't really matter.

But it did really matter, of course it really mattered – although it was to take Tilly four more years to do anything with this new knowledge.

'Here we go,' said the man in the next seat, and Tilly felt the bump of Singapore beneath her.

❄❄❄

'What I can't understand,' said Gladys, for the third time, 'is how you could possibly have forgotten me. It's not like I come to visit every day.'

'I'm really sorry,' Gavin said again.

The way he toadied to the woman. You'd think he was after abandoning her in a lion's den instead of keeping her waiting ten minutes on a pier.

'I mean, it's not as if you have a proper job. It would be different if you were in an office or someplace like that, and you had to be looking for time off to collect me.'

'Another bit of quiche, anyone?' Laura enquired, throwing her husband a look. Don't rise to it, the look said. Three days, the look said, and she'll be gone.

But as usual, he missed the look completely. 'I *have* a proper job, you know I have. I'm self-employed. I don't want an office job.'

His mother waved a dismissive hand. 'You know what I mean, Gavin, don't pretend you don't. I'm just saying you were out and about anyway in your little van. It's not as if Roone is so big you'd be miles away from the pier.'

'I wasn't—'

'Quiche?' Laura thrust the dish practically under her mother-in-law's nose. He forgot you for a few minutes: get over it. Much as you'd like to believe otherwise, the world doesn't revolve around you.

Gladys shook her head. 'No, thank you, dear. One slice was more than enough. I must pass on my quiche recipe to you: once you try the homemade one you won't go back.'

'Gladys, I have three children under three,' Laura replied, knuckles white against the dish. 'I don't have time to make quiche.'

'Oh, but really, it's the easiest thing in the world – and Gavin will tell you how good mine is. He loves it.'

They both turned towards Gavin, who wisely chose that moment to shove a large portion of shop-bought quiche into his mouth, preventing him from doing much more than aiming an apologetic smile in their general direction.

'Doesn't seem to mind that one either,' Laura remarked.

Gladys decided to change tack. 'Ben, do you think you could take that wooden spoon away from your sister, dear? I'm getting quite a headache from all that hammering.'

'I'm Seamus,' Seamus said. She was always mixing up the boys – deliberately, Laura was sure. Anyone could tell them apart if they looked properly. She reached into the playpen and eased the wooden spoon from her youngest child's grasp, causing Poppy to emit a stuttery squawk of protest. Good girl, she thought. Let rip; you might send Gladys out for a walk – but the traitorous child cast about and found Rabbity, and became distracted, in the inexplicable way of very small children, with his left ear.

It was only Gladys's third visit to Roone. The first had been sixteen months previously, for the wedding of her son to the mother of his twin daughters. She hadn't laid eyes on the girls – her only grandchildren – up to then, having turned down an invitation the summer before to attend their christening, and another to join the family on Roone for the Christmas that followed.

It's because we're not married, Gavin had admitted to Laura, who was secretly delighted not to have to put up with a woman who had disapproved of her from the day they'd met in Dublin.

Nothing had ever been said – Gladys was too clever for that – but she'd found plenty of other ways to make it quite plain that, as far as she was concerned, Laura was the scarlet woman who'd seen Gavin as an easy touch, who'd thought nothing of saddling him with another man's children. Laura was the merry widow who'd inveigled poor Gavin into moving across the country with her, far from his doting mother. Laura was the hussy who'd trapped him with more children, forcing him to put a ring on her finger.

Never mind that when Gavin and Laura met, he hadn't been a bit put out to hear that she came complete with two sons. On the contrary, Laura had got the impression that the twins were an added attraction. Aisling said she didn't want children, he'd told Laura, referring to his first wife, who hadn't lost any time getting pregnant with the man she'd abandoned her marriage for. Gavin had bonded almost instantly with Laura's boys, delighted with his ready-made family.

Never mind that once they'd decided to embark on a relationship, Gavin was the one who'd been pushing for the four of them to move from Dublin to Roone, the island where they'd taken separate holidays shortly before they met, the island they'd all grown to love.

Never mind that Gavin had proposed twice, and been turned down twice, before Laura decided she'd better make an honest man of him, now that he'd given her her second round of twins.

Ignore all that: Gladys didn't want to know; she believed what she wanted to believe. Laura gritted her teeth on each of the mercifully few occasions that they met, and did her best to overlook the thinly cloaked barbs, and the subtle but discernible criticism of everything from Laura's housekeeping – fair dues: a tidy home had never been a priority – to her parenting skills, which Laura considered above reproach.

Last December, Laura had sent Gavin to Dublin a week before Christmas to spend a few days with his mother. It was that or invite Gladys to Roone for Christmas again – and after coming to their wedding in September, there was a very real danger that this time she might accept. Her strategy worked and Gladys stayed put; but this year they weren't so lucky. In October Gladys announced that she would be paying them a Christmas visit, and what could they do but agree?

To Laura's great relief, it turned out that their visitor wouldn't be staying for the festivities on the twenty-fifth. I've been invited to a friend's for Christmas dinner, she told them, so I'll go home on Christmas Eve. I presume the ferry will still be running then?

They assured her that it would: Leo Considine, Roone's long-serving ferry operator, always worked a full day on the twenty-fourth to ensure that everyone got home for Christmas. Even if that hadn't been the case, Laura would happily have paid him double time to make a special trip. Come hell or high water, Gladys would be sent packing on Christmas Eve – and Laura had quietly invited a gathering of neighbours around to the house that same evening, in celebration of the event.

Who cared that she had a million and one things still to do? The artificial Christmas tree standing in the sitting room but as yet unadorned, not a single present wrapped, the cake she'd chanced making still without icing, the crackers not bought, the decorations not up. Who cared that the very thought of hosting a party made her weary? She *needed* a party, she'd find the energy, and it would be good to have a few friends around. It might take her mind off things for a while.

She rose from the table now and lifted Poppy from the playpen. 'Time for us ladies to have our naps,' she said. 'Gavin, you'll manage for an hour or so?'

'Course I will.'

'Gladys, don't dream of doing the washing-up: you're the visitor.'

'Of course I'll do it,' her mother-in-law replied, as Laura knew she would: any excuse to contradict her. It was a tiny victory: she found scant comfort in it. What did a few plates and cups matter, when everything else was such a shambles?

She took her leave of them, feeling the familiar heaviness in her legs as she trudged upstairs with her load. Would she ever feel normal again? Would she ever get back to where she'd been before the world as she knew it had been yanked off its axis last March?

Jack had said it would take time. He'd sat her down in his surgery and confirmed her fears as gently as he could. She'd gone to him in confidence, knowing that Gavin would be no help to her if the news was bad – he was hopeless in a crisis.

No B&B for you this year, Jack said. It'll be challenging enough for you to cope with everything else – everything else being one husband, four children, thirty-four hens, a donkey, a pot-bellied pig, two miniature goats and a dog, not to mention whatever treatment would be needed to make breast cancer go away.

Oh, and a fifth baby due in early August, the pregnancy she'd been pretty sure of officially confirmed by Jack on the same day. Some day that had been.

Predictably, Gavin cried when she went home and told him. Well, first he laughed.

I'm pregnant, she said – start with the good stuff – and he caught her up and spun her around, over the moon at the news. Thrilled at the prospect of becoming a father again. Born to be a dad, Gavin Connolly was.

One or two? he asked, and Laura told him just one this time.

There's more, she said then, seeing his happiness drain away as she told him the rest of it.

No, he said, his face collapsing. No, he repeated, his eyes filling and overflowing, his chin trembling. Not cancer, he said, gathering her towards him again, great heaving sobs making any more words impossible as he wept into her hair. Crying the way he always cried, as messily and unselfconsciously as a child, shaking and shuddering against her.

It's OK, she told him. We'll get through this. Offering what comfort she could, as if he was the one who'd been given the diagnosis. Of the two of them she'd always been the strong one: she was the one who'd survived when her first husband Aaron had taken his life a week before his twin boys were born. She'd cried a billion tears after him but she'd survived, and battling against the grief that attacked at every turn had made her stronger.

We'll cope, she told Gavin – because they had to cope. Leaving five children without a mother was simply not an option. But God, the thought of what lay ahead was terrifying.

A mastectomy, as soon as Jack could arrange it. Too late for a lumpectomy, he said, the swelling under her arm ignored by her for too long. Chemotherapy to follow, however much would be needed. Weeks, maybe months of treatment to be endured, running parallel with the usual ups and downs of pregnancy. The prospect appalled her beyond measure.

The surgery was done quickly, at least. Thanks to the premium health insurance policy her father paid for – on the insistence of her stepmother, Susan – Laura was on the road to Cork Hospital less than a fortnight after her diagnosis, a road that was to become wearyingly familiar to her.

According to her oncologist, the operation was a success. Looks like we got it all, he said, a big smile on his overfed face. I'm very pleased with your X-rays, he said, as if he expected her to pin a medal on him. She couldn't look at the mess they'd left behind, couldn't think about it without wanting to dig a hole and bury what was left of her in it.

Cop yourself on, she told herself, you're one of the lucky ones. Look at all those who don't come through it. Look at Francie Keating, dead last Christmas from a brain tumour, leaving three young children without a father. Count your blessings, stay strong. And for the sake of her four children, and the fifth that was waiting to be born, she did the best she could, but the effort almost killed her.

Thank God for her stepmother, Susan, who arrived from Dublin the day Laura came home from the hospital, bringing chocolates and perfume and books. She stayed with them for ten days, fielding visitors, baking Rice Krispie buns with the children, drinking green tea with Laura after everyone else was in bed.

You'll get through this, she said, the night before she returned to Dublin. Half past one in the morning, the house still and silent, the red coals in the fireplace their only light. You'll fight it and you'll win.

Not everyone wins, Laura replied. What if I don't? Susan the only person in the world she could have this conversation with: Gavin would crumble, Nell would probably cry too.

You will, Susan replied calmly. Of course you'll win, you're far too strong not to. Lots of people beat that bastard, and you'll be one of them. Her voice full of certainty, every word like balm.

You needn't think you're going to land me with five kids, she went on. Bad enough making me a grandmother at thirty without expecting me to raise them too – which brought the first smile to Laura's face in days. It was a watery, shaky effort, but it was a smile.

Of course there was no danger of Susan being landed with the children. They'd still have their father – who would surely pack them up and bring them straight to his mother in Dublin, and Laura couldn't bear the thought of them being raised by Gladys. But what could she do? Gavin was their father: the decision would be up to him.

Not that any decision would be needed, of course, because Laura was going nowhere.

When she left, Susan promised to come back as soon as the chemo started. I'm four hours away, she said, that's all.

Gladys had offered to come too, of course, when they'd broken the news to her. We don't need her, Laura told Gavin. We have plenty of help. Susan is coming.

I'll tell her that, he said – but Gladys was having none of it. She bided her time until Susan had left, and then descended on them, bringing with her a crocheted bed jacket two sizes too big for Laura, a stack of colouring books for the children and several loaves of her intimidatingly wholesome brown bread.

And to give the woman her due, she rose magnificently to the occasion. She took possession of the kitchen, rearranging shelves and restocking the fridge with her own preferences. She managed to get the children to eat porridge and brown bread for breakfast – it was only weeks later that Gavin confessed he'd bribed them into it – and for dinner she served up the dishes that the various women of Roone were dropping in each day.

In a whole week she managed to upset only one person, when she remarked to Ita Fennessy – within earshot of Gavin – that the laundry Ita was collecting and dropping back for Laura could do with a bit of conditioner in the final rinse. It makes the towels softer, she said, seeming oblivious to Ita's offended silence. The day she left, Laura served the remains of her bread to Caesar, who accepted it without complaint. Then again, pot-bellied pigs ate everything.

The chemotherapy was horribly sickening but she endured it, got through it, like she'd said she would. She pasted on a smile when the kids were around, and saved her rage and her tears for when they were out of earshot. Susan was a regular visitor, ferrying Laura to and from the hospital, tucking her into bed when they got home, keeping the children at bay until Laura felt human again.

In the middle of it all Poppy was born, blessedly healthy, protected by the placenta from the poison they were pumping into her mother – and finally, at the end of September, her second round of chemo came to an end and Laura was deemed well again.

But Lord, the fight had sucked every ounce of energy from her – she who had been ferociously energetic before. Now, even with her afternoon nap, she felt like a zombie most of the time. And was it really over? Had they really cut it all out? And even if they had, what was to stop it coming back? It had invaded her body once: what if it decided to pay another visit?

The fear was constantly with her. It sat in her head and tormented her. It polluted her dreams, waiting to ambush her the minute she woke.

Her marriage suffered. Maybe it was inevitable: maybe cancer challenged everyone's marriage. Her patience wore thin so quickly these days with Gavin: the characteristics she'd regarded as quirks – his DIY ineptitude, his financial cluelessness, his inability to say no to the children – irritated her now to the point of wanting to scream at him. She *did* scream, a few times, when the children were safely in bed.

She'd screamed at him only yesterday.

You're having an affair with Bernie Flannery, aren't you? I see you, I saw how you looked at her – and as ever, Gavin remained calm and refused to scream back, which only made her want to yank his head off his shoulders.

But she knew he wasn't having an affair, with pretty twenty-something Bernie Flannery or with anyone else. He wasn't the type to have an affair – he wouldn't know how. He'd be as hopeless at that as he was at everything else he attempted, except growing vegetables and looking after animals, and letting his precious mother make a fool of him.

Their sex life was a thing of the past. Laura hadn't let him near her since the surgery. She couldn't bear the thought of being touched in that way now. She turned her back on him in bed, and he made no attempt to initiate anything. Probably wasn't interested either – who'd want her the way she was now?

If Susan had noticed anything while she was around, she'd said nothing. It was a bad patch, Laura told herself. All marriages had them. People married for better or worse, and this was part of the worse. They got through the days, they went to bed at night. They were weathering the storm and presumably, like all storms, it would eventually pass.

Her parents' marriage hadn't weathered the storm it had gone through – but Laura wasn't her mother, and Gavin was nothing like her father. They'd do better: with five children, several animals and two businesses depending on them, they had to.

The main business had taken a back seat. The B&B had stayed closed, no guests at all this year. Their only sources of income had been what Gavin made on his side of things, and the donkey rides that went ahead as usual in the field beside the house from May to September. Money was tight – but this was Roone, and people were wonderful.

In the bedroom Laura laid Poppy on the bed. 'I'm still here,' she told her, pulling apart the fasteners of the miniature tangerine fleecy cardigan. 'I'm not going anywhere,' she said – she wasn't, she *wasn't* – easing off the navy T-shirt and sky-blue trousers, bending to press her face into the irresistible bowl of her daughter's stomach, planting kisses on the tiny chest, squeezing the pudgy knees.

'You're stuck with me,' she said, lifting each foot in turn to nuzzle the velvet-soft soles, inhaling the gorgeous scent of her, marvelling at the glorious *babiness* of the squirming little creature laid out before her.

She changed Poppy's nappy and got her into the pale blue pyjamas sprinkled with white butterflies that Nell Baker had given her last week. Nell showered the child with gifts, bringing something new practically every time she appeared from next door.

Over and above your duties, Laura protested. Godparents are supposed to make sure she says her prayers and makes her first communion, stuff like that – but the presents kept coming.

I'll be taking them all back when I have my girl, Nell promised. One boy so far for her, Tommy heading for his second birthday in February – and Nell making no secret of her desire to give him at least one sibling.

Laura settled Poppy in her cot with Rabbity, who'd begun life ten years earlier as a cradle companion for Ben and Seamus, cherished equally by both. She remembered them asleep side by side, each of them holding tight to a paw.

When her daughters had come along eight years later, they were flooded with toys from Roone residents, the only twins to be born on the island in years, and Rabbity had stayed put in the box of keepsakes that Laura had stored in the attic – but with Poppy's arrival something had made her produce him again, and he'd become her youngest child's furry companion of choice.

More than a little ragged around the edges by now – so many hugs and kisses and squeezes over the years, not to mention hundreds of visits to the washing machine – but cherished none the less by Poppy, who latched onto a long floppy ear now and stroked it dreamily with her thumb as she sucked on her soother and looked up unblinkingly at her mother.

'You have a new dolly,' Laura told her. 'Daddy found her on the beach.' A raggedy old thing: he should have left it alone, but with the children there to witness its arrival, Laura had felt duty bound to say nothing. 'We'll give her a bath and she'll be lovely. She can be Rabbity's friend.'

Parents didn't have favourites. Laura treasured each of her children, felt the same fierce, blind love for them all. She would unhesitatingly throw herself in front of a double-decker bus to save any one of them, would kill without thinking to defend them.

But Poppy. Ah, Poppy. Poppy was special.

It was because she'd had to compete with chemotherapy, even before she was born. It was because Laura had lived in terror that her baby would be harmed by it, despite her oncologist's assurance that she'd be protected. It was because Poppy wasn't a twin: she didn't have another half, like the other four did. Poppy had come to them all alone, unpaired, unmatched. Ben had Seamus, Evie had Marian, Poppy had nobody.

For whatever reason, Poppy had manoeuvred her way into prime position in Laura's heart. You're mine, she'd told her mother the first time they'd come face to face, and I'm yours – and there wasn't a thing Laura could do about it.

She stepped away from the cot and got out of her clothes, avoiding the mirror. No more undressing anywhere near a mirror, not any more. We can do a reconstruction, her oncologist had said. In a few months we can talk about it, when you feel ready – but however they patched her up, Laura didn't think she'd ever be able to look properly at her naked self again.

She'd lost weight. She was a size ten now, after years of struggling to fit into a fourteen. For the first time in her life she had the slender frame she'd envied on others, and all she wanted to do was swaddle it in baggy clothing so she could forget about what lay beneath. The irony of that.

It doesn't change how I feel about you, Gavin had said in the days after the surgery, before she'd driven him away. You're still beautiful, I love you, I always will – but Laura couldn't listen to it, she didn't want to hear it, and eventually he stopped saying it.

She pulled on the grey tracksuit that was waiting on her pillow, and it enfolded her like a mother's embrace. She slid into bed, her tired muscles surrendering gratefully. She tucked the duvet around her, relishing the feathery softness of it.

Within minutes, mother and daughter were asleep.

❄❄❄

'Pardon?' she said, for what felt like the hundredth time since she'd landed, everything needing to be repeated in this alien place called England, where English made no sense at all.

'Fancy anyfink wi' va'?' the woman behind the counter repeated. 'Piestry?'

Not a clue. It had to be English, in London's biggest airport, but it sounded as foreign to Tilly as Japanese. A fellow passenger had said something that sounded like a question as they'd stood next to one another at the baggage carousel, and even though she knew it was English – she recognised the occasional word – all Tilly could do was shake her head apologetically.

'Somefink else,' the saleslady said – did Tilly imagine the hint of impatience? 'A piestry, or anyfink?' Indicating finally the glass-topped display unit to her left, behind which various confections were displayed – slices of cake, round glazed buns studded with raisins, pinwheel Danish pastries.

Pastries. Piestries.

'Oh ... no thanks, just the juice.'

She handed over a ten-pound note, the fifty sterling pounds she'd bought in a bank in town last week already broken into with her purchase of a coach ticket to Stansted airport. A one-way coach ticket: no point in buying a return she might not use.

Everything was so uncertain, everything about this trip so tentative and faltering. She wished she could see what lay ahead, just far enough to know that it was going to be alright. But she had no crystal ball, no way of knowing the reception that awaited her on Roone.

She shoved her change into her jeans pocket and pulled her case behind her to the row of hard plastic seating that was set at right angles to the big plate-glass window overlooking the coach park. People sat or lay across the chairs, their luggage close by. She selected a seat at the end of the row and sank down, placing her bottle of apple juice on the low table that was welded to the floor in front of her and shoving her suitcase underneath. She drew her legs up and wrapped her arms around them, resting her chin on her knees. She took stock.

Here she was in Europe. Here she was in London, England. Home to Sherlock Holmes, and Jack the Ripper – and hadn't Harry Potter got his train to Hogwarts from a London station? She tried to remember anything else she knew about the city, but apart from Prince William's wedding, which she and Lien had stayed up to watch on TV, her fatigued mind refused to yield any more.

Heathrow was thronged this evening, everyone presumably going home for Christmas, wherever home was. Every nationality was here: she watched them tiredly as they swarmed past her. Men in turbans and skullcaps and cowboy hats, women in veils and burkas and saris and kimonos. Every colour skin, from whitest pale to golden to deepest blue-black. Long dark beards and ginger curls and burgundy streaks, earrings and nose rings, tattoos and orange robes. All human life seemed to be passing through, filling the air with countless different tongues.

But it wasn't just the languages that were foreign. Everything was an unknown quantity here, from the quality of the air to the poster ads for products she'd never heard of to the mostly unfamiliar shops she'd passed as she'd made her way through the terminal building, following signs for the coach park.

Good that the bulk of her journey was behind her now. She hadn't imagined that travelling, simply sitting on a plane or in an airport, could be so exhausting. It felt like an eternity since she'd climbed into the taxi outside her house, since she'd watched Ma's face in the window getting smaller as they'd pulled away.

She ran through what was left of her journey. A two-hour trip to Stansted, a ninety-minute flight to Kerry, a bus from the airport to the coast, and finally a ferry to Roone. With waiting times included, another ten or twelve hours.

She checked her watch, adjusted for the second time on landing at Heathrow. Just gone eleven o'clock in the evening here, which meant that she should be arriving on Roone, assuming there were no hitches, by noon tomorrow at the latest.

Nine o'clock the next morning in Queensland right now. Pa already out in the fields, Ma feeding the kids. Both of them expecting her home on New Year's Day.

She couldn't think about that now.

She took her phone from her bag and texted Ma for the second time. *All well, hope everything good at home.* It took a while to send. She watched the screen anxiously – what if it failed? What if she'd made a mistake with her roaming package, and it didn't apply in Europe? – but eventually it went off. Next text, with any luck, would be sent from Roone. Another vague message, telling them nothing. Telling them no lies.

She thought about sending a text to Lien, but they'd agreed not to, to save money. Store it all up, Lien had said, until you get back, and take loads of snaps – and Tilly had said nothing about the fact that she more than likely wouldn't be back, because not even Lien knew that. Not even Lien knew the worst bit. How would she ever explain it to her best friend? How could their friendship ever survive this?

She rubbed her face, yawning. She must look a mess, colourless and drawn, hair uncombed, teeth not brushed in what felt like a century. Her toothbrush was sitting in her toilet bag: she had only to open her case, but she hadn't the energy yet to find a bathroom. Grubby from no shower, crumpled clothes. Awful.

She hadn't slept at all on the second flight, hadn't managed to drift off in the eternity it had taken – thirteen hours, something like that – to get from Singapore to London. She'd watched three films, two of which she'd seen before and hadn't much liked first time round.

Despite not feeling in the least hungry she'd attempted to eat at least some of whatever was placed in front of her: chicken that sat in a pool of greyish sauce, along with overcooked chunks of carrot and a scoop of mashed potato; a plastic tub of watery pink yogurt; slices of rubbery bacon and a rock-hard fried egg, and something that she thought was probably supposed to be a sausage link but tasted a lot different.

The salad that had accompanied the chicken dish was probably the highlight: hard to go wrong with slices of tomato and cucumber, a scatter of olives and a few loops of onion.

Her seat companions on her second flight had been an extremely thin Asian woman who looked to be in her thirties, and two small silent children, no older than five or six, who were definitely siblings and possibly twins.

Hello, Tilly said to the little boy as he'd taken his seat beside her – and he immediately stuck his thumb into his mouth and looked straight ahead. His sister, seated next to him, stared accusingly at Tilly until the mother bent and whispered something, at which stage the child turned her attention to the doll she held in her lap, shooting occasional furtive glances in Tilly's direction until she eventually fell asleep.

The doll reminded Tilly of Betsy. What was it about childhood toys that wedged them in the mind, or in the heart, and made them so hard to forget? Must be nearly a decade since she'd laid eyes on Betsy, but she could still remember every detail of that doll – how she smelt, how she felt, the rough wool of the red dress Ma had knitted for her. She recalled how she'd search for Betsy if she woke in the dark after a bad dream, heart thudding – and how the simple act of pulling the soft little body close could comfort and reassure her.

She remembered all too well the real grief Betsy's loss had caused, the tears she'd shed over her. Ma had been sympathetic at first but had quickly lost patience. It's just a doll, she'd said – but of course it wasn't just a doll, it was Betsy. Left behind in a shopping-mall toilet, no sign of her when they'd returned half an hour later. Some other girl taking her to bed after that, Tilly's childhood friend gone forever. They'd replaced her – Ma had even knitted an identical dress – but it wasn't the same. It was nothing like the same.

She was so tired now, her body clock all mixed up, waves of weariness causing her eyelids to sink, making her limbs feel heavy as wet sand. She regarded the prone figures around her with envy, but she couldn't risk falling asleep. Her luggage might be stolen; she might miss her coach to Stansted.

She tried to read her book, but the lines kept blurring together on the page. And exhausted as she was, the mess she was in refused to go away. It sat stubbornly inside her, threatening to engulf her anytime she relaxed enough to allow it. She'd been so stupid, so innocent and gullible, so easily deceived. She'd trusted him completely – and now she was paying for her stupidity, and would go on paying indefinitely.

She shied away from thinking about the months ahead, each one sealing her fate a little more tightly. She tried not to dwell on the changes she would face, the utterly unknown territory into which she had already been thrown. How was she to cope?

She closed her book and packed it away, and turned her thoughts to more immediate matters. The next coach to Stansted was at half past twelve: hopefully she'd get a bit of sleep on that journey, and once she was landed she might manage to find a quiet spot – it had to be less busy than Heathrow – and relax there till her flight was called at five in the morning.

She opened her handbag again and did another check, constantly fearful that she'd mislay something vital. Passport, coach ticket, boarding pass, all there. Purse with Pa's two hundred dollars still folded up tightly, behind the euro she'd got in exchange for the last of her savings, in a bank where Pa didn't do his business, where nobody knew her.

You shouldn't bring all that cash with you, Lien had said. Use your ATM card as you go, it'll be safer – but Tilly hadn't listened, curious to see the foreign cash, physical evidence of her upcoming trip. The sterling notes were bigger than Australian dollars, and they bore the familiar face of the Queen with her tiara. There was no face on the euro notes, just bits of presumably famous European buildings.

She kept the bag tucked close to her side while she drank the apple juice, which seemed sweeter than at home. She wondered if her taste for coffee would come back. She used to love it, the stronger the better. Now she couldn't even bear the smell, particularly first thing in the morning.

It was raining now; she could see drops spattering the glass windows. Cold too, she was sure, judging by the muffled look of the people who scurried about the coach park outside, most of them pulling cases or wheeling loaded trolleys.

She had yet to experience the elements on this side of the world: they'd walked through a tunnel from the plane straight into the terminal building, which was pleasantly warm. But she'd checked the temperature in Ireland and the UK before she left, and found it to be currently hovering a few degrees above freezing: it rarely dipped anywhere near that in Queensland, even in the middle of winter.

She'd swapped her thongs for socks and boots as soon as she'd reclaimed her case, and put a sweater over her T-shirt. Might need another one beneath her jacket when it was time to move outside.

She'd often seen English winters depicted in films. She recalled snow-covered fields, thatch-roofed cottages with immaculate gardens, quaint little villages. No snow here, nothing remotely quaint about Heathrow airport this evening.

'Seat free?'

She looked up. A man – young, twenties – indicated the chair across the table from hers. She nodded and he sat, tumbling his rucksack onto the floor.

'Phew,' he said, pulling off a navy beanie hat to run a hand across his stubble-short brown hair. 'Hot in here.' He nodded at her case. 'You come a long way?'

His accent was different from what she'd heard so far – and, thankfully, easier to understand.

'Australia,' she told him, and he raised his eyebrows and whistled. 'Whereabouts?'

'Brisbane, in Queensland.' No point in naming her tiny town.

'First time in the UK?'

'Yes.'

'You must be wrecked. How long you been travelling?'

She had to think. 'Um … about a day, I think.'

'All alone?'

'Yes.'

He planted his feet on the table. Sand-coloured desert boots under blue jeans. 'Love to go to Oz some day,' he said. 'Got plenty of mates over there, but …' He shrugged, left the sentence unfinished. He leaned back, hands behind his head.

His jacket was dark brown with a tiny red, white and blue logo at the end of his upraised sleeve. He was sporty, she decided. A runner, or maybe he was into team games. She'd seen people playing cricket in English films, on lawns of impossible green.

'Where you headed?' he asked then, and she told him Ireland.

'Dublin?'

'No – west. Kerry.'

'Ah. Never been myself. Hear it's pretty wild.'

'Oh?' She wondered what kind of wild he meant, but he didn't elaborate.

A short silence fell. She hesitated, not wanting to be nosy – but he'd had no qualms about questioning her. 'Are you English?' she asked.

He grinned, the left side of his mouth travelling upwards, causing a dimple to form in his cheek. 'Would've thought that was obvious. I'm from a place called Bath where Jane Austen used to go on her holidays.' The skin around his brown eyes crinkled when he smiled. He was actually quite good-looking. 'I'm Mike,' he said, sticking out his hand.

'Tilly,' she told him. His hand was warm, his grasp firm. 'Short for Matilda,' she added, in answer to his questioning look.

Same crooked grin. 'Like waltzing Matilda.'

She smiled as if she'd never heard it before. 'Yes, like her.'

'And what do you do when you're not waltzing?'

'I'm still at school,' she said, instantly regretting it. She could have said anything, he'd never have known. She could have told him she was a writer, travelling for research.

'So what brings you to Ireland, all on your own?'

'Um ... visiting family. What do *you* do?'

'I work in IT, very soulless. In London, for my sins.'

She yawned, said *sorry* around it. 'I need to stay awake until I get on my coach.'

'You going to Stansted, then?'

'Yes.'

He took a roll of mints from his pocket and offered her some. He told her he was headed to Luton airport for a flight to Germany. 'Spending Christmas with my kid brother,' he said. 'He lives in Berlin, great city. Great nightlife.'

She was glad he'd sat near her. He was easy to talk to, and it was passing the time. She was glad of the mints too, in case her breath smelt a bit stale.

'Here,' he said then. 'What time's your coach?'

'Half twelve.'

He glanced at his watch. 'You got an hour. Why don't you stretch out, take a kip? I can watch your stuff, wake you on time. My bus doesn't leave till one.'

She hesitated. The thought of closing her eyes, even for a short while, was infinitely tempting – but she'd be entrusting her valuables to a stranger, however nice he seemed.

'Here,' he went on, standing to peel off his jacket, 'put this under your head, it's well padded.'

'Oh no, I couldn't—'

'Course you could. Why not?' He folded it into a cushion-sized square. 'I was just going to take it off – roasting in here. As long as you don't have nits, of course.'

She laughed. 'I don't think so.' He was hardly planning to rob her if he was offering his jacket as a pillow. She took it, feeling suddenly self-conscious at the thought of lying down in his presence.

He indicated her case, under the table. 'Why not pop your handbag on top of that? I'll make sure no one goes near it.'

She'd thought to keep the bag closer – hug it to her chest as she slept – but it seemed a bit rude not to do as he suggested, like admitting she didn't trust him. She laid it on the case and stretched out across the three chairs she had at her disposal. They were hard and not very comfortable, but the very act of lying down, of letting her muscles relax and surrender, was wonderful. And his jacket, still warm from his body, made an excellent pillow.

'Now,' he said, 'close your eyes. If you're not asleep in five minutes I may have to sing you a lullaby – and believe me, you don't want that.'

She closed her eyes, smiling. Almost immediately, she felt her surroundings begin to melt away.

She slept. And when she woke it was hours later, and she was full of pins and needles, and her coach was long gone.

And so was her companion.

And so was her handbag.

✳

WEDNESDAY
23 DECEMBER

✳

'**I**'ll go,' he mumbled – but before he could move Laura shoved back the duvet and slid from the bed, feeling around for her slippers. She wasn't totally helpless.

She lifted the wailing Poppy from her cot and left the room, shuffling swiftly past Gladys's bedroom door. Don't wake the dragon in her lair: don't earn another lecture on bringing up baby.

In the kitchen she plugged in the fan heater and switched on the kettle, her movements automatic even in her sluggish state. She paced the floor while they waited, drawing circles on Poppy's back and singing one of her songs. 'Gerry Giraffe forgot how to laugh,' she sang, 'till Bertie Bunny was awfully funny.'

She used to make up songs all the time for the boys when they were small. Not as small as Poppy: while they were babies she'd been no good to them, still torn up with grief after their father's death. It had been Susan, her stepmother, who'd rocked them to sleep and taken them out in their double buggy while Laura lay in a darkened bedroom or sat in a huddled, weeping mess on the couch. Wanting to die herself, praying for death so she could be with him again.

Susan, just ten years her senior, who'd weathered eighteen-year-old Laura's aloofness when she'd had the gall to marry Laura's father and become her stepmother. Susan, who'd turned into the best friend Laura could have wished for, who'd pulled her through the horror of bereavement. Susan, whom Laura treasured far more than the woman who'd given birth to her.

'Shush,' she whispered, pouring boiled water into the waiting bottle. 'Soon be ready now, nearly there.'

No more breastfeeding, no possibility while she'd been undergoing the chemo. Another loss, the miracle of a little mouth attaching itself to her breast, the small rhythmic tug as it took its sustenance from her. She hadn't breastfed the boys – she'd been in no state for that – but once she'd mastered the technique she'd delighted in it when the girls were born: she'd loved the whole Mother Nature feel of it. No more, not for her.

And worst of all, there was a much-diminished chance of her having more babies. It's not set in stone, was what the oncologist had said when she'd asked. Every woman is different, and it depends on several factors. Your age is on your side, of course, but we'll just have to wait and see.

What he didn't say was *Don't you have enough children already?* – but the question was there in the way he closed her file as he spoke, in the way his eyes darted to the pricy-looking watch that poked from beneath his designer shirt cuff.

And the funny thing was that Laura would have agreed with him – a family of five children was plenty big enough, particularly with the last three so close in age – until she was told she might not be able to have more. Now she wanted to fill the house with her babies. She wanted a football team of them.

She crossed to one of the windows, which was an empty black rectangle at this hour until you stood beside it and tilted your head upwards.

'Look,' she whispered, pointing. 'See all the stars, look.' Millions of them tonight, billions of them jostling for space in the bowl of the sky. She'd hardly seen a star until she moved out of Dublin, had never paid much attention to the night sky. Now, with the nearest street light half a mile away, the sky after dark was a fresh miracle each evening. It was a sight she never grew tired of.

And on this night it was particularly spectacular, hardly a cloud to be seen, the sting of frost in the air when she'd stuck her head outside before going to bed. Nice for the kids if they got snow for Christmas, but Nell, who'd been born and bred here, had told her that snow was pretty much unheard of on Roone. Last year it had rained solidly from Christmas Eve to New Year's Day.

When the milk was ready she fed Poppy on the bench beneath the window. 'The granny in the moon had a pink balloon,' she sang softly, as Poppy watched her mother's eyes and sucked placidly on a rubber teat instead of a nipple. 'She blew it up high and it floated in the sky, she held on tight and they flew through the night, the granny in the moon and her pink balloon.'

From where she sat she could see the Christmas cards, the dozen or so they'd got so far, piled in a tottery bundle on the dresser next to the bench. She'd had no time to do anything with them. Must get the boys to string them up, or stick them to the wall with dots of Blu-Tack, if they had any Blu-Tack.

She slid along the bench and took the top card off the bundle, delivered just yesterday. On the front was a painting of a robin perched on a skeletal branch of a snow-covered tree. Bird, branch, snow – just that, the simplest of compositions – but beautifully, perfectly conveyed. The glimpses of black beneath the blue-white dazzle of the snow, the startling flare of orange on the little bird's breast. Looking at the scene, you could almost smell the pure frozen air.

She turned to the back and read *Detail from Winter's Morning by Luke Potter. Reproduced with kind permission.* She opened the card and scanned again the words beneath the printed greeting. *Wishing the happiest of Christmases to our favourite family on Roone, from Luke and Susan.*

The message was in Susan's writing, like they always were. The line of kisses scattered below were Susan's, not Luke's.

Luke Potter, the famous artist. The household name who had always loved painting more than he loved his only child. Always Luke, never Dad, even when she'd been small.

In the three years since Laura and the others had moved to Roone, Susan had visited them several times. Luke had come once, for Laura's wedding to Gavin. He'd felt like a stranger to her as she'd walked up the aisle on his arm. He'd spent one night on the island and caught a morning ferry back, leaving Susan to stay on for another week.

'He is who he is,' Susan said, and that was pretty much all you could say about him.

Laura pulled another card from the pile. The front of this one featured a photo of a grinning fat baby wearing a white furry nappy and a Santa hat. 'Happy Christmas!' it shouted, in cheerful cartoon lettering that was the same red as the baby's hat.

And on the inside, in black pen: *Hope you're well. Love to all, Mother*. No kiss, no anything else. Laura's mother, whom she hadn't laid eyes on in seven years. Her mother, the highly strung opera singer, who'd stopped screaming at Laura's father a week after Laura's twelfth birthday, when she'd run off with her voice coach.

Love to all: that was a laugh. Her mother had never seen her three youngest grandchildren, had never once set foot on Roone. She'd met the boys on just two occasions, the last time when they were three years old. They wouldn't know her from Adam if they met her now, but she'd have no problem recognising them, thanks to the photos Laura sent each year of all her children. This is your family, the photos said. These are the children of your only child. Not giving her permission to forget them, not allowing her to ignore them.

Her mother didn't know about the cancer. Laura hadn't seen any good reason to tell her.

She regarded Poppy, still working on the bottle. 'Didn't do so well on the grandparents,' she murmured. 'One is gone, and two don't want to know. You're down to one, and I'm afraid she's Gladys.'

Walter, she often thought, would have made the perfect grandfather. Previous owner of this house, their neighbour when she and the boys had rented Nell's place on their first trip to Roone, dead over four years now. When she and Gavin had bought the house, several months after his death, she remembered walking through it and feeling sad that she'd never see him about the place again, digging in his vegetable garden or feeding his beloved chickens, or tending his beehives.

But he came back – or maybe he'd never left. The first time she became aware of him was on a sunny August afternoon, shortly after they'd taken possession of the house and moved in. Gav had gone with the boys to the village for ice-cream, leaving Laura by herself in the little orchard that lay to the side of the house. She was stretched out happily on the grass, bathed in dappled light and marvelling that they'd ended up living on the island she'd fallen in love with, still hardly able to believe that they could call it home now.

And then out of nowhere she'd felt a stirring, a subtle but definite displacement in the air around her. She sat up and looked about. There was nothing to be seen, nothing had changed – and yet she knew that she was no longer alone. And it came to her that Walter was there. She was quite certain it was him. And she felt no fear, not a bit. How could anyone be afraid of such a kindly old soul?

After that he turned up every now and again. She'd never see or hear him, but she always sensed when he was around; she'd feel his gentle presence close by. Looking after them, it felt like, making sure no harm came to them in the house he'd lived in all his life – or maybe making sure they didn't trash it. Either way, for whatever reason, he was there.

She said it to nobody; she saw no sign that any of the others had had a similar experience. It secretly delighted her, the thought that Walter had singled her out, chosen her as the one to come back to.

He was there two summers ago, when her twin girls decided to put in an early appearance. In the midst of the almighty panic – Dr Jack on holidays, the midwife otherwise engaged, Gavin in hospital having his appendix out, nobody around but Eve, the young girl who was helping in the B&B at the time, and one of the guests. In the throes of her contractions, as she'd roared and cursed, hardly able to see for pain, Laura had felt Walter's reassuring presence, had sensed his promise that all would be well, and it was.

He was gone now though; sometime during the past year she'd realised that he hadn't been around for several weeks. He'd drifted away quietly, leaving George, his little donkey, and a handful of the hens as their only living links to him. Maybe he was satisfied that they'd settled in and were a proper part of Roone now. Maybe he was happy that he'd left his house in good hands. Probably just as well he couldn't see the way things were now.

But she wished he was still around so she could talk to him about how far apart she and Gavin had become. He couldn't answer but he'd listen – she'd feel him listening. She couldn't confide in anyone here: Nell was the only one she felt close enough to talk to on that level, but Nell was as much Gavin's friend as she was Laura's; it wouldn't be fair to offload this on her. And she didn't want to worry Susan, who would surely worry if she knew.

The feed came to an end, the milky belches issuing soon after. Laura unplugged the fan heater and left the room. By the time they reached the bedroom Poppy was almost asleep again.

Four twenty-eight, the clock radio told her, as she shucked off her slippers and lay down. With any luck, at least four more hours of sleep. With a little more luck, another two or three hours after that before Gladys decided to get up.

Gavin stirred, turned towards her. 'Everything OK?' he murmured.

She didn't bother answering: he knew damn well that everything was patently *not* OK. She closed her eyes, listening to the rain as it began to pat gently against the windowpanes. No snow this Christmas, that was for sure.

※※※

Her name was Amanda. She was on duty at the airport police desk. She wore a navy trouser suit and a peaked cap, and hanging around her neck was a laminated card with her photo and name on it. She was built to the same generous scale – broad hips, big bust, heavy legs – as Tilly's maths teacher, Mrs Doherty.

'Could happen to a saint,' she said, when she heard Tilly's tearful account of the theft. 'You're not the first, sweetheart, and you won't be the last. Some right scumbags out there – and I'm afraid we get our fair share of them here at Heathrow. Plenty of exhausted travellers, easy pickings.'

Every word made Tilly feel worse. She'd been an idiot and she'd been had, like so many other idiots before her. He was a total stranger – but because he was good-looking and friendly, she'd trusted him. The second man to make a complete fool of her.

'He gave me this to use as a pillow,' she said, showing the policewoman the brown jacket, brushing away the tears that were still running down her face. 'I thought that meant he was OK.'

Amanda shook her head. 'He'll have lifted that from some other poor bugger earlier. They have all the tricks in the book, darling – and, believe you me, we've seen them all. I could tell you stories that'd make the hair stand on your head.'

She led Tilly and her suitcase behind the counter and into a room no bigger than an oversized cupboard. 'Wait here,' she said. 'I'll be right back.'

A tall grey steel filing cabinet took up most of the space in the little room. Tilly leaned her case against the wall and slumped onto it, miserable and exhausted. Kind as Amanda was being, it wasn't making her feel one iota better.

Her passport, her money, her phone, all gone. Everything gone, along with the ticket for the coach to Stansted and her boarding pass for the Kerry flight that was due to take off from there in – she checked her watch – ten minutes. All she had left was the sterling in her pocket. She counted it and got twenty-four pounds and fifty pence.

Her phone gone, and no possibility of replacing it – which meant she had no way of texting Ma now. How long would it be before she managed to contact them again? And how long would they wait before taking action? And what then?

A new and horrible thought occurred: what if Ma sent a text asking Tilly why they hadn't heard from her – and what if the man who now had the phone decided to respond with something vile? She'd heard of that happening, she'd read accounts of it on Facebook. She imagined Ma getting some kind of obscene message; she thought of her reading it in bewilderment, assuming it to have come from Tilly. The prospect of her being upset in that way was utterly appalling – as if Tilly hadn't caused them enough grief already.

She sank her head into her hands, thoroughly defeated. Lien had been right about the money: she shouldn't have got all those euro in advance. They were gone now, every one of them, along with Pa's dollars. Nothing to be done, everything ruined: serve her right for all the lies she'd told.

Serve her right for doing what she'd done with John Smith.

A fresh thought struck her: without a passport, she'd surely be put on the first plane back to Australia. The authorities would probably insist on contacting Ma and Pa to let them know: they'd discover her whereabouts through an unfamiliar voice on the phone. Pa would surely come and meet her at Brisbane airport, she'd have to confess everything to him and Ma, right before Christmas.

The whole thing was unbearable, it was unthinkable; it brought more tears that she didn't bother wiping away. They dropped onto her knees, causing big damp spatters on her jeans.

'Knock knock.'

She looked up.

'Here you go,' Amanda said, handing her a mug, ignoring the tears. 'Nothing like a cuppa to make things look a little brighter. Get that inside you, sweetheart, it'll do you good.'

Tea was the last thing Tilly wanted, but she sipped it obediently.

It was far too sweet and much too milky, but she was hardly in a position to complain.

'Now,' Amanda went on, leaning against the jamb, 'here's what's going to happen. First, we need to get you an emergency passport so you can continue your journey to Ireland. I'm afraid that means waiting until—'

'Excuse me.' A voice, a man's voice, coming from outside, accompanied by a quick rap on the counter. 'Hello? Anyone there?' Authority in the voice, as if he expected prompt attention. An edge of impatience in it, as if he wasn't normally kept waiting.

'Hang on a mo,' Amanda said, and disappeared.

Tilly felt a tiny hope flaring within her. She was being allowed to fly on. She was going to get to Ireland after all, even without a passport or a plane ticket. It might take a lot longer than she'd planned, and she'd be pretty much penniless when she arrived, but it sounded like she was still on her way to Ireland.

For the first time since she'd woken up and reached for the handbag that wasn't there, she felt her spirits lifting a fraction. Maybe all wasn't lost, not completely.

'Tilly? This wouldn't by any chance be yours, would it?'

'Oh—' She laid the tea aside, flooded with relief. 'Oh, yes, it's mine, it's my bag.' She accepted it eagerly, fumbled with the zip. 'Oh, where did you get it?'

'A gentleman found it shoved into a bin, just down the way. Purse missing, I expect.'

She rummaged quickly through the contents as Amanda looked on. 'Yes, my purse is gone ... but I think that's all.'

'Passport? Phone? Credit card?'

'Yes ... they're all here.'

She didn't have a credit card but the other two were there, along with her coach ticket and her boarding pass, her lipstick and her Kindle, her gum and pen and tissues and house key. All still there.

'Good, that's excellent. I'm so pleased for you, sweetheart.'

Tilly looked at her, blinking back new tears. Seemed she couldn't stop crying – but at least this time they were fairly happy ones. She was practically broke, but at least her other important stuff was back. 'Thank you,' she said. 'Thanks very much.'

The words were pitifully inadequate. She wanted to throw her arms around the woman who'd come to her rescue – but she thought she'd better not chance it. Embracing a uniformed member of the British police might well be frowned upon.

'You're very welcome, darling. That's what we're here for – wouldn't want you to think nobody cared in England. Now then, let's sort out the rest of your trip for you.'

In the end, the best she could do for Tilly was a flight to Dublin in the early afternoon – 'No direct flights from here to Kerry, I'm afraid' – and a standby ticket from Dublin to Kerry. 'We could send you to Stansted and put you on standby for a direct Kerry flight from there, but at this stage, so close to Christmas, I'd say it's too risky. At least this way you'll definitely get to Dublin.'

'That's great. I thought I was going to be sent back to Australia.'

'No – we could have got you fixed up with an emergency passport, but it's good we don't need to do that now. You'll probably have a bit of a wait in Dublin, might not even get to Kerry today – not much we can do about that. Can you contact whoever was meeting you, and explain what happened?'

'Yes, I can.' More lies – but it sounded too pathetic to say that nobody was meeting her.

'You sure? Like me to place a call here for you?'

'No, I can do it, thanks.'

Amanda gave her a form to show at the check-in desk in Dublin. 'And bring that Stansted coach ticket back to where you bought it. They'll refund you the price when you explain what happened. It'll give you a bit more cash to keep you going until you get to Kerry.'

'OK.' Twenty-two more pounds: better than nothing. Enough to get her to Roone, and she'd have to take her chances after that. Don't think about it now: just concentrate on getting there.

'And I can also give you this.' The policewoman pulled a slip from a bundle and handed it to Tilly. Food voucher, it said. Eight pounds, it said. 'That'll get you a light meal in any of the cafés while you're waiting – and if your flight to Dublin is delayed, come back to me and I'll issue you another.'

'Thank you.'

'Now, is there anything else?' She cocked a thumb at the brown jacket, still lying across the counter. 'You're welcome to that if you want it, doubt that anyone will come looking for it' – but Tilly shook her head. She never wanted to lay eyes on it again.

'Can't say I blame you.' Amanda bundled it up and pushed it underneath. 'I'll hang on to it then. Some poor sod who needs it will turn up.' She rested her arms on the counter and smiled at Tilly. 'Not too much longer to go now. Be good to finally get there, eh?'

'Yes, it will.'

'You said it was family you were visiting, didn't you, sweetheart?'

'Yes,' Tilly told her. 'My sister.'

Which was the only true bit.

❋❋❋

'All done, nice and tidy again.'

Nell held the mirror to the back of Laura's head. 'Thanks,' Laura said, 'that's lovely,' but it wasn't lovely, not really.

As far back as she could remember, she'd worn her hair long. She'd adored it, loved how it tumbled down her back when it was loose. Her crowning glory, silky to the touch, source of many a compliment. And the colour of it – a wonderful warm bronze that the sun lifted each summer to shades of paler gold and caramel. She'd never gone near a box of dye, hadn't needed to.

Her first husband Aaron would bury his face in it, grab handfuls of it. He'd wind it around his neck like a scarf, giving her no choice but to draw close – and Gavin, when he'd come along, loved it too. You're like a young one with that hair, he'd say, pulling out the clips at night, and Laura would slap him and tell him she *was* a young one.

And then five months ago, the poison that was killing her cancer had begun to kill her hair.

Not everyone on chemo loses it, the oncologist had said. You might be one of the lucky ones, you might get to keep it – but Laura didn't turn out to be one of the lucky ones.

Get rid of it, she'd ordered Nell as soon as it had started falling out, the very day after she'd pulled a brush through it and dislodged a sizeable clump. Unable to bear the thought of its slow decline, not wanting to risk coming away with another hank the next time she ran her hand through it.

Poor Nell, who'd been after Laura for ages to let her at it with the scissors. Just a few layers, she'd say. Take a bit of the weight out of it, that's all. I won't touch the length if you don't want – but until the chemo, Laura was having none of it. No layers, no change. Not even a trim, much to Nell's frustration.

But cutting it all off had never been part of Nell's plan. Cutting it all off was the last thing she wanted to do that day. Laura well remembered her stricken expression, her swimming eyes as she stood in her kitchen, scissors lying on the table beside her.

Come on, Laura said. You've been dying to get your hands on it.

Not like this. Look, I don't have to take it all off. I could do a nice short—

But Laura butted in and told her she wasn't interested in a nice short anything. She was going to lose it anyway, and it was the only bit of this horrible situation that she had full control over, so would Nell kindly get on with it.

So Nell wiped her eyes and took up the scissors and started to cut. The long hanks dropped with barely a whisper onto the kitchen floor as the two of them talked about the ankle Maisie Kiely had sprained coming out of the church after Sunday Mass, and Leo Considine's younger daughter Julie, who had just married a Frenchman, and Nell's father Denis, who was working as a volunteer in a refugee camp in Sudan, and anything else they could think of that had nothing in the world to do with hair.

And when Nell had taken away as much as she could with the scissors Laura said, Now finish it – and finishing it involved an electric razor buzzing its way softly all around her head. And when that was done Nell laid it down without a word, and no hand mirror was produced, so Laura got to her feet and walked into Nell's bathroom and looked at herself in the mirror there.

And after crying quietly for three minutes she washed her face and plastered a smile onto it and pulled a bright pink bandana splashed with green stars from her pocket, one of the ones Susan had brought from Dublin on her last visit, by special request. Get me something bright and fun, Laura had ordered, the possibility that her hair would go still just a possibility then, but she'd needed to be prepared.

The kids took the new look in their stride. The boys proclaimed it cool, and promptly forgot about it; the girls helped Laura to rub coconut oil into her scalp every morning. Gavin insisted it suited her. Takes years off you, he told her – the joke, or the lie, or whatever it was supposed to be, sounding pathetic to her.

Her thirtieth birthday in August had been pretty much a non-event: she'd warned Gavin against any kind of celebration, and thankfully he'd listened, and hadn't rounded up the usual suspects. Susan sent a package from Dublin – perfume, earrings, a cheque – and Nell got James to do a charcoal drawing of the children from one of Laura's favourite photos, but that was it. And in September, two weeks after her last chemo, her hair had started growing back, and this was its first trim since then.

It was coarser and darker this time round. It wasn't the hair she remembered; it felt like someone else's had been transplanted onto her head. More brown than bronze now, no more honey splashes. But it was back, and she was grateful. And sometimes, in some lights, she thought there might be auburn hints in it.

It could have been worse – it could have been much worse.

'So,' Nell said, untying the nylon cape and shaking it out, 'am I allowed to ask how you're coping with Gladys?'

'I'm surviving. She stayed in bed this morning till eleven, so we had great peace. I made her a poached egg when she came down, but it was a little harder than she was used to, God love her. And her own brown bread is far better for us than anything you can buy – I had to hide the sliced pan – so she's passing me on her recipe.'

'How thoughtful. You can get up early tomorrow and have it ready for her breakfast.'

'Tomorrow she can have buck's fizz for breakfast, as long as she goes home after it.'

'What time is she off?'

'The one o'clock ferry, if not sooner.' Laura got to her feet, picked up her bag. 'I left her decorating the tree. I said I knew she'd be far better at it than me. Wait till she sees the state of the decorations. She's roped in the kids to help her – can you imagine?'

'I'm sure it'll be lovely. We can all admire it tomorrow night.'

'Don't even say that out loud – if she heard I was having a party the minute she was gone she'd probably stay, just to spite me.' Laura found her purse and took out the tenner that was all Nell would ever accept. 'Tell me, how's Andy these days? I haven't seen him around much.'

Nell's smile faded. 'He's doing a bit better now – but he took it hard.'

'Of course he took it hard: break-ups always hurt. I remember the first boy who broke my heart. Conor Daly, we were both fourteen. I was nuts about him, but after a fortnight he told me his mother said he couldn't have a girlfriend until after the Junior Cert. Cried myself to sleep for ages, swore I'd never look at another boy. He was only making it up anyway: I saw him with Fidelma Sweeney a few days after.'

Nell hung the cape on its hook. 'This was different, though. Andy and Eve were together nearly two years. He was mad about her.'

'I know, it's a shame.' Laura retrieved her scarf and jacket. Andy was young, he'd get over it. 'Come on, let's call into Fitz's and flirt with your husband for fifteen minutes. I told Gavin I'd be an hour, and I'm damned if I'm going to show my face a second sooner.'

'Can't today, I'm afraid – Tommy was a bit chesty this morning, I told Jacinta I'd look in at lunchtime to check him out. You go in. James would love the company.'

They went downstairs together, the chatter from the bar drifting up to meet them. By the sound of it James had plenty of company – but Laura wasn't about to throw over a chance to avoid Gladys for a while longer.

'See you tomorrow night,' she said, pushing open the bar door. 'Eight o'clock, don't be late.'

'We'll be there.'

The place was warm, and more crowded than normal at lunchtime on a winter Wednesday. People getting into the Christmas spirit, only two days to go. She wished she could feel more festive. She was greeted: glasses were raised in her direction as she made her way to the counter. Roone's population being as small as it was, she and Gavin had encountered most, maybe all, of its inhabitants by now.

James glanced up from the glass he was filling as she approached. 'Look who it is.'

Months since she'd been into the bar – although of course they saw one another often as neighbours. 'Hey there,' she said. 'I thought I'd drop in and say hello.'

'Nell on the way?'

'No – she's gone home to check on your son. Chesty cough, apparently.'

'He's grand. She likes to fuss.'

'That's what mothers of sons are for.' She took possession of a high stool.

'What'll it be?'

'Good question.'

Her taste for wine was returning slowly: she hadn't been able to look at it, or any other alcohol, while chemo was ongoing. But she'd better not order it today – if Gladys got a whiff of it, Laura would be an alcoholic along with everything else.

'Tomato juice,' she said. 'Dash of Tabasco if you have it.'

He raised an eyebrow. 'How times have changed.' Sympathy in the tone: she got a lot of that these days.

'I have to behave,' she told him. 'I'm going home to Mother-in-law.'

'Ah.' He uncapped a tomato juice and decanted it. He set it before her, along with a little bottle of Tabasco. His first wife, whose name Laura had heard but couldn't recall, had died from cancer a year or so before he'd relocated with Andy to Roone. Some won the battle, some lost.

'Something to eat?' he asked, indicating the sandwiches behind the display counter.

'No thanks – lunch is waiting at home.'

Spaghetti hoops and potato waffles on today's menu; she could only imagine what Gladys would have to say about it. No matter: this time tomorrow they'd be waving her off.

'How're you doing?' James asked then, and she told him what she told everyone, which was that she was doing just fine. Nobody wanted to hear how tired she was all the time, how she lay awake and afraid for a long time most nights. Nobody wanted to know about her dysfunctional marriage.

A pair of women approached the counter. She watched James attend to them, remembering how she'd tried to seduce him four years earlier, when she and the boys were on their first visit to Roone.

She'd been on her own for six years by then, and widowed

bartender and artist James Baker, whom she'd met in this very bar, had seemed the perfect candidate for a holiday romance, or maybe a bit more. So she'd invited him over for a drink one evening, and she'd lit a few candles and put Billie Holiday into the CD player, and she'd treated him to a little striptease.

Nothing had come of it, though. One of the twins had woken up before things had had a chance to go any further: nothing like a six-year-old calling for his mother to ruin an atmosphere. James's heart wasn't in it anyway, what with him being in love with Nell at the time. Shame he hadn't thought to mention it to Laura.

And at the end of their fortnight on Roone Laura had returned to Dublin and met Gavin, and James ended up married to Nell, and everyone lived happily ever after.

Until now.

'You all set for Christmas?' He was back, holding another glass under the tap.

'Not a bit of it – still a thousand and one things to do, but hopefully they'll get done. Your mother is coming, isn't she?'

'She is, tomorrow. She has a thing in Dublin tonight.'

Laura had met Colette Baker a few times. At Nell and James's wedding, at Tommy's christening, on various other occasions. Widowed quite a while, well turned-out, younger-looking than her age, which Nell had confided to be late sixties. A full social life in Dublin, by all accounts. Book club, bridge club, you-name-it club.

Laura shook Tabasco into her glass and sipped. Tomato juice and green tea would never have been her beverages of choice, but these days she was all about the antioxidants, so she drank them by the gallon. The things she'd learned since getting cancer, the myriad ways it had changed her.

'No sign of the storm.'

She turned to see Willie Buckley, lobster fisherman, taking up his position on the neighbouring stool. 'What storm would that be, Willie?'

He caught James's eye and nodded for his usual. 'Big one coming, according to Annie Byrnes. Been telling everyone.'

'First I heard of it.'

No sign of any storm on the way today: cold enough for scarf and gloves, the grass white and stiff with frost this morning but calm and dry, not a puff of wind out there. Maybe Willie had called into Murray's pub up the street on his way to Fitz's. Wouldn't be the first time.

'How're the lobsters?' she asked him, and he grinned and told her they were nice and fat. Fifteen pots he put down each time he went out in the bay, sixteen waiting for him every now and again when he collected them – or so he claimed. With Willie, you could never be sure if it was true. On the other hand, this was Roone.

'You're well in yourself?' he asked, and she gave him the same response that James had got.

'Would you ever give us a bar of a song?' he enquired then. 'Something Christmassy?' So to keep him happy she obliged him with a softly sung 'Rudolph the Red-Nosed Reindeer' as the chat continued around them.

Willie had been here the night she'd come in with her guitar, during that same first fortnight, and entertained the whole place for a couple of hours. Nell's idea, after Laura had told her that she sang in her local pub in Dublin once a week.

Happy days. She couldn't remember the last occasion she'd picked up the guitar. Hard to find the time when you were raising five children and battling cancer. Hard to summon the enthusiasm when your marriage was imploding. Maybe she should dust it down for Christmas though, get the kids singing a few carols.

'You'll have another of those,' Willie said, nodding at her empty glass, but she shook her head.

'They'll have the guards out for me,' she told him, sliding off the stool, the familiar weariness coming to claim her as her feet met the floor. Lovely if there was a chauffeur waiting outside in a warm car to whisk her home, but all she had to cover the mile or so of coast road between here and Walter's Place Bed and Breakfast was a ten-year-old bicycle.

These days she rarely drove, although her car still sat at the side of the house, taken out every now and again by Gavin just to keep it running. After her operation she'd found driving a challenge – shifting the gear stick caused a dart of pain on her affected left side – and now she was out of the habit.

She lifted a hand in farewell to James, but he was busy with more orders and didn't see her. 'Happy Christmas,' she said to Willie. 'Make sure you get home before the storm.'

He winked at her. 'Happy Christmas to you, Laura – mind yourself now.'

Outside her breath fogged, the cold catching in her throat. Frost for sure again this evening, but at least it was dry. She pulled her gloves from her pockets and approached the bike, propped where she'd left it against the railing outside the pub. She was reaching for the handlebars when a car drew up beside her.

'Laura – sit in. I'll throw the bike in the back.'

Jim Barnes in his ancient dog-smelling Jeep, pulling behind him the battered trailer that carried sheep to and from the Dingle mart. She thanked him and climbed in while he deposited the bike in the trailer.

A far cry from a uniformed chauffeur behind the wheel of a nice fancy car, but every bit as welcome.

❄✳❄

They hadn't stopped singing since take-off. Every Christmas song Tilly had ever heard of, and quite a few she hadn't.

'What's that one?' she asked Siobhan, who sat beside her.

'It's called "The Fields of Athenry". It's got nothing to do with Christmas, but sooner or later every Irish singsong in the world features it. They sing it at rugby matches too – well, any game, really.'

'I like it.'

'Do you? Think it's a bit of a dirge myself.'

Siobhan was a primary teacher who'd failed to get a job in Ireland when she'd qualified two years earlier. 'Nobody I know got work,' she told Tilly. 'Teaching jobs are like gold dust in Ireland right now. So five of us went to London, and before the week was out we'd all got sorted. We're not teaching, though – Claire and I are in an Irish bar, Maria is a typist in a Japanese trading company, Denise is in a clothes shop and Caroline's a cocktail waitress.'

The friends were all sharing a two-bedroom flat in Kilburn. 'Our landlord thinks there's only three of us in it. We sleep on the couch in rotation, one week in five so it's not too bad. Only time it gets a bit awkward is when someone brings home a man, and then we have to adjust the arrangements a bit. But we all get on – we've been pals since school – and so far we've coped.'

Siobhan was heading home to Dublin for Christmas, and she was alone on the flight. 'Maria and Denise got away yesterday, and Caroline and Claire are working this evening so they have to wait till the morning. We're all meeting up tomorrow night for a session in town. It'll be great crack.'

In the half an hour or so since they'd met, Siobhan had hardly drawn a breath. 'Ireland is a nation of talkers,' she told Tilly. 'We love the sound of our own voices.' Tilly had heard all about her family, living in a part of Dublin that sounded Italian, but that Siobhan assured her had no connection with the Mediterranean country. 'Rialto is as Dublin as it gets – although we do love our pizzas!'

Her laugh was rich and infectious, her way of talking as musical as the voices that sang song after song on the crowded plane. There were quite a few words that Tilly didn't recognise – presumably crack didn't mean the same here as it did in Australia – and some phrases sounded oddly constructed, but thankfully Siobhan's accent was less indecipherable than some of those Tilly had encountered at Heathrow.

Everyone around them was talking or singing or laughing. Tilly wondered if the high spirits were down to the imminent arrival of Christmas, or if it had more to do with the drinks that were being dispensed by smiling hostesses from the trolley that seemed to have been making its non-stop way up and down the plane's aisle since the seatbelt sign had been switched off. Just past two o'clock in the afternoon, and the alcohol was flowing freely.

'Down the hatch,' Siobhan said, draining her second vodka and orange. 'We're a disgrace the way we love our booze – but it's nearly Christmas, and where's the harm?'

Tilly was only half listening, her mind on the challenge of the next few hours. Her coach-ticket money had been refunded, bringing her grand total to forty-six pounds and fifty pence – but shouldn't she hang on to the price of the coach ticket, in case she needed to buy another? Or maybe she'd live dangerously, convert the lot to euro when she landed in Dublin.

According to the Internet, the bus to the pier from Kerry airport was eleven euro with her student card, and the ferry to Roone was seven – eighteen euro to be taken from her precious stash. She resolved to spend nothing more on her journey and hope for the best. Maybe she could hitchhike to the pier and save on the bus fare: was it safe to get into a stranger's car in Ireland? She might take the chance.

Of course, that was assuming she made it to the pier in time for the ferry. She mightn't even make it to Kerry, might have to spend the night in Dublin airport, waiting on her last flight. This journey was becoming endless.

She'd waited as long as she could before using Amanda's food voucher in Heathrow. Eventually she'd spent it on a cheeseburger and fries, washed down with a soda – but she'd barely boarded the plane before she was struck with a raging thirst. She had to sit tight until after take-off, and the second the seatbelt sign was switched off she raced for the toilet – but she saw no signs about the water being safe to drink, so she suffered on until the trolley reached her, and then she broke her no-spend resolution and asked for a bottle of water. It cost one pound fifty, scandalously high when she converted it to Australian dollars – about three fifty! – but she simply had to have it.

She tried not to think about the fact that once she reached Roone, whenever that would be, there was no guarantee, none at all, that a sister she'd never laid eyes on, a sister who didn't even know of Tilly's existence, would want to have anything at all to do with her. What if she didn't? Or what if she simply wasn't there, what if she'd gone someplace else for Christmas? What then?

Tilly would have to find the Australian embassy, which was bound to be in Dublin. She'd have to somehow make her way back there and throw herself on their mercy – and of course all they would do was send her home.

But her sister, though. Her real true blood sister, same mother and same father. She wouldn't turn her away, she couldn't – even when Tilly confessed everything, even when she revealed the real reason for her arrival. She wouldn't turn her back on Tilly – would she?

As the singing continued around her, as Siobhan ordered another drink and talked about London's flea markets, Tilly felt overcome by a wave of fatigue.

So long since she'd slept, afraid to close her eyes in Heathrow after what had happened, moving like a zombie in and out of the airport shops, all the clocks seeming to have slowed to a crawl, until it was time to board this flight. How long had she been travelling now? She had no idea: her exhausted brain refused to come up with the answer.

'Want another?'

She stifled a yawn, dragged herself back. Siobhan was pointing to Tilly's empty water bottle. 'Or something else,' she said. 'Something stronger, for Christmas.'

'No thanks … Actually, I'm really tired. I think I'd better get some sleep.'

'Fire away, if you can sleep with this racket. I'll wake you when we land.'

She closed her eyes – but sleep didn't come. Instead she found herself wandering back to where all of this had begun, and reliving the circumstances that had led to her tracking down the woman who'd given birth to two daughters and abandoned them both.

It was the end of May, and Tilly's seventeenth birthday was still more than six months off, when she'd finally found the courage to broach the subject with Ma again, the one that had been occupying a small but definite space in her head for the previous four years.

I'd like to try to find her, she'd said. My mother, my birth mother.

It was a Saturday morning, and she was helping Ma with the washing-up, and Robbie was pushing Jemima around the yard on his old tricycle, and Pa was off checking on some of the livestock. And Tilly's heart was pattering scared inside her, for fear of how Ma might take it.

But Ma just nodded, lifting a cup from the water. Thought you might, was all she said. Let's have a sit-down.

So they sat down, the two of them, and Ma told her what they hadn't told her first time round. She told her about Diane Potter.

She's Irish, Ma said. Moved to Australia when she was carrying you. Rented an apartment next door to your pa's cousin, Austin. She and Jenny got friendly.

Jenny was Austin's wife. They lived in a small town north of Brisbane. Tilly had met the couple a few times over the years, not often enough to be able to recall either of them with any clarity. But she wasn't interested in Austin and Jenny now.

Told Jenny she was going to give up her baby, Ma continued. Told her she was going to find an agency. Jenny said she knew folks who might take the child. Knew me and Pa wanted one. Said she could do it direct, forget about an agency. So that's what happened.

Again Tilly felt everything shifting, everything taking on a new shape. Ma and Pa had got her direct from her mother. Why didn't you tell me, last time I asked?

Thought you were too young, Ma replied. We were going to tell you, honest we were, when we figured you were old enough – and Tilly had had to be content with that.

So it wasn't a proper adoption, she said – but Ma shook the question away with her hand.

It was as proper as it needed to be. We got your birth cert, just didn't fill in lots of fancy forms, that's all.

But my birth cert wouldn't have said Walker.

Naw, you were Potter on the cert – but we got that changed, soon as we could. Jenny's sister knew someone who could do it for us, all official. We didn't break any law, just took in a child that needed a home. You did alright with us, didn't you? Ma asked, a queer expression on her face, one Tilly hadn't seen on it before. It felt like she was daring Tilly to say no, so Tilly said yes, of course she'd done alright.

But it sounded complicated, and still not entirely credible. She decided to focus on the most important bit. Tell me about my mother, she said. You met her?

Ma shook her head. Never came face to face, just talked on the phone. Jenny brung you to us, when the time came. Your mother didn't want any more contact, we didn't hear from her again. At this point Ma hesitated. I could gather she wasn't all that strong, she said slowly, picking through her words. I could gather from Jenny she was … kinda frail.

Tilly didn't know which frail she meant. Frail could mean weak in body or in mind, two very different things. She turned over what Ma was telling her; she tried to see it from every side.

Jenny and Austin had met her mother, lots of times it sounded like. Jenny had been friendly with her. Tilly could have asked them about her when they'd visited, if she'd known. She felt a curl of anger against Ma and Pa. So much they could have told her, so much they'd kept from her.

You were too young when you asked last time, Ma said again, you were only a child. Tilly must have been wearing her thoughts on her face. We felt we should wait, Ma said, till you were a bit older. We did what was best, Tilly, what we thought was best for you. It was hard to know what to do, we had nobody to ask.

She might have been Matilda Potter. She might have grown up north of Brisbane. She might never have known Ma or Pa, never held Robbie or Jemima in her arms, never gone to the seaside with a girl called Lien. The life she had lived up to this would never have happened if Diane Potter had kept her.

What about my father? she asked. Hadn't he wanted her either?

Again Ma shook her head. I heard no talk of any man. Jenny didn't mention one, and we didn't ask. Seem to remember Jenny saying some woman lived with your mother, but I don't recall ever hearing a name.

Is there no father on my birth cert?

Here, Ma said, I'll show you – and she got the cert and there it was: *Diane Potter* in the mother's space and *unknown* in the father's. Tilly went through the possible reasons for not naming a father on a birth cert, and came up with nothing good.

Clipped to a corner of the cert was another form, with *Change of Name* written in thick black letters on the top and an awful lot of small writing underneath. Tilly skimmed it: *Potter* and *Walker* jumped out at her. It certainly looked boring enough to be official.

Is she still living in the same place – my mother, I mean?

Ma lifted a shoulder. Couldn't say. Jenny doesn't talk of her.

So she could have gone back to Ireland.

She may have, couldn't say.

Tilly sat back, her head spinning with this new information. Her mother had lived three hours away, right next door to Jenny and Austin. She might still be living there, after sixteen years.

Will you find out? she asked Ma. Will you ring Jenny and ask if she's still there?

For a minute Ma said nothing.

Please Ma, will you? Will you ring her?

Tilly, Ma said, are you sure you want to do this? Picking over her words again, like she was looking for diamonds in a jar of broken glass. Because even if she's still there …

She trailed off, and Tilly finished the sentence in her head: even if she's still there she might not want to see you. It was a chance she was willing to take. A chance she had to take.

You're still young, Ma said. You're only sixteen, you still got—

I'm sure, she said. I *am* sure. I want to find her. Will you ring Jenny?

Ma looked defeated. Tilly didn't care. They hadn't told her, and now it might be too late. Her mother might be dead. She'd never forgive them if her mother was dead.

The call was made that evening, after the two young ones had been put to bed. Tilly waited in the kitchen, passing the iron back and forth across Pa's Sunday shirt and trying not to feel too scared as she listened to the muffle of Ma's side of the conversation.

Don't get your hopes up, she told herself, going over the collar for the third time. At least you'll know, one way or the other.

The kitchen door opened, making her start. She'd missed the call ending.

Well, Ma said, she moved into Brisbane, few years back, but she left Jenny her address so they could send on her mail. Jenny's going to drop her a line, ask if she'll meet with you. That's the best she can do, since she's got no number for her.

So there was nothing for it but to wait until Jenny came back to them. In the days and weeks that followed, Tilly thought of little else. What did she look like, this woman who'd travelled all the way from Ireland while Tilly was forming inside her? Did Tilly have her eyes, her skin, her hair, her height? And why had she left her home in Ireland? What had driven her so far away, pregnant and alone?

Or maybe not alone: maybe she'd travelled with the woman Ma had mentioned. Two women, one of them pregnant, journeying across the world. The whole thing made little sense to Tilly. She would just have to wait, and hope to learn the truth eventually.

The phone rang one evening about three weeks later. Pa went to answer it, and came back looking for Ma. He didn't say who was on the line, but from the guarded look on his face Tilly knew immediately.

Is it Jenny? she asked, and he nodded yes, his face still full of caution. Tilly lowered her head and pretended to read the book that was open on her lap. Her eyes went back and forth across the words, just like she'd done with the iron on his shirt, until Ma reappeared.

She'll meet you, she said flatly, no preamble. In Brisbane, next Saturday.

A city-centre coffee shop was the venue. Tilly's mother would be there at half past two. She'll wear a blue coat, Ma said. She'll sit near a window.

It sounded like something out of a spy novel. Was Tilly going to get a password?

I'll come with you, Ma said. We can go on the bus— but Tilly said no, no, she'd be fine on her own. She couldn't have Ma or Pa with her, it wouldn't work. She wouldn't be able to talk properly, with either of them sitting at her elbow.

She looked from one wary face to the other. It's OK, she said. I just want to meet her, that's all. It won't change anything. But she could see they weren't reassured. How could they be? How could things not be changed after this?

For the rest of the week she hardly slept. Was she doing the right thing, or should she have left well enough alone, like Diane Potter had done for all these years?

Matilda Potter. Tilly Potter.

She was up before daylight on Saturday, trying on and rejecting most of her wardrobe. Pa drove her to the bus station as she sat silently beside him, too keyed up to talk, already regretting her choice of red sweater and blue jeans. Too childish, too casual: she should have gone for a dress, and her high-heeled boots.

Pick you up at seven, Pa said at the bus station. Good luck, he added – and some impulse made Tilly reach across and place a kiss on his bristly cheek, causing him to blink in astonishment. They never kissed, never hugged: they weren't that kind of family.

She arrived in Brisbane with forty-five minutes to spare. It took her thirty to locate the café, double-checking the directions she'd found on Google Maps with three different passers-by. Walking along the crowded streets, hemmed in by towering office blocks, she wished for the solid presence of Ma by her side, or Lien, or anyone. But she'd rejected Ma's offer, and Lien volunteered on Saturdays at an animal refuge, and there wasn't anyone else she could think of.

No: she could do this. She'd chosen to do this.

The café was two buildings up from the corner of a block, its name spelled out in cheery orange letters. Tilly scanned the three large windows from across the street and saw no woman in a blue coat behind any of them. Too early: still fifteen minutes to go.

She found a supermarket further down the block and bought Fruit Tingles for Robbie and Jemima, a Violet Crumble for Ma and a pack of gum for Pa. At twenty-five past two, unable to wait any longer, she retraced her steps and pushed open the café door.

She stood inside, heart thudding, legs watery. The café was about a third full, each table occupied by at least two people. There was no sign of a woman sitting alone, or anybody at all wearing a coat in a shade of blue. All the window tables were taken.

A waitress appeared. Table for one?

No, I'm meeting my … someone, but she's not here yet.

She should have waited a bit longer: she should have walked around the block a few times. As she followed the waitress across the floor a few people glanced up, and Tilly could feel herself flushing. Was it obvious? Did she look as nervous as she felt? They might think she was on a blind date. And then she thought: That's exactly what it is.

Here we go, the waitress said, leading her to a table that wasn't too far from the window. It would have to do. She was the only person in that part of the room sitting alone: she'd be easy to pick out.

Something to drink while you're waiting?

Coffee, she said, her drink of choice since Ma had finally let her have some, around a year ago. She loved the burned-nutty smell of it, the dark, almost earthy taste. And it would give her something to do with her hands, something to hang on to.

Two minutes to half past. The door opened and a woman walked in wearing a pale blue coat. Tilly's heart fluttered as she watched her glancing around, a small frown puckering her forehead – but then her face cleared and she moved, smiling, towards a beckoning threesome.

The coffee arrived in a white mug with an orange smiley face on the side. Tilly stirred in milk and sugar, keeping her eyes fixed on the door, everything coiled tightly inside her. In a few minutes, she told herself, I will be looking at my mother. I will be talking to my mother. It didn't seem real.

As she waited, she caught snatches of the various conversations that were going on around her. *He absolutely must do it, if that's what he wants ... Terribly anxious, not having heard a word ... I'd understand if she was allergic, but there was never any evidence ... But they're so alike – it's uncanny!* The words skimmed over her, as meaningless as if they'd been uttered in some unknown language, foreign sounds from different lives that were briefly intersecting hers.

She sipped the coffee, which was considerably stronger than Ma's. She added a second sachet of sugar, sipped again. She tried without success to keep her eyes from drifting back to the clock on the wall every half-minute. Twenty to three.

A couple came in; a trio left. The waitress rushed between tables with menus and plates and glasses. A piece of cutlery clattered to the floor behind Tilly, making her jump. Someone sneezed. Someone laughed. The air was heavy with the smell of food. Fried onions, melted cheese, roasted meat.

A quarter to three. Where *was* she? Why wasn't she here, sitting by the window in her blue coat, like she'd promised? Wasn't she coming? Had it all been a cruel joke?

An awful thought struck Tilly: was this the right café? The idea that she might be sitting in the wrong one sent a bolt of panic through her. With trembling hands she rummaged through her bag, searching for the piece of paper on which she'd written—

Matilda?

She looked up.

Grey bag.

Blue coat.

Pearl earrings.

Pale face.

Dark eyes.

Gold hair.

Tiny.

Are you Matilda? the woman repeated, in an accent that dipped and leaped, like water over stones, in a voice deeper in tone than the slight frame would suggest. One of her hands clutched the shoulder strap of the grey bag.

Tilly got abruptly to her feet, almost knocking over her chair. She towered above the woman, nearly a foot taller. They stood regarding one another, the table between them.

Gosh, the woman said softly, looking up into Tilly's face. Making no movement at all towards her. Tall, she murmured, half to herself, sliding into the chair across from Tilly's. Well, she said, dipping a shoulder to lower her bag to the floor, folding hands that were small as a child's one on top of the other on the table. Her nails were short stubs, bitten away to nothing. She wore no rings. Do sit, she said, in her deep voice.

Tilly resumed her seat, feeling deflated. What had she expected? That they were going to burst into tears and fall into one another's arms, like in a bad soap opera? No, not that, of course not that – but maybe a little more than this, maybe a little less casual than this. Maybe a handshake, at least.

She could see little resemblance to herself in the woman's face. They both had pale complexions, but that, as far as she could see, was their only common feature. A stranger would surely never take them for parent and child.

Well, her mother repeated, her gaze still roaming around Tilly's face. You have his eyes. I might have known you'd get those.

Before Tilly could respond the waitress approached. Green tea, Tilly's mother told her, in the same soft deep lilting voice, and a glass of iced water with a slice of lime. She didn't ask Tilly if she wanted to order anything else, although she must have noticed the coffee mug, must have seen that it was almost empty. If you please, she added, half getting up to shuck off the blue coat and hand it to the waitress, you might find a hanger for that.

Underneath she wore a simple grey shift dress in some stretchy material, its sleeves ending at her elbows. The forearms that emerged were as white as her face, the wrists tiny. Her breasts were little pointed mounds that barely disturbed the fabric of the dress.

So, she said, tilting her head like a bird. Here we are. Her back straight as the chair, her gold hair gathered into some kind of tight arrangement on the back of her head. I wondered, she said, if you would come along.

She looked younger than Ma, or maybe it was the girlish figure that deceived. It all felt unreal. Tilly wondered if she was asleep, if she was about to wake up at any minute and see her yellow bedroom walls, the chair by the bed with her clothes slung across it, the topple of her schoolbooks on the desk in the corner. Just a dream, she'd think, watching a shaft of sunlight falling onto the wooden floor. Never happened.

I suppose, her mother continued, in the same pensive tone, you want to know why I didn't keep you.

Was there something detached about her, as if she was speaking at a remove from Tilly? It felt like she was physically there, but her mind seemed to be someplace else entirely. There was no emotion that Tilly could discern behind her words: she might have been reciting lines from a play.

Tilly found her voice. Yes, she said, the word coming out louder and sharper than she'd intended.

Yes, her mother echoed, nodding slowly several times, her gaze sliding down to study the pale wood of the table top. Matilda—

It's Tilly. Out before she knew it was on the way, and sharp like before.

Her mother looked up. Tilly, she repeated. Tentatively, trying it out.

Their eyes met and held. Neither of them smiled. Tilly, her mother said again. More slow nodding.

The waitress approached. They watched her transferring the items on her tray – pot, cup and saucer, glass, napkin, spoon – to the table. Refill? she asked, looking at Tilly's mug. Anything else I can get for you? Tilly shook her head. She hadn't eaten since breakfast at eight: the strong coffee had left her feeling queasy.

When they were alone again her mother remained silent for several seconds. She lifted the water, took a tiny sip, dabbed her pale lips.

I was very young when I married your father, she said eventually. Her voice was lower now, so Tilly had to slant a little towards her to hear. I was twenty, just a girl. I knew nothing, I was so innocent.

You were married to my father, Tilly said. Trying it out like her mother had tried out her name, feeling her way around it. She was the child of a married couple, not the product of an illicit affair, or a one-night stand, or a rape. Her father not unknown, after all. You were married, she said again.

Her mother didn't react. It was as if Tilly hadn't spoken. I was very much in love with him, she said, in the same faraway voice, one hand coming to rest, as lightly as a butterfly, on the lid of the teapot. He was older, and extremely talented, and very successful. I was … completely in awe of him.

She lifted the lid, allowing pale wisps of steam to trail upwards. She stirred the tea, replaced the lid, poured the yellow-green liquid. A faint scent of something – new-mown grass? – drifted across to Tilly.

Her mother sighed, shifting her gaze to look beyond Tilly's shoulder. It wasn't a happy marriage, she said, not at all. He was … a terribly difficult man, so creative, so … *obsessed* with his work. Her voice rising in tone, the words becoming more deliberate, less dreamy. Her pale face tightening. His work came first, she said. It always came first. It came before everything—

She broke off and raised the teacup to her lips – did her hand tremble? Maybe a little. She reached for her napkin again – but instead of raising it to her lips she began folding and refolding it, drawing deep, slow breaths as she did so. Making a conscious effort, it looked like, to compose herself.

I was completely stifled by him, she said eventually, somewhat calmer now. I was denied the chance to let my own talent blossom. And I had talent, oh yes. She smiled sadly, pressing the napkin between her hands. I could have gone far, if I'd had the chance …

It had begun to feel like she was putting on a performance, with Tilly as the audience of one. She was telling a story, and it sounded well-rehearsed. Tilly wanted to ask what they did, or had done; she wanted to know what jobs they'd had, her creative father and her talented mother, but she remained silent, stifling her question, sensing it wouldn't be welcome. Not now, not yet.

In the end, her mother went on, I left him. I had to – it had become impossible to go on. My health was suffering, I wasn't strong … I had no choice. She pressed the square of folded napkin to her cheeks in turn, just below her eyes. As if she was dabbing away tears, but she wasn't crying. For all that, she said, her voice a near-whisper now, it was hard to leave him. It was the hardest thing I had ever done …

Harder than giving up your child? The question was on the tip of Tilly's tongue but again she held back, her nerve deserting her.

Her mother's words drifted off, her gaze directed towards the thin fingers that were pleating the napkin, and Tilly had the impression that her mind had left the coffee shop and gone elsewhere.

She wondered suddenly if her mother was on medication. Antidepressants maybe, something that blunted sadness, but wiped out other emotions in the process. It might explain the air of detachment, the lack of emotion at meeting the daughter she'd given away sixteen years earlier.

After a while her mother seemed to collect herself. I met … someone, she said then, her voice soft and calmer. I met Trudi through my work. She helped me, she became a wonderful friend – and Tilly remembered Ma saying she'd shared the apartment with a woman.

She helped me to leave him, her mother continued. She brought me here. She's from here, you see, she was coming home, she was leaving Ireland, and she took me with her.

She lifted her glass, sipped water, dabbed her mouth. I didn't know, she said. When we left Ireland, I didn't know you were on the way. She moistened her lips with her tongue. It was a difficult time, she said. My parents had recently died within a few months of one another, and I was so … confused, so terribly uncertain … But for Trudi, I don't think I would have survived … and Jenny, your – here she faltered – aunt, is she?

Austin is my uncle, Tilly said.

Her mother nodded. Yes, yes, Jenny was very good to me too, so kind …

Did you tell him? Tilly asked then, the question refusing to stay in her head. Did you tell my father about me?

A beat passed – and then her mother shook her head slowly, her face clouding. No, she said, voice barely audible. I didn't tell him. He ... filed for a legal separation, right after I left him. And I wasn't well, I was so sick ... and so lonely ...

She bit her lip, reached for her cup, her hands visibly trembling now as she lifted it to sip. You must understand, she said, clattering it back onto its saucer, it was all so ... stressful. I can't ... She raised a hand, fluttered the fingers. I couldn't keep you, she said. I wasn't strong enough to look after a baby.

Couldn't Trudi have helped? Or Jenny?

Her mother made the same helpless gesture. I couldn't ask them – I couldn't expect them to. You were my responsibility.

And yet you abandoned me. Again left unsaid. Silence fell between them. Tilly lifted her mug and drank the last of her coffee, stone cold by now. She wished for water, but she didn't look around for the waitress.

Is he still alive? My father.

A nod. He is, yes.

In Ireland?

Another nod. Look, her mother said then, Matilda—

Tilly.

Tilly, I know this will hurt – but he wouldn't want to know. About you, I mean. He's not ... he should never have married – and he was never cut out for children. There's no room in his life for them.

Every word landed like a thump. Tilly felt a surge of anger for the woman sitting across the table. How could she have just decided not to tell him? What had made her so sure of his reaction? He might have changed – he might have been thrilled to discover he had a child. How could she have written him out of Tilly's life by refusing to name him on the birth cert?

Maybe it had made her feel better, when she'd given up her daughter, to convince herself that he'd have done exactly the same. Maybe it had lessened her guilt to tell herself that neither parent wanted a child. Who knew why she'd done what she had? Certainly not Tilly, who knew nothing at all.

Her mother spoke again, no doubt reading Tilly's feelings on her face. Look, I know how it sounds, how it must sound to you, but I did what I thought was best for you, I did, really.

Everyone doing what they thought was best for Tilly, which basically meant not telling the truth. Ma and Pa saying nothing about the adoption until they'd had to, her birth mother keeping her father in the dark about his daughter. How could any of them think it was best to keep such secrets?

Trudi felt I should give you up, her mother said. She knew I wasn't strong enough to raise you.

Trudi. What was her role in all of this? Was she simply a person who'd befriended a woman at the end of her tether, someone who'd provided an escape route – or had their relationship been more than that? Was it still more?

And what did it matter really? What did any of it matter?

Tilly looked across the table and realised that she felt nothing at all for the person who sat opposite her. No love, no bonding, no pity, no hate. They might have been two strangers who'd simply ended up sharing a table because no other was available. To all intents and purposes, they *were* strangers, nothing in common except a few genes. They probably wouldn't even meet again.

And as she glanced about, searching for their waitress – did she need a bill for her coffee or could she go directly to the cash desk? – her mother spoke again.

Tilly, she said, there's something else …

'Are you awake?'

The voice too close, too loud, made Tilly start. She opened her eyes.

'We're about to land,' Siobhan said. 'Look out at your first glimpse of sunny Ireland.'

Tilly turned her head towards the little window and saw the black of the runway tarmac rushing up to meet them, and a strip of startlingly green grass with a row of long, low concrete buildings, and a sky above it all that was full of dense-looking clouds the colour of stone, and everything was blurred by the silvery needles of rain that were falling.

The wheels touched down and hopped a few times before finally whizzing along the runway – and pretty much everyone on the plane, it sounded like, burst into simultaneous cheery applause.

❄❄❄

'Well,' she said, 'I really and truly think you've done an amazing job.'

They stood around the decorated tree, positioned in the alcove to the left of the fireplace. The baubles – cheap to begin with, and having survived several Christmases plus the move to Roone – were scratched and mismatched, and there were far too few of them. The strands of tinsel were ragged with use, and completely bald in spots. The star at the top was dented. The lights, two sets that flickered weakly, served only to highlight the shortcomings of the whole affair.

'Amazing,' Laura repeated, jiggling Poppy gently on her hip. 'It looks wonderful. Wait till Santa sees it.'

'Evie dropped one of the balls an' it smashed.'

'I didn't dwop it, it *falled*.'

'Doesn't matter, we have plenty – and don't tell tales on your sister, Seamus. Now go and remind Dad that he needs to collect the turkey: I told Jim he'd be over this afternoon.'

'Will it still be alive?' Ben enquired hopefully.

'No.'

'Will the feathers still be stuck on?' Seamus.

'They'd better not be.'

'Can we go with Dad?' Four appealing faces turned towards her.

'Yes please – and tell him there's no hurry getting back. Put on jackets,' she called, in the wake of their scurried exodus.

She turned to smile brightly at Gladys. 'Well done on the tree. I can see you did the best you could with our limited resources.'

'You should have told me you needed decorations: I could have brought some. It could do with twice as many baubles.'

'Not to worry, the lads love it the way it is, and Gavin and I really couldn't care less.'

'Still, you'd be ashamed if anyone saw it.'

There was a small silence. Laura listened to the muffled chatter from the kitchen, wishing she was escaping to Jim's too.

Gladys cleared her throat. 'I hope you won't mind my mentioning this, dear, but those old books are giving out a terrible musty odour. If I were you I'd clear the whole lot out after Christmas, and give the place a few fresh coats of paint to get rid of the smell. I'm not trying to tell you what to do, I'm just giving my honest opinion.'

And there it was, the fundamental difference between them. Gladys looked at Walter's treasured collection of books, many of them leather-bound, many far older than herself, and saw only a pile of rubbish needing to be binned. Laura delighted in lifting out a book, pressing the opened pages to her face and inhaling their glorious rich, ancient scents. There it was, chalk and cheese.

'I love the books,' she said. 'I think they give the place a bit of character.'

Gladys gave her the pitying smile that Laura was well used to. 'But really, how many have you read?'

Cow. 'None,' Laura said firmly, 'but Gavin is working his way through them, and he's begun reading *Treasure Island* to the boys, and they love it.'

Gladys changed tack. 'I would imagine that quite a few of those books are riddled with silverfish.'

Silver fish? What was the woman on about? Did she think Walter's grandfather had hauled them up from a shipwreck?

'And look at all the extra work it must take, keeping them dusted,' Gladys went on, running a finger along one of the shelves before turning it over to inspect it. 'As if you don't have enough to do already.' Knowing full well that Laura hadn't lifted a duster to them in months.

'Oh, I don't bother with any unnecessary jobs these days,' Laura told her lightly. 'Nothing like a bout of cancer to make you realise what's important. No more dusting until we're opening up the B&B again.' Put that in your pipe, you old biddy.

Gladys's smile was full of vinegar, but for once she had no comeback.

'The books were in the previous owner's family for generations,' Laura went on. They'd never once come up in conversation with Walter, but she figured it was a fairly safe assumption. 'I believe that some of them are quite valuable.' Another theory with nothing to back it up, but Madam wasn't to know that.

Gladys gave a sniff. 'The value of anything depends on how much someone is willing to pay for it – and to be honest, I can't see anyone wanting these, apart from some fusty old museum, maybe.'

'Well, they're not getting them,' Laura said. 'They're staying right here.' Jiggling Poppy a little too enthusiastically as she spoke, causing the baby to give out a little squawk of complaint.

Gladys sighed. 'You're the boss, dear. I'm just trying to help.'

'Of course, Gladys. I realise that.'

The women regarded one another, the shakiest of truces achieved, smiles pasted onto their faces. One more day, Laura reminded herself. The thought lifted her spirits.

The back door banged – the others off in search of the turkey – and directly afterwards Poppy chose that moment to emit a blast of wind of heroic proportions from her nether regions.

'Goodness me,' Gladys said faintly.

'Oops a daisy.' Laura struggled to keep a straight face. 'I think that might be my cue to check this little lady's nappy and put her down for a snooze. Make yourself tea, Gladys, if you fancy it. I won't be long.'

In the master bedroom she undressed Poppy and got her into pyjamas, and settled her in the cot. With Gladys unattended, it looked like only one of them was getting a lie-down today.

No need to go straight back down though. She stood by the

window, watching the rain that had begun as Jim had driven her home from Fitz's an hour earlier. Still falling steadily, no sign of a let-up. No sign of a storm either though – for once it seemed that Annie Byrnes's bones were letting her down. The woman must be ninety if she was a day: bones that age were bound to get it wrong once in a while.

The sea, separated from the house by road and field, looked pretty grim this afternoon. Hard to make out the horizon line, sea and sky merged into one dull grey mass. Trawlers sat hunched on the water, fishermen no doubt longing for warm hearths. The beaches empty for sure today, even the gulls missing from the sky. This was the Roone the tourists didn't get to see, the off-season Roone the islanders had all to themselves.

But Laura loved it in winter, for all the harsh winds that blew in from the sea, for all the sheets of rain that hurled themselves against doors and windows. She loved the different character of the island when the holidaymakers went home: the quieter roads to walk on with the children, the deserted beaches for Charlie to race after sticks, the small peaceful pubs with welcome roaring fires in the days when she and Gavin used to get a babysitter and escape for a few hours.

She remembered how she loved the singsongs that happened spontaneously around the pub fires, and the tales of Roone that got retold by old fishermen in sentimental mood on dark evenings. Winter showed them the essence of the island, the parts saved for the natives – and the blow-ins like herself, the lucky ones who got the chance to make this wonderful place their home.

Her three girls had been born here, the luckiest of all. When they were old enough, Laura would get Nell to teach them how to swim. Ben and Seamus had already been taught, soon after the move to Roone. They'd been seven going on eight, irresistibly drawn to the water and frighteningly unfamiliar with it. Nell had brought them out to the harbour in her little yellow rowing boat; she'd taken them one by one into the sea and shown them how to move through the water with confidence, and without recklessness.

It's bigger and stronger than you, she'd told them. It will always be bigger and stronger, so always respect it, and never, ever take a chance with it.

Laura had trusted her completely, knowing the boys would be safe with her. Since she'd fallen from a boat into the sea as a tot, Nell was as much at home in the water as on land. Within weeks Ben and Seamus were like fish, jumping with the local kids off the pier at high tide, clamouring for a boat of their own. No problem, Laura told them. The minute you can pay for it yourselves, it's yours.

We'll save up, Seamus replied, not a bit put out. Clearly unfamiliar with the cost of boats, even a humble little one like Nell's. No harm, let them put their cut of the donkey-ride money aside: by the time they were in a position to buy a boat, they'd be more than old enough to handle one.

By the time they had a boat, all this would be behind her. Good days would come again, she told herself. She'd rediscover happiness, she'd learn to laugh again.

She turned from the window and regarded her sleeping daughter, Rabbity tucked in beside her. Gavin's doll had been duly washed and pegged on the line this morning, still out there in all that rain: not a hope of getting it dry now for at least another day. Poppy probably wouldn't look at it: she only had eyes for Rabbity. They'd pass it on to Charlie – he'd chew on anything.

Laura tiptoed from the room, pulling the door ajar. As she padded downstairs the phone in the hall began to ring.

'Hello?'

'It's me,' Susan said. 'How's everything?'

'Hang on.' Laura ducked her head into the sitting room: empty. She checked the kitchen door: closed. Coast clear.

'We're on the home stretch,' she said quietly. 'She leaves at lunchtime tomorrow.'

'That's good. And it's going alright?'

'As well as can be expected. Biting my tongue a lot, as usual, but we're managing.'

'Glad to hear it.'

'Everything OK there?' Laura asked.

'Everything is fine.' Small pause. 'I just want … Listen.'

Laura listened, and heard nothing. Susan didn't do silences. 'What? Is something up?'

'Laura … I have news.'

Her heart jumped. Something was wrong. Susan was sick. Susan was dying, or Laura's father was. A second went by, two seconds that felt like two hundred. She was holding her breath, she couldn't breathe. 'Tell me,' she demanded finally.

'Laura … I'm pregnant.'

It was so wholly unexpected that she was momentarily struck dumb. Susan was pregnant, after twelve years of marriage to Laura's father. Susan was forty, which wasn't too old these days to have a baby, even if it was your first. Even if your husband was sixty-three next birthday, with no great track record as a parent. Susan was pregnant, when Laura had assumed she never would be, given the man she'd married.

'That's great,' she said, because it was. 'That's wonderful.' A new baby, a cousin for—

Hang on. Not a cousin for the children, an aunt or an uncle. A half-brother or sister for Laura. She wasn't going to be an only child any more, even if she had a thirty-year start on her sibling. Half-sibling.

'You're happy about it, aren't you?' she asked, aware of another stretching silence on the other end.

'Yes,' Susan said, more forcefully than necessary – and it was all there in the single word. The news hadn't gone down well with the expectant father: another child to come between him and his art, the last thing he'd want. Laura wouldn't mention him; she didn't need to confirm what she already knew.

'When?' she asked instead.

'Early June.'

Six months away – no, five. She was nearly four months gone.

'Are you feeling OK?'

'I was a bit queasy for the first while, but I'm fine now.'

'You'll be a mother,' Laura said. 'A real mother, as opposed to my pretend one.'

A small laugh. 'Can you believe it?'

'Can I go public – or can I at least tell Nell?' Too late, she realised she should have said Gavin. He should have been the first person she'd thought of telling.

If she noticed, Susan gave no sign. 'Tell who you want – no going back now.'

Laura wondered if it had been planned, if Susan had quietly stopped preventing the possibility of babies, then called it an accident when she'd broken the news to him. Because she wanted children, Laura was sure of it. Nothing had ever been said, the subject had never come up between them, but Susan undoubtedly wanted them.

Look how she'd cared for Ben and Seamus as babies, when their mother had been too much of a wreck to cope. Look how she doted on the girls when she saw them, how delighted she'd been to hear Poppy was on the way, able to see the joy in impending new life despite the other devastating news.

Look how the children all adored her – and now at last she was getting one of her own.

'Come to Roone,' Laura said. 'We have to celebrate. Come as soon as you can.' *Come on your own*: they both understood.

'I'd love to,' Susan replied, so quickly that she must have been hoping for it. She must have been planning for it. 'I could come on Stephen's Day, if that's not too soon.'

'Oh, do. It won't be a bit too soon – they'll be bored with Christmas by then.'

'Will the ferry be running?'

'Sure will – Leo never takes more than one day off. And stay as long as you like.'

'I'll need to go back on Thursday morning. We have a New Year's Eve thing.'

Of course they had a New Year's Eve thing: Luke would have people clamouring for him to be part of their celebrations, everyone wanting to boast that the famous artist was gracing them with his presence. 'We'll see you Saturday then. Ring when you know what ferry you're getting.'

'I will. Happy Christmas to you, love.'

'And you. Take care.'

She hung up and entered the kitchen. Gladys was sniffing the milk jug, frowning. 'I'm afraid it's turned, dear.'

Hardly surprising, considering who was looking at it.

❄❄❄

Ireland was very wet, and shockingly cold and predominently green. When Tilly rubbed a circle of condensation from the bus window, she saw fields of vivid green bordered with hedges of darker green and dotted sparsely with rather bedraggled sheep and small clusters of cattle.

The air was clogged with the scent of damp wool. The bus was blessedly warm and packed to capacity, with every seat occupied and several passengers standing in the aisle. They hung onto the backs of seats and swayed with the movement of the vehicle and generally didn't look too put out at their plight, even though presumably they'd paid the same as all the people who'd got seats. The Irish, it would appear, didn't sweat the small stuff.

And just like on the plane, everyone was talking. Wherever she looked, people were having animated conversations, some leaning over seats to chat, others conversing on mobile phones. Tilly caught little snatches that meant nothing – *She didn't know who your one was*

... They looked a fright, the cut of them ... He hadn't a bull's notion, but sure that never stopped him – and she was reminded of sitting in the Brisbane café, listening to other strangers' conversations as she'd waited for her mother to appear.

A radio was being piped through the bus, trying to compete with all the other noise. Some kind of chat show or interview was taking place, but everyone involved spoke so rapidly that most of what was being said was lost on Tilly. Was she going to struggle to understand everyone here too?

Although the woman in Dublin airport had had no trouble making herself perfectly clear. *I don't know what they were thinking in Heathrow,* she'd said, holding Tilly's standby ticket by a corner, as if she feared contamination of some sort from it. *All our flights to Kerry today and tomorrow have been fully booked for weeks.*

It was another blow – but strangely, Tilly found herself not too upset by it. She was in Ireland, she'd got this far: she'd find Kerry eventually. Maybe she was high from lack of sleep, and immune to obstacles. *Is there any other way I can get to Kerry?* she asked.

The woman looked doubtful. *I can put you on a bus to Dingle. That's the best I can do.*

Dingle?

The woman waved a hand, as if the place might be located somewhere to the left of her desk. *It's in Kerry, about an hour from the airport. You'll have to tell whoever is meeting you to go to the bus station in Dingle* – assuming, like everyone else, that Tilly was being met. *The next bus leaves at half four,* she said, *it'll get you to Dingle by about nine.*

She wrote rapidly in a notebook. *I can't issue you with a ticket here, but take this to the desk at the bus area* – ripping the page from the notebook – *and they should sort you out. I'd advise you to go straight there: it'll be busy, but hopefully you'll get on.*

So Tilly followed directions and got her ticket, and took her place in the queue at the bus shelter for over an hour, stamping her feet and rubbing her hands together to stop them turning completely numb, and eventually the Dingle bus arrived and they all clambered on, the driver blithely ignoring the maximum allowed number of passengers that was displayed on a sign above the front windshield, for surely there were a lot more than fifty-three of them crowded together.

So she was bound for Dingle, an hour away from Kerry airport – and possibly an hour further from Roone. No matter, it was bringing her closer. And it had to be better than hanging around Dublin airport, which seemed even busier than Heathrow, if that was possible. Full of happy reuniting families, by the look of them. Everyone smiling, everyone embracing. Everyone, it seemed, with someone to meet them, someone glad to see them.

Amazingly, Tilly didn't feel tired any more. Somewhere along the way she'd gone beyond tired. She looked a mess though: deep shadows under bloodshot eyes, cheeks drained of the scant bit of colour she'd had to begin with, hair in dire need of attention. She looked, she thought, like someone coming out of a long illness – or maybe heading into one. In an airport toilet she'd brushed her teeth, splashed her face, slicked on lip gloss. It had made little difference.

She'd lost all track of how long she'd been travelling. Time had ceased to be logical, with planes and airports and sleep and food all messed up, days and nights blurring into one another. She'd work it out when she arrived, after she'd slept, and got her brain back.

She changed most of her sterling in an airport bank, and got sixty euro in exchange. She'd hang on to it like glue.

'Have some more, dear.'

She turned to the proffered bag and helped herself again. 'Thanks.'

In Dublin airport she found a water fountain and refilled the bottle she'd saved from the flight. Refilled it three times, trying to fool her stomach into thinking it was full – but hunger was gnawing again by the time Mrs O'Carroll claimed the seat next to Tilly's on the bus.

Would you mind, dear? she'd asked, her accent different from Siobhan's, different from the airport official's. She'd indicated the two large shopping bags she'd hauled onto the bus. I can't reach to put them up, she'd said, so Tilly had squeezed the bags into the narrow overhead compartment, and Mrs O'Carroll had spent the next ten minutes thanking her, as the bus eased out of its bay and headed for the airport exit.

And they'd barely left Dublin behind – it had probably still been visible in the driver's rear-view mirror – before her companion had learned pretty much all there was to know about Tilly's trip to Ireland, and the reason for it. The reason Tilly gave her, at any rate.

You've got a sister you've never met, living on Roone? And you're after coming all the way from Australia, all by yourself, to find her? I don't believe it. And your money was stolen in London? Do you have any left at all? God bless us, you poor creature – but you're a brave young girl, and no mistake.

Her voice had a beautiful rich musical lilt to it – and much to Tilly's relief, was fairly easy to understand. And by the time they were halfway to Dingle, Tilly had been offered a bed for the night.

You'll have missed the last ferry to the island, it goes around seven in the winter, but you can stay with Paddy and me – we have piles of room since our lads grew up and left. It'll be no bother at all, we love having visitors. And Paddy will have the dinner ready when we get home – I left him full instructions.

Paddy would have the dinner ready. The thought of a home-cooked meal after so long without proper food made Tilly's mouth fill with saliva – and in the meantime the two of them were making their way through a bag of pink mallow candies that were shaped like pigs' heads.

I get these every time I come to Dublin, Mrs O'Carroll had told her. You can only get them in Marks & Spencer's, and we don't have one in Dingle. Aren't they lovely? Go on, have a few more. I shouldn't be eating them at all, the size of me.

She was on her way home from a two-day visit to Dublin. I do it every year, she'd said, come up for the bit of Christmas shopping and stay the night with Sean, our eldest, and his family. I know it's a fair old trip, but it's a chance to catch up with Sean and the lads. We don't see that much of them.

She'd listed her purchases for Tilly. New pyjamas for Paddy – he's nearly coming through the seat of his old ones. A nice jumper for him to give back to me on Christmas morning – he's no good to choose a present, and this way I can be sure he gives me something I like. A scarf for Joan next door, she's great to feed the cats when we're away. A box of the chocolate biscuits Paddy likes from Marks. Jigsaws for Áine's two – Áine is our middle girl. She's married to John and they live in Tralee. Her lads are mad for the jigsaws, bright as buttons the two of them, only four and five. A cardi for Áine and a book for John – Áine told me which one to get. And what else? Oh yes, slippers for poor Nancy down the road. She lost her Eddie during the year – she's in bits since he went, God love her.

Her first name was Breda. It's Bridget in Irish, she'd told Tilly, laughing when Tilly confessed that she'd never heard of a language called Irish. Oh, that's a good one! 'Twas beaten into me by the nuns at school, but I'm afraid they didn't beat me hard enough, because I haven't a word of it left now – although there's plenty around Dingle who have lovely Irish. You'd love to be listening to them. It's not a bit like English, it's much different. You'll have to watch a bit of the Irish-language telly while you're here, so you can hear what it sounds like.

She and Paddy lived just outside Dingle. We're only a mile from the town. I walk in most days, although you'd want to have your wits about you on the road. They fly, some of the drivers – especially the young lads. Mad for speed, they are, and no sense of danger at all. It's probably the same where you are, I'd say. Young fellows are the same the world over, think they know it all. Think they're indestructible, God help them.

She knew Roone; she'd often been there. We used to take day trips across when our lads were small – we're only half an hour from the ferry port. Nice little island, everyone very friendly. The lads loved it, used to nag us to bring them. Paddy will run you to the pier in the morning, get you on the ferry.

A drive to the pier: eleven euro saved. Mrs O'Carroll had brushed away her thanks. Sure wouldn't anyone do it? Wouldn't I want someone to be nice to one of mine if they were all the way over in Australia, and they got robbed like you did?

Yes, Tilly was lucky in her seat companion. She looked out at the continuing rain, the sweet taste of the last mallow pig still on her tongue. 'Any chance it might stop raining before Christmas?' she asked.

No response. She turned and saw that Mrs O'Carroll had nodded off, her rather odd-looking yellow beret tipped askew, her lower lip dropped to reveal a row of bottom teeth that looked too even and regular to be real. Worn out from two days of trekking around Dublin, shopping mostly for other people. Probably came up from Kerry yesterday laden with a whole other set of presents for her Dublin grandchildren.

Cast from the same mould as Ma. Spent her time looking after other people, put herself at the end of every queue.

Tilly sat back and closed her own eyes, and wandered into a place that was halfway between waking and sleeping.

And found John Smith waiting for her there.

Yes, it is my real name, he told them, first day he walked into the classroom. What were my parents thinking? Making them laugh: he was good at that. Making them play with their hair as he talked about Elizabeth Bennet's prejudice and Jane Eyre's passion and the rhyming scheme of the sonnets. Making them shift in their seats under his blue-eyed gaze, making them want him.

Making *her* want him.

He wasn't permanent. He had materialised in July at the beginning of term three, after their regular English Lit teacher, Mrs Harvey, had gone on maternity leave. I'm not sure how long I'll be with you, he'd told them, but let's work on the premise that you'll have me till the end of the year.

It was his smile. It was the way he tilted his chair onto its back legs and folded his arms as they read passages aloud. It was the soft-looking shirts he wore, sleeves rolled to the elbows even in cold weather. It was the way he listened, really listened, as they debated whether Catherine Earnshaw had been right to marry Edgar Linton instead of Heathcliff, as they discussed the tragedy of the doomed love affair between Charles Ryder and Julia Flyte.

It was the scent he left behind when he walked between their desks, a mix of wood and pepper and something dangerous. It was his dark brown leather jacket, scuffed at the seams. It was his teeth, and his laugh, and his long broad fingers. It was everything about him, everything.

He was in his early thirties, they decided. No ring: clearly, he wasn't married. He drove a red Jeep, which wasn't the car of choice for a man with a wife and kids. He'd had his heart broken, they thought. She'd gone off with his best friend, or she'd drowned a week before the wedding – or she was married to his brother, and therefore out of bounds, because he was too honourable to tell her how he felt.

Tilly listened to the conversations and didn't join in. She was afraid her face would give her away if she talked about him. He was all she thought about. He'd come along at exactly the right time, when she was trying to push the mother she'd met a month earlier out of her head, when she was doing her best to forget about a woman who'd clearly forgotten about her, until Tilly had forced her to remember.

No second meeting had been arranged in the Brisbane café, no suggestion of a follow-up communication of any kind. Her mother had simply paid the bill and shaken Tilly's hand – I wish you well, she'd said, just that – and Tilly saved her tears for the bus and cried as quietly as she could all the way home.

Pa had collected her from the bus station. Alright? he'd asked, looking at her swollen eyes and unsmiling face, and she'd got into the car, unable to answer, and spent the seven miles staring out the window, trying not to think. When they'd got home Ma had taken one look at her and said nothing at all, just told her dinner was waiting. Tilly had forced down the bowl of stew and gone upstairs straight afterwards, forgetting about the presents in her bag for them, and cried more tears until she'd fallen asleep.

And while she was still feeling rotten, and trying to convince herself that it didn't matter – hadn't she'd done fine without her real mother up to this, and who cared anyway about a father who knew nothing about her, and an older sister who'd been casually dropped in at the end of their conversation – while she was trying to push the whole thing from her mind, along came John Smith, and thinking about him left room for nothing else.

I like the way your mind works, he said, handing her back an essay on the shared characteristics of literary romantic heroines. It was three weeks into the term. She saw *A minus* scribbled at the top, the first A she'd got in anything. At break time she brought the essay into the toilets and pressed the pages to her face, and fancied she smelt his cologne on them.

A few Saturdays after that she was coming out of the library in town when she almost walked straight into him.

Hey, he said, grinning, watch where you're going, miss. Olive-green shirt, blue jeans. She smelt his toothpaste; for a second they were that close. Blood rushed to her cheeks, she could feel the heat of it. A reader, he went on, pretending not to notice. Might have known. He glanced at her bundle of books – John Steinbeck, Kate Grenville, Thomas Keneally. Nice mix there, he said, can't fault your taste. Tilly remained struck dumb, able only to stand there like an idiot, heartbeats thumping inside her.

She was almost his height. His eyes were blue as the sky, and they were looking right at her.

See you Monday, he said, walking past her into the building, and for the rest of that day she tormented herself with all the witty responses she might have given him.

He must be a reader too: of course he was a reader. They had that in common.

Can't fault your taste.

Thirty-two, or thereabouts. It was a crush, that was all it was. It felt like love but it couldn't be love. He'd leave and Mrs Harvey would return and Tilly would be miserable for a while, and eventually life as she knew it would go back to normal.

And then. And then. And then.

It was the second week in September, the last day of term three. He called her as she was gathering her things together. A word, Tilly, he said, unless you're rushing off. It was the end of the day, English Lit their last class.

He waited till everyone else had left. Tilly stood by his desk, trying not to look too expectant and excited and fearful and delighted, aware of the sidelong glances she was attracting as the others filed out.

I've been thinking, he said, when they were alone. I'd like to give you an assignment over the break, if that's OK with you.

That's fine, she said. If he asked her to go to the moon she'd go.

I want you to write an article, he went on. Five hundred words or so on a subject you feel passionate about, anything at all. I've got a buddy in New South Wales who edits a small literary magazine and I'd like to show him something you've written.

It took her completely by surprise. Of course she was working harder for him than she'd done for Mrs Harvey, but despite the consistent high grades he gave her – nothing lower than a B plus – she'd had no idea he thought that highly of her writing.

You want to? he asked, and she said yes, as casually as she could.

Good. He reached for the leather jacket that was slung on the back of his chair. You've got two weeks, so take your time with it, don't rush it. He stood. And I think it might be best if you kept it to yourself, he added. Wouldn't want people to think I was showing favouritism.

She nodded. Favouritism. Favourite. She was his favourite.

So you could drop it into the staffroom for me, he went on, sometime after the break. OK?

OK, she said.

Lien was waiting at the gate. What did he want?

To talk about my essay, Tilly said, the lie slipping out easily. He said I must try harder. He said I should go back over it during the break, try to improve it.

Too bad, Lien replied, the lie accepted without question, because they never lied to one another.

What are you passionate about? she asked Lien as they walked to the bus stop, and after some thought Lien told her shopping, and animal welfare, and her grandmother's peanut brittle.

Over the next few days she searched for a topic. What did she feel strongly about? What moved her to joy, or to tears, or to anger? In the end, the memory of crying her way home from Brisbane refused to budge, and she decided to write about finding her birth mother, and the sad little episode in the café. Out it poured onto her screen, a lot more words than five hundred; cutting it down took longer than writing it. When it was done she felt scrubbed raw, and lighter.

She read it, and reread it. Was it too personal? Would he prefer something more universal, like the futility of war, or saving the planet? But she liked the idea of sharing this with him; she liked showing him a part of her nobody else knew about – even Lien had been given a very edited version of the episode. She wanted to see his reaction to it.

The two-week break seemed to crawl by, fourteen interminable days without seeing him. On the first day of term four she knocked on the staffroom door at lunchtime. This is for Mr Smith, she told the teacher who opened it, handing over the envelope with his name on it that Lien thought contained her amended essay. During the English Lit class after lunch he gave no sign that he'd received it, or read it.

For the next three days he continued to ignore it. Maybe he hadn't seen it; maybe it was sitting forgotten on a shelf in the staffroom. Or maybe he'd read it and hated it. Or maybe he liked it, but he was embarrassed that she'd revealed so much of herself.

She kicked herself for having written such a personal piece, for having pretty much bared her soul to him. She cringed at the thought that she'd unwittingly given herself away by choosing such an intimate subject. Or maybe it made her sound like a needy teenager, craving a bit of attention.

On Friday, when she'd given up waiting for a response, when English Lit had become something she dreaded rather than looked forward to, he asked her to stay back at the end of class, like he'd done before. She rolled her eyes at Lien and waited with him again until the room was empty. Here it came, whatever he had to say.

He pulled her envelope from his leather satchel and laid it on his desk. Sorry I've taken a while to get back to you, he said. I sent it to Doug to see what he thought; I wasn't sure if it was what he'd want.

She said nothing. Her toes curled in their shoes. He hated it.

Is it true? he asked then, and she nodded.

So you just met your mother recently?

June.

Wow. He shook his head slowly. Tilly, this is powerful writing. It's not for Doug – it doesn't fit in with his magazine – but that's not to say it doesn't have worth. It's a wonderfully written piece. Doug thinks so too. We think it could be the kicking-off point for a short story, or even a novel … You have a lovely writing style, and you write from the heart, which is so important.

She sat immobile, the words filling her with delight. Doug didn't want it but he liked it; they both did. They thought it was wonderfully written.

Tell you what, he said, let's talk about this further. Can you meet me tomorrow to discuss it? There are some books I'd like to lend you – and just like that, they arranged that he'd pick her up outside the library where they'd met by chance several weeks before.

98

Feedback on the essay, she said to Lien. He said it's an improvement, he's upped my grade – and Lien totally believed it.

The following day she told Ma she was going to the library to study for her end-of-year exams. She took the bus into town, every bit of her jangling. She stood on the library steps in her favourite blouse and cleanest jeans, mouth dry, stomach churning. What if he didn't turn up? What if this was all a big joke, and he was making fun of poor pathetic Tilly Walker, with her all-too-obvious crush on him?

But he did turn up, just a few minutes after he'd promised. Hop in, he said, and she hopped into the red Jeep. We need to be careful, he said, pulling away from the kerb. If people saw us together, they'd get the wrong idea, you know? Best not give them the opportunity to jump to the wrong conclusion, right?

He left the town behind, drove out into the countryside. Somewhere quiet, he said, where we won't be disturbed. His car smelt of him. His hands on the steering wheel were tanned. He wore a red check shirt she didn't remember seeing before. The radio was on, tuned to a talk station. She heard the words, but they meant nothing to her.

He left the main road and took a series of turns, driving past fields and trees and farmhouses. She had no idea where they were. She didn't care. She leaned her head back and waited for what was to come. For what she wanted to happen, but didn't dare think it might.

Eventually he pulled up by a small copse of trees. I come here sometimes, he said, when I want to be alone. It's so peaceful. Come on, he said, pulling a rug from the back seat. You'll like it.

They walked into the little wood. Her heart was thudding so loudly he must have been able to hear it. He spread the rug on the ground in the middle of a small clearing. Now, he said, we're completely private.

And then he seduced her. Just like that.

I know this is so unprofessional, he said, drawing a finger slowly along her cheek and across her lips, leaving a burn behind – but I find you completely irresistible, Tilly. Beginning to unbutton the blouse she'd put on an hour before. You're like a flower about to bloom, he whispered, so delicate and untouched. Bending to graze the skin of her throat with his mouth, making her shudder as his hands worked their way down the buttons. Opening her up.

You have a truly passionate heart, Tilly. I could see it blazing out of every sentence you wrote. Drawing her blouse down from her shoulders, bending to kiss the bare skin he uncovered. You need to be loved … You deserve to be loved. Reaching around behind her, his breath hot on her neck as he undid hooks, as he slid straps away – and with every word, every touch, she could feel herself melting, crumbling into the fire he'd lit in her.

I won't hurt you, he murmured, when he'd stripped her bare. I'll be careful, he promised, when nothing was hidden from him any more. God, look at you, when she lay exposed and trembling beneath his gaze. You're so beautiful, he said, as he shed his own clothes, as they fell one by one to the ground beside her. This will be wonderful, he whispered, as he dropped to his knees and eased her apart, as he laid his body on hers. Trust me, Tilly, he breathed, as he went where nobody had gone before.

Hurting her, despite his promise not to. The pain taking her by surprise, making her cry out. Shush, he said, sweeping her into his rhythm, a hand gripping her hair, shush, Tilly, his skin tasting of salt, their limbs tangled together, sssh, the rug becoming bunched and damp beneath them, his smell mingling with hers, oh, oh, the leaves shivering on their branches above her as she came to a boil, pleasure mixed with pain, oh, oh—

And when it was over, as she was clinging to the aftertaste of it, as he lay beside her, his palm resting lightly on her thigh, he turned to her and said, This must be our secret, Tilly: we'd both be in serious trouble if anyone knew. We must tell nobody, no one at all, not even your best friend. Promise me, Tilly.

And of course she promised.

Come back here with me, he said, after she'd dressed, after

she'd run unsteady fingers through her hair, her mind still trying to comprehend what had just happened. Next week? Will you come back?

So she went back. Six more Saturdays she took the bus into town and met him outside the library, pretending she was going there to study – and he drove out to the countryside, his hand on her thigh, and in the same little forest they did what they'd done the first time.

And every Monday to Friday in between, Tilly sat in his class and tried not to picture his naked body, or think about the things he did when they were alone. The things he said to her.

You don't realise how beautiful you are.

You don't know what you do to me.

I look at you and I'm lost.

I'm so glad I was your first.

Age doesn't matter when you find someone you connect with.

He didn't talk about her writing again. She wondered if he'd made up the whole story, if Doug or the magazine even existed. She found the idea exhilarating, that he would have gone through that charade simply to get close to her.

It occurred to her that what they were doing was probably illegal. At sixteen she was a minor, and he was a figure of authority, charged with her care during the English Lit class. This she found exhilarating too: they were flouting the law in the name of love – because of course it was love. There was no doubt now in her mind.

In bed at night she made plans. They would marry as soon as she was old enough. He'd still be under forty, not old at all. Ma and Pa might have some reservations about the age gap, but the fact that he was a teacher would help them get over it.

They'd have children, one of each at least. She would be a writer; she'd start with magazine features and progress to short stories, maybe novels.

In class he treated her the same as everyone else, giving her precisely the same attention as every other student. She hugged her secret to herself, counting the days till they could go to the forest again.

And then, the Monday after their seventh Saturday, Lien said, There's a rumour going around.

It was the sixteenth of November. School was over for the day. They were walking to the bus stop. What kind of rumour? Tilly asked, her heart tightening.

About you and John Smith. Abigail Carson's mother says she saw you getting into his car on Saturday, outside the library.

Tilly laughed, the sound coming out all wrong. A kind of crowing, not her usual laugh at all. Abigail Carson made that up, she said. You know she fancies him.

But why would she say she'd seen him with *you*?

I have no idea. Maybe her mother saw someone who looked like me.

She didn't sound convincing, even to herself. It's rubbish, she said. It's not true.

People think it might be though, Lien said, not looking at Tilly, staring straight ahead as the bus stop came into view.

Well, I'm telling you they're wrong.

OK.

She'd wear a scarf on Saturday: she'd wrap her hair in it, make herself different. She'd tell him they'd been seen. They'd change where they met. They'd work it out.

For the rest of the week she kept as much distance as she could between herself and Abigail Carson. She became aware that people stopped talking as she approached – or did she imagine that? In English Lit she took care not to look at him, even if he addressed her directly.

On Saturday she pulled a turquoise scarf from her bag as she approached the library steps and wrapped her head in it. As she waited she kept glancing around, but nobody seemed to be watching.

He was late. Ten minutes passed, then twenty. After an hour she went home, her skin itching with dread, convinced that someone had said something to him too. That evening she went to do her usual shift in the Indonesian restaurant, but she was so absent-minded, mixing up orders and bringing the wrong bills, that Nadia's mother sent her home early, saying she must be sickening for something.

On Monday morning there was no sign of his red Jeep in the school car park when she walked through. She told herself it meant nothing: he was late, that was all. The day crawled along, English Lit straight after lunch. She couldn't eat the sandwich Ma had made; when Lien asked if she was OK, she told her she had period pains.

On the way back to class she realised that her period was five days overdue. She was like clockwork, never late by more than a day.

The bell rang. She sat at her desk, her palms damp, her stomach bubbling with acid, her head aching.

The door opened and Mrs Harvey walked in. Surprise, she said – but it came as no surprise. Hands up who missed me. A few heads swivelled towards Tilly, who pretended not to notice.

When she got home from school Ma and Pa were waiting for her in the kitchen. This came, Ma said, holding up a letter that didn't have a signature on it. And as Tilly read the few short typed sentences of condemnation, from Abigail Carson or her mother, one or the other, she felt something bursting inside her – and it all came washing out then, along with a torrent of tears.

I'm sorry, she wept, as they stood dumbfounded before her. I'm so sorry, I know it was wrong, I know we shouldn't have done it, I know I've let you down, but it's over, he's gone, it's all over.

He's your *teacher*, Ma said faintly.

He's not – he's not any more. He's gone, Mrs Harvey is back – I'll never see him again.

She begged them to take no action. She said it would ruin her in school, that she'd definitely be expelled if it came out. She told them they'd been careful, that there was nothing to worry about. And because they were uncomplicated country people they believed her, and agreed to leave it in the past.

But she'd broken their trust: she'd betrayed it every Saturday for weeks. She could see it in the careful way they looked at her after that. Something had been lost between them: it was one more thing to mourn.

It was 23 November, with two weeks left of the final term of the school year. She went through the motions each day. She sat through exams she didn't remember afterwards, she responded to questions in class. She walked to the bus stop every afternoon with Lien, just like they'd always done, and John Smith's name never once came up.

She didn't tell Lien about her missed period. She made no mention of the anonymous letter. And she didn't tell her best friend that a few mornings after the letter's arrival, she'd had to run to the bathroom to throw up the breakfast she'd just eaten.

❄

THURSDAY
24 DECEMBER
CHRISTMAS EVE

❄

✳✳✳

Nobody had died. She had to keep reminding herself that nobody had died. If she didn't keep doing that, there was every chance that she would slap a child – or two children – very hard, or collapse in a dead faint, neither of which sounded like particularly sensible courses of action just then, given that there was a baby clamped to her hip.

She lowered Poppy into the playpen and turned back to the offenders. 'How many times have I forbidden you two to go anywhere near those cliffs?'

Silence. Two lowered heads.

'Well? How many?'

'Dunno.'

'Dunno.'

'I'll tell you. Too many times to count, that's how many. I've told you over and over to stay well away from there.'

More silence. Shuffling of four feet.

'Haven't I?'

'Yes.'

'Yes.'

'Because they're dangerous, that's why.' More silence. 'Aren't they dangerous?'

'Yes.'

'Yes.'

'And still you went – and in this weather too. Can you *hear* that wind? *Listen* to it.'

The three of them listened to the wind as it whipped and shrieked outside. In her playpen, Poppy grabbed Rabbity by his long-suffering ears and whacked him against the bars, and yelled in delight at the sound.

'Wasn't so windy when we went out,' Ben mumbled – and even in her agitated state Laura had to acknowledge the truth of that. How terrifyingly quickly it had blown up: not a breath when she'd risen this morning, not much more when the boys had gone on their usual ramble just after lunch.

She imagined what it must have been like on the cliffs once the wind really got going, how easily two skinny ten-year-old boys weighing less than five stone apiece could have been picked up and tossed—

She cut the thought off sharply. Nothing had happened. Nobody had died.

I thought I should bring them home, Dougie Fennessy had said, landing the boys on the doorstep not five minutes before. It's a wild one: Leo's just called a halt for the day.

This time of year, it wasn't uncommon for Leo to suspend ferry operations for a time due to stormy conditions, stranding people on or off the island until more clement weather returned. Visitors to Roone could be put out at having to change their plans without warning, but locals accepted it as a matter of course, and adapted accordingly.

Praise the Lord Gladys had got away, by the skin of her teeth it sounded like. Gav had driven her to the pier for the one o'clock ferry, the wind only starting up then, but still it must have been the last one to go across. How lucky were they?

Laura had thanked Dougie and sent him home with a bottle of apple juice. The beauty of living on a small island, everyone looking out for everyone else's children. No shortage of guardian angels here, both heavenly and human varieties.

But Roone, for all its wonderful community spirit, was not without its dangers for children and adults alike. Chief among them had to be the Atlantic Ocean, washing up on every side. Benevolent when it chose – offering a livelihood, between fishing and tourism, to a goodly proportion of Roone's population – but unpredictable as a wildcat, demanding always to be respected. Nell Baker's grandfather and Walter Thompson's father were among the many islanders whose lives had been claimed by the sea: both seasoned sailors but no match, when it had come to it, for a storm-tossed ocean.

Then there were the cliffs, to the west and south of the island, the closest of them less than half a mile from the house. The bane of every parent's life despite the safety fence, which could be scaled easily if you were any way nimble – Ben and Seamus were like monkeys.

Still, all things considered, Roone had to be one of the safest places in Ireland to raise a child. I wandered all over it with my friends when I was young, Nell had told Laura. There wasn't a square inch we didn't explore. We knew every rock in the place, every cove, every lane.

And that was the kind of childhood Laura wanted for her children; the kind she'd never had growing up in the heart of a city. She wanted them to enjoy the freedom of Roone, to roam about it until they knew it like Nell did. She just didn't want them taking chances in the sea, or going anywhere near the cliffs, in any weather, until they were old enough and sensible enough to handle them with care.

But she was lucky: most of the time they were good boys. They did their bit around the place – they took it in turns to collect the eggs and feed the livestock each morning and evening. When the B&B was running at full tilt at the height of the summer they'd pitch in when she asked them, and they helped out with Gavin's deliveries when they had holidays.

But they were boys, and a month ago they'd turned ten, and with the school closed for Christmas it was inevitable that they'd get up to some tomfoolery now and again.

'I have a good mind to send you to bed before the party begins,' Laura said.

Their faces fell. The deal had been that they could stay up beyond their usual bedtime, in return for helping with the food distribution. It wasn't the party they'd mind missing, with its wholly adult guest list: it was the coins that would undoubtedly get slipped to them as they offered seconds of mince pies and held out dishes of cream.

'We're sorry, Mum,' Ben said.

'Yeah, please can we stay up?'

She looked at their beseeching freckled faces. 'I'll think about it,' she told them. Of course they'd be staying up: Gavin wouldn't manage all the running around on his own, and Laura had no intention of doing it.

As if the thought of him were enough to conjure him up, she heard the click of the back door opening – and almost immediately it slammed shut again, making the cups jump on the dresser, and Poppy start in her playpen. 'Sorry – wind grabbed it,' he shouted from the scullery.

His hair, when he eventually appeared, was tossed about his head. Laura should have sent him to Nell earlier in the week for a cut: now he'd have to wait till the salon opened again after Christmas. You'd think he'd remember things like that himself: sometimes it felt like she had six children.

'Hey there,' he said, feet already shed of his wellingtons, shucking off his jacket. 'Going to be the mother of all storms tonight. Sea is whipping up like you wouldn't believe. Mam was lucky she didn't leave it any later to go – the ferry is cancelled for the rest of the day.'

'I know.'

As he was hanging his jacket on its customary hook he spotted the Christmas cake sitting on the dresser, the one Laura had iced the minute Gladys was out of the way.

'Hey,' he said, 'you finished it.'

'I did.' She waited.

'It's wonderful. Well done, your first cake. Good for you.'

He must be blind. The icing was a disaster, messy and lopsided, the silver balls she'd plunked on top unevenly spaced, the whole affair as far from a thing of beauty as it was possible to get. Wonderful my foot.

'Did you remember the green tea?'

'I did.' He dipped into the jacket pocket and handed the box to her before turning to the boys. 'Hear that wind?' he asked, but they didn't reply.

He took in their abashed stance. He glanced at Laura. 'Something happen?'

She told him, and he did his best to look shocked. 'I'm very disappointed,' he said. 'You know you shouldn't go near the cliffs, you've been told often enough. What would Santa have to say?'

She could see his words floating away unheeded. She was definitely the bad cop in this family: he was a hopeless softie, incapable of disciplining them. Even at two years old, the girls were running rings around him.

'Your mother went off OK?'

'She did, no problem.'

'Did you check on the animals?'

'They're in the shed.'

'And the hens?'

'Inside.'

He loved animals. He'd been working at Dublin Zoo when they met. He'd fill their place here with four-legged creatures, open up a Roone Zoo if she gave him half a chance.

He wasn't doing too badly as it was.

To be fair, he couldn't be directly blamed for any of the livestock they'd acquired since moving to Roone. When they'd bought Walter's house, the farmer who'd been looking after George the donkey and the hens returned them. They belong here, he'd told Gavin and Laura, it's only right that they should come back – so they'd had little choice but to accept them.

And Laura herself was wholly responsible for acquiring Charlie, the half setter, half Lab pup she hadn't been able to resist when his owners had been looking for homes for the litter two years earlier. Since then, Charlie had shed his adorable puppyish pudginess and was eating everything they gave him and more, but he'd tail-wagged his way into the hearts of the entire household.

Caesar the pot-bellied pig had been a raffle prize the Christmas before that, and since Laura had insisted on Gavin buying a ticket – the raffle had been organised to fund new Christmas decorations for the village street – there wasn't much she could say when he'd arrived home with piglet Caesar in the van.

And when Cheryl and Maddie, the miniature goats, were left ownerless after Morgan O'Rourke from two doors down died last winter, it had seemed like the Christian thing to take them in. Morgan had kept them supplied with goat's milk for Evie, who couldn't stomach the regular stuff, and he'd never accepted a penny in return.

So even if Gavin hadn't set about developing his very own animal kingdom in their back garden, one was quietly coming into being. Of course, there were returns to be had – eggs, goat's milk, donkey rides – and between them, George and the goats kept the grass down in the field.

In fact, Laura used to feel secretly that there was something rather satisfying about a garden full of animals. In a way, it seemed the perfect complement to a house full of children, despite the frequent chaos that both entities could cause. Now there were times when she was tempted to let them all go, animals and children, to the highest bidder.

'Girls napping?' Gavin enquired – and the words were hardly out of his mouth when they heard the familiar high-pitched babbling from upstairs that heralded the joint awakening of his toddler daughters.

Laura turned to the boys. 'You have exactly half an hour,' she told them. 'Go upstairs with Dad and help him to get the girls up, then change the sheets on Granny's bed and put clean towels in her bathroom. When that's all done, clean your own room. If everything is OK when I check, you can stay up tonight.'

'Thanks, Mum.' They sped from the room and thumped up the stairs.

'Take Poppy,' she said to Gavin. 'Do whatever you have to do to keep them all out of my way for half an hour. I'll be wrapping presents.'

'No problem.'

'And you should have got your hair cut for Christmas,' she added, unable to resist. 'I'm surprised your mother didn't mention how awful it looks.'

In the small silence that followed, she heard the sharp echo of it, heard how nasty it sounded.

He bent and gathered Poppy into his arms. 'Well,' he said mildly, 'that's me told.'

She opened her mouth to tell him not to mind her, but he was gone, the door closing behind him. He'd get over it.

She stood on a chair and retrieved the presents, wrapping paper and ribbon she'd hidden in two black bin bags on top of the dresser. She brought everything out to the scullery, which was little more than a passageway from the kitchen to the garden, used mainly as a storage area for egg boxes and juice bottles, and a dumping ground for wellingtons, umbrellas and items waiting to be recycled.

Out here the storm was even more in evidence, the wail of the wind even louder than in the kitchen. Annie Byrnes's bones had been right after all: she should never have doubted them.

So early in the day, not yet three o'clock, the light was already beginning to fade. She peered through the little side window that looked out on their half a dozen apple trees, and saw the wet gleam of the branches as they slapped and whipped about in the wind. She remembered Nell telling her, not long after she and Gavin had moved in, that her grandfather had helped Walter's father to plant the trees, when both were young men. That must make them ... what? Eighty years old, maybe more?

She thought of the boys clambering up the gnarled branches in the summertime; she imagined the girls in years to come having dolly tea parties in the dappled shade beneath. They were so lucky to have those beautiful trees as part of their playground. She wondered what the life span of an apple tree was: would this lot still be standing when her grandchildren were running around outside? Would the magic tree, as the children called it, still be offering its apples all year round? Amazing how they'd all come to accept that as completely normal, nobody commenting any more on apples that ripened in February or March.

She made out the shed standing just beyond the trees, where the animals were harbouring for the night. Thank goodness they'd got Damien Kiely to build it after Gavin's poorly constructed pigsty had finally collapsed last year, nearly flattening poor Caesar: let the wind huff and puff all it wanted, it was hardly likely to blow down a shed made of bricks.

As she began to wrap Evie's princess dress, the back door rattled on its hinges in response to a sudden fierce gust, and she felt the accompanying draught at her ankles from the sizeable gap between door and floor that had been there since Walter's time, and that Gavin had yet to address, despite his frequent promises. Mind you, given his DIY history, he might well make the problem worse.

Hopefully the storm wouldn't wreak too much havoc while it was in full swing. It had better not put paid to her party this evening. The closer it got, the more she found she was clinging to the thought of it. A few hours of relaxed company and entertaining conversation, not to mention a couple of glasses of mulled wine. Not a lot, not enough to make tomorrow torturous – hangovers and excited children didn't belong in the same sentence. Just enough to soften the edges and send her floating off to sleep when everyone had gone home.

When the last gift was wrapped she stowed everything back in the bin bags and stood them in a corner. Anyone looking would take them for recycling, and ignore them.

She thought of all she still had to do before her guests arrived. Locate the crib – where on earth had they put it after last Christmas?

– mop the kitchen floor, get dinner cooked and eaten, make the turkey stuffing, put the three small ones to bed, give the sitting room a quick run around with the Hoover, change her clothes, prepare the—

'Mum?'

She hadn't heard them coming back downstairs. She pushed open the kitchen door – and there among the children stood Gladys, handing her coat to Ben.

Gladys, back again.

Gladys, not gone home on the one o'clock ferry after all.

Laura's heart plummeted to the floor. She smothered her dismay and did her best to look merely surprised. 'Gladys – I thought Gavin had put you on the ferry.'

But one look at him, skulking with Poppy by the dresser, told her he hadn't done any such thing. He wore the abashed expression of someone caught robbing a neighbour's bottle of milk from the doorstep.

'I asked him to leave me off in the village,' Gladys said, sinking into a chair. 'I wanted to pick up a magazine for the journey. Oh, I'm exhausted. Seamus, you make sure to use a wooden hanger with that coat now.'

'I'm Ben.'

'You should have waited with your mother,' Laura told Gavin. Keeping the words even, but giving him a look she knew he'd recognise. 'You should have brought her to the pier and made sure she got safely onto the ferry.'

'I offered to wait, but she said she wanted the walk.'

Pathetic, truly pathetic. Could he do *nothing* right?

'Ah, don't be at him,' Gladys said, setting Laura's teeth further on edge. She was the nagging wife now, a new string to her bow. 'I told him he didn't have to wait, wasn't I well able to make my own way to the pier? And I was so full after that breakfast you gave me, I needed to walk it off.'

The breakfast that Laura had cooked, the sausages and rashers she'd grilled, the egg she'd poached because Gladys didn't care for it fried – *and maybe the yolk could be a tiny bit softer than yesterday's, dear* – in the middle of trying to soothe a peevish Poppy and feed Charlie, who was snuffling hopefully at his empty bowl, and keep the girls from squabbling while Gavin and the boys were out doing his deliveries.

'But then I was delayed in the shop. There were three ahead of me, and that girl with the red hair behind the counter is so slow – is she a bit retarded? And the woman ahead of me took *ages* to make up her mind between a mint Aero and a Crunchie – it wasn't as if she needed either of them, the size of her – and to cut a long story short, I ended up missing the ferry by a few minutes. It was just pulling away when I got down. I waved at the man – I *know* he saw me, it wouldn't have taken him a minute to come back, but he couldn't be bothered. So then I tried to ring Gavin, but he didn't answer his phone.'

'Mam, I told you I had things to do after I left you.'

'Didn't you see my number coming up?'

'My phone was in my jacket – you know I don't answer it when I'm on the road.'

Gladys pinched her lips together. 'I would have thought you'd have been looking out for a call from me, in case anything went wrong – and it wouldn't kill you to pull over for a minute. You must have heard it ringing.'

In the accusatory silence that followed, Poppy passed one of her famously loud blasts of wind, which caused the assembled children to erupt into merriment, and brought a small grin even to Gavin's face.

'Well,' Gladys said, shifting indignantly in her chair. 'I'm glad you all find my troubles so amusing.'

'Mam, we're not—'

'So then I thought all I had to do was wait for the two o'clock ferry, so I went back to the village and into that little café beside the post office, whatever the name of it is …'

Laura had stopped listening. Her mind had snagged on the fact that he'd dropped his mother in the village. He hadn't offered to run into the shop and get her damn magazine. He hadn't waited to make sure they got rid of her. He'd dropped her and then gone on his merry way.

Wait till she got him on his own.

'... and the scone was as hard as a rock, it really was. I said it to the proprietor, and she was quite sniffy. Someone should tell her the customer is always right. Of course I insisted on a replacement, which I was *perfectly* entitled to do ...'

Lelia. She was criticising Lelia's scones, which were fêted throughout Roone. The woman was unbelievable.

'... and then, after all that, when I got down to the pier I found the two o'clock ferry had been *cancelled*, without a blind bit of notice, just because it was windy. What kind of a service is that?'

'Mam, Leo has to use his—'

'And then I tried your phone again, and *still* got nowhere—'

'I was probably—'

'And so I had to double back to the village yet again and at this stage I was being blown out of it, and so cold, nearly frozen *solid* ...'

Frozen solid, in her cashmere and wool coat.

'... that I headed into the hotel and ordered myself a little hot port, which will tell you how bad I was, because as you know I hardly *ever* ...'

A little hot port. While Laura was imagining her halfway back to Dublin she'd been swigging port half a mile down the road.

'... and then I got them to ring me a taxi, which took *forever* to arrive – it must be nearly three o'clock now, is it? I can't believe there's only one taxi on the whole of the island – you really need to do something about that.'

Silence.

'And now it looks like you're stuck with me for Christmas.'

More silence.

'Well,' she said tartly, 'it's nice to know I'll be welcome anyway.'

'Of course you will,' Gavin said hastily. 'We're delighted to have you.' Looking beseechingly at Laura, who ignored him. 'We're just surprised, that's all.'

'It's terribly awkward, it's throwing out all my plans. Joyce is expecting me back – we were to have Christmas dinner together, it was all arranged. I'll have to ring her when I've recovered. She'll be very disappointed.'

Or delighted. One or the other.

'I don't suppose,' she went on, looking mournfully at Laura, 'there's any hope of a cup of tea?'

'Gavin will make it,' Laura replied, whisking Poppy from his arms. 'This little lady needs her nappy changed.' She was damned if she was going to be waiting hand and foot on the Duchess of Dublin over Christmas.

He followed her out to the hall. 'Laura, hang on—'

She rounded on him. 'How *could* you?' she hissed. 'How could you do this to me?'

'I'm sorry – she was in plenty of time to get the ferry.'

'Clearly, she wasn't, or she wouldn't be here now.'

'I would have waited, but she insisted—'

'For God's sake – one thing you had to do, and you messed it up. You're *useless*.'

'Look, I don't know what you want me to say—'

'Nothing,' she shot back. 'Say *nothing* to me, unless you have to.'

She started up the stairs with Poppy. On the landing she heard the kitchen door open and close. Back to mother, who thought the sun shone out of him.

In the bedroom she changed Poppy's nappy, which didn't need changing. What a calamity. Gladys not gone, and the party only hours away, no choice now but to make her part of it. And Lelia was coming, Lelia whose scone had been rejected by Gladys earlier. A fine Christmas Eve this was turning out to be.

She imagined tomorrow's dinner. Gladys would be full of criticism: the turkey would be on the dry side, the stuffing would be better with a little sausage-meat or chestnuts or *something* added to it. The children would drive her mad: she'd wonder if Laura could ask them to be a little quieter. The pudding, Betty Buckley's finest, would undoubtedly give her heartburn. The crackers would bring on a migraine.

The room was dim, twilight taking a firmer hold now, leaching the colour from everything. The patch of sky she could see through the window was a peculiar greyish-mustard shade, lending a vaguely sinister air to the storm. What was that song about the bleak midwinter? They'd sung it at the carol service in the church last week. Winter was bleak, and no mistake. Winter needed parties, lots of them.

She looked down and met her youngest daughter's eyes. 'What's your opinion on the whole thing?' she asked. 'Are you as fed up as me?'

Poppy met her gaze solemnly. 'Gah,' she told her mother. 'Mmff,' she added, grabbing onto the thumb Laura offered, encircling it with her tiny hand and holding on tight. The world got a small bit brighter.

Nobody had died. They'd all survive a few more days. And Gladys or no Gladys, Laura was going to enjoy the evening ahead. She was going to eat and drink – maybe more than a couple of glasses – and keep as far from her husband as she could, and maybe Lelia would oblige by throttling Gladys with a string of tinsel before the night was out.

'Twas the season to be jolly. She'd be jolly if it killed her.

❄❄❄

'Just missed it,' Paddy said placidly, as if missing a ferry happened to him every other day, and wasn't anything at all to get bothered about. Tilly didn't imagine Paddy O'Carroll got bothered about very much, which she supposed was a good way to be.

She watched the Roone ferry pulling away from the little pier. So close and yet so far: three minutes earlier and she'd have made it. But there it went, leaving a wide trail of white foam in its wake. Nothing to do but bide her time until the next one.

And look at the sea, look at the Atlantic Ocean washing up not twenty feet from the car. Her first time to set eyes on it, her first glimpse of the sea that would soon be surrounding her. Listen to it, the pounding of waves against stone loud even with the car windows rolled up. Despite her disappointment, the sight of it, so majestic and wild, lifted her heart. She longed to get out: she was greedy for the scent of it, for the wet feel of it on her face.

'The half one, that was,' Paddy said. 'Be another one along at half two, if the wind don't get any worse.'

But the wind had been getting steadily stronger since they'd left Dingle half an hour ago, later than planned because Joan from next door had called in just before noon, the same Joan who looked after Breda and Paddy's two enormously hairy tabby cats anytime they were left unattended.

I heard you had a visitor, she'd said, setting something wrapped in tinfoil on Breda's table, pulling off her purple bobble hat, taking in every bit of Tilly with her red-rimmed, watery blue eyes. Where's this you're from again? she'd asked, shrugging her arms out of her olive-green waxed coat, pushing a cat off a chair to plonk down next to Tilly. America, is it?

And by the time Breda had made and poured her third pot of tea of the morning, and they'd cut the still-warm apple tart Joan had brought, and Tilly had answered every one of her many, many questions, it was coming up to one o'clock, and Breda was ushering Tilly out the door and telling Paddy to be sure and get her to the pier by half one, the day wasn't looking good.

But they hadn't quite made it by half one, although Tilly's knuckles had been white from gripping the side of her seat as they'd hurtled along roads that didn't look wide enough for one car, let alone two.

Paddy, his seatbelt left untouched, bounced over potholes and overtook anything slower than him with terrifying abandon, and whizzed by all oncoming vehicles – cars, vans, tractors – with equal nonchalance, whistling gently through his teeth the whole time, seemingly unaware of the extreme trepidation of his passenger.

There was a strong whiff of cat in the car: clearly he and Breda didn't always leave them at home when they travelled. The back seat was piled high with a jumble of books and magazines and what looked like plastic fertiliser bags and assorted items of clothing, wellingtons and hats.

The night before, when he'd collected them from the bus station, the clutter had merely been shoved aside to make room for Tilly. The boot was equally full – a set of golf clubs, a camping gas stove, what looked like a rolled-up tent and several other plastic bags. We'll make it fit, Paddy had said equably, hefting Tilly's case, and he'd somehow squeezed it in, along with his wife's bulging shopping bags.

They'd driven through Dingle on the way to the house. People crowded the narrow streets, calling and waving to one another, and crossing to the other side whenever they felt like it, forcing oncoming cars to stop. There seemed to be an awful lot of bars, most of which had a Guinness sign hanging outside: Tilly caught snatches of lively music as they passed.

Breda and Paddy lived on the side of a country road that was dotted with other lit-up houses. Their kitchen was cluttered and cosy, with a big open fire in front of which the two cats sprawled, ignoring the humans. The roast-chicken dinner that awaited them had never been so welcome: it had taken all of Tilly's willpower not to wolf down the slices of succulent breast and gloriously crunchy-on-the-outside roast potatoes and little mound of minted garden peas, and the irresistibly buttery sauce that Breda poured generously over everything.

I have him well trained, haven't I? she said, winking at Tilly. When he puts his mind to it, he can dish up a grand dinner.

Give over, Paddy replied. He was a man of few words, possibly because he'd lost the knack of talking after sharing the past forty years or so with a woman who rarely stopped. He'd been good-looking in his younger days too – you could see that in the still-strong line of his jaw, the sculpted cheekbones, the coffee-brown eyes.

And there was no mistaking the affection between the couple. Tilly had noted the tender smile he gave his wife when they were reunited at the bus station, the way he'd held the car door open for her, the way he'd settled her in. Love that had lasted, maybe even grown stronger with the years. Tilly wondered if she'd ever know it.

After dinner Tilly was shown upstairs to a room at the rear of the house. Navy carpet swirled with purples and blues, cream wallpaper splashed with roses, mahogany wardrobe, matching dressing table on which lay a lace cloth, and a giant double bed covered with a crocheted blanket in pale blues and pinks and lemons. Window veiled with heavily patterned netting and framed by burgundy velvet curtains.

This was the girls' room, Breda told her, pulling the curtains closed. Áine made the crochet blanket in school when she was twelve. The two of them would fight like cats and dogs by day, and you'd come in at night and they'd be curled around one another in the bed.

She led Tilly into the bathroom across the landing and turned on the hot tap in the cast-iron bath. I bet you can't wait to have a proper scrub after all your travels, she said, shaking in a fistful of salts that caused a musky scent to waft around the steamy little room. I'll put a hot jar into your bed while you're soaking – and Tilly pictured one of the big mason jars Ma used to store her pickled onions in sitting in the centre of the bed, and thought it a strange way to heat it.

When Breda had disappeared she dropped her clothes one by one onto the tiled floor and eased her way into the hot bath and lay back. She could hear the soothing gurgle of water through the pipes, and the murmur of Breda and Paddy's voices in the kitchen directly below. Two people she hadn't known existed until a few hours ago, two complete strangers who'd opened their home to her and made her welcome.

She yawned, breathing in the fragrant air. It was becoming an effort to keep her eyes open. Better not stay too long, never do if she drifted off; mortifying if they had to bang on the door to wake her.

She rippled the water, thinking about all that had happened since she'd waved goodbye to Ma through the taxi window and set off on this journey across the world. So much to think about, good and bad.

She'd be on Roone now if she hadn't fallen asleep and missed her connection in London. She might be lying in a bath in her sister's house instead of here. But then she wouldn't have met Breda and Paddy, who'd shown her such kindness. Maybe everything really did happen for a reason.

And after more than forty-eight hours without access to one, the bed when she slid into it ten minutes later was like a gift straight from Heaven. The hot jar turned out to be a regular hot-water bottle, the kind Pa used on chilly nights; her feet had barely made contact with it when she sank – literally dropped straight – into the deepest sleep of her life.

She didn't stir till Breda tapped on her door almost twelve hours later and presented her with the first of several cups of tea Tilly was to have before leaving for the pier with Paddy.

Don't be long, Breda said, your breakfast is ready below, and the forecast isn't great so you'll need to get going for the ferry in a while – and Tilly felt again the stomach-flip of anticipation that every mention or thought of Roone caused. Just hours away now from her destination, nothing more to delay her.

Pulling on clean clothes, she suddenly remembered that she hadn't texted home since Heathrow, which seemed ages ago: better do it now. Half past ten in the morning here, almost bedtime at home but Ma would still be up.

Hope all is well, she typed. *Will miss you for Christmas, have a lovely day*. She imagined them gathering without her around the table on the veranda where they always ate the roast beef Ma cooked on Christmas Day. What did the Irish eat for Christmas? She'd find out tomorrow: another stomach lurch.

Breakfast was a feast, a dinner plate loaded with fried egg and thick bacon strips and plump sausages, and two tasty little circles, one beige and one so dark brown it was almost black. Pudding, Breda called them, black and white.

A full Irish breakfast you have there, she said. We have it on Sunday mornings, and on special occasions. The rest of the time it's porridge, and my own brown bread. Her brown bread was the colour of toasted macaroons, and bore no resemblance, in taste or texture, to any bread Tilly had come across. It was soft inside, with a hard crust and a pleasant nutty flavour. It was also warm.

I made a bit before you were up, Breda told her. Easiest thing in the world, could do it in my sleep. A mix of brown and white flour, a fist of bran, a splash of buttermilk, a shake of salt and a spoon of bread soda. Every woman in Ireland makes it the same way and every one of them gets a different loaf. If you were staying a bit longer I could teach you.

Paddy was nowhere to be seen. Out on the farm, Tilly presumed. She wondered, but didn't like to ask, when he would be taking her to the pier. Now that Roone was so close, she was seized with a desire to be there, to discover finally what reception awaited her on the island.

We thought you'd better go for the half twelve ferry, Breda eventually said, in case they have to stop early with the weather. The forecast isn't great for later. Spooning yet another round of loose tea into a pot as she spoke, splashing boiling water on top. Paddy is just gone to check on the sheep. He'll be back to drive you.

But then Joan had called, and the apple tart was cut, and they decided the half one ferry would be time enough. And now Tilly and Paddy climbed out of the car and watched the ferry moving further and further away from them. Beyond it, Tilly could make out a faint dark hump of land rising from the line of water at the horizon. 'Is that Roone?' she asked Paddy.

'It is, that's it. 'Tisn't far … but 'tis different from here.'

She turned to him. 'Different?' A gust snatched her hair and swept it across her face; she pinned it back.

He shoved his hands into his armpits, gave a toss of his head. 'Ah, they're grand, but they have their own ways. You'll see when you're there a while.'

He'd been told what Breda had been told, that Tilly was going to find her sister. He had no idea how long Tilly was planning to stay on Roone, if things worked out.

The breeze coming off the sea was sharp and bitingly cold, but she'd never breathed anything so clean and pure. She remembered standing at the edge of the Pacific seven years earlier, on the far side of the world. She thought there was something wilder about this ocean, something dangerous and exciting. It flung itself against the pier, it pelted icy drops onto her face: she licked them and tasted salt.

Paddy nodded in the direction of a grey cabin, slightly bigger than an average garden shed and set a little way back from the pier. A small green Jeep was parked by its door. 'We can wait in there,' he said, 'out of the cold.'

'You don't have to wait,' Tilly said. 'I'll be fine on my own.' He'd done more than enough already.

He looked doubtful. 'I'd say Breda would want me to stay, make sure you get off OK.'

But Tilly sensed he had plenty at home to keep him busy. 'Give me your number,' she told him, 'and if I run into any problem I'll call you.'

She wouldn't call, of course: she had no intention of it. If she had to spend Christmas right there in that cabin she wouldn't presume on their generosity again. But it wouldn't come to that. The ferry would return and she'd get on, and finish her journey.

He scribbled the phone number on the back of a leaflet he found in the car. Handing it over, he still looked unsure. 'Getting rough now,' he remarked, looking out to sea.

'Honestly,' Tilly said, 'I'll be fine. Really.' Hoping to God she was right.

'Nearly forgot,' he said then. He stuck a hand in his back pocket and it came out with a banknote. 'Here,' he said, thrusting it towards Tilly. 'Breda wanted you to have that, over you being robbed.'

She backed away from it. 'No, I couldn't take it, you've been more than—'

'You have to,' he insisted, reaching for her hand and pressing the money into it. 'She'll have my guts for garters if I come home with it. Take it, you might be glad of it.'

'Give me your address then,' she said 'so I can send it back to you when I get home' – but already he was turning for the car, raising a hand in farewell.

'Safe journey now, and a happy Christmas to you if we don't see you.'

'Thank you so much,' she called. 'Happy Christmas,' waving until he was out of sight. She unfolded the note and saw that it was twenty euro. Their kindness brought tears to her eyes.

She tucked the money into the inner pocket of her bag and wheeled her case across to the cabin, and pushed open the door. A youngish woman with long auburn hair sat behind a desk at the far end. Jacket, scarf, hat. Book held in hands that emerged from some kind of knitted cuffs. A fan heater humming at her feet.

'Hello there,' she said to Tilly, lowering the book. 'Do close the door, keep in the little heat I have.' Her accent was strange; elements of it similar to Breda and Paddy's but a twang that had been missing from theirs. 'You want to go to Roone.'

'Yes please.'

'You just missed the half one ferry.'

'I know – I saw it going. But I'll wait for the next.'

The woman lifted a hand, doubt on her face. 'Let's hope there is one: it's getting wild out there. Leo will let us know.'

'Leo?' She thought of the star sign. Were Irish ferry schedules dictated by a celestial lion?

'The ferryman. He'll give me a shout if it gets too bad.'

This sounded ominous. Through the window Tilly could see the water tossing about, as if some giant hand was swishing it around, like Breda had done to the bathwater last night to dissolve the salts she'd thrown in. It was getting stormier out there, that much was clear.

But today was Christmas Eve. Her skin tightened with anxiety. She began to wish she'd hung on to Paddy. 'What happens if there isn't another ferry?'

A grimace. 'Then I'm afraid you're stuck on this side. There's no other way to Roone, unless you have a private jet.'

'And tomorrow? Christmas Day?'

'Nothing. No ferry again until the twenty-sixth.'

The twenty-sixth, two days away. Two nights to spend still in transit. Tilly cast another look out the window. 'How bad does it have to get?'

'Not much worse than this, to be honest.' She nodded at Tilly's suitcase. 'Have you come far?'

'Australia.'

She whistled. 'Long, long way. You got people on Roone?'

Tilly hesitated. 'Yes, I have some family there.'

Should she keep telling people about the sister she had yet to meet, or would it be better to keep the information to herself in case it all went horribly wrong?

'If you don't get over today, what then? Do you have any other contacts here, on this side?'

'Not really ... Well, I have a phone number of a couple in Dingle, but I only met them yesterday, and they let me stay in their house last night, and I wouldn't want to bother them again ...'

How awful was it to have come so far, to be so close to her final destination and maybe not get there after all? She thought of the man in Heathrow who had promised to look after her things, and felt a hot rush of anger. It was all his fault; he'd messed it all up.

If she hadn't met him she'd have stayed awake and got her coach to Stansted, she'd be on Roone now. And even if Roone didn't work out and her sister didn't want to know, she'd still have money; with funds she'd be able somehow to manage. It would be miserable, of course, to have to spend Christmas alone in a foreign country, but it wouldn't be impossible.

Now everything was different. With just a few euro to her name – eighty now, with Paddy's twenty – the story was very different. How long could you live as a tourist on eighty euro?

'There is a village,' the woman told her, 'about half a mile up the road. It's called Kilmally.'

'I saw it.' They'd passed through, Paddy hardly slowing his pace. A single street, a scatter of houses, a shop or two, petrol pumps.

'There's a pub there, they have accommodation, and as far as I know it's open all year round. You could stay there if you were stuck.'

'Yes ...'

She was assuming that Tilly had the money to pay for it, because nobody travels from Australia to Ireland in the middle of winter without enough money to get by. Tilly had no idea how much an overnight stay cost in Ireland: presumably a pub would be cheaper than a hotel, but she still doubted that she had enough to pay for two nights anywhere.

Outside, conditions continued to worsen, the waves crashing in earnest now against the pier wall. It was looking more and more likely that Tilly would be stuck on this side of the sea. In a while the phone on the woman's desk would ring and it would be Leo telling her to go home, that the ferry had stopped running for the day.

She'd have to phone Paddy, she was left with no choice. She hated the thought of having to impose on him and Breda again – and this time she'd be barging into their Christmas. They mightn't even be staying at home for it: they might have been invited to one of their children's houses. Or they might be hosting; everyone might be coming to them for Christmas dinner. How could Tilly expect them to make room for her?

They would, though. Knowing the kind of people they were, she was fairly sure they'd come to her rescue for a second time. She just hated having to ask them.

'You may as well take a seat,' the woman said. 'Would you like some tea?' She indicated a large flask sitting on a shelf behind her. 'I also have cookies.'

'No thanks.'

At least she wasn't hungry – and she'd drunk enough tea in the last few hours to keep her hydrated until at least the following day. She sat on the wooden bench that ran the short length of the cabin and studied the array of posters that were displayed on the wall that faced her. Blasket Island Cruises, Dingle Peninsula Walking Holidays, Ring of Kerry Coach Tours. Not too many people taking a cruise to the Blasket Islands or walking around the Dingle Peninsula today.

She turned back to her companion. Might as well make conversation, as long as they'd been thrown together. Might help the time pass.

'What part of Ireland are you from?'

The woman's face broke into a wide gap-toothed smile. 'I'm not Irish, I'm Dutch.'

'Oh – but your English is so fluent.'

'We learn it in school, and most of our TV shows are UK or American imports, with subtitles, so we hear it all the time. I am Isa,' she added, 'short for Isabella.' She made it sound like *Ee-sah*.

'I'm Tilly, short for Matilda. Have you been living here long?'

'I came fifteen years ago. I was travelling around Europe with my boyfriend, and this was our last stop. We had planned to stay a week.' She laughed. 'When the week was over he went home.'

'And you stayed here alone?'

She shrugged. 'We were heading that way anyway – the few weeks' travelling together made up my mind.' Another smile. 'And soon after that I met an Irishman, a farmer. We're married now – we've been married for nearly ten years. We have two boys.'

'Wow ...'

She'd come for a week, and never gone home. Her life was here now, her family, her work. Her children were Irish. Tilly remembered the uncertainty she'd felt when she was booking her flights to come here, wondering if she was doing the right thing, unable to see an alternative. Still tormented with heartache after John Smith's abrupt disappearance, still filled with the new, terrible fear that had gripped her in its aftermath.

Isa had come here and stayed. She'd made a new life here. It was possible.

'Another one,' Isa said then – and mixed with the wailing of the wind Tilly heard the slam of a car door outside, and the hard clack of heels on stone. The door swung open, bringing a gust with it that swept up pages on Isa's desk. A woman entered, or was whooshed in, dark hair tousled, handbag clamped under her arm.

She had to lean against the door to close it, shutting out the elements. 'Lord, such weather,' she said, running fingers through her hair as she approached Isa's desk. 'I hope the ferry is still operating.'

She was older – maybe sixty, maybe more – and elegant, with boots encasing slender legs, a pale grey coat that looked expensive, a scarf in rusty oranges with the sheen and fall of silk that trailed from her hand.

'I'm waiting to hear,' Isa told her. 'This young lady –' indicating Tilly with a tilt of her fingers '– is also trying to get across. She's travelled all the way from Australia to spend Christmas on Roone.'

'Goodness,' the woman said, turning to regard Tilly. 'Let's hope you get there. I thought Dublin was a long way to come, but it's nothing in comparison.'

She had a polished, precise way of speaking that suggested a good education, or maybe lots of money, or both. She took a seat next to Tilly on the bench, bringing with her a scent that reminded Tilly of the white jasmine that was in full bloom everywhere at home.

'I flew into Dublin yesterday,' Tilly told her. 'I was supposed to fly direct to Kerry from London but I fell asleep in the airport and missed my flight, so they put me on a Dublin one, and then I got a bus to Kerry.' She'd say nothing about the stolen purse; she was ashamed of her carelessness.

'Oh dear, poor you – as if your journey wasn't long enough. Travel can be so exhausting, can't it? But you're almost there now.' She opened her bag and took out a gold-coloured powder compact, and gazed critically at herself in its mirror. 'Lord, I look a fright.'

She dabbed at her face, found lipstick and stroked it on, pushed her hair into place. 'I have a son and a grandson living on Roone,' she said, snapping the compact closed, crossing one ankle neatly over the other. 'They moved to the island a few years ago, after my son's wife died.'

'I'm sorry ...'

'Yes, it was very sad. She was young, of course, it was cancer ... but my son met an island girl, and they married two years ago. He's very happy now.'

She didn't ask, but Tilly felt obliged to supply information in return. Isa was tapping on a mobile phone now, and paying no attention to them.

'My sister,' Tilly began. 'She lives on Roone, but I ... Well, we've never met. I was adopted. It's kind of a long story. I'm going to find her.'

The woman's eyes widened. 'My goodness,' she said softly. 'What an amazing journey you're making.'

And completely without warning, Tilly's face crumpled. She dipped her head, mortified, and scrabbled about in her pockets, but found nothing.

'Here—'

She pulled a tissue from the offered pack and blotted away her tears. How ridiculous. 'Sorry,' she said, 'it's just been a long trip—'

'My dear, don't dream of apologising. It's simply lack of sleep. I can never function if I don't get my eight hours.'

Tilly pressed the tissue to her eyes. *What an amazing journey you're making.* If she knew what had prompted this trip – if she knew it was as much about running away as it was about trying to find anything, or anyone – she might have something entirely different to say.

'Tilly?'

She raised her head. Isa handed her a dark green mug from which curls of steam were rising. 'Tea,' she said. 'Drink.'

Tea, it would appear, was the drink of choice on this side of the world. Tilly thought of Breda's pot that never got a chance to empty fully, and Amanda in Heathrow saying there was nothing like a cuppa to make things look brighter.

Isa's tea was different. There was no milk here, just a pale golden liquid that tingled with cinnamon.

'Vanilla chai,' she told Tilly. 'Good to keep the cold out.'

'It's nice … thank you.' As she raised it to her lips again the phone on the desk rang.

Isa pushed up a sleeve to glance at the oversized watch on her wrist. 'Leo,' she announced. 'He'll be over there by now.'

She lifted the receiver. 'Yes,' she said, and then 'OK,' and then, 'OK. Happy Christmas to you.'

Happy Christmas. If it was Leo, and she was wishing him happy Christmas, it was because she wouldn't see him again until it was over.

She replaced the receiver with a soft click. She regarded her two companions. 'I'm sorry,' she said simply. 'He can't risk another crossing today.'

'Oh dear,' the dark-haired woman said. 'What a shame. Oh well, these things happen, I suppose.'

She was so matter-of-fact about it, so resigned about having to turn around and drive all the way back to Dublin. Despite having half expected the news they'd just received, Tilly's stomach plummeted in dismay. Nothing for it but to give Paddy a ring.

The older woman turned to Tilly. 'What about you, dear? You're in a bit of a pickle now, aren't you?'

'I told her about the village pub,' Isa put in. 'They have accommodation.'

'You mean the next little village, on the way to Dingle?'

'Yes, Kilmally. The pub is O'Loughlin's, halfway along the street on this side.'

The woman wound her scarf around her head. 'Come along then,' she said to Tilly. 'You can sit in with me and we'll check it out. I thought I'd have to go all the way to Dingle, but this would be so much more convenient. We can hole up there until the ferry gets going again.'

Tilly got uncertainly to her feet. 'You're not going back to Dublin?'

'Certainly not – one of those journeys a day is more than enough.'

Now was the time to admit that she probably couldn't afford to stay in a pub, that she was going to have to make other plans. But even if it was only half a mile away, the village was in the right direction, and she could wait there until Paddy was able to return to fetch her. At least she could save him having to come all the way back to the pier.

The three of them left the little place together, Isa locking the cabin door behind them. They bowed their heads against the wind that whipped around them and the icy spears of rain that were now falling. Tilly wrapped her jacket tightly about her and followed her companion to the black car that was parked neatly behind the green Jeep.

'Happy Christmas!' Isa shouted cheerfully, climbing into the Jeep – and Tilly wondered exactly how happy it was going to be.

❄❄❄

By the time the girls and Poppy were being put to bed, just before seven, the phones had been down for quite a while. The first they'd known of it was around four o'clock, when Gladys had attempted to ring Joyce, the friend who'd invited her for Christmas dinner, to tell her of the change of plan.

I can't get through, she'd said. I'm getting no sound at all – so they'd tried to call Joyce on the landline, and on Gavin and Laura's mobiles, with similar results.

There must be a mast down on the mainland, Gavin had told his mother. It's happened before. They'll get it up and running again, but it might take a day or two.

Gladys, of course, had been most put out. Why would mobile phones and house phones be gone at the same time? That makes no sense. Don't they work on different systems?

The storm might have knocked a telegraph pole here too, he'd explained, but really he didn't have a clue. Neither he nor Laura concerned themselves unduly with technology: when they'd been setting up the B&B it was Nell who'd put it online for them, using the same holiday-accommodation website she'd used to advertise her own house rental a few summers earlier.

But how am I to contact Joyce? Gladys had demanded, and they'd had to tell her there was no way. Mobile phones down meant Internet gone too: when Roone lost its phone signals, it became to all intents and purposes cut off from the outside world.

Generally not a problem for the island community, well used to the quirks of their surroundings – and such problems tended anyway to be short-lived, service generally resumed within a day. Of course, this being Christmas Eve, they might have to wait a little longer than usual for things to get back to normal.

It's simply not good enough, Gladys had said crossly. Joyce will be so worried. I can't believe there's no other way to get a message out in this day and age.

Maybe she expected them to have a stock of carrier pigeons at the ready in case of communication emergencies. Honestly, the fuss she'd made. Joyce would no doubt get over the trauma of being deprived of a dinner guest – and the turkey breast, or whatever she'd planned to dish up, would last her twice as long. The world as Gladys knew it would spin on, phones or no phones.

But for the moment it looked as if everything was spinning a little out of control – or at any rate, the weather was. The storm had been gaining intensity all afternoon, no sign of it abating. Looked like they were in for a wild night of howling gales and lashing rain. More than one telegraph pole down on the island, Laura guessed, pulling closed the curtains in the girls' room. A few trees too, possibly. Hopefully nobody hurt.

She turned back to her toddlers, who were clambering into the bed they'd been sharing since they'd vacated their cots six months earlier. Two separate beds they'd been put into – but from the start they'd favoured sharing, and after two weeks Laura had given in. Fewer sheets to wash, if nothing else – and she was pretty sure that it wouldn't be long before they were demanding their own space.

She sat on the side of the bed, just below the hump of their intertwined legs. 'Now you know who's coming tonight, don't you?'

'Thanta!' they chorused, eyes sparkling.

'That's right, and he's on his way now. So you need to go straight to sleep after Dad's stories.'

Gavin was the unacknowledged king of the bedtime story, working his way patiently each evening through as many books as it took to close all four eyes. It was Laura's time to stretch out on the sitting-room couch as the boys watched television or read their comics for a further hour.

She wouldn't be stretching out on anything this evening, not with Gladys already parked in the sitting room with her bag of knitting. She wouldn't be doing anything much for the rest of the night, the storm putting paid after all to her party hopes. With the phones down, nobody had been able to cancel – but who in their right minds would venture out on a night like this, unless they had absolutely no choice?

Shame, particularly as she'd already broken the news to Gladys, who as usual had had plenty to say. Why on earth would Laura draw a party on herself on Christmas Eve – hadn't she enough to be doing getting ready for tomorrow? And of course – the incredulity replaced now with martyrdom – it wasn't Gladys's place to say, but wouldn't it have been nice to arrange a little something *during* her visit, instead of waiting until she was supposed to have left? But now that she wasn't gone after all, maybe Laura would prefer if she stayed out of the way while the party was going on. She was the last person to barge in where she wasn't wanted, she'd be quite happy in the kitchen. And so on, and so on, all of Laura's protestations and assurances in vain, now that it wasn't happening.

Preparations had been abandoned. No point in assembling the mince pies on a baking sheet, ready for the oven; no need to whip the accompanying cream. And the big pot of mulled wine, four bottles' worth, that had been sitting at the back of the cooker since early morning, complete with Nell's instructed additions of cinnamon stick and orange slices, was also surplus now to requirements. Such a waste.

Still, it *was* Christmas Eve. Maybe she'd decant some of the wine into a smaller pot in a while. Gladys might even be persuaded to have a glass, might knock some of the contrariness out of her. Despite her frequent declarations that she wasn't much of a drinker, she could swill with the best of them when she had a mind to. Look how she'd had no bother ordering herself a hot port in Mannings Hotel earlier.

Laura got to her feet. 'I'll send Dad in,' she told the girls. 'See you in the morning.' She bent and kissed two warm cheeks, rested her hands briefly on their identical mops of blonde curls, her exact hair colour before the chemo. 'Sleep tight, sweethearts. Happy Christmas.'

On the landing she met Gavin emerging from their room. 'She's asleep,' he told her – but he was still in the black books so Laura ignored him and tiptoed in. Poppy lay on her back, her face lit softly by the fuzzy glow of the little lamp that sat on the floor by her cot. Blankets kicked sideways, limbs spread starfish-like, the whole of her small body surrendered to sleep. Rabbity rested as always in the crook of one arm. Her pale blue soother bobbed gently, mouth working on it even in her dreams.

Laura rearranged the bedding, tucking it around the tiny toes. Impossible to hear the puffs of Poppy's rapid exhalations above the howling of the wind, but she placed her palm lightly on the little chest and felt the rise and fall. She crossed to the room's side window and parted the curtains an inch to peer out. Below were the black shapes of the apple trees, branches being flung about even more wildly than before. Like the whips of a dozen lion-tamers they were, lashing and thrashing madly, the small solid hump of the shed just visible beyond them. She hoped the animals weren't too nervous.

Nell and James's house sat across the field, the light from their sitting-room window blurred by rain. On a clear night Laura would see fainter lights from other houses further along, but tonight nothing much was visible.

She could only imagine what the sea must be like by this, churning and leaping like a mad thing. Hopefully the buildings closer to the village, separated from the water only by the road and a low wall – the church, the hotel, the line of fisherman's cottages – wouldn't suffer any consequences.

She checked her watch, squinting in the dim light: twenty past seven. Might as well face the music downstairs. She left the bedroom and pulled the door ajar. As she passed the girls' room she heard Gavin say, 'I'll huff and I'll puff and I'll blow your house *down!*' Pretty appropriate sentiment for the night that was in it.

In the sitting room Gladys's knitting needles clacked busily, a strip of something navy emerging from them. 'Would you fancy a glass of mulled wine?' Laura asked. 'I'm putting some on to heat.'

Gladys looked mildly shocked. 'Oh no, thank you, dear. A cup of tea will be fine for me, if you don't mind making it. And you might put another little bit of coal on the fire too, as you're up.'

Poor helpless Gladys. Well able to get herself and her suitcase from Dublin to Roone, but incapable of hauling her backside off the couch if there was a way at all to avoid it. At least she'd stopped giving out about the smell of the books.

The coal scuttle was down to its last shovelful: Gavin could refill it when he came down. Laura tipped what was left into the fire, causing a small flurry of sparks to leap onto the hearth. Gladys pulled her feet hastily out of the way – 'Oh, *careful*!' – presumably because they might spontaneously combust if a spark dared to land on one: now *there* would be a Christmas to remember.

In the kitchen Laura found the boys kneeling side by side on the bench by the window, elbows propped on the sill as they gazed out. Charlie was stretched out behind them, front paws resting on Seamus's calves – pretending, as he always did, to have forgotten the no-dogs-on-the-furniture rule.

All three heads turned at her approach. 'Down, Charlie,' Laura ordered, and down he hopped, throwing her a baleful look, and padded to his basket.

'Why don't you come into the fire?'

'Nah – we're alright here.'

Maybe avoiding Gladys too. She ladled some of the wine into a smaller pot and lit the gas under it.

'What if the wind makes Santa's sleigh crash into something?' Ben asked.

'Yeah – or what if it blows all the stuff out?'

She regarded their anxious faces. Bless them, ten years old and still concerned about Santa. 'He's well used to storms,' she told them. 'There's a storm much worse than this somewhere in the world every single day.' She wondered if this could possibly be true. 'Has there ever been a Christmas when Santa didn't come?'

'No, but—'

'In fact, maybe you should start getting ready for bed now, in case the wind gets him here a bit early. You could read your comics until you feel sleepy.'

'We forgot to collect the eggs,' Ben said.

She held the kettle under the tap. 'Well, they'll have to wait until tomorrow – there's no way you can go out in that.'

'How 'bout Charlie? He might be scared if we leave him down here all by himself tonight.'

At the mention of his name Charlie's tail wagged. He didn't seem particularly scared. His basket sat by the stove, his water dish nearby. He wasn't a pup any more: she was pretty sure he'd be perfectly content in the kitchen for the night, wind or no wind.

But it was Christmas Eve.

'You can bring him up, just this once,' she said, 'but he sleeps in his basket, not on a bed. You can tell Dad I said it would be OK.'

'Thanks, Mum!'

They grabbed the basket and scampered off, whistling for a delighted Charlie to accompany them. When the water in the kettle rumbled she made tea in the little china pot that Gladys had given her the previous Christmas. She filled a single glass with warm mulled wine and left the rest simmering. Let Gavin get his own, if he wanted it.

By eight o'clock the three adults were settled in the sitting room. Gavin sat with his mother by the fire, Laura on the smaller couch in the bay window, her feet on a little low stool, her eyes half closed as she listened to the rain still lashing against the window, the wine sitting pleasantly inside her. Christmas might just pass off peacefully, if she could manage to hold her patience with mother and son.

'Refill?'

She hadn't noticed him getting to his feet. She handed him her glass wordlessly, and off he went. He was trying, she'd give him that.

'Such a night,' Gladys said. 'I'd say I won't get a wink of sleep.'

Laura hid a yawn behind her hand. 'You should have a glass of wine,' she replied. 'That would do the trick.'

'Yes, I've just told Gavin I might have a tiny drop.'

Hadn't taken her long. 'And there's no rush in the morning, Mass isn't until eleven.'

'Oh, I'll be up early, dear, to give you a hand. You couldn't possibly do it all on your own.'

'Whatever you like, Gladys.' Deep breaths, serene thoughts. She ran through the morning tasks. Get the kids washed and dressed and fed as usual. Stuff the turkey, prepare the vegetables, boil the ham. Ready the pudding for steaming. Scoop balls from the melon, the least complicated starter she'd been able to come up with.

Whip the cream for the pudding; make the brandy butter that Gavin preferred. Find the crackers and the red candles and the candlesticks. And have another hunt for the crib if there was time. Christmas wasn't the same without a crib.

Find a minute to run across to Nell with the present she would have been getting tonight, if the party had gone ahead. And no doubt there were plenty of other jobs she hadn't yet thought of.

She yawned again as Gavin reappeared. She'd have this glass and then she'd head up to bed, and maybe even sleep.

The doorbell rang.

Laura sat up. The doorbell? What time was it?

'I'll go,' Gavin said, setting his glass on the mantelpiece.

He left the room. She heard the front door opening, an eruption of voices in the hall.

'Who on earth—?' began Gladys.

Laura scrambled to her feet, smoothing down her skirt, thinking fast.

The sitting-room door opened and in waltzed Lelia, owner of Roone's most popular café, baker of scones and a lot more. 'Sorry we're late,' she cried, festive in a red and white party dress, flicking drops from her dishevelled hair before planting a kiss on Laura's cheek. 'You can blame the minibus, I told Pádraig to check it yesterday but I may as well have talked to the wall – and tonight not a dicky bird until he got the jump leads out.'

'You came in the minibus?'

'Of course we came in the minibus – how else would everyone fit?'

Lelia's carpenter husband Pádraig was the proud owner of an ancient twelve-seater vehicle that he dusted down every summer in order to ferry visitors around the island on a historical tour. According to Nell, most of the history had only happened in Pádraig's head, but the tours were very popular.

'Here we are—'

'Hello there—'

'Such a night—'

And in they all surged, laughing and exhilarated after their dash in the wind and rain from the minibus to the front door. Thrusting bottles and gifts at Laura, filling the place with perfume and chatter and a whiff of the outside. In they all crowded, Nell and James, Imelda and Hugh, Ita and Dougie and Pádraig, exclaiming over the tree, shaking hands with Gladys, perching wherever they found a place – ledges, couch arms, windowsills – as Laura fled to the kitchen after hissing at Gavin to keep everyone talking.

While the wine was heating she whipped the cream and tumbled the mince pies into the microwave – no time to wait for the proper oven – and assembled plates and glasses, listening to the bursts of laughter and snatches of chat from the front room.

'Can I help?'

Nell in blue, her hair pinned up with sparkly clips.

Laura indicated the trays, stacked on a shelf under the worktop. 'Grab a couple of those, and get out forks and napkins. And bags of nuts in that press – you can dump them into dishes. I would have had it all done, but I was sure nobody would make it with the weather.'

Nell pulled open the cutlery drawer. 'You haven't been living here long enough. Takes more than a bit of a storm to stop us coming to a party. Did you notice, by the way, that Colette is missing?'

'I didn't, with the shock of you all arriving – where is she?'

'Never got here. She was aiming for an afternoon ferry, so she must have been stranded. We can't contact her with the phones gone.'

'Ah no, that's a shame.'

'It is – I know James was looking forward to having her for Christmas, the first time she would have spent it on Roone. We're assuming she headed back to Dublin, so she'll be on her own for Christmas. Tim and Katy are gone to Donegal with the kids.'

'Ah, too bad.'

Tim, the man Nell nearly married, before she realised she preferred his brother James. Katy, the woman Tim found when Nell deserted him.

The microwave pinged. Laura lifted out the pies and tossed in another handful. 'What about your father? What kind of Christmas is he going to have?'

Nell's father Denis, who'd abandoned Nell's mother Moira, his wife of over thirty years, and his long-standing job as principal of Roone's primary school, when he'd fallen in love with someone else a few years earlier. The whole island, not surprisingly, thrown into a state of disbelief.

The new romance hadn't lasted – apparently she was married too – but there had been no reconciliation with Moira, who had since died. And for the past several months Denis had been volunteering in a refugee camp in Sudan. Making amends maybe, for past hurts.

Nell tucked napkins around forks. 'He says they're planning a slap-up meal tomorrow. I'm not sure I believe him.'

A slap-up meal in a refugee camp didn't sound very likely. Probably wouldn't feel remotely like Christmas either, under the blazing African sun. And Nell would miss him: those two had a strong bond.

'Has he any plans to come home?'

'He says Easter. We'll see.' She paused, a napkin halfway around a fork. 'The weird thing is, I think he's genuinely happy now. Sounds crazy, doesn't it? Considering where he is, and the conditions he must be living in. I'm sure he doesn't tell me half of it. But he does seem to have found … I don't know, some kind of peace of mind there. After all that had gone before, I mean.'

'He's helping others,' Laura said. 'He's making a difference. I think that always brings its own happiness.' She ladled steaming wine into glasses. 'Go out to the scullery and look at my cake, see what you think.' Give her a laugh.

A moment of silence from the scullery, and then: 'Wow. That's … some cake.'

'I know it looks shocking. Hopefully it'll taste OK.'

'You're not cutting it tonight?'

'I can't – the icing isn't set, we'll have to wait till tomorrow. Imagine the look on Gladys's face when she lays eyes on it – I've managed to hide it from her so far.'

'Never mind Gladys – well done to you, your first Christmas cake. There'll be no stopping you after this.'

'You must be joking; never again. You can make ours next year – I'll be happy to pay you in apples and eggs, or you could have one of the goats.'

'Tell you what – you bake it, I'll ice it.'

'Done.' She put the last of the glasses on the tray. 'Well, this is thrown together, but it's the best anyone is going to get tonight, so let's bring it in.'

And for the next few hours she forgot about everything else as they talked of the progress of the new community centre, and agreed that the street decorations in the village were charming, and bemoaned the cutbacks that had reduced the mobile-library visits to once every three weeks, and marvelled at Annie Byrnes for her accurate weather predictions, and laughed at the notion of Santa's toys being blown from his sleigh.

And mercifully, Lelia and Gladys seemed to have forgotten the earlier scone incident – or if it wasn't forgotten, it was being tacitly ignored by both of them. Gladys must have decided to behave herself for Christmas.

Outside, the storm raged on, the rain and wind showing no sign of lessening. And then, shortly before midnight, just as people were starting to talk about going home, the various lamps in the room gave a few simultaneous rapid flickers before finally blinking off, leaving the place lit only by the fire.

And while everyone was exclaiming in dismay, Gavin called, '*Shush* – listen!'

They stopped. Laura became aware, beneath the noise of the storm, of a peculiar creaking sound, like a heavy ancient door being pushed slowly open. Increasing in volume, becoming too loud to be nothing. Too loud not to be working up to something bad.

'What is it?' she asked – but before anyone could respond there was a gigantic deafening crash, so intense and booming that it caused the floor to vibrate beneath their feet, it rocked the old house to its foundations.

When it stopped, there was a second of total silence in the room.

'What was that?' Nell breathed – and as if the words released her, Laura leaped from her seat, banging her thigh painfully against a table, sending plates and glasses crashing to the floor as she stumbled in the flickering light towards the door.

The hall was in complete darkness. Over the shriek of the wind, over the sound of the various alarmed voices behind her, she could hear something far more chilling: a child's scream.

Her children.

Heart in her mouth, terror beating in her chest, she rushed blindly up the pitch-black stairs.

❄❄❄

It was just after two o'clock in the afternoon when they pushed open the door of the pub. Tilly's first impressions were of heat and noise and a pleasant sweetish burned smell, and lots and lots of people – every one of whom, it seemed, turned to stare as Tilly entered with her companion, who had introduced herself by then as Colette.

They approached the bar counter, the sea of people parting like water to let them through, nobody making any secret of their curiosity. Did they *never* see strangers here?

One of the two men behind the counter nodded cheerfully at them as he skimmed foam from the top of a pint glass and delivered it to a nearby customer. 'Bad day,' he said, through the bushy gingery beard that covered the bottom half of his face, and a good proportion of his torso. 'But ye're not too drenched.'

His eyebrows, as bushy as the beard, shot wildly from his forehead and ran together above his flame-red nose, as if trying to compensate for his completely bald and very shiny head. 'Ye weren't heading to Roone, by any chance?' he asked, shoving coins into a cash register and slamming it shut. 'I'd say Leo had to cancel the ferry, had he, with the weather?'

'He had,' Colette replied, their first opportunity to get a word in. 'I've been trying to phone the island and I can't get through. Leo rang from there about ten minutes ago, but now there seems to be no service.'

'Hold on,' he said, 'I have a cousin there.' He pressed keys on the phone he took from his breast pocket and listened for a few seconds before shaking his head. 'Nothing – must be a mast down. We usually go when the island goes.' He tried another number, shook his head again, returned the phone to his pocket with a shrug. 'What can you do?' he asked.

The same fatalism Tilly recalled Paddy displaying when they'd arrived at the pier to see the ferry disappearing. The same acceptance Colette had shown when the ferry had been cancelled. Probably the most sensible reaction, in the face of unchangeable circumstances.

'What'll ye have?' he asked them, and Colette said they were looking for accommodation, but in the meantime she'd like a Baileys, no ice. Tilly chose apple juice, wondering how much it cost but feeling obliged to order something.

She needn't have worried. 'On the house,' he said, 'for Christmas. I'll get Ursula to show ye the rooms in a while.' Winking at Tilly as he spoke, turning away to attend to someone else before they had a chance to thank him.

Colette lifted her glass. 'Isn't that nice of him? I wonder what the rooms will be like – we might have to stay after this.'

Tilly sipped her juice. She hadn't said anything on the short drive there about her money situation, still trying to decide what her best option was. Should she enquire about the nightly rate before she bothered Paddy and Breda? Maybe she could do one night here if it wasn't too expensive, and take her chances on the next.

'I don't know about you,' Colette went on, 'but I could do with something to eat. Let's see if they do any food, when I can catch his eye again.'

Food now: this was getting out of hand. Time to come clean. 'Listen,' she began, and told her companion as briefly as she could about her misadventure in London, and Breda and Paddy's hospitality the night before. 'I need to find out how much they charge here,' she said. 'If it's too dear I need to go back to Dingle.'

But Colette shook her head. 'There's no sense in dragging that man out again in this weather. I'm happy to cover your stay here, it's not a problem.'

Tilly looked at her in astonishment. 'Oh, I couldn't possibly expect you to do that.'

Colette smiled. 'My dear, it's nothing at all. I can well afford it – and to be honest, I'll be glad of the company, especially if the lodgings are a bit … haphazard, which I suspect they might be. Now,' she went on, raising a hand in the barman's direction, 'let's see if they can feed us first, will we?'

'Ye're in luck,' the barman told them. 'We don't normally do food, only crisps and peanuts – but we have grub in today for the Christmas, for this lot of rowdies, and we were just about to throw it out to them' – and with that, he and his companion produced little baskets that were filled with sausages and French fries and chicken wings. They made their way through the bar, depositing their offerings on tables and counter, to the delight of the locals, who had plenty to say about it:

'Ye must have won the Lotto, lads.'

'They'll be hikin' up the price of our pint after this.'

'I hope them sausages aren't past their sell-by date, Bernard.'

'Eat up,' a man close to Tilly and Colette advised. 'These savages will have them polished off if ye don't' – so Tilly took a sausage.

'You're not from around here,' the man remarked, and Tilly told him she was Australian.

'Is that a fact now?' He turned towards the crowd and yelled, *Tony MacMonagle!* in a bark that carried easily above the conversations that had resumed all around them.

An equally loud *What?* came back from somewhere to their left.

C'mere – you're wanted!

And presently a man emerged from the knots of people, half a sausage in his hand. Small and bony and weather-beaten, he wore a raggedy cable-knit bottle-green jumper that ended halfway down his thighs, and trousers so stained with numerous splashes of paint that it was difficult to be sure of their original colour.

'This young girl is from Australia,' the first man told him. 'I think you might have a song for her, would you?'

A song? Tilly was bemused, but Tony MacMonagle showed no surprise. He solemnly finished his sausage and wiped both hands on his trousers before offering Tilly his right to shake.

'Delighted to meet you,' he told her. 'Welcome to the kingdom of Kerry. You've come to the best part of Ireland' – and immediately he threw back his head and launched into a song, which prompted instant shushing among the crowd.

He sang in a most unexpectedly soulful tenor voice. He was word perfect and unselfconscious. He sang with eyes closed of his true love who had black hair and lips like roses; he sang of his sadness because they were apart – and for the few minutes that the song lasted, nobody at all made a sound.

When he had finished, his audience broke into enthusiastic applause. He gave a little bow to Tilly and vanished once more into the crowd before the whoops and cheers had fully faded.

'Now so.' The bearded barman, whose name they now knew was Bernard, materialised behind the counter again. ''Tisn't every day you get serenaded, I'd say.' Cutting slices from a lemon, flinging them into a glass, tumbling ice in after it, moving swiftly away before she could respond.

As she and Colette ate, they were drawn into conversation by those around them, who plied Tilly in particular with questions. Many of her interrogators seemed to think there was every possibility that she'd met their various relatives who'd emigrated to Australia, and she felt almost apologetic when she had to admit to not knowing them.

At one stage a man approached the counter and introduced himself, while he waited to be served, as Kieran McHugh, owner of the village newsagent's and petrol pumps.

''Tis quiet here in the winter,' he told them, 'although it can be lively enough in the summertime. Kerry is a popular spot with the tourists, and Roone in particular gets its share – and most of them have to pass through here on the way to the island. We like having it to ourselves when the season is over, but 'tis nice every now and again to see a few new faces.'

Somewhere along the way, Tilly learned that the smoky smell was from the turf that burned in the fireplace, turf that had been growing in a nearby bog. 'That fire hasn't gone out in over ninety years,' a man in a knobbly cream sweater told her. 'Bernard and Cormac build up the new one from the old ashes every morning.'

Bernard and Cormac were brothers, and joint owners of the bar. 'Ursula is Cormac's wife,' the man went on, indicating a woman in a tight red blouse – improbably black hair, lipstick the colour of blueberries – who was taking a turn behind the bar with her husband while his brother went around collecting the empties. 'Bernard is still a bachelor,' the man added, 'no woman has been quick enough to catch him yet, though plenty have tried, including Ursula.'

Tilly looked at him in astonishment.

'Oh yes – before she married Cormac she was doing a strong line with Bernard. We thought it was only a matter of time, but then we heard it was all off – and within six months wasn't she walking down the aisle with Cormac.'

Had she thrown Bernard over, or had it been the other way around? Tilly watched the barman as he gathered up the glasses, stopping often to exchange a smiling remark with his customers. She wouldn't have taken him for a ladies' man, but by the sound of it he and Ursula had been pretty close. She wondered how Cormac felt, married to a woman who'd chosen his brother first. Maybe it didn't bother him. Maybe he only cared that she'd ended up with him.

Then again, maybe Ursula had planned it that way all along, going out with one brother only until she'd figured out how to get her hands on the other. Who knew, when it came to love? Certainly not Tilly. She hadn't a clue how it worked.

The afternoon wore on. The food baskets were cleared away, and more songs were sung, and an old man recited a poem with several verses on the theme of winter. At one stage a group of men came in carrying fiddles and guitars, and something that resembled an outsize tambourine. They were enthusiastically welcomed, and space was made for them to the left of the giant fireplace.

The music they played was similar to the snatches Tilly had heard coming from the Dingle pubs the evening before. Lively and cheerful, dipping and swooping, and accompanied by many yips and yahoos from the listeners. The tambourine, she was told, was a type of Irish drum made with goatskin, whose name was very peculiar. Its owner beat out a tattoo using both ends of a stubby stick, his hand moving so fast that at times it became a blur.

After twenty minutes or so the music stalled, and various drinks – mainly Guinness – materialised in front of the musicians; and in the interval that followed, the guitar player took a narrow metal flute from his breast pocket and played a plaintive solo tune that sent a fresh stillness through the room.

Every so often someone would leave the pub, calling a general goodbye, and more would arrive, wet and windswept. Everyone seemed to know everyone else: it was like a giant family gathering. Tilly wondered what the bar was like the rest of the year. Could it possibly be as crowded and as lively, could its clientele be as good-humoured as this, all year round?

'Ye wanted to see our rooms.'

It was Ursula, Cormac's wife, taking them in as she held a glass of amber liquid to her tight red front. 'Follow me,' she said, leaving Tilly and Colette to weave through the crowd after her.

She left the bar through a door marked 'Private' and led them along a carpeted hallway that smelt of polish. The air was much colder there. 'Dining room,' she said as they passed a glass-panelled door on the right. 'Ye can let us know when ye want breakfast.'

They followed her up two flights of narrow stairs, past a family of ceramic geese making their way in formation along the wall, past a painting on the first landing of a thorny-crowned Jesus, and another of a pope Tilly didn't recognise who looked out wearily at them. The higher they climbed, the mustier it smelt. At a bend in the stairs Tilly caught Colette's eye: the older woman's smile was resigned.

'Number five,' Ursula said on the second landing, standing back to allow them to enter a room with a pink-covered single bed, a sink in one corner, a narrow wardrobe in another, and no sign at all of an adjoining bathroom. 'And six,' she went on, as they gazed silently around the chilly, bare space, 'is up those stairs.'

Tilly hadn't noticed the trio of even narrower steps that led off the landing to an unpainted wooden door. Behind it she discovered a tiny room whose ceiling slanted almost to the floor on one side, with a patchwork quilt covering a narrow bed that was pushed up against the window. There was a small locker at the foot of the bed and two clothes hangers suspended from a hook on the wall, and absolutely nothing else. No wardrobe, not even a sink.

The place was as shockingly cold as a fridge. She couldn't stand upright in most of it. She felt like Gulliver in Lilliput. She knelt on the bed and peered out.

Even this early, the light was fading. Far below was a yard to the rear of the pub, metal barrels piled up against a breeze-block wall. Beyond it, giant slabs of black rock onto which sheets of water were being periodically dashed from the sea below them.

She looked out past the shoreline, across the immensity of roiling water, and saw again the dark, humped shape of Roone in the distance. She thought of her sister somewhere on the island, preparing for Christmas. Wrapping presents, or stringing fairy lights around a banister, or doing some last-minute shopping. Planning to watch an old film on television later, or meet friends for a drink, like the people in the bar below.

Or maybe she didn't drink, maybe she never met her friends in bars. So little Tilly knew about her, so little information she'd been given. Nothing really, except that she was several years older than Tilly, and lived on Roone. Tilly hadn't asked, too bewildered at this unexpected information, and her mother hadn't volunteered any more.

She pulled back the patchwork quilt, and the blankets underneath. The sheets looked clean at least, but they were icy to the touch. She wondered if she could request a hot-water bottle – what had Breda called it? A hot jar, maybe they'd have one downstairs.

She left the room and pulled the door closed. No key was in evidence, and she hadn't seen one in the other bedroom door either. Didn't people lock rooms here? After her experience at Heathrow, the thought of leaving herself vulnerable again was dismaying.

This was different, she told herself. This wasn't an airport, with all manner of strangers passing through. And anyway, her case was still locked into the boot of Colette's car, and her handbag hadn't left her side since the robbery.

Colette and Ursula were talking in the corridor. They turned at Tilly's approach. 'Everything alright?' Colette asked, and Tilly said yes, everything was fine, determined to make the best of what was, after all, a godsend.

'Bathroom is down there,' Ursula said, indicating a door at the far end of the corridor. 'Ye're the only ones staying, so ye'll have it to yourselves.' Her breath smelt richly of alcohol.

'Is there a bath?' Colette enquired, and was told that there was, but that something called an immersion would have to be turned on, and there would be a wait.

'And maybe one of the men would bring in our luggage?'

'No bother; give me your keys and I'll get it sorted' – and Tilly watched Colette handing over her car keys, just like that. She found it reassuring that the older woman, who presumably valued the contents of her luggage, didn't seem in the least concerned about their safety. It would appear they were in a place where people could be trusted not to run away with your valuables when your back was turned.

'I'll bring up a couple of fan heaters too,' Ursula said. 'The rooms get a bit chilly when they're not used in a while. If that's everything so ...' Already edging towards the stairs, and when Colette said it was, she made her escape.

They remained silent until the sound of her footsteps had faded. Colette rubbed her hands together. 'Cold up here, isn't it? And it's a bit rough and ready – but we'd best stay put, for tonight at least. The fan heaters will help; and make sure you wear a few layers in bed. We can head into Dingle tomorrow, when the storm has passed.'

Tomorrow was Christmas Day: hard to keep remembering that, with everything so different and uncertain. And then she reminded herself that things could have been much worse. If she hadn't met Breda on the bus, if Colette hadn't come along to the pier, who knew what dire straits she might be in now?

'Thank you so much,' she said. 'For offering to pay for me here, I mean. I'll pay you back if you give me your address. I'll send you the money when I can.'

Colette smiled. 'There's really no need for that: I don't imagine our bill here is going to break the bank. Consider it a Christmas gift.'

'Well ... thank you.'

The sound of the revelry below could be faintly heard: maybe that was why they'd been given rooms two flights up. Tilly didn't imagine the crowd had any plans for an early night this Christmas Eve.

'Listen to that wind,' Colette said, and that could be heard too, even though the corridor had no window. The storm raged on, no sign of it losing any of its power. 'Christmas will be interesting,' Colette murmured. 'Your first Christmas in Ireland – you'll certainly remember it.'

Tilly laughed. 'I sure will.'

She should be keeping a diary, she thought. She should be recording all the happenings, good and bad, of this strange journey she was on – although she doubted that she'd forget any of it, written down or not. When I was seventeen, she'd tell her children, and later her grandchildren, I had the most unusual Christmas ever. She might tell the story every Christmas – it might become a family tradition.

Footsteps sounded on the stairs, and a minute later Bernard appeared, bearing a pair of small electric heaters and two hot-water bottles.

'Take these,' he told them, doling them out, 'before ye freeze to death. I'll get the cases' – and he was gone, thumping down the stairs again. They plugged in their heaters and stood cradling the hot-water bottles until he reappeared with the luggage.

'I hope we're not putting you out,' Colette said. 'I imagine you don't normally have people staying at this time of year.'

'Not at all – we couldn't see ye homeless at Christmas. We're officially closed tomorrow, but the three of us live on the premises, so we'll be around – and there'll be plenty of turkey, so ye won't go hungry. But ye never know,' he went on, folding his arms across his chest, 'we might manage to get ye out to Roone tomorrow if it clears up.'

Colette regarded him in surprise. 'But there's no ferry on Christmas Day.'

'You're right there, but we might find an obliging soul who'd run ye across in his boat.'

'Really? That would be wonderful – wouldn't it Tilly?'

'Yes,' she said. 'Wonderful.'

'I'm making no promises, but we'll keep an eye out for ye.' And off he went again, back to his noisy, happy bar.

'Would you mind if I had a little lie-down?' Colette asked when they were alone again. 'I'm feeling rather tired.'

'Of course not.' Tilly didn't feel in the least bit tired, but she could read her book. They agreed to rendezvous in a couple of hours – 'tap on my door,' Colette said, 'if there's no sign of me by seven. We'll find something to do for the evening, I'm sure.'

Tilly's little room was warming up. It was pitch black now beyond the window, rain pelting hard against the glass. She drew the thin yellow curtains together and pulled off her shoes and slipped under the blankets with her book – but as soon as she lay down, sleep claimed her as swiftly as it had the night before.

She was woken by a tapping. She blinked as she hauled herself from the bed – the light on, the room uncomfortably stuffy, the fan heater still whirring out its hot air, her clothes damp with sweat.

Ursula, not Colette, stood outside. 'You've been invited to dinner with the Corbetts out the road,' she said, taking in Tilly's crumpled appearance with a lightning glance. 'Joseph will be over to collect ye in half an hour.'

Tilly had no idea who Joseph was, and no explanation was offered. She squinted at her watch and discovered it to be a little after seven. She peeled off her sweaty clothes, planning a quick shower – but to her dismay there were no towels to be seen in the room, and she didn't want to risk racing down the corridor in a state of undress, in case she encountered either of the brothers.

She blotted herself dry with the shirt she'd taken off and pulled fresh clothes from her case, and attempted to smarten herself up by combing her hair and spritzing on perfume. Probably just as well there was no mirror in her room.

Colette by comparison looked immaculate. She'd had a bath – the air in the corridor was scented with whatever she'd put into the water – and she'd changed from her jacket and skirt into a grey trouser suit. 'Isn't this nice?' she said when Tilly appeared. 'Aren't people very good? We'll have a proper dinner after all.'

Joseph Corbett, it turned out, had been among those who had chatted with them earlier in the bar. 'When I went home and told Sheila about ye, she put your names in the pot', he told them, as they lurched in his well-worn Land Rover over the rain-puddled roads. 'We're not far, just a mile or so …' and Tilly tried not to wonder, as they swerved sharply around another bend, as she grabbed the back of Colette's seat in an effort not to be sent flying against the door, how much he'd had to drink before he'd gone home to Sheila. Did all Irishmen drive so recklessly, or had she just happened to meet the two who seemed to court death at every turn in the road?

Thankfully, he managed to ferry them to his big old farmhouse without mishap – and after they ran through the wind and rain, skirting puddles on their way to the back door, after they were welcomed by Sheila, who took their coats and put them sitting straight at the table in the mercifully warm kitchen, the dinner was served. Thick slices of very salty bacon whose pink was striped with wide ribbons of fat, accompanied by scoops of mashed potato as soft as ice-cream that had bits of green mixed in with it.

'Colcannon,' Sheila told Tilly. 'Cabbage and scallions, a drop of cream and a good knob of butter. There's a song about it' – and she launched into it as she filled plates with food for the three small girls with Joseph's dark red curls who stared silently across the table at the visitors all the way through. The Irish, Tilly decided, loved to sing.

The bacon, with its preponderance of fat, was a challenge. Seeing the rest of them, including Colette, eating it up without complaint Tilly did her best, but was forced to abandon the last slice, unable to stomach any more of its greasy taste. Seeing her push it to one side, Joseph reached over and transferred it to his plate.

'Give it here,' he said, without a trace of embarrassment. 'Sheila will tell you I'm a divil for the streaky bacon.'

'Oh, he is.' Sheila ladled out seconds of colcannon. 'He never leaves a bit behind. You'll have another spoon of spud, dear?'

Dessert was stewed gooseberries topped with warm custard. 'I freeze the gooseberries in the summer,' Sheila told them. 'We all love gooseberries in this house, don't we?'

The oldest of the girls, who looked about ten, and whose name Tilly had forgotten, spoke up suddenly.

'Did you ever see a kangaroo?'

Tilly smiled. 'Yes, lots of times.'

'Have you a pet one?'

'No.'

'But *could* you?'

'I suppose I could, if I wanted.'

Pause. 'Did you ever see a crocodile?'

'Yes.' She didn't add *on television*; she suspected that part wouldn't be half as satisfying.

'And snakes?'

'Oh yes. Lots of times.'

'Could they kill you?'

'Some of them could.'

The other two listened solemnly to this exchange.

'I got bitten by a snake once,' Tilly told them. 'I was young, about five or six.'

'I'm five,' the smallest girl said.

'Was it very sore?' the middle child enquired.

'It was,' Tilly replied, although she couldn't remember how painful or otherwise it had been.

'Did you nearly die?'

'I did. Everyone was very worried.' More artistic licence – the snake wasn't poisonous, and was probably far more frightened of her, but where was the drama in that?

'I got stinged by a wasp,' the five-year-old announced. 'It got in my sandal an' it stinged me on my toe.'

'It wasn't a wasp,' the middle girl said disdainfully. 'It was just a *fly.*'

'No, it *wasn't.*'

'Yes, it *was.*'

Sheila got to her feet. 'I think it's time for bed. Santa will be here soon, and he won't want to hear any fighting. Joseph, will you put the kettle on while I bring them up? Say goodnight to our visitors.'

By the time Tilly and Colette were dropped back to the bar it was almost ten o'clock, and the storm was still at the height of its power. The cars that had been parked outside when they left were all gone now, although the lights still blazed from within.

'Ye'll get some sleep tonight,' Joseph remarked, pulling up. 'Looks like they've cleared the place.'

They thanked him and sped inside, where they found the pub deserted apart from Bernard, who was wiping down tables.

'There ye are,' he said. 'Bit of peace and quiet for ye. We close early on Christmas Eve.'

'I thought you were in for a long night,' Colette replied.

He shook his head. 'Stephen's Night will be the busy one – we'll never get them home. Will ye have a nightcap before ye turn in?'

'Only if we can pay for it,' Colette said, and he grinned and put up his hands.

'What'll it be so?'

Colette asked for a brandy, Tilly opted for water. 'Sit yourselves over by the fire,' he told them, and they settled on the seat that had been occupied earlier by the musicians.

'You'll join us,' Colette said when he brought their order across – but he told them he was off to bed.

'Making up for late nights this past week,' he told them, bolting the front door, flicking switches that extinguished the main lights, leaving only the warmer glow of the wall lamps. 'Help yourselves to seconds if ye want them – and ye might turn off the rest of the lights before ye head up.'

And so they were left alone, every drink imaginable within their reach, if they felt like it, and possibly a good deal of money in the till too, or on the premises at least – for where were the brothers going to deposit it tonight?

'It's been an interesting day,' Colette murmured.

'Yes, it has … We didn't tell them what time we wanted breakfast in the morning.'

Colette smiled. 'Something tells me breakfast will be pretty informal.'

They sat without speaking for a bit, the silence easy between them. Colette made another attempt to ring Roone, with no more success than her first time. Tilly gazed into the dying fire and wondered again if they would make it to the island the following day, and what the outcome would be whenever they did.

'Do you know many people on Roone?' she asked eventually.

'I know a few at this stage,' Colette replied, not taking her eyes from the fire. 'My daughter-in-law is a hairdresser, the only one on the island. She's lived there all her life, she knows just about everyone. And my son manages one of the bars, so of course he meets a lot of the locals too. I've met a fair few of them in the past few years.'

'My sister,' Tilly began – and then stopped. Even in this softly lit peaceful space, the phrase felt awkward in its unfamiliarity; it didn't settle easily into a sentence. 'It's just … you might have met her.'

'I might,' Colette agreed. 'It's quite possible.'

Putting no pressure on Tilly at all to say any more, leaving her completely free to drop the subject again and move on – except that Tilly didn't want to move on. She said it then, the name that had imprinted itself on her brain when she'd heard it in the Brisbane café six months earlier. This was the first time she'd uttered it aloud, the name of the woman who shared a mother and a father with her.

Colette nodded. 'I know her. I've met her often. In fact,' she said, 'she lives right next door to my son and his wife. She's lovely,' she added.

And just like that, Tilly jumped another step closer. She was talking with someone who knew her sister, whose son was her neighbour. It felt surreal.

Tell me about her, she wanted to say, hungry for more – but something stopped her. Maybe she wanted to find out for herself when they met. Maybe she wanted them to come together on an equal footing, neither knowing anything about the other. Although Tilly was already at an advantage, aware at least that she had a sister.

The subject was left alone. Colette said nothing further, and Tilly was grateful for her discretion. Here was a person, she imagined, who could be entrusted with the most precious of secrets.

And later, as she lay under the patchwork quilt in her little attic room, as the storm gusted on outside and sleep evaded her for a change, as Christmas Eve turned without fuss into Christmas Day, Tilly went back over everything that had occurred since she'd touched down in Dublin, and she came to the conclusion that even if things were a little unorthodox here, Ireland was undoubtedly a place where you could depend on the kindness of strangers.

❅

FRIDAY
25 DECEMBER
CHRISTMAS DAY

❅

'**W**ho's for another sausage?'

'Me.'

'Me too.'

'Me too.'

'Me too.'

'And what,' she enquired, jabbing a sausage with her fork, 'is the magic word?'

A simultaneous 'please' came from the gathering around the table. Laura doled out the second helpings, marvelling at the resilience that had allowed the girls in particular to bounce back from their fright of the night before.

All four of them had got a shock. The boys and a barking Charlie were already out on the landing when she got upstairs; in the darkness she'd collided with them.

Are you OK?

Yeah.

Nothing happened in your room?

No – we just heard a really loud noise, like an *explosion*.

And the light doesn't work.

Their voices small and scared, but themselves unhurt. Wait here, she ordered. Stay here. Dad's coming – because he had to be following close behind, he had to. She felt her way along the wall to the girls' room, from which terrified screams continued to issue. Every instinct urging her to hurry, hurry *up*, get there, get to them, pushing away nightmare scenarios of exploded gas pipes

163

and collapsed walls and rubble-strewn rooms and broken bodies as she patted her way along with trembling fingers. I'm coming, she called. It's Mum. I'm coming. Praying it was fear and not pain that was causing their shrieks.

She felt the outline of their door and threw it open. Pitch black – but as far as she could see, still intact. It's OK, she told them, shouting above their screams. It's OK, it was just a bang. Flicking the light switch on and off repeatedly and uselessly – forgetting, in her agitation, that it wouldn't work. She groped her way towards them until her foot collided with their bed. She crouched and gathered them both into her arms and told them it was OK, it was OK, they were alright, it was just the silly storm knocking something over.

And as she was stroking hair and patting backs, as their cries began to abate, she was thinking, Poppy, Poppy, Poppy, and fighting against the urge to leap from the bed and hurtle back into the pitch black corridor. Poppy, Poppy, Poppy, who was in the room just across the way, and who was making no sound at all that her mother could make out.

I'm here— Gavin's voice at last, at last, in the doorway.

Poppy, she said. Check on Poppy. He vanished, and even as she continued to hush and soothe the other two, she strained to hear the cries of her youngest daughter.

I dot a big fwight, Mama, Evie whimpered woefully.

Me too dot a big fwight, Mama.

I know, I know you did, darlings, it was very scary. But it's OK now, it's all over now, and you're safe with me. She went on crooning to them, every sense alert for his return. Where was he? Why wasn't he coming back?

It wasn't all over, far from it. Something big, something huge had happened to cause that noise: something had exploded, or collapsed, or been flung by the wind into a place it had no right to be – and the longer Laura didn't know what it was, the more terrified she was becoming.

Why in God's name was Poppy still making no sound? What devastation had he found in their room?

Gavin! she shouted finally, unable to bear it any longer – and at that instant, thank the sweet Lord Jesus, she heard Poppy erupting into outraged bawling, and it was music, it was a symphony that brought silent tears of relief and gratitude pouring out of her.

She's fine, he called from across the corridor. She was asleep, she never woke – and he was there, the two of them were at the door, Poppy still yelling her protestation at having been woken, their faces lit now by the candlelight that had arrived, courtesy of James.

We're thinking it was one of the apple trees, he told them, his face ghostly in the candle's glow. Hugh and Pádraig have headed out to investigate.

And as soon as he said it, Laura had thought, Yes, of course, that was it, that was what they'd heard. The noise of a tree falling, the creaking and groaning of its timber as it had toppled, the enormous crash as it had landed – that was it, that was one of the trees. The size of it, the weight that must have been in it. Thank God, it was just one of the trees.

Only a few hours ago she'd looked out at them and wondered if they'd still be there for her grandchildren – and now one of them was gone, just like that. Far enough from the house not to have damaged it, whichever way it had fallen, but she dreaded to think what the aftermath must be like.

And then she thought of the shed, on the far side of the orchard, right next to it. The animals sheltering inside, George and Caesar, Cheryl and Maddie. Let it have toppled the other way, she prayed silently. Let it not have come down on the shed. Let the animals be safe, let us not have lost those too.

Eventually order was restored. The four older children were placated with reminders of Santa, who was still on the way, and promises of imminent hot chocolate that Gavin had been despatched to make. James, with his candle, was left on corridor duty until torches could be located, and Poppy was sung back to sleep by her mother.

When Laura eventually returned downstairs it was to find the partygoers drinking tea, Nell having located the stovetop kettle every Roone kitchen kept tucked away to use during power cuts. Hugh and Pádraig were still absent. The mood was sombre, the earlier merriment banished by what had happened. It felt to Laura like a gathering of mourners, except there was no body.

Within a few minutes the investigators returned, their findings grim. The shed had taken a direct hit and as far as they could see, had been pretty much demolished. We won't know the full extent of the damage until it gets light, Hugh reported.

Laura's heart sank. The four animals crushed to death; they must be. She mourned their loss, particularly gentle-natured George, who had carried countless children without complaint around the field for the past two summers. No more donkey rides, or none anyway that involved poor old George.

On foot of this dismaying news the party had broken up. Coats were retrieved, goodbyes and happy Christmases exchanged. Gladys was despatched to bed with a torch as Laura and Gavin stood in the doorway, waving until the minibus had disappeared.

Dying down a bit now, Gavin said, but Laura couldn't see any lessening of the storm's ferocity. I think I'll go out and take a look—

No, she'd said fiercely, pulling him back inside and closing the door. It's still too wild – you won't be able to see anything. You heard what Hugh said: wait until morning.

Her recent anger towards him had been swept away in the face of this calamity. She couldn't have him finding what was left of the animals in the dark on his own; it would kill him. The men had promised to come back at first light, and no doubt a few others would turn up as well when they heard, Christmas Day or no Christmas Day. The island community would rally, like it always did in times of trouble.

By candlelight they'd given a desultory tidy to the sitting room and arranged the presents around the tree. Upstairs they'd stood by the window in their room, looking down at the enormous dark muddle that was the fallen apple tree, and the destroyed shed beneath it.

And to her sorrow, Laura realised it was the special tree that had been taken from them. Yes, it had stood just there, on the furthermost edge. No more apples all year round, the magic gone from the orchard.

They'd gone to bed in silence, no more words passing between them. For the first time ever, Poppy had slept through the night: a phenomenon that Laura decided to regard as her child's Christmas present to her. And now it was the morning after, it was Christmas Day, and mercifully the storm had passed over and left them with a morning that was icy cold and perfectly calm. Santa's presents had been opened, the children were being fed, and the turkey was stuffed and ready for the oven.

Gavin had given her a necklace. She'd found it sitting on his pillow when she woke, a package wrapped in paper stamped with holly leaves, her name on the accompanying envelope.

'Happy Christmas from your useless husband, who loves you', he'd written in the card, the words bringing a wry smile to her face. The necklace was sweet, a little guitar suspended on a slender silver chain. She wondered where he'd got it. She slid it into her locker drawer: Poppy would only pull at it and break it if she wore it.

Her present to him had been new wellingtons, handed over a few days ago when his old ones had finally sprung a leak. She'd got James to buy them for her in Dingle: he was going anyway, it made perfect sense. She supposed wellingtons were a bit functional for a Christmas present, but Gavin needed them and they didn't have money to spend on fripperies.

She hoped the necklace hadn't cost too much. She wished he'd got her something less … pretty.

No sign of Gladys yet, despite last evening's promise – or threat

– to get up early to help. No sign of Gavin either since they'd come downstairs, out the back probably since first light. He'd been joined a little while ago by James and Pádraig; Laura had spotted them arriving together.

She was praying that none of the children would enquire about the animals. They didn't know that the tree had fallen on the shed, only that it had been knocked over in the storm. We can't go out just yet, she'd told the boys, not until Dad and the others make sure there are no more wobbly trees – and thankfully they were still preoccupied enough with their presents not to pursue it.

She dreaded breaking the news of the animals' fate to them: they'd be heartbroken, particularly for George, whom they'd all loved. They might buy another donkey; it might soften the blow. She had no idea how much they cost.

When the children were finishing breakfast the back door opened, and they heard the men's voices in the scullery. Laura waited in dread for them to appear – and Gavin's face, when the kitchen door was pushed open, told her all she needed to know. He gave a small shake of his head, and the last faint hope she'd been hanging on to flickered out. All gone then, no survivors.

She made them coffee and handed round some of last night's mince pies. 'Nobody is to go out the back,' Gavin said to the children. 'Not until we make sure it's safe.' And for once, not one of them argued or tried to get around him.

'Jim Barnes will be over shortly,' Pádraig told Laura. 'I called into him on my way here. He's bringing the trailer and the chainsaw. And Hugh is coming too, he'll be along in a while.'

She was glad to hear the extra help was coming: this would take some clearing up. She had no idea how the animals would be disposed of – were they to be buried, was there some protocol to be followed? Whatever it was, it had to be done before the children got wind of what had happened.

But it could happen so easily: all it would take was for Ben or

Seamus to remember that Caesar hadn't yet been fed, or for one of them to look out a window on that side of the house and figure out where the tree had landed, and the questions would begin. She'd face it when it happened.

At least the hens were safe: the henhouse had survived, its flock intact. What kind of a storm uprooted a tree, and spared a henhouse at the other end of the same field? It made no sense.

Within minutes, the sound of Jim's Jeep was heard. The men pushed back their chairs and left. Laura cleared the table and found crayons and paper for the girls, and sent the boys into the sitting room – which faced away from the orchard – with a notebook and a pen.

'This is a special Christmas game,' she told them. 'I want you to write down all the things you can find in this room that begin with C, starting with the Christmas tree. I'll give you ten cents each for every one you find – and if you spell them right I'll make it twenty.'

Bribery, she realised, probably didn't feature in the top five recommended strategies for bringing up children, but it certainly worked for her. Back in the kitchen she changed Poppy's nappy – prompting noises of disgust and much finger-flapping from the older sisters – and settled her with Rabbity in the playpen.

She'd better deliver Gladys's morning tea, or they'd never hear the end of it. Normally that task fell to Gavin, but not surprisingly he'd forgotten it today. Getting on for half past nine – Gladys would want to be up by ten if they were to make Mass by eleven. So much for her early rising. Laura filled the kettle and set a cup and saucer on a tray, and added a Ferrero Rocher in an eggcup for the day that was in it.

As she waited for the water to boil she peeled Brussels sprouts, half listening to the girls' chatter as they covered their pages with scribbles. She thought of Susan, and wondered what kind of Christmas she and Luke were having. Would they dine alone today, or had they arranged to eat, like they normally did, with other childless couples?

They wouldn't be childless next Christmas. Let's see how that went.

Susan would attempt to ring later – she always did on Christmas morning – and she would have no luck, the phone lines still as impotent as the electricity cables. Tomorrow at the earliest, Laura reckoned, before either of them came back. Little wonder every house on Roone had a gas cooker: the islanders had learned over the years not to depend on electric power.

Laura's early memories of Christmas, with her mother still around, were vague. She supposed they'd done the usual present exchanges and turkey dinners that everyone else did, but none of them had left any lasting impression on her. She did remember the dinner-table rows, her father's black moods, her mother's tears – but they happened all the time, not just at Christmas.

After her mother's departure, Christmas dinners became anonymous hotel affairs for her and Luke, during which he ate little and smoked a lot, and tried not to look at his watch too often as his daughter scanned the room and made up stories in her head about the occupants of the neighbouring tables.

She wondered if he and Susan fought like her parents used to, and thought that they probably didn't. She couldn't imagine Susan staying with him if he made her miserable. She wondered if leaving him had caused her mother to be any happier, and hoped that it had.

The kettle boiled. She made tea. 'Want to come up and see Granny?' she asked the girls. Strength in numbers.

They laid down their crayons and pattered on all fours, like little monkeys, up the stairs. They slapped Gladys's door with their palms. 'Wake up, Gwanny!' they chorused. Hopefully the poor woman was already awake.

Laura reached past them to turn the handle and push open the door. The girls spilled into the room ahead of her.

Gladys lay on the floor by the bed, the duvet half tumbled around her, as if it had reached out to catch her in her fall.

'Go down to the boys,' Laura said quickly, dread pricking her all over. 'They're in the sitting room. Go down the stairs on your bottoms.'

'What's wong with Gwanny?'

'Mama?'

Small scared voices, like her boys' last night.

'She'll be fine, just go downstairs. Be careful, go slow' – and away they scuttled.

And as Laura set the tray on the locker and stepped towards the prone figure of her mother-in-law, Ben shouted up the stairs, over the heads of his descending sisters: 'Mum, the tree fell on the *shed*! It *squashed* all the animals!'

And directly afterwards, as the girls burst into simultaneous shocked tears, the doorbell rang.

❄❄❄

Such a difference, such a transformation. She sat on the bed, swaddled in blankets, and surveyed the scene beyond her window, trying to take it all in.

The storm was gone. The sea was like glass this morning. Not a ripple, not a white cap to be seen. And the colours, the incredible colours of it, the rich shades of blue and green she had no names for. Swathes of colour, turning the sea into a thing of indescribable beauty.

The strip of Roone lay on the horizon, dark and squat. Much too far away to make out any of its features, no matter how she squinted. Maybe with strong binoculars she'd see buildings, fields, roads, beaches. Or maybe not, until she got closer.

The sky was a uniform blue-white, not a single cloud to mar it. No sun visible from her vantage point, but it must be somewhere behind her because the light was like nothing she'd witnessed before. Everything gleamed, everything sparkled, everything looked freshly rinsed. Birds wheeled and swooped across the clear sky, their cries muted through the glass.

Her little sash window was edged with frost. She tugged and wriggled the paint-encrusted catch until it gave. She pushed the window down an inch, and the air that rushed through was icy and delicious. She breathed it in, listening to the louder shrieks of the birds.

A movement on the sea below caught her eye. A boat had appeared, grey and functional, a working boat. Someone fishing on Christmas Day? The chug of its engine carried easily to where she knelt. She watched it cutting through the water, saw the white frill it left behind. She recalled Bernard promising to try and get them to Roone today, and she wondered if he'd remember.

She checked the time: just after nine. Her eyes felt gritty. She hadn't slept much, jet-lag catching up with her maybe. The thin mattress on her bed hadn't helped, or the little room that was too stuffy with the fan heater turned on and too cold without it.

But she didn't care: it didn't matter in the least. She was here, she'd made it this far – and today, or tomorrow, she would finally get to Roone.

She might sleep on Roone tonight. The thought brought a surge, half-fear, half-excitement, that made her throw off the blankets. She grabbed her toilet bag and the clothes she planned to wear, and pattered barefoot down the narrow steps and along the corridor past Colette's room to the bathroom.

It was as arctic as the bedroom – hadn't they heard of central heating? There was a single white towel, hard and thin, hanging on the rail. The shower was above the bath and disappointingly feeble, but the water at least was hot. She washed quickly and dressed before she was fully dry, teeth chattering.

On her way back, Colette's door was ajar. 'Tilly, is that you?'

'Yes.'

'Come in.'

She was zipping her case closed, dressed in the same grey trouser suit she'd worn the evening before. 'Happy Christmas,' she said. 'Looks like a nice day out there.'

'Happy Christmas,' Tilly echoed. 'The light is amazing.'

'Yes, it's always good here – makes up for our mediocre weather.' She set her case by the door. 'I have a feeling we'll get to Roone today,' she said.

Tilly was unable suddenly to speak.

'Don't worry,' Colette said. 'It'll be fine, I'm sure it will.'

'… Hope so.'

'Will we go down? Are you ready?'

'Just give me a minute.'

In her room she rummaged in her suitcase and found the package Ma had given her the day before the trip. Save it for Christmas, she'd ordered. Beneath the wrapping Tilly found the linen tunic she'd admired a few weeks ago in the mall with Lien: Ma must have asked her advice.

She held it up. Sky blue, sleeveless, cute little pleats at the hips. Perfect for the sunshine in Bali, or in Queensland: out of the question in the middle of an Irish winter. She folded it carefully and replaced it in the case.

Early evening at home now. The presents long since opened, the dinner eaten, Ma watching TV in the front room, spared the washing-up because of Christmas. Pa doing it on his own this year, no Tilly to lend a hand. At eight, Robbie was plenty old enough to help, but he was Ma's golden boy, and not generally called on for chores.

She opened a new text box. *Happy Christmas*, she typed, *love my present, thank you. Miss you all.* She pressed *send* – but nothing happened. She'd forgotten about the phones being out. No way to contact Ma until they came back, whenever that would be. They'd wonder why she wasn't getting in touch on Christmas Day – or maybe they'd think she was having too much fun to bother with them.

Downstairs the dining room was deserted and chilly. They looked into the bar, which was exactly as they'd left it the night before. Tilly glanced at the fireplace, remembering someone saying that the fire hadn't gone out in ninety years. Looked well and truly out now.

'I think we need to find the kitchen,' Colette said, 'and make our own breakfast,' so they poked around until they found it to the rear of the bar. Tilly ran upstairs for her fan heater, and by the time they'd scrambled eggs and toasted bread a yawning Bernard had appeared, so they fed him too.

'I'll give Kieran McHugh a shout in a while,' he said, holding out his coffee cup for a refill. 'He has a little boat, he'd run ye over, I'd say. He's the newsagent, ye met him last night.'

Tilly had a vague recollection of someone telling them he owned the newsagent's in the village, but they'd spoken to so many, she couldn't recall a face for him.

'Could I leave my car at the pier?' Colette asked. 'I could collect it tomorrow when the ferry is running again.'

'You could, to be sure – or someone from here would bring it over for you, no problem.'

No problem, nothing a problem here.

After breakfast they loaded the dishwasher while Bernard tried to ring Kieran before remembering that the phones were down. 'I'll walk up the street to him,' he said, pulling on his jacket: another obstacle brushed away.

There was no sign of Cormac or Ursula. Maybe Christmas Day was the only lie-in they got in the year. Tilly went upstairs to brush her teeth, and by the time she came down Bernard had returned.

'Kieran is bringing his mother to eleven Mass,' he reported. 'He'll run ye over after that, around half twelve-ish.'

'Wonderful, thanks so much.' Colette turned to Tilly. 'I'd like to get to Mass myself – what about you?'

Tilly was Presbyterian. She'd never set foot inside a Catholic church. She wondered what Reverend Johnson would have to say. On the other hand it was Christmas, and she couldn't see Jesus objecting to her paying a visit to any of His churches.

'Sure,' she said. 'I'll go.'

They decided to use up the half-hour before Mass with a walk around the village. They piled on layers – Colette lent Tilly a green scarf – and set off. Despite the sun, the day was bitterly cold: Tilly's fingers soon stung. She shoved them into her pockets, thinking of the stifling heat of Queensland. On balance, she decided she preferred this sharp air that didn't suffocate you – but a pair of fur-lined gloves sure wouldn't go amiss.

The village was tiny and charming, one side of its single street comprising a neat row of white cottages whose front doors and windowsills were painted in bright blues and pinks and greens and reds.

Across the road from them, on the sea side, was the bar they'd spent the night in, the café that closed for the winter, a small supermarket with a post office sign hanging overhead and a green-painted slot for letters set into its wall, a pharmacy with a big poster for flu medication in the window, and Kieran McHugh's newsagent's with its two petrol pumps outside.

At the far end of the street, beyond the cottages, was the church – set back off the road and approached by a short paved drive – and directly next door to it a small school with a single basketball post in its front yard.

No bank, no ATM, no boutique or shoe shop, no library, no music store or mobile-phone outlet. Dingle, presumably, their nearest port of call for all that. As they walked, they encountered little children on brand new bicycles, and older people who smiled and wished them a happy Christmas, and hoped they'd slept well at Bernard and Cormac's, and wondered if they'd managed to get someone to take them across to Roone. Everyone seemed to remember them from the night before – had the entire adult population been in the bar?

Tilly was enchanted by it all. This was where her mother had grown up, this small country of singers and wild storms and simple, instinctive kindnesses. This was where her sister had grown up, and where she still lived.

Tilly herself might have been born and raised in Ireland, if her parents had remained together for a few more months, if her mother had realised that she was pregnant before deciding to leave him. She might have waited then; she might have had the baby in Ireland. The thought was intriguing. With a small change in timing, Tilly might have been Irish by birth instead of by descent.

'So,' Colette said, as they walked slowly towards the church, 'how are you feeling about meeting your sister?'

'A bit nervous,' Tilly admitted. 'I'll be a shock for her.'

'A surprise, I'm sure – and when it sinks in, a very pleasant one.' She paused. 'If you like, I could go with you when you meet her. If you thought it might make it easier.'

Tilly considered this. Better to have someone there, or better for her to go alone? Either way, she felt, it would be momentous.

'Of course, it's entirely up to you. Think about it, you have plenty of time.'

'I will, thank you.'

In bed the night before, when sleep wouldn't come, she had tried to imagine it. She'd pictured herself standing before her sister and announcing who she was – and there it had ended, her mind unwilling, or unable, to predict what might happen after that.

And in the dead of night, as the storm continued to rattle the little attic window in its frame, it had suddenly occurred to her that her sister might not even be there. Wasn't it possible that she had gone to Dublin to spend Christmas with their father, the man Tilly's mother had told her wouldn't want to know of his second daughter's existence? And then she'd thought: how did he feel about his first daughter – were they close? So little she knew about them, so ignorant she was.

She should have written. She should have written a letter, given her sister advance warning. She shouldn't have embarked on this crazy journey without some kind of preparation. But she hadn't thought, she'd acted impulsively, out of fear and heartbreak – and now she'd have only herself to blame if it all went wrong.

Just then bells began to peal, their notes as pure as the air. People emerged from the houses and made their way towards the church. Cars were arriving too, parking willy-nilly on the street. People clambered out of them, calling to others, wishing them happy Christmas, voices carrying clearly.

Mercifully, the church was fairly warm. They found seats halfway up the aisle, between a scarlet-cheeked woman in a tangerine coat with an enormously fat baby on her lap, and a pair of teenage boys in identical black leather jackets and blue jeans, their hair completely hidden under woolly hats – one maroon, one brown – their hands red and raw-looking with the cold.

A bell pinged. Everyone stood. The priest walked out to the altar and the Mass began. There was singing, of course – but strangely, not from the congregation. At home, everyone joined in the hymns when Tilly attended a service, but here they stood silently and listened to a small choir of a dozen or so elderly females, who were accompanied on an organ by a slightly younger man. Not at all what she would have expected, given the enthusiastic singing of the night before.

Ten minutes into the proceedings, the baby beside her began to whimper. The woman reached into a shopping bag at her feet and drew out a bottle whose rubber teat was covered with a twist of aluminium foil. She removed the foil and offered the bottle to the child, and peace was restored.

Tilly found herself covertly examining the little face, what she could see of it, the chubby fingers that encircled the bottle, the fat legs that periodically kicked out at nothing. She heard the little noises it produced, the wet smacks of its sucking, the swallows of the milk going down. She studied it all like it was knowledge for an exam she was soon to take.

Which it was, in a way.

'Now Nelly will do the readings,' the priest announced, and a woman from the top seat in a bright yellow coat walked to the altar and read from the Bible. People coughed and shuffled feet. Offspring fidgeted and were hushed.

A toddler escaped from a seat and made a chuckling race up the aisle before being hastily retrieved by his grinning father. Tilly's infant neighbour released its grip on the rubber teat to belch solemnly, prompting an eruption of delighted titters from the younger members of the congregation who were within earshot.

'Now we'll have our Christmas pageant,' the priest said, and a group of small children emerged scarlet-faced from various seats – six or seven years old, Tilly thought, slightly younger than Robbie – and enacted an abridged version of the Nativity at the top of the church.

The production was overseen by a woman who crouched at the side of the action, and whom Tilly presumed to be their teacher. '*Shepherds!*' she hissed audibly, when the actors in question missed their cue and failed to appear. On they darted, looking remarkably like the innkeepers who had denied shelter a few minutes before to Mary and Joseph. They arranged themselves in a jostling huddle beside the happy couple and their swaddled doll baby, one or two waving at members of the congregation.

As the performance drew to a close, one of the shepherds proclaimed loudly that he needed to do a wee, causing general merriment as he was ushered rapidly down the aisle by his mother, shaking her head in mock shame.

The pageant was roundly applauded, the grinning actors hopping back to their various seats. As the Mass proceeded, Tilly stood and sat and knelt along with the others, her gaze wandering up to the stained-glass windows, the softly glowing red light that hung on a long chain above the altar, the priest in his colourful robes, who raised a silver cup high as a bell tinkled and everyone bowed.

Among the people in the seats around her she recognised a few faces from yesterday. She saw the small thin man who'd sung for her in the bar, whose name she had now forgotten. He was in a navy coat today, sitting next to a dark-haired woman in purple and an assortment of children, every one of them wearing spectacles.

Across the aisle she spotted Sheila Corbett, who'd cooked dinner for them the night before, sitting with Joseph and their three girls, the smallest perched on her father's lap.

Glancing behind her, Tilly glimpsed Bernard standing with a huddle of men just inside the door of the church. She wondered why, with a couple of unoccupied rows of seats at the rear.

She remained where she was as people shuffled up to communion, Colette among them, the choir singing carol after carol until all seats had been resumed. At the end of the Mass the priest wished everyone a happy Christmas, and warned of a fallen tree on the way to Dingle, a few miles beyond the village. 'It made a big hole in the road,' he told them. 'The guards are looking into it' – and the smile that followed this announcement caused the whole place to erupt. Laughter in a church!

By the time Tilly and Colette were leaving their seat to join the slow shuffle down the aisle, Bernard and his companions had vanished. As they emerged from the church Tilly felt a hand on her arm. She turned to see a man whose face she recalled from the previous day.

'You're all set,' he said, 'for the trip across. 'Tis a fine day for it' – and she realised it was Kieran McHugh, who owned the newsagent's, and who had agreed to take them to Roone.

'My mother,' he said, and Tilly and Colette shook hands with the small bundled-up woman by his side, and agreed that it was bitterly cold, but a lot better than yesterday. The four of them walked slowly down the street as people climbed into cars and drove off.

'I'll see ye down at the pier so,' Kieran said when they reached the newsagent's. 'About half an hour.'

'But would ye not come in for a cup of tea first?' his mother enquired as he turned the key in the door next to the shop.

'I think we should keep moving,' Colette told her. 'We're anxious to get to Roone as soon as we can,' and Tilly was aware of a small and steady internal fluttering that had started up inside her.

About half an hour.

Back at the bar Cormac materialised to bring down their cases and load them into Colette's car. They went in search of Bernard and found him peeling potatoes in the kitchen, a striped apron tied around his waist.

'Ursula is gone to visit her sister,' he told them. 'She lives three miles out the road. We're under strict orders to have the vegetables done before she gets back. I'm leaving the sprouts to Cormac – can't be doing with the little feckers.' He shot a grin at Tilly as he swept potato skins into a bin. 'Excuse my language, ladies – we're not used to civilised company around here. I'd say ye'll have tea before ye go.'

So they had tea, and prepared the sprouts between them as the kettle boiled. Afterwards, as Tilly waited by the bar door, she couldn't help overhearing the brief argument between Colette and Bernard, the gist of which was that the amount suggested by Bernard for payment was considered by Colette to be far too low.

'Yerra, not at all,' he insisted. 'Isn't it Christmas, the season of goodwill to all men? Ye can come and stay again in the summer, and I'll charge ye full price, I promise,' and that was that.

'Safe trip now,' he said as they got into the car. 'I hope ye can swim,' he said, laughing through the big bush of his beard. He and his brother stood waving as they left, and Tilly waved back until they disappeared from view.

Colette shook her head. 'He hardly covered the cost of the breakfast with that bill. Then again, it wasn't exactly the Ritz.'

She didn't say how much, or how little, he'd charged: by the sound of it Tilly thought she could probably have footed her own bill after all, but she felt awkward about offering money now, which would surely, anyway, be refused.

'I still appreciate your paying,' she said instead, and was told it was nothing, nothing at all.

They met no car on the short drive to the pier, which was deserted. They parked by the side of the cabin and sat looking out at the sea while they waited.

'Look how still it is this morning,' Colette said. 'So different from yesterday. I hope there was no damage on Roone. It's very exposed, being so tiny, and having the sea all around it.'

'Does it get many storms?'

'Quite a few in the winter, I believe – but I imagine last night's was far worse than normal.'

A beat passed. 'They'll be glad to see you,' Tilly said. 'It'll be a nice surprise.'

Colette laughed. 'Let's hope so.' She seemed about to say something else, but just then they heard the sound of a motor, and a small blue and white boat came into view. They got out and unloaded their cases, and Tilly caught the end of the fat rope that Kieran threw out to them and wound it on his instruction several times around a low stone pillar.

He helped them to climb on board. The sensation felt most peculiar to Tilly – like being on a trampoline, solid ground gone from under her feet. She grabbed at the rail to steady herself, making Kieran laugh.

'I've never been on a boat before,' she told him.

'Is that a fact? Not to worry, you'll find your sea legs in a minute. It's nice and calm, we'll have no bother going across. Head into the cabin,' he added, 'it'll be chillier out to sea' – and they stepped into the tiny cabin, where there was just enough standing room for them.

He lifted on their luggage and retrieved the rope and flung it into a corner. He squeezed past them to the controls and turned the little boat around until they were facing out to sea. 'Now,' he said, 'Roone, here we come.'

He gunned the engine and they puttered away, leaving the pier behind. Tilly gripped the ledge that jutted beneath the cabin's window and watched the boat cutting through the water, and the hump of the island as it got steadily bigger. After just a few minutes she could make out the green of fields, and pale dots that must surely be houses, and slender strips of beaches where water met land.

She lifted her gaze and saw the wide blue arc of the sky, barely a cloud interrupting it this Christmas morning. The sun out of sight behind them, but casting a dazzle on the water that was almost too bright to watch. Such a perfect day to arrive: surely that boded well.

'Your first visit to Roone?' Kieran asked.

Tilly nodded. She hadn't mentioned the reason for her trip to anyone last night, just told them she was travelling around.

'It's a grand little spot,' he said. 'They're friendly enough, the island folk. You'll enjoy it. You staying at the hotel?'

'Not sure yet,' she replied, hoping he didn't ask any more. After an eternity of travelling she was almost there – and the closer they got to the island, the more anxious she was becoming. Her stomach churned even more than it usually did in the mornings these days: she felt jumpy and apprehensive. Her eyes brimmed with sudden nervous tears – she blinked them away before they had a chance to fall.

She felt an arm going around her waist. 'It will be fine, believe me,' Colette said softly into her ear. 'You have nothing to worry about, I'm certain of it' – and because she did sound certain, Tilly tried to take comfort from her words. They were far from true, of course – she had so much to worry about – but maybe, hopefully, her sister would help.

The island was rushing towards them now, beaches and cliffs and rocky outcrops encircling the shoreline, houses and roads and trees and hills clearly visible behind them. Fields with animals and red barns and other outbuildings, cars and Jeeps and tractors parked here and there.

'Damage to Mannings,' Kieran remarked. 'Looks like you won't be staying *there*, anyway' – and Tilly saw a badly torn roof on a large two-storey building with an apricot façade that lay a short distance from the pier. *Mannings Hotel* she read, in fancy black lettering on a big cream sign at its entrance.

A long metal ladder was propped against the hotel wall, beneath the damaged portion of the roof. A figure in a fluorescent orange jacket was making his way up; a second, similarly clad, stood below holding the ladder.

Adjacent to the hotel was a church, and a terrace of ten or twelve white cottages beyond it, all with identical dark blue doors and window frames, and other houses after that, set back a bit further from the sea, and separate from one another.

On the other side of the pier were buildings that looked commercial – shops or galleries of some kind, names painted above windows that she couldn't make out from this distance – before the road veered left, and out of sight.

It struck Tilly that all the buildings were on the far side of the road, with nothing to impede the sea view of anyone staying in the hotel, or emerging from the church, or living in any of the houses. Nothing between them and the sea but a road and a low wall that seemed to be constructed of stones piled on top of one another, and strips of sand or pebbles or giant black rocky slabs where water met land.

'The village is in that direction,' Colette told her, pointing to the bend in the road. 'It's just around the corner, but we're going the other way, past the hotel and the church.' Tilly wondered if there was a bus service, but saw no sign of a stop – and anyway, what bus would run on Christmas Day?

The air was different here. It seemed to have a new scent to it, one that reminded her of the crisp smell of just-washed sheets after they'd been left outside to dry. It was as if the whole of the island had decided to do the laundry on Christmas morning. She found herself taking deep gulps of it, almost drinking it in.

Kieran brought the boat in by the long pier and stopped by a set of stone steps, behind a huddle of bigger boats already moored there. The ferry they'd missed the day before sat apart from the others on the far side of the pier. *Roone Crossings* it declared, in giant red lettering. No cars on its deck now of course, its engine silent today. They'd got here anyway, without its help.

She climbed from the boat and went up the steps and stood on Roone for the first time. She was finally here, she'd made it. The journey from Australia had taken nearly four days, twice as long as it should have, but she was here now.

Kieran accompanied them the length of the pier, their cases bumping along behind him. After twenty minutes or so on the sea, after accustoming herself to the rhythm of the water, the ground felt oddly solid now to Tilly: she found herself anticipating a tilt that never came, a dip that was no longer there.

'Ah no,' Colette said, 'that looks like Nell's little boat' – and Tilly saw a mess of shattered yellow timber that was strewn along the pebbled beach to the right of the pier. 'Oh dear, what a shame.'

Nothing left intact but the curved tail of it, *Ju* in blue lettering all that was still legible at the broken-off edge. Tilly wondered what had come next – Julie? Judy? Weren't boats usually given female names?

When they reached the road she looked back. The mainland was reduced now to a ragged dark frill above the water, as insignificant as Roone had been when she'd looked out at it from her attic window a few hours earlier.

'How will you go from here?' Kieran asked, and Colette told him they could walk, it wasn't far.

'Thank you so much,' she said. 'You've been more than kind.'

'No bother, happy to help.' He shook their hands, wished them a happy Christmas and retraced his steps to the boat, and they watched as he turned it around and headed back.

Once the sound of his engine had faded, all they heard was the soft rumble of the sea, and the calls of the gulls that flew above it. Despite her jangling nerves Tilly stared at the water, hypnotised by its rhythmic roll and fall. Would she ever get tired of looking at it?

'Now,' Colette said, 'we have a short walk, about twenty minutes. Good job the day is dry.'

They set off, pulling their cases behind them. The road was quiet; in the few minutes since their arrival no car had driven past, not so much as a single bicycle had appeared. Christmas Day: everyone at home with their families.

Tilly felt another nervous leap inside her. I'm walking to my sister's house, she thought. In twenty minutes I'll be there. Every footfall sounded unnaturally loud, their suitcase wheels thundering over the ground like a herd of stampeding buffalo. They walked past the hotel and the church, and were just approaching the terrace of white cottages, in front of which the path they were on seemed to peter out, when Tilly heard a car approaching from behind. She glanced around to see it pulling up beside them.

A window was rolled down. 'Ye look like ye could do with a lift,' the middle-aged woman in the passenger seat said. 'Did ye just come over?'

'We did,' Colette told them. 'Kieran McHugh from Kilmally brought us across.'

'Ah yes, Kieran has the petrol pumps.' By now the male driver had got out and was opening the boot. 'His brother Joe is married to Vinnie's sister-in-law,' the woman went on. 'We know them well. So ye were stranded yesterday, were ye?'

'We were. We stayed in a pub in Kilmally.'

'O'Loughlin's, that would be, Cormac and Bernard. Their cousin Frank is here.' The man was silently loading their cases into the boot. 'And where are ye headed now?'

'James and Nell Baker's house – you probably know it.'

'Of course I do. Sure everyone on the island knows Nell. We all go to her for the haircuts.'

'We know James as well,' the man remarked, slamming the boot closed.

'You do anyway,' the woman shot back. 'Never out of Fitz's pub, that fellow,' she said to the others, but her voice was good-humoured. 'Hop in, ladies, throw those wellingtons onto the floor.' She waved a hand at the pair on the back seat.

They slid in, moving the boots out of the way.

'So who have we here now?' the woman asked, craning in her seat to examine them as they set off. Like Paddy, neither of them wore seatbelts.

'I'm James's mother,' Colette replied, 'down from Dublin, and this is a friend of the family, just visiting from Australia.' The lie came out so smoothly that Tilly almost believed it herself.

'I'm Avril and this is Vinnie. We live on the high road, just down from the lighthouse.'

Tilly only half listened to the conversation as she looked out the window at the passing trees and houses and fields, at the cattle and sheep and barns and sheds. My sister knows all this, she thought. This is her home ground, this is where she lives. She probably travels this road every day.

'Ah, 'twas shocking, that storm. Trees down all over the place – and the phones gone, and the power out too, since last night – and ye saw the damage to the hotel roof, did ye? Poor Henry had to go around this morning farming out his guests. They can't keep them until it's repaired – Health and Safety wouldn't allow it – and he had nearly a full house. He does a good three-day package over the Christmas, always gets a lot. We're just after visiting my cousin Sinéad – she's taken two into her B&B for him. Here we are now.'

They drew up in front of a whitewashed bungalow with a gleaming red front door onto which a Christmas wreath had been pinned. 'Now so,' the man said, lifting the luggage from the boot. 'Happy Christmas to ye, they'll be glad to see ye.'

They stood by the roadside as the couple drove off. Tilly regarded the white house that was full of people she didn't know. There was a large red candle in one of the windows, and two cars parked in the driveway, presumably belonging to Colette's son and his wife. She looked to right and left of the house, searching for her destination.

'It's that one,' Colette said, pointing right. They'd just driven past it. Tilly saw a field, and beyond it a big old stone house set back slightly from the road. A sign at the gate read *Walter's Place B&B*.

'That's it,' Colette said. 'That's where your sister lives.'

'I didn't know she had a B&B,' she replied. Trying to spin out time, now that there was no more travelling to do. Trying to gather her courage for what was ahead.

'Want me to come with you?'

Tilly took in a shaking breath, let it out. Took in another. 'No,' she said. 'I'll be OK on my own.'

'You will.' Colette hugged her. 'Go on: the quicker you do it, the better. And come and see me when you can. I'll be here for a few days at least. I'll be dying to know how you get on.'

'Don't tell the others,' Tilly said, 'if you don't mind. Not yet, not until I see how things go.'

'Of course not,' Colette promised. 'Not a word. This story is yours to tell.'

'Thank you so much, for everything.'

'Go. Best of luck. See you soon.'

Tilly walked off, pulling her case behind her. Her legs felt unsteady, like when she'd stepped onto the boat. Halfway to the other house she suddenly remembered that she was still wearing Colette's green scarf: she looked back, but the road was empty. She'd return it later.

She passed the field: its five-bar gate was wide open. She glanced in and saw a Jeep with a trailer attached to it parked beside a small white van that had something – a fruit basket – painted on its side. The drone of machinery – a drill? a chainsaw? – came from somewhere behind them.

And then she was there. She was in front of the stone house. As she stood by the small gate a chattering group of children – two curly-headed girls wearing long dresses, two older boys in matching red football jerseys – emerged onto the road from Colette's son's house, followed by a woman with a baby in her arms, and a dog that trotted along beside her.

Tilly stood and watched as they turned en masse into the field she'd just passed, nobody looking in her direction at all. They disappeared behind the vehicles, presumably making for the back entrance of the very house she was headed for.

Was the woman Colette's daughter-in-law, dropping in for Christmas with her children? Or could she be Tilly's sister, just back from a call to her neighbours? Tilly stood uncertainly for another several seconds, and then she opened the little gate and walked up the path, pulling her case behind her. She stood before the big wooden door – no wreath hanging here – and wiped her damp palms on her jacket.

She took another deep breath. She pressed the bell. Inside, a dog started barking. She had the urge to turn and run.

The door was flung open by an irritated-looking silver-haired and deeply tanned man wearing a grey suit and very shiny black shoes. 'About time!' he barked – and abruptly, his expression darkened further.

'That's *not* my suitcase!' he yelled. 'Can't you goddamn people get *anything* right around here?'

And as quickly as he'd opened it, he slammed the door in Tilly's face.

✳✳✳

'For Heaven's sake, don't *fuss* – I'm perfectly alright. I got a dizzy spell, that's all. It only lasted a second or two.'

Dr Jack inflated the blood-pressure cuff that was wrapped

around Gladys's arm. 'With all due respect, Mrs Connolly, you were unconscious when Laura found you—'

'I came *round*. She *told* you I came round right away.'

'Yes, I realise that, but we still need to find out what caused you to collapse. I see your blood pressure is quite high, which probably had something to do with it—'

'My blood pressure is high? First I've heard of it. It's always fine when my own doctor checks it.'

He deflated the cuff and removed it. 'Well, it's definitely high now, and I'd be much happier to admit you to hospital as soon as—'

'Hospital? On Christmas Day? Nonsense, I won't hear of it.'

'Mrs Connolly,' he persisted, 'you may have had a mini-stroke. It's not uncommon in women of a certain age—'

Bad mistake. Poor man had no way of knowing what any mention of age did to Gladys.

'Mini-*stroke*? I've never heard of anything so ridiculous! How *dare* you insinuate that I'm old enough to have a stroke!'

'Actually, Mrs Connolly, strokes can happen at any age – and I'm only saying it might be that. It could also be your heart—'

'My *heart*? Rubbish – my heart is perfectly sound. Gavin, tell him.'

'Mam, maybe you should listen to what Dr Jack—'

'Oh, for Heaven's sake.' She folded her arms crossly and glared at the doctor. 'I'm telling you now I haven't a notion of letting anyone cart me off to a Kerry hospital. I'll make an appointment to see my own man when I get home, if that'll keep you quiet.'

The doctor snapped his bag closed. 'Well, I can't force you—'

'You certainly can *not*.'

'—but I'm telling you now that I'd be happier to see you being properly checked out—'

'Which I will be, in Dublin.'

'Fair enough.' He withdrew a pad from inside his jacket. 'In the meantime I'm going to prescribe some pills for your blood pressure, which I would urge you to start taking as soon as possible, and I would also recommend that you stay in bed for the rest of today at least.'

He wrote. Gladys watched silently, mouth pursed. Laura wanted badly to shake her. She was like a misbehaving child, refusing to listen to reason. Had it even occurred to her that Gavin had had to leave the other men sorting the chaos outside while he'd driven to Dr Jack's house to summon him on Christmas Day?

Did she for one second consider thanking anyone for looking after her, or acknowledging that they had more than enough on their plates as it was, like a quartet of children who were mourning the sudden wipe-out of their animal friends, and the arrival of an unexpected and very agitated house guest?

Hotelier Henry Manning's timing could not have been worse – or better, depending on the way you looked at it. After managing to get a somewhat revived Gladys back to bed, Laura had sped downstairs to find Henry and another man having been admitted to the hall by the boys, and surrounded by children in various stages of distress.

Stay here with Mr Manning, Laura had ordered everyone, not even saying hello to the poor man – 'Emergency' was what she said – and barely registering his companion before rushing off to find Gavin and tell him his mother needed the doctor.

Chaos. Small wonder Mr Rachmaninov, or whatever his name was, was put out. By the time Gavin had gone for Dr Jack and Laura had ushered the visitors and children into the kitchen, Poppy was demanding to be fed in the only way she knew how.

And while Laura was preparing a bottle of formula and spooning instant coffee into mugs, and Henry was apologising for landing in on top of them, and explaining that he wouldn't be bothering her only he was in dire straits, what with the hotel roof being damaged in the storm, and he knew she was officially closed but could he prevail on her to take in just one guest, it would only be for a couple of nights, while all this was going on Charlie trotted in from the scullery with his latest toy in his mouth – Gavin's doll, which Poppy had duly rejected in favour of Rabbity – and dropped it right onto the shiny shoe of Mr Whatever, who kicked it off with as much enthusiasm as if it had been radioactive material, and hissed something to Henry that included the phrases *can't possibly expect* and *must be some place more suitable.*

And Henry whispered something back to him, which Laura couldn't hear at all, and they carried on in agitated undertones for some time, as Laura made coffee and found milk and sugar and cooled formula and assured the children that all the animals had gone straight up to Heaven – Santa had probably delivered them himself on his sleigh – and pretended to be wholly unaware of the other conversation.

And the long and the short of the whole thing was that they'd been landed with Mr Whatshisname, who turned out to be from America, for two nights, until he was due to leave the island. Laura couldn't bring herself to say no to poor Henry, who kept a stack of leaflets advertising the donkey rides on the hotel reception desk all through summer. She supposed it was a bit like Mary and Joseph looking for a place to stay in Bethlehem: she couldn't be like the no-room-at-the-inn ones who'd refused to give them shelter.

Mind you, her guest wasn't anywhere near as nice as she imagined the other two to have been. He didn't seem at all thrilled to have got a room at her inn. In fact, he looked as enthusiastic at the prospect of staying with them as Laura felt – and to be fair, he had good reason to be put out. Not only, she learned, had he been woken in the small hours by over half of the hotel roof being wrenched off, doing a fair bit of damage to his bedroom ceiling in the process, but his luggage had somehow managed to get lost in the subsequent kerfuffle, and was being urgently sought by hotel staff, who were no doubt feeling every bit as harassed as the suitcase's owner.

It must have been delivered to someone else by mistake, said poor Henry, who kept glancing at his watch, and who really did look at the end of his tether. I'm sure it'll turn up in no time at all – and of course it would, Roone being far too small for a missing suitcase to stay missing for long.

By now the boys had migrated to the scullery, where Laura knew they were craning to see what was going on outside, and the girls, still in the princess dresses that Santa had brought, were squabbling over crayons, having apparently forgotten about the animal tragedy, and Charlie was under the table finding fallen bits of sausage from earlier, and Gavin had yet to return with Dr Jack for Gladys, who might well have passed away peacefully by now, unattended by anyone.

Thank God for Nell, who appeared like a mirage at the scullery door and bundled all five children into jackets and ushered them and Charlie back to her house for 'Christmas surprises', leaving Laura free to see Henry off the premises and show Mr Newcomer to his quarters – Lord, what on earth had Henry called him? She couldn't admit she'd forgotten his name: he was bad enough. She brought him to the second-best guest room (Gladys, naturally, was in the best) figuring that the man probably deserved a bit of pampering after what he'd been through.

And while she was putting sheets on his bed and stuffing pillows into cases and finding towels for his bathroom – you'd think he'd offer to help all the same, instead of scowling out the window while she worked: it wasn't as if he'd lost the use of his limbs, just had a bit of plaster fall onto his bed – Gavin finally arrived back with Dr Jack, allowing Laura to make her escape, and let him sulk alone.

Do check out our library in the sitting room, just by the front door, she suggested. Unlike Gladys, he might appreciate the old books. Make yourself a snack in the kitchen if you're peckish, just have a rummage in the fridge – wondering, as she spoke, what there actually was in the fridge that might constitute a snack. Cheese, maybe. Tub of yogurt.

I'll be serving Christmas dinner at six, she told him. I'll give you a shout. She left the room swiftly before he could tell her he was vegetarian, or lactose intolerant or something. And he'd eat in the kitchen with the rest of them: he needn't think she was going to cart trays into the dining room.

And now it was heading for eleven, and it looked like Gladys wasn't about to shake off her mortal coil anytime soon, and none of them was going to get to Mass for Christmas this year. Pity: she liked the church on Christmas Day, all decked out in holly and ivy and whatever bit of colour Maisie Kiely and her cohorts had been able to scavenge from the island's bushes and fields.

She enjoyed seeing the women dressed in their finery, the farmers and fishermen of Roone scrubbed and polished for Christmas, the children still bubbling with the excitement of Santa. Above all, she never tired of Father William taking the phone call from the North Pole midway through the proceedings, as he always did.

The first time she'd witnessed it, their first Christmas on Roone, she'd been appalled. A mobile phone rang just after the sermon, and she wondered who'd forgotten to silence it – and then Father William broke off the prayers with an abashed face. I'm terribly sorry, he said, but I'd better see who this is – and he hunted about in his vestments and pulled out the ringing phone.

Really, Laura thought indignantly, that's a bit much – and she looked around to see if anyone else disapproved, but nobody seemed at all put out, which she found unbelievable. Didn't anybody mind that a mobile phone – the *priest's* mobile phone – was disrupting the Mass, on Christmas Day of all days?

Hello? Father William said – and immediately his troubled face cleared. Oh, it's you! he cried, and lots of smiling and nodding and yes, yes-ing followed, while Laura continued to fume silently. The *nerve* of him, to carry on a conversation just like that – and to think she'd *liked* him. To think they'd given him a trio of potted hyacinths for Christmas.

And then he said, Hang on, they're all here, I'll just ask them – and he held the phone to his chest and told them it was Santa, just arrived back at the North Pole and wondering if they were all happy with their presents.

It was so perfectly executed, the pretence fooling Laura completely. She looked at her boys' enchanted faces, at all the happily surprised children around her, at the smiling parents who'd known what was coming – and she thought yet again how glad she was that they'd decided to relocate to Roone.

And every Christmas the same trick fooled the island children afresh. It was as if they entered into a conspiracy each January to wipe the previous phone call from their collective consciousness. They were as newly charmed by the ruse each time it happened – and as she came to be familiar with the benevolent magic of Roone, Laura thought it wasn't outside the bounds of possibility that their memories of the call had indeed been gently erased by whatever force was at work on the island.

Of course, Santa wouldn't be able to phone this year, not with the lines down. But he'd contact them another way, she was sure. A letter might be delivered by someone running excitedly up the aisle in the middle of the proceedings, saying he'd found it in a bottle washed up on the beach, or dropped by a seagull on the road outside the church – and the surprise would delight the children like it always did.

After seeing the doctor off the premises, and before Gavin returned to the business of restoring order in the field, Laura told him about their unexpected guest. The news didn't go down well.

'What? Henry landed someone in on top of us, just like that? On Christmas Day? As if we don't have enough to cope with.'

'Gavin, the man was desperate – half the roof blew off the hotel last night and he has to rehouse all his guests. He kept apologising.'

Gavin wasn't mollified. Of course he wasn't, his mind still on his dead animals, and his mother who might have had a mini-stroke, or possibly a heart attack. Still, there wasn't much point in kicking up a fuss.

'Well, it's done now. I've taken him in, and that's all there is to it.'

'I'm only thinking of you,' he said. 'The extra work.'

'I'll manage,' she told him. 'You should get back to the others' – and he turned and walked out without another word. She watched him go, remembering too late that she'd forgotten to thank him for the necklace. Some Christmas this was turning out to be.

The tree looked woefully shabby in the daylight. They really must invest in a few new baubles, and maybe a string of decent lights for next year. She plumped cushions, straightened rugs, ran a duster around the place, retrieved a forgotten plate from the floor by an armchair, got the Hoover from under the stairs and plugged it in before remembering that the power was out.

She cleared the ashes from the grate and brought them to the metal bin that stood near the gate into the field. The air was icy and calm, not a puff of wind – no wind left to puff after yesterday. Her steps crunched on the frosty grass. She tipped the ashes into the bin and paused to survey the scene of last night's calamity, shoulders hunched against the cold.

One small corner of the shed was still standing; the rest had collapsed beneath the fallen tree, and was still pretty much inaccessible. Jim Barnes was in the process of dismembering the trunk with his chainsaw, section by section; the others were hauling the chunks away and piling them up by the far hedge. The rest of the orchard seemed mercifully intact, none of the other trees affected by the fallen one. It would leave a sad space behind though.

Hugh spotted her and walked across, brushing leaves and twigs from his jacket. 'I'll come in and get a bag,' he said, 'and gather up the apples. You may as well have them.'

Everyone on Roone knew about the tree that bore fruit most of the year, and everyone accepted it as just another of the island idiosyncrasies. 'How soon before you can get the animals out?' Laura asked as they walked back together to the house.

'Hard to say. It's slow work – and even when the tree is cleared there'll be the blocks to shift … There's more help on the way, though. Jim met Dougie and Leo on his way here. They're coming later, and they'll bring anyone else they can get.'

'People are very good, on Christmas Day too.'

He shrugged. 'We help each other out, that's all.'

'I know … I suppose there's no hope that any of the animals survived?'

He shook his head. 'Not under that lot, I'm afraid. They wouldn't have had a hope. It's an awful shame.'

Laura gave him her shopping basket for apples and brought firelighters and kindling inside, and started a new fire in the sitting room. She picked up the empty coal scuttle and carried it out to refill it – and almost collided with a fully dressed Gladys outside the door.

'What are you doing up? The doctor told you to stay in bed.'

'Oh, I couldn't, I'd be a nuisance to everyone. Anyway, I wouldn't get a bit of sleep with that chainsaw.' Gladys eyed the scuttle. 'You have the fire lit?'

'Just this minute.'

'I'll pop in there then. I'll sit quietly and bother no one. I think I left my knitting in there last night.'

'You did – I put it on the sideboard.'

'Thank you, dear, that's all I want. I suppose we've missed Mass – was the eleven o'clock the only one?'

'It was, I'm afraid.'

A martyred sigh. 'On Christmas morning too. I've never missed Mass at Christmas before.'

Nor had the rest of them. 'Would you eat a bit of breakfast?'

'Ah no – although I suppose I should keep my strength up. Maybe just something small, with the big dinner ahead of us.'

'What about a boiled egg?'

'That'd be nice … or maybe I'd manage a sausage, and a small rasher if you have it, and if you could scramble the egg, you know I don't care for them fried. And a bit of toast, I think, just the one slice. I can come out when it's ready, if you like – or you could bring it in, if it's easier.'

'You stay put. I'll bring it in.'

Easier to leave her parked in the sitting room, out of everyone's way. It occurred to Laura, as she took the frying pan out of the sink, that Gladys hadn't enquired about the fallen tree, or the fate of the animals in the demolished shed. Not a single question.

Could she possibly have forgotten? Might Dr Jack be right in his suggestion of a mini-stroke, one that might have affected her memory?

And then she thought: No, of course Gladys hadn't forgotten. She'd mentioned the chainsaw: she knew exactly what was going on. No interest then, no concern for anything that happened outside her own selfish little orbit. Some things didn't change.

She made the breakfast, reminding herself that it was the season of goodwill to all men, and mothers-in-law. Approaching the sitting-room door, she was surprised to hear voices within. Who on earth—? And then she remembered Mr Scowling Visitor, who must have found his way to the sitting room, and who had now been thrown into the company of one Mrs Gladys Connolly: let's see how that went.

'Well, I must say—' Gladys broke off as Laura entered. 'My dear, you never told me we had a guest. Mr Kawalski has just been telling me of his terrible ordeal in the hotel last night.'

Kawalski: that was it. And look at Gladys – the woman was practically glowing, the knitting bag thrust aside in honour of her companion. Ankles crossed demurely, hands clasped together in her lap. Butter wouldn't melt.

'Thank you *so* much, dear,' she said, as Laura set the tray on a little table by her chair. 'I'm an awful nuisance to her,' she added, twinkling at Mr Kawalski, who sat across the fireplace from her with a face as long as a horse's. Didn't look like he was quite as captivated by Gladys as she appeared to be by him.

'Can I get you something to eat?' Laura asked him, wondering if she was going to spend the day running around after the two of them, but to her relief, he shook his head and told her he was good.

'At least have some tea,' Gladys said, 'and then I won't feel too shy about eating my breakfast in front of you. Laura won't mind bringing in another cup, will you, dear?'

'Not at all.' It wasn't as if she had anything else to do today.

'I guess ...' he said doubtfully – and when Laura returned with the cup he was examining the shelves of books, and Gladys was telling him that her son was very proud of his collection, making it sound like Gavin had put the library together all by himself. Not a mention of a silver fish now, no talk of the books smelling up the room. Say nothing, Laura told herself, and left them to it.

In the kitchen she boiled the kettle again and made a cup of green tea, relishing the unaccustomed emptiness of the place. She sat on the bench by the window, picturing the boys there the night before, remembering how they'd looked out at the storm and worried that Santa would crash his sleigh. Bless them, bless their innocence: they wouldn't have it for much longer.

She sipped tea, her eyelids heavy, listening to the intermittent drone of the chainsaw outside. A nap would be wonderful, but out of the question with the children returning at any time, and two visitors in the other room. She'd soldier on, and hopefully get a reasonably early night.

She finished her tea. She stretched her arms above her head and yawned. Shame not to just stretch out on the bench for a few minutes, even if there wasn't time for a nap.

She was awakened by the children bursting into the kitchen, the girls eager to show her the paper swans James had made for them, the boys clamouring for a place to hang the rings board that Nell had given them, Poppy beaming at her from Nell's arms. Laura checked the time and was amazed to find that over an hour had passed since she'd lain down.

'I would have held on to them for longer only Colette has just this minute arrived,' Nell told her. 'Would you believe she stayed in O'Loughlin's in Kilmally last night – they got someone to bring her across just now. Oh, and I heard Con Maher found a door, of all things, on the beach this morning when he went for his swim.'

'A *door*?'

'The storm must have ripped it off an outhouse or something. And James told me about Gladys – how is she?'

Laura lit the oven before reclaiming Poppy. 'Fine, apparently. She's in the sitting room talking to the hotel guest that Henry delivered to us earlier. You heard the roof was damaged?'

'Oh dear, I did, Colette said it's in a right state. Poor Henry. And you've been saddled with one of his guests – will you cope?'

'Doesn't look like I have a choice, does it? At least I have the space – and of all dinners, the Christmas one can stretch to feed a few more.' Just then the doorbell rang again, making Charlie bark as usual. Laura made a face. 'Lord, that better not be another refugee.'

'I'll leave you to it,' Nell said, opening the back door. 'Shout if you need anything.'

'I will – thanks for the break.' When she'd gone Laura turned to the children. 'Wait here,' she ordered. 'Remember what Dad said: *no* going out in the garden. Ben and Seamus, take off the girls' jackets please.'

'Can we just hang the board for the rings?'

'No – jackets first.'

She went out to the hall, Poppy still in her arms, just in time to hear Mr Kawalski snap: 'That's *not* my suitcase. Can't you goddamn people get *anything* right around here?' and slam the front door loudly, causing Poppy to burst immediately into startled tears.

Laura was outraged. 'You *rude* man!' she cried, above Poppy's wails. 'How *dare* you slam the door – *my* door – in anyone's face! *Look* what you've done to my daughter!'

His mouth dropped open. She took advantage of his speechlessness – momentary, she was sure – to reach past him and open the door again.

A tall, slender teenage girl stood there, a look of bewilderment on her pale face, her lips blue with cold. She wore a navy jacket that didn't look warm enough for the weather, and a green scarf that might be silk. Black jeans, black ankle boots. Beside her sat a large suitcase covered with thin stripes of blue and beige, an Aer Lingus label looped around its handle.

'I'm so sorry,' Laura said, wondering how long she'd been working for Henry. He hadn't mentioned taking on anyone new, least of all someone not even from the island. 'It seems the case doesn't belong to this gentleman' – laying special emphasis on the word, hoping he'd recognise the heavy sarcasm. 'Perhaps if he gave you a description—'

'I *gave* a description,' he muttered. 'I filled out a goddamn *form*—'

Laura spun towards him. 'Watch your language,' she said sharply. 'It's quite clear your description didn't get passed on to this young lady, who's only trying to do her job – so you might trouble yourself to let her know what she's looking for.'

He looked pained, but at least he wasn't yelling any more. 'It's *brown*, plain brown leather, and it's got my *name* tag, for Chri— for Pete's sake: Larry *Kawalski*.'

'Actually,' the girl said quietly, 'I have no idea where this gentleman's case is.'

Australian, the accent sounded like, or maybe New Zealand – Laura could never tell the difference. She shifted Poppy from one hip to the other, thinking of the turkey that should be going into the oven around now.

'So,' she said, 'you'll let us know when you locate Mr Karpotski's luggage.'

'*Kawalski*,' he growled.

Laura ignored him. 'Brown leather,' she said to the girl. 'Name tag. Thanks so much.' She made to close the door.

'But this is *my* suitcase.' The same soft voice. 'I haven't … I don't know anything about the gentleman's.'

Laura halted. 'You're not employed by the hotel?'

'No.'

'Are you looking for a place to stay then, is that it?' Was she to be inundated with all of Roone's waifs and strays today? It wasn't on, really it wasn't.

The girl's pale face turned pink. Was she going to burst into tears?

But no tears came. 'Are you … Laura? Laura Connolly?'

'I am.' Henry must have sent her, afraid to come himself in case Laura said no this time. 'You need a bed, is that it?'

'Well …'

'Come in,' Laura said. What else could she say? It was one more, and they had the room, and she didn't look like she'd be any trouble. Talk about opening her doors at Christmas though: at this rate she might as well be running the B&B properly.

Henry would owe them, big-time.

Out of the corner of her eye Laura saw Mr Katorski slink back into the sitting room – good. Let him cool his heels, or whatever he needed to cool. Let Gladys and himself have a good old moan, if that's what he wanted.

The girl was still hovering uncertainly on the doorstep. 'I'm not exactly … that is, I haven't just come looking for a place to stay—'

But Laura could hear a commotion in the kitchen. 'Sorry, I need to— Look, come with me, will you? Leave your case and follow me. And close the front door.' At least Henry hadn't landed Laura with two crosspatches – and this one might even be of some use.

A cacophony met them in the kitchen.

'Mum, Ben won't hold the board straight. He's doin' it on purpose, so all my rings drop off.'

'Am *not*!'

'Are *so*!'

'Mum, Challie ate my—'

'Stop,' Laura ordered. 'Behave yourselves: we have company.'

They all stared at the newcomer, who gave them a small weary smile. She looked as tired as Laura felt. She looked like she could do with a week of sleep.

'What's your name?' Laura asked.

'Tilly. Short for Matilda.'

'And you need a place to stay.'

'Well, I—' She broke off, biting her lip, her glance darting from the silently watching children to Laura. 'Yes please,' she said then, 'if you have space.'

'As it happens, I'm officially closed,' Laura replied, 'and I've already taken in one hotel guest – that delightful man you just met – but I can't very well turn you away on Christmas Day. I'm wondering why Henry didn't bring you in person, though.'

'I don't know who Henry is,' the girl said apologetically.

'The hotel owner.' This was becoming confusing. 'Aren't you here because the roof fell in?'

'Actually, I … I haven't come from the hotel. I've just … arrived on Roone.'

Laura's eye caught the clock just then: the explanation would have to wait. 'Could you take the baby for a minute? I have to get the turkey into the oven, or we'll have no Christmas dinner.'

The girl took Poppy, who regarded her warily. 'Shall I take her jacket off?'

'Do, please – you can sit on that bench.'

Yes, she might turn out to be quite useful. Laura took the stuffed turkey from the fridge and shoved it into the oven. She removed the bundle of coats from their hook on the back of the door to the scullery and hung the boys' rings board there: that would keep them quiet for a while. She changed the water in the saucepan that held the ham.

And as she worked, she listened.

'What are your names?'

'Ewie.'

'Mawian.'

'Those are pretty princess dresses. Did Santa bring them?'

'Yeth.'

'And what's the baby's name?'

'Poppy.'

'That's a pretty name, like a flower.'

'Poppy dot a dweth too.'

'She did, I can see that.'

'Not a pwintheth one.'

'No, but it's still lovely.'

'Right.' Laura turned from the cooker. 'Boys, be good while we're upstairs, OK?'

'OK.' The rubber rings thwacked against the board. Clever Nell, finding a game that was relatively quiet, and needed no electricity to function.

'Girls, come with us while we find a room for ... Tilly.'

They trooped upstairs, Evie and Marian hopping on ahead, Poppy back in Laura's arms, the girl carrying her suitcase. A low murmur from the sitting room as they passed – Mr Kamalski moaning about his case to Gladys, no doubt, and the abuse he'd suffered at the hands of his landlady.

Have to apologise to him later for the sharp words, in the interests of diplomacy. Not that he hadn't deserved them: ignorant man. Hopefully the brown suitcase would show up before long, might thaw him out a bit.

She brought her new guest to the third-best room. No sea view, overlooking the hills of Roone instead, which did look pretty spectacular in today's frosty brightness. 'Girls, show Tilly her bathroom,' she instructed, while she went to the airing cupboard for more clean sheets and pillowcases and towels.

'I'll do it,' Tilly offered, when Laura returned. 'I'm sure the girls will help – could you put the pillowcases on for me?'

She was used to children; maybe had younger siblings at home, wherever home was. Laura sat with Poppy on the armchair by the window and watched Marian and Evie pushing pillows into cases.

'Australia or New Zealand?' she asked, and again the teen's face flushed lightly as she tucked in the bottom sheet.

'Australia – Queensland. A small town near Brisbane.'

Brisbane was where her mother lived; that was the sum total of what Laura knew about it.

'What brings you to Ireland? Do you have family here?'

The questions seemed to fluster the girl. 'I ...' She stopped what she was doing, the colour deepening in her cheeks. 'Yes, I ...' she tried again, and failed again. Family skeletons, maybe.

'Forget it,' Laura said. 'None of my business. We're a very nosy lot round here.'

'Look,' Tilly said, crossing her arms, uncrossing them, 'I didn't mean to ... that is, I wasn't trying to *mislead* you downstairs ...' She stopped, darting a look at the girls, who were paying them no attention. 'You just,' she went on, 'I mean, that man just *threw* me, and I didn't know ... and then you brought me into the kitchen, and I couldn't—' She broke off again, clearly very ill at ease. What on earth was up with her?

'Hey,' Laura said, 'forget I asked. It doesn't matter.'

But the girl said, 'No, no, it does, I must tell you,' giving another quick look at the girls. 'I mean, I have to, I had it all – but maybe we could do it in private? I – I mean, I think it might be—' She broke off again, her eyes filling with sudden tears.

There was more to this than someone looking for a bed for the night. It was beginning to look like the girl hadn't happened accidentally on Walter's Place, although Laura still couldn't for the life of her imagine what was going on.

She got to her feet. 'You'll find tissues in the bathroom,' she said, and the girl fled. Laura turned to the twins. 'Marian, Evie, I just remembered that Granny never saw your beautiful swans – would you go down and show them to her? I know she'd *love* to see them.'

Off they scampered, so easily distracted. 'Careful on the stairs,' Laura called automatically. 'Down on your bottoms' – and as she turned back Tilly was emerging from the en-suite, looking a little more composed.

'Sorry,' she said quietly. 'I'm making such a mess of this … and I'd planned it over and over, what I'd say to you. I'd practised it, and then—'

She was several inches taller than Laura. Her hair was the colour of pale straw, her skin as freckly as an Irish person's. Her green scarf had come undone, half of it trailing down the back of the jacket that she was still wearing. Deep shadows darkened the skin under her blue-green eyes.

Her eyes.

Inside Laura, something stirred. She felt the scratch of a premonition, or maybe it was the tug of a memory. Something reached for her, but didn't quite make it. She was grateful, all of a sudden, to have the comfort of Poppy's warm little body nestling into her.

They stood facing one another, watching one another, six or seven feet apart.

'Who *are* you?' Laura asked.

She waited, listening to the girls' excited *Gwanny! Gwanny!* as they thumped with little fists on the sitting-room door.

❄❄❄

Her sister had pale brown hair, cut short as a boy's. Pretty face, blue eyes, a lighter colour than Tilly's, the whites shot with fine red lines. Short, only about Lien's height, or maybe an inch or so taller. Slim probably, hard to be sure under the bulky orange sweater that came to the middle of her thighs and looked more like a man's.

An accent different from the people in Kilmally, different from the couple who'd given them the lift from the pier. More like Colette's accent, but not quite the same.

Her sister was a mother with five children. Two sets of twins, it looked like. A pair of red-headed freckle-faced boys, another of blonde curly-headed girls, and one plump cherub called Poppy. Tilly hadn't known that about her: children hadn't been mentioned. She'd been told so little about her sister.

Married, their mother had said. She's Laura Connolly now. Living on a small island called Roone, off the west coast of Ireland. She'll be thirty on the first of August. And that had been all, and Tilly hadn't asked any more, still trying to absorb the fact that she had a sister.

Five children. Tilly had three nieces and two nephews.

A big old house, a bed and breakfast business. A husband Tilly had yet to meet.

The angry man who'd opened the front door had been so unexpected, so shocking. He'd sent the words she'd been rehearsing flying right out of her head, leaving her completely thrown. And then the door opened again and Laura was suddenly there: Laura Connolly was suddenly standing there. Tilly knew immediately who she was, who she had to be.

Laura, her sister, who still didn't know, but who was beginning to realise, who *must* realise, that Tilly – stuttering and stammering and making a total mess of it, because now that they were face to face, it was the hardest thing in the world to say – Laura must realise at this stage that Tilly wasn't just a stranger looking for a place to stay.

'Who *are* you?' she asked, eyes narrowing.

Say it. Say it. Just say it.

'I'm your sister,' Tilly said.

'We're sisters,' she said.

'You're my sister,' she said.

Three times she said it, in case once wasn't enough.

The news was greeted with dead silence, apart from the baby's rapid little breaths as she gawped, from the safety of her mother's arms, at the person who was in fact her aunt.

Then Laura began to shake her head slowly. 'Oh dear,' she said. 'I'm sorry, I'm afraid you've made a mistake. I don't have a sister, I'm an only child. My parents separated when I was twelve and my mother went to—'

She stopped dead. She blinked a few times.

'Australia,' Tilly finished. 'She went to Australia.'

The skin between her sister's eyes pleated.

'Her name is Diane Potter,' Tilly went on. 'I met her last June, in Brisbane. I was adopted. She put me up for adoption.'

'No,' Laura said, shaking her head again, more decisively. 'I mean, no, sorry, you can't be. My parents separated a long time ago, they're divorced now, they didn't have any more children. She *left* him.'

'She didn't know,' Tilly said. 'She didn't know when she was going away, she didn't know she was pregnant.'

More silence. Laura's face impassive now. Impossible to know what she was thinking, how she was taking it.

Tilly combed through her memory, trying to drag out what little information her mother had given her. 'She came to Australia with a woman. She said she knew her through her work. She said her name was … Trudi. I didn't meet her.'

At the mention of the name, something changed in Laura's face. She stepped back until her calves bumped against the chair she'd been sitting in. She sank onto it again, her gaze never leaving Tilly's face. She adjusted Poppy to sit on her lap. Mother and daughter observed Tilly with the same grave expression.

'I didn't know,' Tilly said. 'I didn't know I was adopted until a few years ago. I didn't know anything. I hadn't a clue. My parents, I mean my adoptive parents …' she hesitated, wanting to be kind to them '… they did what they thought was best. I asked them about our family tree – we were doing a school project, I was twelve or thirteen

– so they told me then … They're good people, they're decent and hardworking. They took me when they thought they couldn't have their own children, but then they had two.'

Still not a word from Laura, one thumb absently stroking the back of her daughter's pudgy hand as she listened.

'My real mother,' Tilly began, wanting to say *our*, but maybe it was too soon for that, 'she didn't do it officially, the adoption I mean. It was arranged through my uncle and aunt – she lived beside them when she came to Australia. Last June I told Ma, my adoptive mother, that I wanted to meet her. I just, I don't know, I just wanted to, and … my aunt and uncle arranged it, and I met her in a café in Brisbane—'

Her mother's white face flashed for an instant in her head, throwing her off-course. Unnerved by Laura's continuing scrutiny she dropped her gaze to the floor. Old wooden boards, polished to a mellow nut-brown sheen. 'It wasn't … what I hoped, when I met her. We didn't really … connect.' When the silence stretched she glanced up again. Laura hadn't moved, hadn't taken her eyes off her.

'I haven't met her since,' she said. 'We didn't make any arrangement. But she did tell me about you. I was … amazed to learn that I had a sister, in Ireland.'

Still no reaction, no word from Laura. Why didn't she say something?

'She told me that my father … She said he doesn't know about me, that she didn't tell him. She said … he wouldn't want to know. She didn't tell me much of anything about him, except that he's still alive. And that he's successful at whatever he does. She didn't name him on my birth cert. It says "unknown" for the father.'

She halted again, out of words. She wanted to sit down. She wanted a drink of water. She wanted Laura to stop staring at her.

At last, a response came. 'You have your birth cert?'

'Yes, I made a copy.' She tugged at the zip on her case, her fingers made clumsy by Laura's silent scrutiny. After an eternity she found the envelope and pulled out the cert and handed it over. Laura studied it, her expression unchanged.

She looked up. 'How old are you?'

'Seventeen. My birthday is December the seventh.' It was there on the cert. Laura didn't believe her; she was testing her.

'What year were you born?'

''Ninety-eight.'

It felt like an interrogation. Poppy's mouth stretched in a yawn.

'Your mother. What was she like?'

Your mother, not ours. Still not convinced. Still not able – or not willing – to accept that they were related.

'She was small and thin. Her hair was gold – I mean, sort of … blonde.'

Laura shook her head, mouth tight. 'How did she *seem*? How did she come across?'

Tilly thought back to the café, remembered the fluttering movements, the jerked-out sentences. Recalled wondering if her mother was on medication of some sort. 'She was a bit … highly strung. She seemed … vulnerable. On edge.'

Laura sighed, but didn't comment. A long silence followed, during which Tilly couldn't think of anything else to say that wouldn't sound pathetic: please believe me, I'm telling the truth, I've come so far to find you. I need you.

Poppy had fallen asleep, her lips slightly parted, her cheek squashed against her mother's breast. Watching her, Tilly became aware of feeling unaccountably tired herself. She remembered her night of little sleep in the small attic room while the storm raged outside.

Eventually Laura got to her feet, shifting Poppy to settle against her shoulder, leaving Tilly's birth cert on the chair. 'It's a lot to take in,' she said, 'what you've just told me. It sounds like it's true, but it's a lot to get my head around. And to be honest, you could have chosen a better time to arrive unannounced.'

Tilly's heart sank. 'I'm sorry, I should have let you know.'

'Yes, you should.' There was no anger in the words, more a weary resignation. 'But you're here now, and I can't very well turn you away.' She stopped. 'How did you get here on Christmas Day?'

Tilly told her as briefly as she could about missing the ferry and meeting Colette and staying in the bar. 'We came across together,' she said. 'A man brought us in his boat.'

'Did you tell Colette who you were?'

'Yes,' Tilly replied, her face hot. 'I didn't know she knew you. I just – it just came out.'

It had been a mistake to confide in Colette, she could see that now. She shouldn't have told anyone before telling Laura. She should have kept the reason for her trip to herself, until she saw how the news was received. Another blunder.

'I asked her not to say anything,' she said. 'She promised she wouldn't.' Did they need to keep it hidden though? Why should it be a secret, now that Laura knew?

'How long,' Laura asked, 'are you intending to stay?'

Again, no rancour in the words. No anything at all in the words. She might have been addressing a stranger, or the angry man downstairs.

'I have a return ticket,' Tilly said, 'for the thirtieth. Next Wednesday.' She wondered if she dared to reveal the rest. Not now, certainly not now.

Laura nodded, her expression unchanged. 'The electricity is out, it was cut off last night in the storm, so your shower won't work, and you'll have no hairdryer either. Feel free to run a bath if you want, in the main bathroom out on the corridor. There's plenty of hot water – it heats from the kitchen stove. And I'll send you up a torch for when it gets dark.'

Exactly the information a paying guest would get. 'Thank you,' Tilly said, her hopes dimming with every word she heard.

'I'll call you for dinner around six. You'll have to take us as you find us: we don't stand on ceremony around here, even on Christmas Day.'

'Thank you,' Tilly repeated, wishing she'd give some tiny indication that the notion of having a sister wasn't so unwelcome.

In the doorway Laura turned. 'Look,' she said, 'you were probably hoping for a warmer reception, but you can't just … arrive like this and announce that you're my sister. You can't do that to someone. It's not fair. I'm going to let people think you're another hotel guest, like the American man, at least until I have a chance to get my head around it myself, and we'll just have to hope Colette keeps her promise and says nothing. OK?'

Tilly nodded, unable to speak.

And then she was alone, Laura shutting the door quietly behind her, leaving Tilly standing in the centre of the room on the verge of tears. That had gone just about as badly as it could, despite Colette's assurances that everything would be fine.

She should have broken the news in a letter, and waited for an invitation before coming to Roone. But she'd had no address for Laura, just her name, and the name of the island. She couldn't have let her know; it wasn't possible.

She paced the wooden floor, trying to think. She hadn't been turned away, but she hadn't been made welcome either. She was to be introduced as another displaced hotel guest, her true identity hidden, like a shameful little secret. And unless that situation changed – and she had no reason to think it might – she would be waved off on the thirtieth, sent back to where she'd come from. It was like meeting her mother all over again, one big disappointment.

What was she to do now? Should she stay and pretend to be someone she wasn't? The prospect was awful – but with so little money, what choice did she have?

Maybe Colette, who'd been so kind, so understanding, would give her a loan, if Tilly could bring herself to ask for it. She could find cheap accommodation – maybe go back to Bernard and Cormac's pub, ask them if she could stay until her return date. Even without a loan she could do that: she was fairly sure they'd agree to her sending them money as soon as she got home.

But she quickly dismissed this idea: the village was too close to Roone, literally within sight of the island. She needed to get further away, put more distance between her and a sister who'd prefer that she hadn't come.

She thought about Paddy and Breda in Dingle again. She could ask if they'd take her in until it was time for her to fly home. Yes, she'd phone them right now, leave the island tomorrow on the first ferry.

She opened her bag and found the leaflet – an ad for a pizza restaurant in Dingle – that Paddy had scribbled his number on. She entered the digits into her phone, but when she tried to connect, *no service* showed up on her screen. Of course it did: the phones were down.

She could get the ferry tomorrow anyway: she could leave the island and ring them from the mainland, or from Dingle itself. But what if the phones were down all over Kerry, or what if Paddy and Breda had indeed gone away for Christmas?

Oh, it was such a mess. She put her head into her hands. She had to think, she had to think what to do.

What about their father? He lived in Dublin: she could get his address from Laura, make her way there and look him up. But by the sound of it he wouldn't want her either. Nobody, it would appear, wanted her.

She stopped pacing: this was getting her nowhere. She crossed to the window and looked out, and saw a line of raggedy hills patched in purples and blues, and below them a scatter of houses and ramshackle russet barns spaced between fields in rough rectangles of brown and green and yellow, some of them dotted with cattle or sheep.

Closer to home she saw the top section of the field that lay to the side of the house. There was a wire enclosure there, twenty or thirty feet across, in the centre of which sat a little wooden hut that was painted white with a green door that appeared to be split horizontally in two. Several hens with different colouring – reddish brown, cream, black, speckled combinations – were wandering about within the enclosure, pecking at the earth.

And then Tilly spotted a man standing in the enclosure, close to the little hut. Elderly, on the plump side – portly, she'd call him – with ovals of pink in his cheeks. He wore a jacket of heathery tweed and neat grey trousers. His black shoes were polished and a flat grey cap sat on his head. He wasn't doing anything much but standing there, hands behind his back, observing the hens.

And just as she was about to turn away, the man raised his head slowly and looked directly at her. He brought his right arm around to lift his cap an inch or so off his head, and he gave a little bow and smiled. There was a delightful quaintness about him, and a gentle quality to his smile that brought an answering one to Tilly's face. There was a world of comfort in that smile. She raised a hand and waved, and he acknowledged it with a second little bow.

He moved off then, leaving the enclosure through a metal gate, closing it carefully behind him, walking out of her line of vision. She wondered who he was. An elderly relative maybe, or a neighbour pottering about, waiting to be called home for his Christmas dinner.

As she turned away, her gaze fell on the birth cert she'd copied in the town library. She lifted it and read the words she knew by heart before returning it to its envelope and replacing it in the suitcase. She rummaged among the clothes until she found the present she'd brought for her sister. She wondered what to do with it now. She couldn't hand it over: it would look like she was trying to make Laura feel guilty if she presented it to her just before she left. Maybe she should give it to Colette instead, or Breda, if they met again.

She yawned, overcome with another wave of weariness. She

closed her case and slipped off her jacket and shoes, and slid Colette's scarf from around her neck. She finished making the bed, taking the pillows from the floor where the girls had left them.

She got in, fully clothed, and burrowed under the duvet, whose white cover was splashed with giant yellow and orange and red daisies. The sheets felt cool where her skin touched them, but the room was warm. She closed her eyes. She'd get through the rest of today, and tomorrow she'd find somewhere to go.

It was Christmas Day. She kept forgetting.

She slept.

❆❆❆

Her sister.

She laid the sleeping Poppy in her cot. She went downstairs and basted the turkey and made ham sandwiches and coffee and brought them out to the party of eight men now assembled there who had cleared the tree and were beginning to tackle the mound of shed debris underneath.

She had a sister.

She made more coffee and took it into the sitting room, where she found Gladys dozing by the fire and no sign of Mr Kablinski. She basted the turkey and gave the children bags of popcorn and cream crackers topped with peanut butter to keep them happy until dinnertime.

Her sister was here. She was upstairs.

She peeled potatoes and scrubbed carrots and cut crosses into Brussels sprouts. She basted the turkey and set the ham to boil and put Betty Buckley's plum pudding on to steam. She made brandy butter and got Poppy up again and sat her in the playpen with Rabbity. She basted the turkey and took the Christmas cake from its shelf in the scullery and placed it on one of the bone-china dinner plates that Gladys had given them for their wedding, and sat it on the dresser.

And all the while, as she worked her way through the afternoon, as she picked up fallen toys and discarded socks and splayed picture books, as she washed small hands and wiped runny noses and changed nappies and scolded and cajoled and praised, as she swept the floor and located the red tablecloth at the back of the airing cupboard, as the kitchen filled with the tantalising aroma of roasting meat, as she lit candles in the fading light and placed them safely out of reach, all the while the revelation of her sister – she had a *sister* – was the only thing she could think about.

She didn't doubt that the girl's story was true. Everything tallied. The times matched, and the description of the meeting with Diane – highly strung, hadn't she'd said, vulnerable? Laura could identify with that, oh yes, that sounded about right. And the mention of Trudi: where on earth would she have heard about Diane's voice coach, if not from Diane herself?

And the eyes, of course. She had Luke Potter's blue-green eyes, and his height, which had passed Laura by. But it was the eyes that clinched it.

For seventeen years her sister had existed, and Laura had been completely oblivious to the fact. What kind of mother didn't tell her firstborn child that she'd had another? What kind of selfish monster didn't let her daughter know that she had a sister?

Laura thought back, dredging up memories of times she normally preferred to forget. The years before her mother's departure, the rows, the slamming doors, the sobbing that Laura had tried not to hear as she pretended to do her homework in her room. The silent mealtimes afterwards, her father glowering, her mother red-eyed as she drank herbal tea and ignored the food.

How had they lasted so long, the two of them? What had kept them together for over thirteen years, while they'd been busily ripping one another apart on a regular basis? Was it love that had held them in place? Could love really have been that warped, that devoid of happiness?

Whatever it was it ran out, a few months after Diane began working with a new voice coach. Trudi, Laura was told, from Australia – and she shook hands with the woman whose cheekbones were high and sharp, whose many bracelets rattled when she moved, whose dark hair was swept into a stiff tower on her head. Trudi, who smelt of baby powder, and who called Laura's mother Di – the only person Laura had ever heard addressing her in this way.

Trudi became a frequent caller, spending hours closeted with Diane in the room off the kitchen, the scales and exercises and arias drifting out and filling the house as Luke painted in his big purpose-built studio at the bottom of the garden, safely out of earshot.

And then one day Diane left, a few weeks before almost twelve-year-old Laura finished primary school. She simply packed a bag and walked out without a word to anyone, leaving only a brief note on Laura's pillow for her to find when she got home from school.

I've gone away with Trudi, I felt I had no choice. I deeply regret leaving you, but you will be better off without two parents who cannot live together. I hope you will be happy with your father, and I will see you when I feel able.

Three stilted sentences, the only evidence of real emotion to be seen in the splotched mess that had been made of the word *hope* when a drop of liquid, presumably a tear, had fallen onto it. No mention of where she was going, no contact information at all.

Life was easier without her; there was no denying it. With nobody screaming or throwing bits of crockery about, no doors being slammed, the house was an infinitely more peaceful place. It was lonelier too for a while, of course, and disconcerting to become suddenly motherless, but before a week was out Luke had engaged the services of a live-in housekeeper, who took care of the practicalities, and he enrolled Laura in a boarding school at the end of the summer that she immediately took to, and life moved on.

Months passed, years passed. No letter arrived for Laura, no phone call. It was as if her mother had simply walked out and left the world behind. Laura assumed her father hadn't heard from her either, but she was wrong.

Your mother and I have legally separated, he told her, completely out of the blue, one time she was home for the holidays. It was a year or so after Diane's departure, and the first time he'd mentioned her.

Where is she? Laura asked.

Australia.

She wanted to ask more, so much more she wanted to know, but his expression forbade it. What did it matter anyway, when her mother clearly didn't care about her any more? She determined to put it to the back of her mind – and largely she succeeded, thanks to the cheerful bustle of boarding-school life. Every hour of the day filled with classes and sports and study and meals, and nightly whispered chats after lights out. She could get on without her mother; she could manage fine.

And then, three years after Diane's departure, Laura was called out of class and told she had a visitor – and there, in the smaller of the family rooms, sat her mother. Thinner, paler, altogether more subdued than Laura remembered.

They embraced, mother and daughter. It seemed like the thing to do. They spent barely ten minutes together, during which time they managed not to mention Luke once. Diane asked Laura how she was doing, and Laura told her about school, and her friends, and the schools' basketball league they were involved in, the semi-finals of which were coming up at the weekend, and the trip to France she was taking with a friend's family during the summer holidays.

Diane didn't offer much information, didn't really say anything about the years since they'd met, apart from telling Laura that she was living in Australia now, that she'd gone there with her friend Trudi, and that she wouldn't be moving back home anytime soon.

Laura didn't say she already knew about Australia. She accepted the gifts her mother had brought – hair ornaments, a brooch, a pen – and told her she'd better get back to class.

I'll write, her mother promised, and Laura shrugged and said OK, and that night she avoided the other girls and wept under the bedclothes for a mother who couldn't, or wouldn't, love her, and a father who had shipped her off to boarding school rather than have to look after her himself, and who never turned up on family days.

By then Tilly had been born. Tilly had been two and a half or thereabouts when her mother had come back to visit Laura. The thought butted into her reminiscences, bringing her up short. Her mother had had a second child, and neither Laura nor her father had had the slightest inkling. And, by all accounts, he still didn't know he'd fathered two children with her.

Three weeks after the encounter, a letter arrived at the school with an Australian stamp, the first of several over the ensuing months. They were generally sad little affairs, filled with trivia that told Laura nothing of any worth. *A neighbour's cat had kittens, all white except for one that has a grey and black tail ... A convenience store at the end of our block burned down, the police think it might have been deliberate ... A little boy went missing in the neighbourhood; he turned up safe and well hours later on the other side of town ... We watched a film set in Ireland on television, Meryl Streep was in it ... Very hot this past week, hard to get to sleep ...* and so on.

A return address had been written in the top corner of the first envelope, and Laura dutifully wrote back with whatever happenings she could summon. After some months they both ran out of steam, and all Laura got from then on was a card at Christmas that never included her father in its greeting, and all she sent was one in return.

When she left school Laura signed up for a childcare course, and her father provided her with an allowance that enabled her to move out of home and into a flat that was shared with two others. They met rarely after this, their lives moving on different tracks. Laura would occasionally call by the house, where she'd drink coffee and they'd make small talk. Luke never got in touch with her: she knew their connection, such as it was, would be lost completely if she stopped calling in.

And six months into her childcare course, out of the blue one day her phone rang and it was her father. I'm getting married, he told her.

She was completely stunned. She had no idea he was even seeing someone. But then, how would she? They were practically strangers to one another.

Aren't you still married to my mother? she asked.

No, he replied shortly. We're divorced.

Another bombshell. Her parents had divorced, and nobody had thought to let her know. She felt a surge of real, cold anger towards him. He was her *father*, for Christ's sake. She was his daughter, not some casual acquaintance who dropped in for coffee now and again. She bit back her resentment, tried to tell herself it didn't matter.

Two months later, while she was still smarting from his casual indifference, she acquired a stepmother just ten years her senior. She sat stiffly in the register office; she congratulated them politely. She left the ensuing cocktail party, full of people she knew only slightly and had no interest in, as soon as she could.

And not long after that she met Aaron, and fell immediately and thoroughly in love with him.

She married him a week before her nineteenth birthday, much against her father's wishes. Looking back, she could hardly blame him. Aaron was an unemployed bricklayer living in a council flat; Laura was the daughter of a highly successful artist. But she was deeply in love for the first time in her life, and she was loved in return, she was certain of that. They were made for one another, she and Aaron. They would have lots of babies, and grow old and crotchety together.

Happiness made her generous, made her want to share it. I'm

getting married, she wrote to her mother. I'd love it if you could come. They weren't planning a big wedding. A scatter of Aaron's family, a few friends from either side, an aunt of Laura's – her father's sole sibling, who lived in Galway and whom she rarely met – and a couple of cousins, her aunt's children. Luke and his new wife were also attending. Laura had hoped they'd turn down the invitation, which she'd felt obliged to send, but they hadn't.

I wish you all the very best, her mother wrote back. I can't be there, but I wish you every happiness. She enclosed a cheque for one hundred Australian dollars and a silver bangle that winked with small blue stones. So Laura got married without her, while her father scowled his way up the aisle, and she determined to have nothing more to do with either of her parents from then on.

The months passed. Laura quit her childcare course and got a waitressing job, and kept inventing reasons to refuse her stepmother Susan's regular dinner invitations. Aaron's efforts to find a job proved fruitless, and he spent long hours alone in their flat, becoming increasingly morose. Laura would bring home doggy-bag dinners from her workplace; she'd spend her tips on scented candles and bottles of cheap wine; she'd tell him all the time how wonderful he was and how much she loved him and how happy he made her, and eventually she'd be rewarded with a smile, and a lifting of his spirits.

A week before Christmas, when they'd been married two months, Susan rang and invited them both to Christmas dinner. No thank you, Laura told her, we have plans. And there was a brief silence before Susan wished her a happy Christmas, and hung up.

Laura was well aware of how petty she was being, how immature and unfair it was to take out her anger towards her father on his innocent second wife. From their limited interaction, Susan came across as pretty inoffensive; but becoming her friend was a step too far.

In May Laura did a pregnancy test, and for a while their good news brought about a real improvement in Aaron's outlook. He made a wooden cradle – and when Laura found out they'd need two, he made another. No one was as happy as them: they were lucky, they were blessed. She wrote again to her mother, and phoned her father's house and gave the news to Susan, who heard it with what sounded like genuine delight.

Her mother's response, when it eventually arrived, was more circumspect. Congratulations to you and your husband, she wrote. Your husband – she couldn't even use his name. I hope everything goes well, she wrote. I hope you are feeling well, and looking after yourself. No evident happiness, no reference to her becoming a grandmother, no indication of impending travel plans. Laura shouldn't have let it bother her, but she did.

And then, with just over two weeks to her due date, Aaron's demons finally got the better of him, and there was to be no growing old together, and no more babies with him.

And the first person who rushed to be with her was Susan. As soon as the news reached her she came, whisking an incoherent Laura back home from the council flat, putting her to bed in her old room, every so often bringing her tea and tiny things to eat – two thin crustless fingers of buttered toast; a palm-sized omelette; three halved strawberries drizzled with honey; a few spoonfuls of homemade soup.

She sat for hours at a time by Laura's bedside, holding her hand silently while Laura cried her heart out. She accompanied her to the hospital when Laura's pains began – a week to the day after his death – and stayed with her throughout the whole heartbreaking, wonderful, excruciating, exhausting hours that followed. She looked after Aaron's baby sons in those first grief-ridden weeks and months as if they were her own.

And even in the face of such devastating news Laura's mother stayed away, returning to Ireland only when the boys were three. Bringing boomerangs and T-shirts and jigsaws, too late for Laura to forgive her. Much too late for anything but the most stilted of conversations while the boys flung the boomerangs about and knocked pictures off the walls.

And now Diane Potter's second daughter had materialised. Just as abandoned as Laura – no, worse than that. Given away soon after she was born, by the sound of it, passed on to other people to raise. More rejected even than Laura had been, no experience at all of her real mother.

But given the mother in question, maybe the best thing that could have happened. Hadn't she been spared two pretty useless parents? Better surely to have no contact with them at all, better to be handed over to strangers who wanted you.

And what was Laura to do now with this teenager who'd landed on her doorstep, this timid creature with their father's eyes who'd travelled halfway around the world in search of her? What on earth was she to do? How was she to treat the second child of her parents, whose very existence had been unknown to her just a few hours ago?

She hadn't the energy for this new development. She couldn't face the questions that would inevitably follow a disclosure of the girl's identity, the explanations that would be demanded. She simply wasn't up to their dysfunctional background being laid bare for all to inspect. With everything else she had to contend with, a sister was the last thing she needed right now.

In a week, in less than a week, the girl – Tilly – would be gone home, and they could forget about her. She'd hardly be making a return visit, with the lukewarm reception she'd got this time.

But she'd come all the way from Australia. She'd found her way to Roone, all alone. She clearly *did* want a sister. And it wasn't her fault, none of it was. Like Susan, Tilly hadn't been the cause of any of the upheaval in Laura's life.

'Stop it,' she said sharply – aware that she'd said it aloud only when the girls' heads lifted in unison to regard their mother, when the boys turned from the complicated rings tournament they'd devised.

'Sorry,' she said, 'I was just talking to myself,' and they went back to their various activities, too young to wonder about the implications of that.

Tilly wasn't her responsibility, she told herself fiercely. She wasn't under any obligation to her – she had *enough* on her plate without that. Wasn't she putting a roof over her head? Wasn't she feeding her for as long as she was staying here?

She's seventeen, and looks younger. She flew thousands of miles by herself, and I'm refusing to acknowledge her.

Stop it, stop it. This time she was careful to shout it only in her head. Stop making me feel guilty. I'm doing the best I can here.

Colette knew who she was. Colette knew and, despite her promise not to say anything – and Colette was nothing if not discreet – it was surely only a matter of time before Nell and James knew too. Laura would deal with that if it presented itself.

Just then she heard a shout from outside, where the men were still working. Lord, what now? She glanced around the room, but the children seemed to have missed it.

A second shout followed, and another. In the act of retrieving rings from the board, Ben stopped.

'What was that?'

'Nothing,' Laura said quickly. 'Just someone calling someone else outside.'

Probably giving up for the day, too dark by now to see what they were doing properly. Had they unearthed any of the casualties? Had they taken any of them away yet?

'Ben! Seamus!' Gavin's voice, nearer. 'Everyone! Come out here!'

What was he thinking, calling them outside? 'Stay where you are,' Laura ordered – and a minute later there he was at the door, his hair grey with dust, his grimy face alight with happiness.

'Quick, everyone!' he cried. 'Big surprise outside! Big surprise from Santa!'

They followed him, hurried through the scullery and went outside, blinking and shivering in the dusk – and there, to everyone's astonished delight, were all four of the creatures they'd assumed lost to the storm, looking very much alive. George the donkey pulling placidly at the grass, like he always did, the goats bleating – presumably to be milked – Caesar snuffling hopefully in his feeding trough. Evie gave a screech and flung her arms around Maddie the goat, causing the little creature to skitter away in fright.

'They just reappeared,' James said, his face every bit as dirty and happy as Gavin's. 'Just walked in the gate this minute, all together.'

'But how could they?' Laura asked, as the children continued to race around, yelling happily. 'Weren't they in the shed?' She turned to Gavin. 'Didn't you say you locked them in last night?'

'I did – but the door seems to be gone.'

Her mouth dropped open. 'What?'

'There's no sign of it.' He regarded the goats. 'I'd better milk these two before they burst.'

And as he went in search of his milking bucket and stool, Laura wondered what was snagging on her memory – and then it came to her: Nell said that Con Maher had found a door on the beach. It must be from the shed, wrenched off in the storm. Could the wind possibly have been strong enough to rip a door from its hinges and whisk it away?

Of course it could. Hadn't it ripped an apple tree from the ground? 'Con,' she said.

James looked at her. 'Con? Con Maher? What about him?'

'The door.'

'What about it?'

'It's on the beach. Con saw it this morning.'

The comedy of it – a door flying through the night, like those whirling animals and bicycles in the *Wizard of Oz* tornado – struck her suddenly. Dangerous, of course – imagine if it had collided with anyone. But it hadn't: they'd have heard by now if it had.

'Must've fancied a swim,' James said, completely deadpan – which was all she needed.

'What are you laughing at?' Ben asked, and as Laura told them about the flying door, making them all giggle, a new thought came to her.

It wasn't Santa. Santa hadn't had anything to do with it. It was Walter. Suddenly she was certain of it. He'd kept the animals safe, his beloved donkey and the others. Walter had got them out of the shed before the tree had fallen on it. That was exactly the kind of miracle that happened on Roone.

'But where did they *go*?' Seamus wanted to know. 'Where *were* they all night?'

'Who knows?' Laura replied. 'They must have found shelter somewhere. Get the vegetable peelings for Caesar, they're on the draining board' – and they sped inside and came out with the basin of peelings and tipped it into his trough, while the men packed up and set off for their respective turkey dinners.

Laura ushered everyone back into the warmth of the house. Going to be a bitterly cold night: Gavin would have to farm the animals out to neighbouring sheds. No problem, with places a-plenty to choose from, right on this road.

The turkey was cooked. Laura hauled it from the oven and left it to rest. She put the dinner plates in to warm and made the gravy.

'Call the others,' she told Ben and Seamus. 'Granny is in the sitting room, Mr ... Treblinka is in number two, and Tilly is in number three. Tell them dinner will be ready in five minutes. Bring up two torches, give them one each.'

As they went off, she said, 'No – stop.'

They stopped.

'I'll go,' she said. 'You set the table, put out side plates and cutlery – and make sure the girls don't go near the oven.'

She climbed the stairs, still marvelling at the turnaround of events, still convinced that Walter had had a hand in it. Gone-but-not-forgotten Walter, who might still be in the vicinity after all.

Walter, who would never, she was sure, disown a member of his family, for whatever reason. Walter, who would be shocked and saddened at the notion of Laura refusing to acknowledge a sister, simply to get back at a mother who had hurt them both.

She decided to do what Walter would do. She summoned Gladys and the American to dinner. She changed hurriedly in her room, selecting the blue dress she'd been planning to wear for the party the night before. She left the room and stopped outside Tilly's bedroom door and stood for a few seconds, listening to the silence from within.

She knocked.

❄❄❄

She was woken by someone tapping on the door. She lay in the darkness, completely disoriented. Where was she? Which bed, whose house? She groped for a lamp and eventually found one. She located a switch and clicked it, but nothing happened, no light shone.

And then it all came back, accompanied by a wave of despair. She was on Roone, she'd made it to her sister's house, where there was no electricity, and where she wasn't wanted. It had all been for nothing: the whole trip had been a mistake of epic proportions. The three plane rides, the bus from Dublin, the drive from Dingle, the boat to the island, all wasted, all useless.

The tapping continued. She threw back the duvet and groped her way through the absolute darkness, the floor cold against her bare feet. She opened the door to find a light shining blindingly in her face; she put up a hand to shield her eyes.

The light was instantly lowered. 'Sorry,' her sister said. 'You caught me at a bad time. We're having a few ... problems right now. It's generally a bit of a ... well, and you arriving when you did – I reacted badly, I should have been more welcoming. After you coming all that way, I mean.'

The words were thrown out in quick, awkward bursts. In the dim light from the torch that was now aimed at the floor between them, her sister's expression was unclear, but her tone was different from before. It was warmer, softer.

Tilly cast about for a response. 'I should have let you know. I shouldn't have just arrived.'

'No, that's not – it doesn't matter—'

'I didn't have an address. I only knew your name—'

'Well then, how could you? You couldn't have let me know.'

'Still, it was wrong to just turn up like I did—'

'What choice did you have though?'

'Well—'

'Look, it's fine, it's – and now you're here.'

Their words stuttered to a halt. Tilly became aware that she was covered all over with goosebumps.

'Anyway,' Laura said, 'I just wanted to say sorry for not being nicer – and of course I'll tell people who you are. I'll tell them as soon as you come downstairs. Dinner's ready,' she added. 'Don't be long. Oh, and take this.' Tilly felt the torch being passed over, and then she was alone, her sister vanishing back down the dark corridor.

In the en-suite she splashed icy water on her face and brushed her teeth. She combed her hair with her fingers and applied a little eyeliner as carefully as she could in the torchlight. She spritzed perfume onto her wrists and behind her ears, and from her suitcase she pulled clean but crumpled jeans, two long-sleeved T-shirts and her favourite pink pullover.

As she put them on she allowed herself to hope that it would work out after all. She'd caught Laura at a bad time. Maybe the baby was teething, maybe the American had been making demands. It was Christmas Day, surely a busy time for any mother, especially a mother with so many small children.

She left the room and followed the torchlight along the corridor to the stairs. A savoury smell wafted up, making her mouth water. She realised that she hadn't eaten a thing since breakfast in Cormac and Bernard's kitchen; so long ago that seemed.

The kitchen door was closed, the chatter of voices and the clatter of cutlery coming to her from the other side. Was she late? Had they already started? She stood in the hall, feeling unaccountably shy, remembering the children who'd stared curiously at her earlier, and the solemn unblinking gaze of the baby Laura had given her to hold. Poppy, like the flower.

And who else was on the other side of the door? The grumpy American – she'd forgotten his name – and Laura's husband, and maybe the elderly man she'd seen by the henhouse. A lot of strangers to face.

Get it over with. She pasted on a smile, turned the handle and walked in.

The room glowed softly with the flames of several fat red candles in glass jars. They were everywhere: three of them clustered in the centre of the table, two more on a high shelf of the dresser, one on top of the fridge, another on the draining board, a pair in each of the deep windowsills. The candlelight made faces rosy, made jewels of the berries in the sprigs of holly that were dotted throughout the room, made shadows dance and leap about.

The big table was covered with a red cloth that Tilly was pretty sure hadn't been on it earlier. The four older children sat at its far end, the two little girls facing one another, strapped into some kind of booster seats, the boys next to them.

Closer to Tilly was a woman who looked around Colette's age but with none of her trim elegance – tightly permed grey hair, plain features, plump, matronly figure – and across the table from her was the American in a navy suit, with just as dour an expression as Tilly remembered on his face.

There was no sign of the other man, the one who'd smiled up at her from the hen run. She would have liked him to be there.

Next to the matron there was a vacant place setting, and two more at either end of the table. Poppy sat propped with cushions in a wooden playpen, similar to one Ma and Pa had used for Robbie and Jemima. She was sucking on the ragged ear of a brown rabbit, an assortment of other soft toys assembled around her.

Laura was at the cooker, tipping vegetables into dishes. An apron was tied around her waist; beneath it she wore a dress that was blue, or maybe purple. A tall sandy-haired man stood next to her, in the act of drawing a carving knife repeatedly across a steel block. An enormous turkey sat on a platter nearby.

Everything stopped when Tilly walked in. A hush fell over the entire table as faces turned towards her. The carving knife was halted in its track. Even Poppy seemed to draw an expectant breath as she looked up. The only sound in the room was the gentle bubble of something on a hotplate. Under everyone's scrutiny Tilly felt her face grow warm. She stood rooted to the spot, her hands curling of their own accord into fists, grateful for the soft forgiving light of the candles.

'There you are.'

Laura approached, wiping her hands on her apron. She took Tilly's arm and drew her a little further into the room.

'Everyone,' she said, 'I have an announcement to make.'

They were all still looking at Tilly.

'I'd like,' Laura said, 'to introduce my sister, Tilly.'

For what seemed like an awfully long time nobody moved – unless you counted Poppy, who went on chewing her rabbit's ear, oblivious to the drama that was unfolding.

'She's my sister,' Laura repeated to the room at large, 'if you can believe it. I have a sister I never knew about until today.'

Tilly felt her throat tightening, tears threatening. No, she thought, don't – but she might as well have asked the turkey to fly around the room. As the first tear rolled down her cheek, as she dashed it away, mortified, Laura said, 'Hey, no need to cry, we're not that bad' – which of course made her ten times worse.

Laura laughed softly and offered her a gold-coloured paper napkin from the table – and while Tilly was dabbing her eyes and trying desperately to pull herself together, aware of all four older children watching her with similarly opened mouths, the tall man, who had to be Laura's husband, materialised beside her.

'Gavin Connolly,' he said, a broad smile on his lean freckled face, 'your very surprised brother-in-law.' His hand outstretched, before he changed his mind and gave her a quick hug. 'Welcome to the family,' he said, the words almost undoing her again.

'Tell her who everyone is,' Laura said, returning to the cooker – so he led Tilly around the table and began with the older woman, who turned out to be his mother, Gladys.

She shook hands and said, 'Well, that's a bit of news alright', her dubious tone leaving Tilly in some doubt as to whether it was welcome or otherwise.

The American got to his feet and shook Tilly's hand solemnly. 'Larry Kawalski,' he said. 'Larry might be easier for everyone to remember. Pleased to make your acquaintance properly, miss.' He actually looked in rather better humour now – maybe the turn of events had softened him up a bit. 'Apologies about before,' he added, in an undertone. 'I was … not in the best of spirits.'

'It's nothing,' Tilly murmured, which was quite true. His outburst on the doorstep seemed trivial now, washed away as it had been by what had followed it. She suspected it was something she might use to amuse people in years to come: her first encounter with her sister, right after the door had been slammed in her face.

Then it was the turn of the children. 'This is your auntie,' Gavin told them, 'Auntie Tilly.' The little girls went on staring solemnly at her, thumbs by now installed in mouths, while Ben lifted his chin to display a thin zigzag line – a legacy, it transpired, from a tumble off his bike the previous summer: 'I got five stitches, it was *pumping*.' Tilly gathered it was his stock form of introduction, the easiest way for newcomers to differentiate between the brothers.

'You're their only aunt,' Gavin said, bringing Tilly to her seat next to his mother. 'I don't have siblings' – a sudden gap-toothed grin – 'unless I have yet to meet them, of course.' The last bit under his breath, audible only to her – maybe to ensure that his mother didn't catch it, and be offended by the implication.

And after that, the evening pretty much sailed along. After that, the evening was, well, quite wonderful. The turkey was applauded and carved and doled out – 'Free range and organic, like all the island meat,' Laura told them. The vegetables were distributed, the gravy and cranberry sauce passed around, and the dinner was eaten as Tilly filled in the people around her – Gavin, his mother and Mr Kawalski – on the events that had led to her discovery of an Irish sister.

At the other end of the table Laura kept order among the younger diners, in between offering seconds and mopping up occasional splashes and wiping dribbles from chins as the dog, hovering about that area, enjoyed his own Christmas dinner from whatever dropped to the floor.

And in due course Poppy demanded that she be fed too, so Gavin prepared her bottle while Tilly retrieved her from the playpen and tried to teach her how to say 'Auntie Tilly', with little success.

And later, after the plates and dishes were piled up on the draining board and the pudding set alight to more applause, after it was sliced and doled out, and the accompaniments – brandy butter, cream, ice cream – passed around, two little princesses migrated to their father's side and demanded that he make room for them on his lap, necessitating Poppy, who was by now gnawing contentedly on the handle of a wooden spoon, being passed back to Tilly.

And after the Christmas cake was produced, prompting yet more applause, after it was cut and sampled – Laura's first ever, Gavin told Tilly – after the crackers were pulled and their jokes groaned over, the boys left the table to resume throwing their rubber rings at a numbered wooden board, and Evie and Marian were brought up to bed by Gavin, and Poppy fell asleep on Tilly's lap and was taken upstairs by Laura, and Tilly played with a little plastic fish that had come out of a cracker as Mr Kawalski quizzed her about the route she'd taken from Australia, and Gavin's mother grimaced every time one of the boys' rings slapped against the board.

And when Gavin and Laura had both returned to the kitchen, and the boys had been sent up to bed with torches, and warnings about dire consequences if they didn't brush their teeth, and if they weren't asleep in ten minutes – when all of that had happened, Larry Kawalski, who looked in his late sixties, and who they'd learned was a recently retired car dealer from Cincinnati, accepted a glass of port from his hostess and told them why he'd come to spend Christmas on Roone.

'Friends of my wife and I – Max and Ruthie Sherman, we lived across the street from them forever – they came to Ireland on vacation, maybe fifteen years ago. Toured around the west coast, took in a trip to Roone, stayed in the hotel for a coupla nights. Got home, showed us their snaps, told us we had to come see it. Paulina, my wife, fell in love with this place, this island, just from the pictures. She wanted so bad to come – she'd always wanted to see Ireland, even though we got no connection here, no family. But now it was Roone she wanted most of all.

'I said yeah, yeah, sometime we'll go, but we never did get round to it. I was busy with work, and we had the kids, three boys – and then in April I retired, and passed the business on to our middle kid, and I thought I'd surprise her for our fortieth wedding anniversary, which was day before yesterday. I had no idea what it might be like here in the wintertime, but I knew she wouldn't mind about the weather, so in September I bought the air tickets and booked us into the hotel for a week.'

Here he paused, and was silent for so long that Tilly wondered if that was it. But where was his wife? While they waited, one of the candles on the table spluttered and fizzled out.

'End of October,' he said then, more quietly, more slowly, his eyes on the thin trail of smoke that curled upwards from the extinguished candle, 'she was driving home from visiting a friend on the other side of town, speeding ambulance went through a red light, drove into her at an intersection. She died a few hours later in the hospital.'

His hands cradled the glass of port that he hadn't yet touched. His face had an emptied-out look to it, his gaze on one of the remaining candles.

'Max and Ruthie said no way should I come, our boys said it too. Nobody thought I should take this trip, everyone told me I was crazy, but I came anyway, because it's what she woulda wanted, plain and simple. It's what she woulda wanted,' he repeated, lifting a hand to run it across his empty face.

Nobody at all spoke. Tilly thought of him packing his brown leather case and making his way to the airport. Maybe being driven there by a disapproving son, who might have shaken his father's hand at the departure gate and told him it wasn't too late to change his mind.

She imagined him getting on the plane and seeing the empty seat beside his. She thought of his angry face at the front door earlier, his rage that hadn't been rage at all but loneliness and grief, and maybe terrible regret that he'd never brought her to Ireland, that he'd left it too late to make her dream of seeing a small Irish island come true.

At length he looked around the table and attempted a smile. 'Sorry, folks,' he said. 'Guess I sorta spoiled the party' – and they told him, no, not at all, but it was quieter after that. Gavin got up to put the kettle on, and Laura produced her guitar and led them in a few Christmas carols. Her voice reminded Tilly of Joni Mitchell's.

And later, after coffees and teas had been drunk, and the dishes piled up by the sink – 'The washing-up can wait till morning,' Laura said firmly – after they'd trooped upstairs with an assortment of candles and torches and hot-water bottles, and whispered their goodnights on the landing, Tilly got into pyjamas and stood at her bedroom window, arms wrapped tightly around herself, and thought of Australia where Christmas Day was already long over, and looked out into the black, black night, with a sky that held stars in formations she didn't recognise, and she watched pale wisps of something – ashes from a fire? debris of some kind? – fluttering softly and silently to the ground.

❄

SATURDAY
26 DECEMBER
ST STEPHEN'S DAY

❄

❄❄❄

I n living memory, it hadn't happened. Ninety-two-year-old Patsy McDonagh, officially Roone's oldest resident since the death of one-hundred-and-one-year-old Gerry Bannagher two years earlier, had never seen snow on Roone, and he'd been fairly sure his parents hadn't either – which meant, if his memory could be trusted, that it was well over a century since the island had experienced a white Christmas, or a white any other occasion.

Maybe it had never happened at all. Certainly there was no historical record of it that anyone knew about. Maybe this was Roone's first ever snowfall.

Thnow! Thnow! Evie and Marian had cried, as they'd come trotting in as usual to wake their mother. Well used to seeing it on DVDs and in picture books, no trouble identifying it this morning from their bedroom window.

Shush, Laura had whispered, eyes still closed, don't wake Poppy. She'd pulled back the duvet to let them climb in as usual – but for once her bed didn't interest them. Thnow, they insisted, Mama, wook, wook – and nothing would satisfy them till Laura had given in and dragged herself upright, and allowed them to lead her to the window to see it for herself.

And she had to admit it was worth the trip. In the morning light it gleamed softly, the powdery white that had settled on everything, trees, fields, barns, roofs. It must have fallen all night. It must have emptied itself out of the heavens hour after hour as they slept.

The sky was a swipe of yellowish grey above it, the rising sun a pale, shimmering disc spilling its lemony light into a sea that was dotted with the dark hulks of familiar trawlers. Fishermen putting Christmas behind them already, business as usual, thnow or no thnow.

It was magical, no other word for it. It was a morning to rejoice in, a morning to count your blessings in. It was a morning to hope fervently that you were spared long enough to appreciate lots of other similar magical mornings.

Snow had been predicted, for the north and west of the country only: Dublin was probably as green and as grey as ever. And it wasn't expected to last – even as they were forecasting it, the weather people were urging children to make the most of the snow. Gone as soon as it arrived, they said. A thaw setting in this afternoon, rain on the way tomorrow, they said.

But today it was here.

'Come on,' Laura whispered, 'let's get dressed' – because even though it was far too early, and she could as usual have done with considerably more sleep, having been up with Poppy in the night, there was going to be no more rest with the girls so keyed up. No matter: she had plenty to get up for, with the house full of people, Gladys leaving and Susan—

Her thoughts snapped to a halt. Gladys. Dear God, would the snow change her plans? Would they be stuck with her for another day? Presumably the ferry would be operating as usual, with the trawlers out and the sea so calm – but there would need to be public transport on the other side to bring her back to Dublin. Let the buses and trains be running today, let the country not have ground to a standstill, like it sometimes did when the snow came.

She checked her phone and found it still useless. They'd have to consult with Leo later on: he'd know what the story was on the other side. Whenever Roone was cut off, Leo was their link to the mainland. Gavin could go to the pier after breakfast and talk to him.

And Susan, who was due to arrive from Dublin today. Would the weather change her plans too? Would she hear about snow in the west and decide to postpone her trip? With the phones still down they had no way of communicating, but Laura hoped fervently she'd show up.

She needed someone to talk to.

All very well to acknowledge Tilly publicly last evening, to welcome her into the household, but she was still a virtual stranger. Presumably the notion of having a sister would eventually become less startling, but so far Laura was still feeling her way around it, still trying to come to terms with this astonishing information and all its repercussions.

You might have told me, Gavin had said as they'd been getting ready for bed. Not sounding cross, more disappointed.

Told you what? But she'd known what.

That you had a sister.

I was busy, she replied. I was up to my eyes. I was coming to terms with it myself. All true, nothing he could argue with – but he was right, she should have told him; he shouldn't have had that sprung on him, along with everyone else. He was her husband.

And her father, their father, he needed to know. It would be unforgivable to keep the information from him, even if his ex-wife had chosen to do just that. Ironic that he was acquiring two new children at this time, one as yet unborn, the other an unknown quantity until now. Laura wondered what his reaction would be to Tilly, coming so close on the heels of Susan's pregnancy. She might run the idea of telling him by Susan, see what she thought was the best way to handle it.

And of course Susan herself was involved too, having just come into possession of a new stepdaughter. So many ramifications, so many people affected by Tilly's arrival. But she existed, and she was here, and they would have to make space for her. And to give her her due, she was doing what she could to fit in. Laura had seen her helping Gavin with Poppy at the dinner table last evening, and she'd given a hand when Laura was doling out the pudding and cake too. She was trying her best; you had to acknowledge that.

And she'd definitely got Evie and Marian's vote. See the way they'd drifted to her end of the table as soon as Laura had released them from their seats, see how they'd climbed onto their father's lap just so they could have a good look at her – fascinated, no doubt, by her exotic accent.

At one stage, Laura had seen Evie reach across and give Tilly's hair a series of light little pats with her hand, in exactly the same way that she used to pat Laura's hair, before Nell chopped it off.

And when you thought about it, wasn't it good to discover that you had a sister, a full blood sister, whatever the circumstances of your discovery? Wasn't it marvellous to find someone with such a strong genetic connection to you, regardless of the hows and whys?

Wasn't it?

After breakfast Laura would bring her next door, introduce her to Nell and the others. She'd been planning to call there anyway with the bag of apples from the fallen tree – Nell was far better at making tarts, and with any luck she'd send one back to Walter's Place. And maybe it was just a case of getting used to Tilly, maybe a bond would develop as they got to know one another. Not that they'd have much time to do that, with Tilly leaving in four days, but they could try.

Laura finished pulling on her clothes, the girls practically dancing with impatience. Amazingly, Poppy slept on, undisturbed by their excitement. Gavin was up and gone, sneaking out as he generally did while Laura was still asleep. Checking on the animals, no doubt, who'd spent the night in Donal Murphy's shed down the way. Plenty of clearing up still to be done outside too.

He should talk to Damien Kiely about getting a new shed built across the field, well out of range of the remaining trees. Maybe with a sliding door this time, something that couldn't be torn away like the last one. She'd say it when she saw him.

Laura shepherded the girls back to their room, where she dressed them in plenty of woolly layers, explaining that their princess dresses would get too wet in the snow. The corridor as they tiptoed through was silent, everyone still asleep. Passing Gladys's room, Laura was reminded of the previous morning's drama, and wondered whether to put her head around the door now to make sure the woman was still alive. No, that would be fussing. Gladys would outlive them all, just to annoy her.

No sound from Tilly or Larry's room. Poor old Larry – who would have guessed his sad story? Coming here to pay tribute, you could say, to his dead wife's wish – and then to have to deal with the storm, and his hotel ceiling falling in, as if he'd needed anything else to go wrong. Thank God the brown leather suitcase had shown up, less than half an hour after Tilly's arrival.

Gavin had lit the kitchen stove; the chill was ebbing from the room. He'd also tackled the considerable amount of washing-up that had been waiting – but the kettle sitting on the cooker was still cold to the touch, which meant he'd used lukewarm tap water, the heat gone out of it since the night before. Laura would have to give everything another wash when she got the chance.

He'd meant well. He always meant well.

As she was tipping Sugar Puffs into bowls and filling plastic beakers with orange juice she heard sounds from the room directly above.

'That'll be the boys,' she said – and in less than a minute she heard the small thump of their footsteps on the stairs. They burst into the kitchen, every bit as excited as their sisters.

'We don't want breakfast, we're not hungry.'

'Yeah – can we go out now?'

Laura filled two more bowls with cereal. 'The snow will still be there when you've eaten,' she told them. 'It's not going to vanish in ten minutes.'

'But Mum—'

'Eat,' she commanded, and they gave up and grabbed spoons and plunged them in. How many more years, she wondered, leaning against the sink to watch them, would they submit to her? How long before one of them – or more likely, both of them simultaneously – simply refused to do as they were asked? Three years away from teenagers, new territory for her. Cross that bridge when she came to it.

She turned to look out the window. She spotted footprints in the snow and followed them until she found him, wheeling a barrow of blocks from the fallen shed across to the far side. No sign of the animals: he must be leaving them in Donal's shed until the weather softened, or until the field was back to normal.

That wasn't his wheelbarrow – Ben had painted ladybirds on his – and then she remembered that he'd kept it in the shed. Flattened, it must have been, not able to flee to safety like the animals. He must have borrowed this one, from Donal probably.

She waited until he had dumped his load and was on the way back before rapping on the window. He looked across and waved, nose and cheeks pink above the new navy scarf Gladys had finished knitting for him the day before, his breath fogging in the still air.

She kept forgetting to thank him for the necklace. She must do it, the very next time they spoke.

'Finished!' Ben pushed back his chair and darted out to the hall for his jacket, leaving a good third of his cereal behind in the bowl. Laura remained silent, not having the energy to argue.

'Finished!' Seamus clattered down his spoon and followed suit. Not to be outdone, the girls scrambled from their chairs and clamoured for freedom. Laura wiped hands and faces and bundled them into jackets, hats, scarves and gloves.

'Stay where Dad can see you,' she instructed, 'and keep your gloves on' – and out the four of them rushed, Charlie scampering after them, barking delightedly, leaving Laura to catch her breath and eat something.

She put an egg on to boil. She took a slice of bread from the loaf and slotted it into the toaster and pressed down the lever, but it refused to engage. She'd forgotten again about the electricity being out. She transferred the bread to the grill of the cooker, and boiled the kettle and made green tea.

She ate standing up out of habit, listening to her children's high-pitched squeals carrying clearly across the blanketed field, and hoping that her various guests didn't hear them too. Not much she could do about it if they did: asking excited children not to make noise was like asking the tide not to come in twice a day.

She finished her breakfast and added a shovel of coal to the stove. She cleared the table and mopped up the milk splashes and set three new places. She boiled the kettle again and washed and dried the dishes. She made a fresh cup of green tea and sank into the chair by the stove with it.

No sound yet from upstairs. Twenty minutes until she needed to make Gladys's morning cuppa. Check on Poppy then too: she'd be due to wake.

She set her untouched tea on the floor. She let her head tip back and closed her eyes. Not sleeping, just taking a breather. Just gathering her energy for the next bit.

❄❄❄

She slept with the abandon of a child, surrendering herself completely. Head tilted to the left, mouth dropped open. Hands resting loosely on her thighs, palms up, fingers curling inwards. Legs in navy trousers jutting in a straight line from beneath her loose grey sweater, pink-slippered toes aimed at the ceiling.

In her sleep she looked defenceless, and as young as Tilly. Each of her exhalations slid out like a sigh of relief.

The kitchen was warm, a fire glowing in the stove by Laura's chair. The red tablecloth of last evening had been removed. This morning the table held three place settings, a huddle of cereal boxes, a milk jug, a sugar bowl and a butter dish. Tilly wondered where the children were – not still asleep, surely?

'Come on,' she whispered, 'let's find you some breakfast.' She knew from last evening that Poppy was bottle-fed – already weaned, or maybe Laura not a fan of breastfeeding.

Ma hadn't breastfed either of her babies – Tilly had no idea why not. She'd been nine when Robbie was born, too young to be privy to that kind of information. But even with Jemima, five years later, Tilly hadn't asked, and the subject had never come up. It wasn't the kind of thing you talked about with Ma.

She remembered being told about menstruation. Her monthly visitor, Ma called it. Instructions are on the pack, she said, presenting eleven-year-old Tilly with a brown-paper bag of sanitary napkins, warning her never to leave it around where her father might see it, and always to dispose of used ones discreetly.

The exchange had left Tilly feeling vaguely ashamed, and more than a little confused. She assumed that the phenomenon was peculiar to their family, or at least limited to certain unfortunate female souls. She awaited her first monthly visitor with apprehension, terrified that her awful secret might be discovered. When the topic was more comprehensively covered a few months later by the school's sex-education programme, and she learned that every female in the world experienced periods, the relief was immense, even if the periods themselves weren't exactly welcome.

Until they stopped coming.

She tiptoed with the baby around the kitchen, opening haphazardly filled cupboards in search of the tin of baby formula that Gavin had used. She pushed aside cans of spaghetti and rice pudding and packets of biscuits until she eventually found it. The instructions were pretty much the same as at home.

As she was filling the kettle she became aware of high-pitched voices outside. She looked out and there the four of them were, piling snow into a little mound, building what she assumed would be a snowman. And there was Gavin, wheeling a barrow across the field.

'Look,' she whispered, 'snow' – but Poppy was more interested in trying to grab at the blind cord. 'Snow,' Tilly repeated, gazing at the scene that had so mesmerised her when she'd seen it for the first time upstairs.

A voice, she'd thought, had woken her, someone speaking in the corridor outside – but by the time she'd surfaced fully from sleep it was gone, and there was nothing to be heard but the faint cries of gulls outside the window.

She'd lain in bed, going back over the events of the previous day, reliving them one by one. A day full of firsts, it had been. Her first time in a Catholic church, her first boat trip, her first time to step on Roone soil, her first encounter with her sister.

It must be late: the curtains were edged all around with light. She reached for her watch and squinted, but it was still too dim to read the hands. She pushed back the duvet and got up, and walked in bare feet to the window.

She parted the curtains.

The sight was breathtaking. Snow everywhere she looked, her first sight of real snow. The hills cloaked in it, not an inch of colour to be seen on them. Hedges and trees capped, fields hidden beneath a white coating. It was magnificent, it was enthralling. She stood there, ignoring the cold floor, and drank it in.

The roof of the henhouse was topped with snow. Two hens wandered about, the rest presumably staying indoors. Someone had already paid them a visit – a mess of footprints churned up the snow about the gate, and more were evident in the enclosure. The old man of yesterday maybe, coming around to see them again.

The window was an old-style sash one. She undid the catch and pushed up the bottom half until she could poke her head and shoulders out. The crisp air was as shocking as splashing her face with icy water. She scooped snow from the ledge and touched it with the tip of her tongue. She got her phone from the bedside locker, shivering now, and took photos – wondering even as she clicked who would see them, or when.

Don't think about that now. Not yet.

She had to get out in the snow, she had to walk in it. She had to discover how it felt under her feet. She pulled clothes from the suitcase she had yet to unpack, and dressed hurriedly. As she was brushing her teeth she heard a sound nearby that she recognised. She lifted her head and listened for several seconds. It dipped and fell, and didn't stop.

She spat and rinsed. She left the en-suite and opened her bedroom door gingerly and made her way along the corridor, following the sound. The door of the room it was coming from was ajar: she pushed it open slowly and stuck her head inside.

'Shush, shush—'

Laura and Gavin's room, it had to be. The curtains still drawn, just a tiny gap letting in a chink of light. She crossed to the cot and stooped over it. 'Shush, Poppy,' she whispered, but Poppy wept on.

She felt about among the tangle of blankets and located a blue soother and inserted it between the parted lips. Poppy latched on immediately, whimpering still, her tearful eyes fixed on Tilly's face.

She crossed to the window and pulled the curtains apart. A wicker basket in a corner held the supplies she needed: she lifted Poppy from the cot and lowered her onto the unmade bed, pushing aside a grey tracksuit that had been flung across it.

She undid and wiped and powdered and replaced, her movements practised and confident. Jemima had been a smaller baby, her limbs more slender, her cry less robust than Poppy's – but a baby was a baby, and changing a nappy was the same the world over.

She took fresh clothes from a bundle that sat on the chest of drawers. She wrapped the damp nappy in a bag and retrieved the brown rabbit from the cot and they made their way downstairs, encountering nobody in the process, and found Laura asleep in the kitchen.

The kettle boiled. Tilly found a bottle on the draining board and made up the formula – just over four months old, Gavin had told her – all the while humming softly as Poppy sat on her hip, sucking steadily on the soother and making occasional grabs at Tilly's hair. She'd forgotten that about babies, their fascination with anything that dangled. She'd had to tie up her hair around Robbie and Jemima for about six months.

She filled a mug with cold water and sat the bottle in it. Maybe that was why Laura wore her hair so short, surrounded by small children as she'd been for several years.

She glanced at her sleeping sister again. My parents separated when I was twelve, Laura had said the day before. Diane Potter had walked away, had kept going until she got to Australia. How could a mother leave her child just like that? What must it have been like for Laura? At least Tilly had never had to cope with a vanishing parent; she'd had Ma and Pa all her life.

She lifted the bottle from the water and wiped it dry. She tested the milk on her wrist, like Ma had taught her. She moved to the window seat and eased the dummy from the baby's mouth and inserted the bottle's teat – and immediately felt the little body relax and settle into the serious business of feeding. The same basic instinct the world over.

They gazed at one another as Poppy drank. 'Hello,' Tilly whispered. 'Remember me? We met yesterday. I'm Auntie Tilly.'

She'd forgotten how she used to love this, how she used to look forward to the feeds almost as much as Jemima had. She loved everything about babies: the solid warm weight of them as they lay cradled in your arms, the trusting way their eyes would fix on you as they drank, the indefinable, irresistible smell from the top of a baby's head when you pressed your nose to it and inhaled. She did it now: Poppy's head smelt precisely the same as Jemima's.

She wondered how she'd feel about her own. She hoped she'd love it, this creature she hadn't planned, hadn't anticipated. She wondered what kind of a mother she'd make. She couldn't think about having a baby for long: it made her too scared.

'Morning.'

She looked up quickly to find Laura awake and watching them. She felt suddenly flustered. 'I hope it's OK,' she said, 'that I brought her down. She was crying – I heard her. I didn't want to just leave her.'

Laura hid a yawn behind her hand. 'Of course it's OK. And you've made up a bottle: I'm impressed.'

'I found the formula in that cupboard.' Her words were tripping over one another. 'I boiled the kettle. I let it cool.'

'Sounds like you did everything right then,' Laura said mildly. 'And I see you've dressed her too.'

'I got the clothes on the chest of drawers.'

'And the nappy?'

'I changed it upstairs. I found the things in the basket—' She stopped. Was she overstepping the mark? Barging in on them yesterday, taking over today. Going where she hadn't been invited. 'I forgot to bring down the used one,' she said, 'but I did put it in a bag.'

Laura didn't seem concerned. 'You've done this before,' was all she said.

'I used to help look after Jemima, when she was a baby. My sister, she's three now.' *My sister*: for the first time it sounded not quite right. 'My adoptive parents' daughter, I mean. Their real daughter.'

'I know what you mean,' Laura said. 'You told me about her yesterday – I'd forgotten. Thanks for helping out, I appreciate it.'

'You're welcome. I love babies.' She opened her mouth to say more, and closed it without a word. Too soon.

Silence fell. Poppy lifted a languid hand, let it drop: Jemima all over again. Tilly couldn't shake a feeling of self-consciousness. Despite Laura's declaration of the night before, despite Tilly being acknowledged as an official family member, she still felt like a visitor. But that was bound to happen, wasn't it? It would take a while, that was all.

More shouts from outside. 'You saw the snow,' Laura remarked.

'I did – it's wonderful.'

'Your first time?'

'Yes.'

'The girls' too. They were so excited.' Laura got to her feet. 'Bet you're keen to get out in it. We've been told it's not going to last.'

'I was thinking I might take a walk – and I'd love to go to the sea.'

'There's a beach not ten minutes down the road: turn right when you go out. Have something to eat first.' Laura opened the fridge. 'You like eggs? We have lots of eggs, piles of them, our ladies never stop laying. You could have scrambled egg on toast. And there are sausages and rashers to go with them.' She rummaged about, her face hidden. 'Yogurt, strawberry or cherry, and there's pudding, black only, I'm afraid. Oh, and we have cheese. You like cheese? Cheddar and feta.'

Was she talking too much? Was she ill at ease too? Were they both feeling their way? Tilly found this possibility somewhat comforting.

'Toast is fine,' she said. 'It's all I usually have at home. And I can do it myself – you don't have to look after me.'

But Laura took a wrapped loaf of bread from a metal bin and pulled out two slices. 'You stay where you are: I can pretend I have a nanny.'

'I love babies,' Tilly said, remembering as soon as the words were out that she'd already said it.

'I can see that.' Laura pulled out the grill pan and laid the bread on it. She came to sit on the bench next to Tilly. There were dark shadows under her eyes.

'You're tired,' Tilly said.

'I'm always tired,' Laura replied lightly, reaching out to encircle Poppy's fat ankle with her hand. 'Aren't I?' she asked the baby. 'Mama's always tired, isn't she?' She ran a finger along Poppy's cheek while the baby pumped her legs.

'You must let me help,' Tilly said. 'While I'm here. I'd like to help.'

Laura turned to her. Their eyes met. Outside in the field, someone shrieked.

'That's kind of you,' Laura said. A second passed, and a few more. 'This will take some getting used to,' she said. 'Won't it?'

Tilly didn't know what to say.

'Us, I mean.'

'Yes …'

'But you're staying such a short time. Wednesday you said you're going home?'

Here was her chance. Now she should say it, she should tell Laura what she was planning, what she was hoping would happen. She should tell her everything right now, while nobody was there, while she had the chance.

She couldn't. She couldn't say it. The words wouldn't come.

'Wednesday,' she said. 'The thirtieth.'

A nine-day trip was what she'd booked. The question hadn't been whether to buy a one-way or a return ticket – with a holiday visa a return ticket was mandatory. She'd settled on nine days, which was short enough not to have Ma and Pa asking questions, and long enough to get to know the lie of the land in Ireland, and to gauge whether her plan was going to work.

'I wasn't sure how long to book for,' she said, 'when I hadn't told you I was coming, I mean.'

'You thought I might send you packing,' Laura said.

'No.' The colour rose in Tilly's face. 'I thought … you mightn't be here, or something—'

Laura smiled. 'Relax, I'm teasing. Just seems an awfully long way to come for such a short time, that's all.'

'I know. It is.'

Laura yawned again. 'Sorry,' she said. 'Tired.'

In the short silence that followed, Tilly smelt burning. 'The toast,' she said, and Laura leaped to her feet and pulled out the grill pan.

'It's OK,' Tilly said, 'I can scrape it' – but Laura threw it into a battered plastic basin that sat next to the draining board.

'Caesar will eat it,' she said, placing two fresh slices under the grill. 'He's not a bit fussy.'

'Caesar?' Tilly had thought the dog was called Charlie.

'Our pot-bellied pig. You'll meet him soon – he's away at the moment. Here, pass over that child, you've done enough. And put the kettle on for tea. I forgot it.'

Tilly surrendered Poppy and got to her feet. As she brought the kettle to the sink the baby burped loudly.

'Oops,' Laura said. 'Watch your manners, missy, in front of Auntie Tilly.'

Auntie Tilly: already it was starting to sound familiar. She wondered what Ma would say if she knew that Tilly was an auntie to three girls and two boys. She lit the gas ring under the kettle and kept an eye on the bread until it was toasted. The butter was a deep yellow.

'Lemon marmalade in the press beside the cooker,' Laura said. 'A woman with a café in the village makes it.'

'Thanks.'

Lelia's Lemon Marmalade was handwritten in blue ink on the label. The kettle began to whistle.

'You want tea?' Tilly asked, dropping a bag into a cup.

'No thanks – but you might fill that little white pot on the worktop for Gladys. She likes a cup in bed before her breakfast.'

'I can take it up to her.'

'No, you have yours. I'll do it.' She settled Poppy into her playpen. 'By the way,' she said, 'I don't think I told you yesterday. Our father remarried ten years ago. I don't imagine our mother mentioned it.'

Tilly stared at her. 'No,' she said faintly.

'No,' Laura repeated. 'Well, you have a stepmother. Her name is Susan. She's supposed to be coming today.'

'Coming here?' Another hurdle to cross, someone else to meet. 'Is our father coming too?' But of course he wasn't, or Laura would have said so.

'No, just Susan. And there's something else you should know.'

A beat passed. Poppy hiccuped, a comical little high-pitched yip. Upstairs a toilet flushed. In the field someone shouted: *Dad!*

'She's pregnant,' Laura said. 'Susan. I only found out a couple of days ago.'

'Oh ...'

Their father's wife was pregnant. Tilly looked into her tea and thought about this. Another baby on the way, a half-brother or -sister for her and Laura. 'When—'

'Hang on,' Laura said. 'I'll bring this up and then I'll fill you in.' She left the room with the tray.

Tilly listened to the soft thump of her steps on the stairs. A stepmother. A pregnant stepmother. A twist, a development she hadn't expected. She thought about the implications for her own situation, but it was impossible to gauge how this new information would impact on her.

She glanced at the clock on the wall and read half past nine, and added on ten hours. Early evening, dinner just over. Jemima being prepared for bed, Robbie watching TV or playing in the backyard with Markus from the next farm, who cycled over every few days.

She felt a sudden piercing dart of homesickness. If she was there she'd be doing the washing-up right now. She closed her eyes and pictured the kitchen at home, so different from this one. Roughly the same size, but plainer and less cluttered. The unvarnished wood cabinets, the well-worn salmon-coloured linoleum that covered the floor. The table, round, not rectangular, its olive-green oilcloth patterned with cherries. A fan on the ceiling, screens on the windows. Cockroach traps by the fridge and under the sink, a rolled-up towel at the back door to keep out snakes. Ma's apron slung over a chair.

She opened her eyes and twisted the top from the marmalade jar. It was pulpy, more like a thick citrus sauce. Poppy gabbled in her playpen. Outside there were more shouts. Tilly added milk to her cup. She fished out the teabag and left it sitting in her spoon.

Laura returned and took the chair next to Tilly. 'So,' she said, 'our father is an artist, a very famous one – well, on this side of the world anyway. He lives in Dublin – that's where I grew up – and he's loaded. His pictures sell for Monopoly money, as in they cost a lot.'

The sentences came out dispassionately. She might have been describing a little-known acquaintance, or a celebrity she'd never met and had little interest in, rather than the man who'd fathered her. She said his name. It meant nothing to Tilly.

'We're not close, we never have been. He's not what you'd call …' her mouth twisted '… child-friendly.'

It was an odd thing to say about her father, but it tallied with what their mother had told Tilly. He was never cut out for children, wasn't that how she'd put it?

'Susan is forty,' Laura said. 'She's over twenty years younger than him. She's lovely.'

'When is she coming?'

'Afternoon, probably. I can't get in touch without the phone.'

'You have no Internet here?'

'It works off the mobile-phone network on the island: if the phones go down so does the Net. We're completely cut off.'

Completely cut off: for some reason, this appealed to Tilly. No contact with the outside world. Whatever catastrophes might be happening elsewhere, Roone would remain in blissful ignorance, at least for a while.

But then she remembered Ma, waiting in Australia for the next text from Bali. The last one sent on Christmas Eve, two days ago, from Breda and Paddy's house. Nothing to be done, the situation out of Tilly's hands. She hoped they weren't worrying though.

'I was married before,' Laura said then. 'The boys aren't Gavin's. I married him two years ago, after Evie and Marian were born.'

'Oh …'

'My first husband died, a week before the boys came along.' A frown on her face that wasn't really a frown. Looking at the table, not at Tilly. Frowning at the butter dish. 'He killed himself. He suffered from depression.'

Tilly was horrified. She wanted to reach out to Laura, but she was too shy. 'I'm so sorry,' she said. It was horribly inadequate. 'I can't imagine what you went through.'

'It was hell,' Laura said calmly, raising her eyes to meet Tilly's again. 'Susan was marvellous. I don't think I'd have survived without her. And then six years later I met Gavin, and here we are.'

Her smile too bright. Tilly searched for words. 'Thank you,' she said finally, 'for telling me.' So much sadness. She'd been so young when she'd endured that heartbreak.

'So,' Laura said, getting to her feet, 'you're all caught up. Now have your breakfast before it gets cold.'

They heard footsteps on the stairs just then. 'That'll be Gladys,' Laura said, bringing the kettle to the sink.

The door opened. It wasn't Gladys.

'Hi there,' Larry said. Navy trousers, grey sweater, very white trainers. 'Guess this is where I get breakfast.'

'Have a seat,' Laura told him. 'Hope you slept well.' Back to normal, no sign that she had just shared her tragic history with Tilly.

'Yeah, not bad, thanks.' He took the chair across the table from Tilly. 'How are you today?' he asked.

Tilly smiled, remembering his own sad story of the night before. He needed smiles. 'Fine, I'm fine.'

'Get that snowfall – came outta nowhere.'

'I know – isn't it lovely?' Laura replied, her head in the fridge again. 'You're certainly getting a mix of weather here. I have eggs, sausages, bacon and black pudding for your breakfast. That sound OK?'

'Sure.'

'And there's cereal on the table. Help yourself.'

He made no move towards the boxes. 'You got juice?'

'I have orange.'

'Sure, that's good.' She filled a glass for him and he nodded his thanks.

'How d'you like your eggs?'

Tilly finished her toast, only half listening, still thinking about Laura's first marriage, and the awful way it had ended. A week before the boys had been born – how did anyone survive that?

Their mother had made no mention of it in Brisbane – but then, she hadn't exactly been a fount of information on any front. Tilly wondered if she knew that their father had remarried. And what about Susan, arriving on the island in a few hours? How would she react when she heard about Tilly, the stepdaughter she never knew she had? Hopefully she'd be as nice as Laura said.

She brought her cup and empty plate to the sink. 'Leave those, go for your walk,' Laura told her. 'Don't be too long. I want to bring you next door to meet Nell and James.'

Nell and James, presumably Colette's son and his wife. She was going to be introduced: Laura wanted her to meet the neighbours. Optimism surged through her. It was going to be alright, it was going to work out.

She smiled at Larry again, but he was looking through the window at the snow and didn't notice. She ran lightly upstairs and put on another sweater and her jacket, slipping her phone into her pocket for photos. She wrapped Colette's scarf around her throat; wouldn't have it for much longer. Stupid not to have packed a scarf – not that any of her flimsy things would have been a match for this cold, but they'd have been better than nothing.

She let herself out the front door, not wanting to go through the kitchen again, and pulled it closed behind her. She stood on the step watching her fogged breath drift upwards, feeling her spirits lift again.

She regarded the short path to the gate, covered now in white. Was it only yesterday she'd wheeled her suitcase up that path, butterflies going crazy inside her? She looked beyond it to the field across the road. From here the sea wasn't visible but it was there, just a short distance away. She could smell it – the air was full of it.

She walked to the gate. The snow felt crunchy, like walking on gravel. She looked back at the footprints she'd made. She reversed into them, stopping at the front door again. She turned and made her way past the bay window, which was still curtained. Already her toes and fingertips tingled with the cold, but she didn't care. She looked back again at the footprints she was leaving behind.

She rounded the bend and saw the children, scattered about in the centre of the field. She laughed and broke into a run, the ground bumpy under its snowy covering. She felt about six years old again, chasing after Lien in the school playground. She waved at Gavin, coming back across the field, and he lifted his arm in return.

She reached the first little girl and stopped, panting. She could feel the blood zinging around inside her. The child was adding a small handful of snow to the column that was now about eighteen inches high. Like her sister, she wore a red padded jacket. Her hands were encased in bright green mittens. Curls poked from beneath her blue woolly hat to frame her face, which was rosy with cold.

'Hello,' Tilly said. 'Are you making a snowman?'

She nodded, patting the snow into place, and Tilly was reminded of one of them reaching over to pat her hair at the dinner table last evening. So sweet.

'It's lovely.' Tilly pulled her phone from her pocket and took a snap. 'Are you Marian or Evie?'

'Mawian.'

'Here—' Tilly fished a tissue from her pocket and wiped her runny nose, the little girl submitting without comment.

Nearby Evie, in a yellow hat and orange mittens, was kicking up little bursts of snow with her boots, evidently having decided her work was done. Tilly took more snaps, then turned to the boys, who were moulding snow into a rough basketball-sized sphere a short distance away.

'That's the head?' she asked.

'Yeah. Can you put it on top?'

'Sure.'

Auntie Tilly, playing in the snow with her nieces and nephews. She crouched and lifted it, and placed it carefully on top of the column. She stood back, wiping her wet hands on her jeans.

The five of them regarded it silently. It was short and squat, about the same height as the girls. The head was out of proportion and slightly lopsided, but Tilly didn't dare touch it again.

'We need a carrot,' one of the boys said.

'Yeah, an' a hat.'

Off they sped towards the house, leaving Tilly with the other two. 'What's the snowman's name?' she asked.

A few seconds passed. Then: '*Daddy*,' Evie said decisively.

'Daddy,' Marian echoed, hopping about and giggling delightedly. 'Daddy!'

Tilly laughed along, filled with a pure happiness she didn't think she'd ever experienced before. She wanted to grab them, she wanted to throw her arms around them and squeeze, but she thought she'd better not: an excess of affection from their brand-new aunt might alarm them.

She scanned the field and saw the trees – apple, she thought – to the side of the house, and the large crater in the ground, the mess of bricks and branches. A fallen tree – and something else, some structure it had damaged when it fell.

The boys came running back with a red baseball cap, a small tomato and a fistful of raisins. 'Mum had no carrots,' they said, pushing the tomato into the centre of the head, causing a sizeable wedge of snow to fall off and land with a splat on the ground. Tilly attempted to patch it back together while they poked in raisins for eyes and mouth, and perched the cap on top.

They stood back again. It was a snow clown, with an uneven mouth, crooked eyes and a nose that threatened to tumble to the ground at any second. As snowmen went, it was a disaster.

'It's wonderful,' Tilly said, careful to keep her face straight.

'*Daddy!*' Evie cried again, causing Marian to erupt into renewed giggles.

'Daddy! Daddy!' she cried, skipping in joyous little circles – and here he came, his barrow full of bricks, stopping as he approached to examine their creation.

'That's a great snowman,' he said. 'But why is his nose a tomato?'

'Mum had no carrot.'

'Hang on.'

He strode up to an area near the hen run, the little girls trotting and skipping after him. He crouched and fumbled about in the snow, and then yanked something out with a shout of triumph. Back he came, brandishing it high, the girls running along beside him.

When they drew near enough Tilly saw that it was a small carrot, about five inches long. He removed the tomato and stuck the carrot in its place, packing the snow firmly around it. 'Now,' he said, stepping back, wiping his hands on his jacket, '*that's* a snowman.'

'You grow carrots?' Tilly asked.

'I do, and lots of other vegetables – that's my job here. I sell veg and eggs around the island. I do the houses and the cafés.'

He and Laura had the same accent. 'Are you from Dublin too?'

He nodded. 'That's where I met Laura – although we'd both just been on holidays here, we'd narrowly missed meeting up. I'll tell you the story sometime, when this lot give us a chance.'

The boys had begun to wrestle; the girls were each leaning into their father, arms about his thighs, observing Tilly.

'What happened there?' she asked, pointing to the orchard, and he told her about the storm damage, and the miraculous escape of the animals. 'I'm transferring the bricks,' he said, indicating the pile he'd already formed at the opposite side of the field. 'We'll get a new shed built there, out of harm's way.'

'Daddy,' one of the girls said, pulling at his trouser leg. 'Daddy,' she repeated, pointing at the snowman. Her sister tittered, looking up at Gavin to see his reaction.

He looked shocked. 'What? You mean that's *me*?'

They nodded, giggling. He growled and reached down and scooped both of them into his arms. He lunged at them, making munching sounds while they screamed in mock terror and tried to bat him away. 'Nom, nom, nom,' he said, as they ducked their heads, laughing. Lucky girls, whose father clearly adored them.

Tilly took more snaps. She was warming to him, to them all. After only one day, after less than a day, she was becoming connected.

I want to stay here, she thought. I want to live here.

She'd barely arrived. She'd seen virtually nothing of the place. She knew nobody on Roone outside this family, apart from Colette, who was only visiting – and yet she was convinced she could happily spend the rest of her life here, on this island.

What was it about the place that made it somehow feel like home? Impossible as it was, it felt *known*, it felt familiar to her. Maybe she'd lived here in a previous existence. Maybe she'd been born on Roone a few hundred years ago.

Time to get to know it a bit.

'I'm going for a walk,' she told Gavin, who was still trying to eat his shrieking daughters, and he lifted his head just long enough to tell her that it was impossible to get lost. 'The coast road winds in a circle all around the island,' he said, 'and everything else links up with it. Village that way,' he said, nodding left, 'but you won't get anything open today.'

'I want to go to the sea,' Tilly said, and he directed her to the beach that Laura had spoken of. She walked from the field and onto the road. She saw tyre tracks in the snow, but there wasn't a sign of a vehicle now.

She looked towards the house next door, where Colette was staying and where Laura would be taking her later. There was someone in the front garden: she could see a form inside the waist-high stone wall. She could hear the clank of metal on stone.

She drew nearer. He – it was a he – wore a dark green woolly hat and a brown padded jacket. He was shovelling snow from the path.

He looked up at the sound of her footsteps. Their eyes met for an instant.

Her heart stopped. It literally stopped dead.

She felt something, some sensation, sweeping through her, from her head to her fingertips to her toes. Lighting her up as it went, making everything in her jump to attention. Cranking her heart up again, making it thump a million beats to the second.

He was her age, or thereabouts. He was tall, like her. His face was the most beautiful thing she'd ever seen.

He nodded hello before dipping his head again and resuming his shovelling. Tilly walked on, her legs suddenly unsteady. She was shaking, every part of her was literally shaking with … what?

With love.

She had just fallen in love.

She'd fallen in love at first sight with a boy – a man – who was shovelling snow.

Stop. Stop that. There was no such thing as love at first sight. It didn't exist, except in books or films. You couldn't fall in love with someone you didn't know. It simply couldn't happen.

She walked on, head in a whirl. She didn't dare look back in case he wasn't watching her. She could hear the repeated scrape of his shovel on the ground.

She had to look back.

She couldn't look back.

She looked back.

He dipped his head: he *had* been watching. Her heart sang. She walked on, taking big gulps of the frosty air, trying to calm her racing pulse.

Assuming he wasn't just working there, he lived next door to Laura and Gavin. He lived in the house where Colette's son lived. He lived, she realised with an actual *gasp* of shock, in the house Laura was bringing her to later. She would meet him – she would be introduced to him. This is my sister, Laura would say, and he would say – what?

Who was he? He was about the right age to be Colette's grandson. Had she mentioned a grandson? Tilly couldn't remember – she'd forgotten everything in the shock of encountering him.

His face, though. His face was imprinted in her brain; it was saved in her memory. She closed her eyes as she walked and there he was.

Blue. Blue his eyes were, beneath the woolly hat that had covered his hair. No scarf. Faint scar running down one cheek – oh yes, she hadn't missed it. Biggish nose, pink-tipped like the girls' from the cold, tiny dark freckles dotted on the bridge. Mouth perfect, skin on the pale side. Chestnut-brown jacket, blue jeans, hiking boots. Black gloves on the hands that held the shovel. Every detail right there, memorised as surely as a snapshot she'd taken.

What was his name? She wanted to hear his name. What did his voice sound like – what accent did he have? She wanted to know everything, every *single* thing about him. She kept walking past houses and fields and barns, none of which registered.

Snow? What did that matter?

She turned for the beach, still in a trance. She stood by the water's edge, unable to remember getting there from the road. She walked by the shore, unable to focus on anything but him.

She'd never felt like this before. She hadn't fallen in love with John Smith the first time she'd seen him. She'd thought he was nice-looking, she'd certainly fancied him, but there'd been nothing like this, nothing like this *avalanche* of emotion, this tornado that had engulfed her the instant she'd looked into his eyes.

She walked up and down the beach, paying scant attention to her surroundings. Eventually she thought to check the time, and was astonished to find almost half an hour gone by since she'd left the house. Laura would be waiting for her.

Her anticipation grew as she drew closer to the garden where she'd seen him. Would he still be there? Would they talk – would he say something this time? She could feel her heart thumping in her ears as the house came into view. Her skin tingled. She walked closer, rehearsing her smile.

There was no sign of him. The path was clear of snow, he and his shovel gone. But it didn't matter: she was going to meet him later. Please let him be living there, please let him be at home when they called.

She turned in at the gate of Walter's Place, everything still whirling and fluttering inside her.

❄✳❄

Would you credit it? This she had not seen coming.

Love was in the air.

I'm getting up, Gladys had announced when Laura delivered her tea, the bottom half of her already dressed in green tweed. It's too nice a day to stay in bed.

Too nice a day? Her curtains were still closed, her room in near-darkness. Had she even looked out?

It snowed last night, Laura told her, setting her tray on the bedside locker. Everyplace is covered. She went to the window and pulled the curtains apart.

Isn't that lovely? But Gladys didn't even glance in the window's direction as she buttoned her white blouse.

I'm hoping it won't upset your travel plans, Laura said.

That got her attention. My travel plans? She strode on her support-stockinged feet to the window and looked anxiously at the scene outside. Isn't the ferry running?

I'd say it is, but we'll have to enquire about the buses and trains on the other side. I'll send Gavin down to talk to Leo in a while.

Lord, Gladys muttered, crossing to the wardrobe and taking out a grey cardigan, pursing her mouth at it before putting it back in favour of a paler grey one. Grey was Gladys's default shade.

There's a thaw expected this afternoon, Laura said. I'd say you'll be alright.

No response. Gladys had pulled on her cardigan and patted her hair into place in front of the dressing-table mirror. Distracted, without a doubt. Could she be working up to another collapse?

I'll leave your tea, Laura said. You might have it while you're getting ready.

Hmm? Gladys looked vaguely at the tray. Oh. Yes. Thank you, dear, I'll be down shortly.

And as Laura was leaving the room, her hand on the doorknob, Gladys asked, her voice *drenched* in unconcern, turning this way and that as she smoothed her skirt, Is Larry up yet, I wonder?

Ah. *Ah*. Larry.

I think he's getting up. I heard him moving around when I passed his door just now.

Laura waited, but no more was said. Gladys was locating her shoes, slipping her feet in – was she *humming*?

I'll see you below so, Laura said, and went back downstairs, where she filled in a few gaps in the Potter family history for Tilly – and when Larry appeared shortly afterwards, she wondered if she should give the poor creature some advance warning.

No, of course she shouldn't. He was a grown man, able to look out for himself. Besides, what would she say – run for the hills, my mother-in-law has taken a shine to you? Hardly.

Anyway, it might well be just what Larry needed right now, someone to massage his ego with a bit of attention. Not that it would last long, with Gladys heading off, all going well, in a few hours. But maybe Laura had got it wrong: maybe she'd imagined any romantic notions on her mother-in-law's part. Maybe Gladys was simply bothered about the trek back to Dublin.

She had not got it wrong.

Gladys appeared in the kitchen five minutes after Larry, wafting clouds of lily-of-the-valley. She bade them good morning and took her seat at the table. She small talked with Larry and Laura until she was halfway through her breakfast – and then she made her move.

So you're off home on Monday, she said, and Larry agreed that he was. He had two more days in Ireland.

And didn't you say that your flight is from Dublin?

Yeah, that's right.

I'm just thinking, she said, forking up her scrambled egg, the picture of innocence, you should come back with me today.

Pardon? Today?

Why not? I'd be glad of the company – and you could stay in my house, save a bit of money.

Larry looked a little cornered, as well he might. I made a hotel reservation.

Gladys waved away the hotel. You could cancel that, I have lots of room, you could come and go as you please. The island is all very well for a few days, but at this time of the year – breaking off to throw a glance at Laura, who was pretending not to listen as she scrubbed egg from a saucepan – at this time of the year, it can be a little quiet.

As if she knew Roone well, as if she came often, in winter or summer. Laura wasn't entirely without sympathy, though: Gladys had been on her own for donkey's years, since Gavin's father had gone to work one day and never come home, tumbling off scaffolding instead and breaking his neck. Could you blame her for latching on to widowed Larry now? Her last chance, she was probably thinking.

He'd turn down her offer, of course. Laura couldn't see him gallivanting across the country with a woman he'd laid eyes on for the first time yesterday. Anyway, the poor man had hardly been widowed a wet week. And he'd surely prefer an anonymous hotel to a place where he'd have to make constant small talk. Larry wasn't exactly the king of small talk.

But he hadn't turned down her offer. Far from it.

Well, sure, he said. I guess I could do that, if it's OK with you.

Of course it is. And I could take you around, show you a bit of Dublin if you wanted.

So Laura had sent Gavin to the pier, and he'd come back to say that public transport was running as normal on the other side, so the pair of them were heading off into the sunset, or off on the two o'clock ferry anyway. Could you believe it?

And then Tilly had reappeared, all pink and sparkling from her walk, and the two travellers went upstairs to pack, and while Laura was making up Poppy's next bottle the girls ran in and demanded that she come outside to look at their snowman, so she'd left Tilly in charge and gone off to admire their heroic, amateurish efforts.

And by the time that was done it was after eleven, and Gavin went off to check on the animals, and brought the children with him.

'When are we going to Nell's?' Tilly asked now, Poppy feeding in the crook of her arm, and Laura told her as soon as the bottle was empty. Keen to meet the neighbours, obviously.

'I saw the fallen tree,' Tilly remarked. 'And Gavin told me about the animals escaping. That was wonderful.'

Laura almost mentioned Walter, and her belief that he'd had some part to play in their survival, but decided against it. Might spook her to think there was a ghost around, even one as harmless as Walter.

She thumped damp coffee grounds from the cafetière into the bin. 'Larry sure drinks enough of it,' she remarked. 'He had three mugs for breakfast.'

'You don't drink coffee,' Tilly said.

'I used to love it, but I lost my taste for it.' She rinsed the cafetière under the tap, letting the silence grow, wondering whether to explain. And then she thought, *Why not?* It wasn't a state secret: everyone on Roone knew it.

'I was diagnosed with breast cancer earlier this year,' she said. 'I had a mastectomy in April.'

Tilly's mouth fell open.

'I'm OK, it's just that it changed my tastes – the treatment did, I mean, the chemo. No big deal. These days I'm all about green tea.'

'You had *cancer*?' Her face, suddenly so stricken.

Maybe Laura shouldn't have mentioned it. 'I'm over it now. I've got the all-clear.'

'Have you? When?'

'In September, when I finished my chemo. They just have to keep an eye on me for a while. I'll be checked out every six months.'

'And *are* you OK? Really?'

Laura turned to her, the cafetière still in her hands.

'Sorry,' Tilly said, 'it's just … It must have been awful.'

Her concern was genuine, you could see that. They might have just met, but she seemed to really care.

And just like that, Laura realised that she'd met someone she could tell.

'Honestly,' she said, 'I'm scared. I'm terrified it'll come back.'

'It keeps me awake at night,' she said. 'The worry.

'I can't bear to look at myself,' she said. 'I hate how I look now.'

'I had long hair before,' she said. 'I loved it, I really miss it.'

'I'm hell to live with,' she said. 'I can't believe Gavin is still here.'

It was such a relief to be able to tell someone the truth. So good not to have to pretend she was fine, she was coping.

And Tilly just listened. She sat there and listened.

And eventually, while she was still telling the truth, Poppy finished her bottle and emitted one of her impressive gassy explosions, which Laura took as her cue to belt up.

'Right,' she said, stowing the cafetière in the press, taking Poppy from Tilly's arms. 'Let's get you changed, missy.'

'How can I help?' Tilly asked. 'What can I do?'

'You can cut a bit of that Christmas cake and find tinfoil for it in the dresser drawer. I promised Nell I'd bring her a bit to taste.'

'I meant,' Tilly said, taking a knife from the block, 'how can I help *you*?'

Laura looked at her gratefully. 'You've already done it. But you could give me some of that hair too.'

Tilly smiled as she cut the cake. 'You'll be OK. You're strong, I can tell.'

'I *am* strong. I've had to be.'

'And your hair will grow again.'

'It will, I know.'

It was good, how they could talk like this. It was making a difference – it was lifting her spirits.

'Do you like baking?' Tilly asked, wrapping the cake in tinfoil.

'Hate it – Nell badgered me into making that. I'm useless. You could build a wall with my rock buns.'

'I could make cookies while I'm here,' Tilly said, 'if you like. Ma says I make the best cookies.'

'That'd be good. The kids would love you.'

She was pretty, in a way. There was a – what was it? – a kind of fragility about her that was appealing. The slender frame, the long legs, the pale skin. The fair lashes above those almost turquoise eyes, the quick smile that poked a dimple into her left cheek. The blush that came and went, often.

She was smiling now as she pulled on her jacket, the fresh sparkle still in her face from her walk. She looked, Laura thought suddenly, like something that was blooming, or about to bloom. Maybe it was her age, everything still ahead of her at seventeen.

'We'll go out the front way,' Laura said. 'The field might be too tricky in the snow, with Poppy' – so they left the kitchen and went through the hall.

'I saw him,' Tilly remarked.

'Who?'

'That man.' She pointed to James's painting of Walter, which Laura had hung outside the sitting-room door. Walter in a white shirt and dark green bow tie, smiling out at them.

Laura looked from his face to Tilly's. 'You saw him? Where? When?'

'Yesterday. He was in the henhouse. I saw him from my bedroom window, not long after I arrived.'

Walter in the field, yesterday.

Walter.

She couldn't have seen him. Walter was gone. Walter had left the building.

Laura could think of nothing to say in response, nothing at all. What could she say – that Tilly had seen a ghost, that she must have imagined it?

But Walter hadn't gone away, had he? He was still here, still watching over them. He'd saved the animals. It was just that the past few months had been so fraught and busy and frightening, Laura hadn't had time to notice him. It had taken Tilly, a newcomer, to do that.

But Tilly had *seen* him. Laura had never seen him. She'd known he was there, but he'd never made himself visible to her. Maybe Tilly was more susceptible to that.

She pulled up Poppy's hood, feeling Tilly's eyes on her. 'Come on,' she said, 'or we'll never get there.'

They left the house, pulling the front door closed behind them. Laura searched for something to say to break the silence as they walked down the snowy path. 'The apple tree that fell,' she said, 'bore fruit all year round, pretty much.'

Tilly turned to stare at her. 'What? But that's not possible.'

'I know. September is the time for apples here. All our other trees bear fruit then, but this one was different. It was special. And now it's gone.'

Tilly said nothing. Probably didn't believe her, probably thought it was a story to impress the Australian visitor.

'So what are their names again?' she asked as they approached the house. 'Colette's son and his wife.'

'James and Nell. And you'll probably meet James's son Andy, from his first marriage. He's seventeen, or maybe eighteen now. And

Tommy, who's nearly two. It was originally Nell's house: James and Andy moved in when she married James.'

Someone had cleared the snow from the path. They walked to the door and rang the bell. Tilly hung back slightly. Shy, Laura thought. Not used to meeting so many new people.

Colette appeared, looking as smart as she always did – cream tailored pants, blue fitted jacket, patterned scarf in violets and blues. Laura imagined all her immaculate clothes on padded hangers covered with cellophane. They wouldn't know a wrinkle if it shook hands and introduced itself.

'There you are,' Colette said, smiling broadly. 'All well?' Looking brightly from one to the other.

'All fine,' Laura replied. 'I know you two have already met – I wanted to introduce Tilly to the others.'

They were ushered in and brought straight through to the kitchen. Tilly met Nell, who seemed genuinely astonished – it appeared that Colette had kept her promise not to tell – and Tommy, who abandoned his toy cars to stare solemnly at Poppy, who stared right back at him from her mother's arms.

'Isn't this the most amazing thing?' Nell said, taking jackets and laying them across the small settee by the far wall. 'I can't believe it. James will be sorry he missed you, but he had to open up.'

'He manages one of the village pubs,' Laura explained. 'You'll meet him soon enough. Hi, Tommy. Did Santa come?'

He nodded.

'What did he bring?' He waddled off and returned clasping a chunky wooden train. James's eyes, Nell's smile. Good combination.

'Sit,' Nell said, opening a tin and lifting out cubes of a dark brown cake. 'Tea? Coffee? Hot chocolate? Juice?'

Tea for Laura, juice for Tilly. 'Could I take Poppy?' Tilly murmured, and Laura handed her over. She still seemed a bit ill at ease – had Laura upset her by ignoring her reference to Walter?

'Is Andy about?' she asked Colette. Nice for Tilly to meet someone her own age while she was here.

'He went walking with the dog – he should be back soon. My older grandson,' she added to Tilly, who seemed more interested in smoothing Poppy's bit of hair. Maybe she had a boyfriend back home, and wasn't bothered about meeting Irish boys.

'So tell me,' Nell said, taking the chair next to Tilly's, 'how did you discover you had a sister?' and Tilly told the story again in her quiet, hesitant way.

As she spoke, as they questioned her, she played with the cake she'd been given – which turned out to be gingerbread – crumbling it between her fingers but actually eating very little. Watching her figure, no doubt, like seventeen-year-old girls the world over.

When Tilly told her about meeting up with Colette, Nell turned to her mother-in-law. 'You never said a thing.'

'Tilly asked me not to,' Colette replied, throwing a smile in Tilly's direction.

The front door opened. They all heard it. 'That'll be Andy now,' Nell said, getting to her feet.

'Hi,' he said to the room in general, bringing a whiff of the outside in with him, bending to undo Captain's lead. 'Hi, Laura,' he said. Poor thing, his smile still a bit subdued after Eve breaking his heart.

Introductions were made. He and Tilly shook hands. 'Saw you earlier,' he said. Funny, Laura thought, she'd made no mention of it. 'You're sisters?' he asked, eyebrows rising. 'No way.'

'Hot chocolate?' Nell asked him, already pouring milk into a saucepan.

'Thanks.' He pulled out a chair and sat – and immediately Tommy clamoured to get onto his lap. The adored older brother, despite the gap of sixteen years between them, despite them only having a father in common. 'Hey, buddy,' Andy said, hoisting him up.

Good-looking boy. Wouldn't be long before another girl gave him the eye. His first term of college just over: maybe some of his fellow students were already sizing him up. Wouldn't take him long to forget Eve.

They talked of the storm, and the damage it had done. Nell told them about the roof that had blown off Annie Byrnes's hay barn and landed in Tony Kennedy's yard, six fields away, and the telegraph pole that had toppled outside the creamery, narrowly missing Phil Doran's van that was parked a few yards away, and *Jupiter*, her own little boat, which had been smashed to pieces on the beach.

'Ah no,' Laura said, 'your lovely boat. We had many a trip in it,' she told Tilly. 'My boys loved it – they'll be sorry to hear it's gone.'

'It was the worst storm I remember,' Nell said. 'Lots more trees are down around the place too, and of course the hotel roof will take a few weeks at least to repair. Poor old Henry.'

They marvelled at the snow, and enquired about winters in Tilly's part of Australia. In the middle of the chat, the radio sprang suddenly to life: power had been restored to Roone.

'How long will you stay here?' Laura asked Colette.

'I'm not sure. They're trying to persuade me to hang on for New Year.'

'You must,' Nell put in. 'You missed Christmas, or practically missed it.' She turned to Tilly. 'New Year is great here. Everyone gathers at the pier and Father William rings the church bells at midnight, and there's a big singsong. You'll love it.'

'She would,' Laura said, 'if she was here. She's flying home on Wednesday.'

'What?' Nell exclaimed. 'But that's only a few days away, and you've only just arrived. And such a long trip, too – you must still be jet-lagged.'

'And to have your money taken as well,' Colette added.

A beat passed. 'What money?' Nell asked.

Laura looked at Tilly. 'Your money was taken?'

She flushed. 'I – my purse was stolen,' she said. 'In Heathrow, when I fell asleep.' She looked deeply uncomfortable, wouldn't meet anyone's eyes.

'I'm so sorry,' Colette said. 'I assumed you would have told her.'

'I meant to, I just …'

But she hadn't told Laura. She'd told Colette, who wasn't related to her at all, and she hadn't said a word to Laura.

Tilly ducked her head towards Poppy. Laura regarded the pale hair that screened her face from them. 'Was anything else taken?' she asked.

'No, just the money.'

'All your money?'

'I had some in my pocket, and I got a refund on a coach ticket … But it's OK, I don't need money, it was just in case—' She broke off.

Laura waited.

'In case I needed it,' she finished.

In case Laura had sent her away. In case she'd had no place to stay.

Nell stood. 'Refills,' she announced, but Laura got up too.

'We need to be getting back. I must feed our two travellers before they head off.' She reached for Poppy, and Tilly handed her over without a word.

Nell accompanied them to the front door. 'Come for brunch tomorrow,' she said. 'Bring Susan.'

'Lovely – elevenish?'

'Perfect.'

They walked down the path, the snow already going slushy. The sky was clear, a thin sun doing its best to soften the chill.

'You should have told me about your purse,' Laura said, as soon as the front door closed after them. 'Why didn't you tell me?'

Tilly walked out the gate and turned towards Walter's Place, slightly ahead of Laura. 'I didn't want to be a nuisance. I didn't want you to feel you had to give me money. It was enough that you took me in.'

'Hang on,' Laura said, and waited until Tilly stopped. 'Look at me.'
Tilly turned.

'Listen,' Laura said, 'I know we've only just met, but we *have* met, and we *are* sisters, and I thought we were getting on pretty well. I told you things this morning. I said things that I haven't said to anyone else. So stop thinking you have to be this perfect person or I'll send you away. I'm *not* going to send you away. Whatever you say, or whatever you tell me, that's not going to happen.'

Tilly said nothing.

'OK?'

'OK.'

'So is there anything else,' Laura asked, 'that I should know?'

For a second Tilly made no response. And then she said, in a kind of a slithery rush, 'I'm pregnant. It was an accident, and my parents don't know. I don't want to go home, I want to stay here.'

✳❋✳

They prepared lunch – cold turkey, potato croquettes, grilled tomatoes – and fed everyone.

After that they all stood on the doorstep and waved as Gavin drove Gladys and Larry to the pier.

And now Laura was settling the four older children in front of a *Shaun the Sheep* DVD in the sitting room, and Tilly was waiting in the kitchen, her heart in her mouth, for her to reappear.

We'll talk, she'd said, after lunch. That was all, four words, not nearly enough to give any clue as to what she was thinking, or how she'd taken the news.

Had Tilly ruined everything? Despite Laura's promise that she wouldn't send her away, was this just too much? Was Tilly about to be packed off and told never to show her face on Roone again?

She swept the same bit of floor she'd been sweeping for the last several minutes. There was nothing else she could think of to do, and she had to do something. If she sat down and thought about it she'd feel sick.

Laura had had cancer, just a few months ago. Tilly knew people who had died from cancer – everyone knew someone who'd died from it. And even though Laura had got the all-clear, she was still terribly anxious about it. She'd told Tilly as much – and now Tilly had dumped a whole new worry in her lap. Who could blame her if she washed her hands of it?

The door opened. Tilly almost dropped the broom.

'Right,' Laura said, depositing Poppy in her playpen, taking a seat. 'Tell me everything, the whole kit and caboodle.'

So Tilly propped the broom against the wall and told her everything, and Laura listened without interruption until she'd finished.

'So,' she said then, 'let me get this clear. This teacher – what did you call him?'

'John Smith.'

The name, Tilly realised, had lost its power over her. Somewhere between Australia and Ireland it had become meaningless: it had gone back to being simply the name people used when they were trying to become anonymous. It was actually, she thought, a really boring name. It was a name designed to be forgotten.

'So this John Smith took advantage of you—'

Tilly felt a wash of heat on her face. 'No,' she said. 'I can't blame him. I – I wanted it too. I didn't object when it happened.'

'Tilly, you were sixteen.'

'... Yes.'

'And he's what – late twenties? Thirty? Older?'

'I don't know ... around that.'

'So this older man, in a position of authority, asked you, one of his sixteen-year-old students, to meet him outside school hours, to talk about, what – something he'd asked you to write?'

'An article, he said his friend had a magazine ...' She trailed off, cringing again at the thought that she'd bared her soul to him with the piece she'd written. She remembered wondering if the friend even existed, or if John Smith had invented him. She remembered being thrilled at the notion.

'So,' Laura was saying, 'he got you to meet him under false pretences, and then he initiated sex with you.'

'... Yes.'

'And I'm going to assume it was your first time.'

Tilly nodded quickly.

'And it happened more than once.'

'Yes.'

'And did he ever use protection?'

'No.'

How sordid it all sounded now. She recalled her devastation when he'd vanished, when Mrs Harvey had walked into the classroom instead of him. She remembered how she'd held in her tears until she got home, how she'd sobbed her heart out in the shower so nobody would know. How she'd cried herself to sleep for ages afterwards.

She could hardly remember what he looked like.

'And when was your last period?'

'Around the middle of October.'

'I presume you've seen a doctor, or done a pregnancy test?'

'I did a test.'

The terror of the twin blue lines had made her retch. Up to that minute she'd been tamping down her dreadful suspicions; she'd been telling herself she was being ridiculous. The blue lines had taken away her hope. The blue lines had thrown her into a panic. She'd booked her ticket to Ireland the next day, reaching blindly for the only escape route she could see.

'Give me your hand,' Laura said, and Tilly put it into her sister's.

'It wasn't your fault,' Laura said. 'You were sixteen. He was the adult. He behaved abominably. He took advantage of the fact that you were young and innocent, and probably making it clear that you fancied him, but you did nothing wrong.'

Tilly looked at her wordlessly. It wasn't true, of course. She'd gone to meet him hoping for something to happen. She'd wanted it as much as he had. She hadn't resisted when he'd begun.

'You should report him,' Laura said. 'You should tell the head of your school what happened. He'll do it again, unless he's stopped. He'll do exactly the same to another girl in the next school that takes him in. Tilly, he should be facing criminal charges.'

Criminal charges: that meant a court case. The thought horrified Tilly – everyone discovering what had happened, what they'd done. What *she*'d done.

'Look,' Laura said, 'we can leave that aside, but you do need to think about it.'

'I will.'

She wouldn't.

'Now,' Laura went on, 'as to your staying here …' She paused, holding Tilly's gaze. 'Am I to take it,' she asked, 'that your parents know nothing about this pregnancy?'

'Yes,' Tilly whispered.

'And they're expecting you home in a few days.'

'… Yes.'

'And can you imagine,' Laura asked softly, 'how they'd feel if you didn't go home?'

Tilly couldn't answer. She didn't want to think about it, didn't want to consider the hurt she'd cause. But of course she *had* thought about it, couldn't help thinking about it, couldn't help remembering Pa handing over the dollars the day before she'd left, Ma getting up in the small hours to wave her off, neither of them dreaming for a second that they might not see her again – or not for a long time.

How could she do it? How could she be so despicable? But what choice did she have, when her reappearance, and all that would follow, was bound to cause them even more hurt?

There was a faint booming sound – an explosion, a collision – from the sitting room, followed by a spatter of laughter.

'I can't,' Tilly said. 'I can't go home and face them, I just can't. It would kill them.'

'So you're going to – what? – call them and say you've decided to stay in Ireland, just like that?'

Tilly took a breath. 'They don't know I'm here.'

Laura frowned. 'What? They don't know you're on Roone?'

'They don't know I'm in Ireland. I was afraid they wouldn't let me come if I told them.'

'So where do they think you are?'

'Bali.' She told her about the family who owned the restaurant where she waitressed.

'Good Lord,' Laura said faintly. 'So your parents don't know you're pregnant, and they think you're thousands of miles from here.'

'Yes.' Tilly looked down at their still-connected hands. 'I've made such a mess of everything,' she said. 'I bet you wish I'd never come.'

'You can cut that out right away,' Laura said sharply. 'Feeling sorry for yourself won't help a bit. It's true you're in a mess, so now we need to figure out what to do.'

Tilly clung to the 'we'. She looked up. 'Thank you.'

'Don't thank me yet – I haven't done anything. I need to think about all this. How are you feeling, by the way?'

'I'm OK.'

'No morning sickness?'

'I did at the start, a bit, but it's gone now. I've gone off coffee.'

'I went off oranges when I was expecting the boys. Couldn't look at them. It might be no harm to let Dr Jack have a look at you.'

'A doctor?'

'Yes, just to make sure things are OK, and to give you some advice.'

'Yes … OK.' The thought of being examined by a doctor, of having to answer his questions, was unnerving, but she could hardly refuse.

'I'll give him a ring tomorrow – or we can drive to his clinic if the phones are still out.' Laura glanced at the clock on the wall and got to her feet, releasing Tilly's hand. 'Right. Susan will be here in an hour or two. Can I leave you in charge while Poppy and I grab a nap?'

'Of course.' That much at least she could do.

'Send one of the boys up to wake me if we're not back down by half four, or if Susan arrives before then.' Laura lifted Poppy from the playpen. At the door she turned. 'You should ring your parents when the phones come back,' she said, 'and tell them where you are. You should do that much anyway.'

And without waiting for Tilly to respond, she left. Tilly sat on, watching the flickers behind the stove window as occasional small eruptions of sound – crashes, bangs, more laughter – continued from the sitting room.

She thought about phoning her parents and telling them where she was. Admitting that she'd lied to them again, shattering their trust in her once more. She'd have to call them, she knew that – she wasn't simply going to disappear, she wouldn't be so cruel – but not yet, not until she had to.

Eventually she rose and got the coal bucket from the scullery and added another shovelful to the stove. Charlie, dozing in his basket, lifted his head and looked at her.

'It's a dog's life,' she told him, and he stretched all four legs at once and yawned. She replaced the bucket and looked through the little scullery window and saw Gavin, back from the pier and heading towards the henhouse. The sight reminded her of the old man she'd seen there, and Laura's rather strange reaction when Tilly had mentioned him. He must be a relative, with his picture hanging in their hall. Maybe they'd fallen out.

Back in the kitchen she resumed her seat at the table and sank her head into her hands. This trip was so full of *happenings*: it was pulling her in every direction, making her feel so much. She was worn out from it.

But at least now Laura knew about the pregnancy, and she

hadn't sent her away, and she was going to help. Laura, she realised, knew more about her than anyone else, even Lien – and Laura, she suspected, was very good at finding solutions.

Of course, there was one thing Tilly hadn't shared with her. Couldn't share.

Saw you earlier, he'd said in Nell's kitchen, his smile making her want to turn somersaults all around the room. His hand when he'd shaken hers was cold after his walk: she'd had the urge to tuck it under her layers of T-shirts and sweater, to press it to her stomach and warm him with her skin.

And his face, anytime she'd dared to glance at it. And his voice, and the way he'd lifted his little brother onto his lap – *Hey, buddy* – and the way he'd thanked Nell when she'd put the hot chocolate before him. Not a bite of gingerbread could she eat, even before he'd appeared, such havoc he'd been playing with her insides.

She was in love, or something, with a boy – a man – she'd set eyes on for the first time today. She was pregnant. As far as hopeless situations were concerned, this one deserved a medal.

❄❄❄

'Look at us,' she said. 'Ladies of leisure.'

Beside her, Poppy waved her arms about and pumped her fat little legs in the air.

'Aerobics,' Laura said, 'very good. Twenty minutes of that every day, you won't go far wrong. And never, ever smoke, or I'll ground you until you're sixty.'

Poppy brought her fists to her nose and rubbed, and sneezed – and immediately afterwards yawned.

'I know,' Laura said, around her own answering yawn, 'but we have to get up in a minute, because your nice granny is coming to see you – and guess what? You're not going to be the only baby in the family for much longer, so make the most of it.'

What time was it? From what she could see, twilight was well advanced outside: it must be four, or after it. The clock radio was tilted the wrong way; she reached across and adjusted it, and saw that it was twenty past four. She'd slept, they both had, for nearly two hours. Now they were lolling in the double bed, having a somewhat one-sided chat, and Laura was taking stock.

Gladys and Larry would be on the train to Dublin by now. She tried and failed to imagine their conversation. She and Gladys had never become properly acquainted. They'd never sat down and had a heart-to-heart about anything. She knew nothing about her mother-in-law's interests: did she ever go to the theatre, was she a member of any club, did she have friends other than the Joyce she'd been planning to have Christmas dinner with?

She had a gentleman friend for the next couple of days. Presumably she'd take Larry out and about a bit, show him a few art galleries maybe, take him to a play or a concert. They could have quite a time, the two of them.

She turned her thoughts to Tilly and her revelations. Pregnant at sixteen, seduced by her teacher. Running away to Ireland, letting on to her parents that she was going to Bali. Telling the whole thing to Laura, looking at her with the same hopeful expression that Charlie wore when he thought she had a treat for him. Did she expect Laura to wave a magic wand and make it all go away?

Booked her flight to Ireland in a panic, no doubt, when she found out she was pregnant. Travelling to the only place she could think of, travelling to the only *person* she could think of who might help her.

She had a return ticket, but she didn't want to return. She wanted to stay here, presumably to go on living with Laura and Gavin until the baby came. She probably had some romantic notion about them all living happily together, like some hippie commune.

She'd make a good mother, though. Look at her with Poppy – she was a natural.

'What'll we do at all?' she asked aloud – and at the sound of her mother's voice Poppy tossed her legs about some more.

Just then Laura's phone rang. She plucked it from the bedside table and pressed the answer key before the significance of it ringing dawned on her.

'Finally,' Susan said. 'I've been trying to get hold of you since yesterday.'

'The phones have been down – you're the first call I've got since Christmas Eve. Where are you?'

'On the ferry. We've just taken off.'

'Did you drive?'

'No, train and bus.'

'Great, I'll send—' She broke off. 'No, I'll come and collect you myself.' She'd tell Susan about Tilly before she brought her home, give her a bit of advance notice.

She dressed hurriedly, dabbed on foundation and blusher, added lipstick, coaxed some life into her hair with wax. She put Poppy into a clean dress and tights and brought her downstairs.

The sitting room was deserted, and smelt of crisps. She found everyone in the kitchen, the boys playing with the football board game that Gladys had given them for Christmas, the girls sitting on either side of Tilly on the window seat as she read to them from *Chicken Licken*. Charlie was under the table, gnawing happily on his new dolly.

'I'm heading to the pier to collect Susan,' Laura said to Tilly. 'We might stop off for coffee – can I leave you on duty here for another while?'

'Sure.'

'Do you know where Gavin is?'

'Out in the field.'

Still working, in the near darkness. Laura placed Poppy in the playpen. 'She'll need feeding in a little while,' she said, 'twenty minutes or so. I'll get Gavin to come in—' but Tilly said no, no, she'd do it after the story.

'I feel like I'm putting you to work,' Laura said, pulling on her jacket.

Tilly smiled. 'Go to the pier.'

More at ease, it seemed, since she'd opened up to Laura. Her problems shared, two of them now to find solutions.

'By the way,' Laura said, her hand on the scullery door, 'the phones are back' – and by the slight dimming of Tilly's smile she knew she was thinking of her parents, and the call Laura had suggested she make. She'd say nothing more, let Tilly make that decision.

She found Gavin in the vegetable plot, forking up the frozen earth between the rows, banishing the last of the snow from them.

'We have phones again,' she told him. 'Susan rang, she's on her way. I'm going to collect her.'

'I can go.'

'No, I want to do it. Tilly will stay with the lads, and she's going to do Poppy's next feed. You might put your head in in a while, make sure they're not killing her.'

'OK.'

'I'll bring Susan to Lelia's,' she said, 'for a chat on our own.' She hadn't mentioned Susan's news to him, plenty of time for that. Now there were two babies he didn't know about.

'Fine.'

'And I have a turkey casserole in the fridge, I forgot to say it to Tilly – will you put it in at gas six at five o'clock?'

'I will.'

'You won't forget?'

'No.'

He was still in a huff about Tilly. Let him, she had bigger things to worry about. Driving the short distance to the pier, skirting the slushy puddles, she remembered that she still hadn't thanked him for the necklace. Maybe that's what had him in a huff.

She drove past Andy, walking in the direction of the village with Gary O'Donnell and Clive Mason and the boy of the McDowds whose name she could never remember – Ollie? Donny? She tooted the horn and they waved.

The ferry was approaching. She parked and sat watching as Leo steered it smoothly onto the ramp. She got out and waited while the few cars drove off – and here came Susan in their wake, the only foot passenger, pulling a navy blue case behind her.

Grey coat, dark hair hidden under a black hat, pushing a red scarf down from her face as she approached. Not looking any different, now that she was pregnant.

They embraced like they always did on meeting and leaving one another, hard, warm hugs that lasted. Susan smelt of the grapefruit scent she'd worn for years. 'Good to see you,' Laura murmured.

'You too. Wish you weren't so far away.'

They drew apart. 'How are you?' Susan asked.

'Can't complain – you?'

'Fine.' But the word had little conviction in it. Before Laura could comment Susan said, with some surprise, 'You had snow here too. I wouldn't have thought it could.'

Laura reached for the case and began pulling it towards the car. 'It never did before, as far as I know. You missed the snowman at Walter's Place – he's practically a puddle now. We're getting weird weather this Christmas: we had a bad storm two nights ago that toppled one of our apple trees.'

'Ah no, that's too bad. It didn't damage the house?'

'No.' She'd tell her the story of the shed later. She deposited the case and slammed the boot shut. 'Let's go to Lelia's and have a chat. Once we get back we'll have no time on our own.'

'How was Christmas?' Susan enquired as they walked the short distance to the village, and Laura filled her in on the party that had been interrupted by the storm drama, and Gladys's collapse the following morning, and the unexpected arrival of Larry. She waited until they were sitting in the café with two glasses of Lelia's hot cinnamon fruit punch in front of them before telling her about Tilly.

'Can you believe it? A sister I never knew about, turning up on the doorstep.'

'A sister,' Susan said. 'A full sister.'

'Yes – it seems my mother didn't know she was expecting before she left Ireland.'

She'd leave out Tilly's pregnancy, let her digest this much first.

Susan took a sip of punch. The café was full of walkers in brightly coloured jackets, none of whom Laura recognised. A group from the mainland over for the day.

'Or maybe she did know,' Susan said then, so low that Laura hardly heard it above the chatter.

'What?'

'She might have known. Your mother.'

'What do you mean?'

No response.

'Susan, why did you say that? Do you know something – has my father said something?'

She shook her head. 'I don't know anything about your mother, Laura. All I know is that Luke definitely doesn't want another child.'

Her voice calm, the words steady, but her face all of a sudden wretched in its sadness.

'Oh, Susan …' but of course it came as no surprise to Laura, none at all. He'd never wanted to be a father. He'd all but washed his hands of Laura after her mother left.

'What has he said?'

Susan rubbed at the creases in her forehead. 'He wants me to get rid of it.' The words had a crisp, bitten-off sound to them. 'It wouldn't surprise me if your mother had known, and told him, and got the same reaction I got.'

Was it true? Had they known about the pregnancy before Diane went away? Laura raced through the implications, each more depressing than the last.

It would mean that he was aware he'd fathered another child, whom he presumably had no desire to meet.

It would mean that he'd issued some kind of an ultimatum to his wife – what? 'Me or the child'? – that had caused her to leave.

It would mean that their mother had lied to Tilly when she'd claimed not to know she was pregnant when she was leaving Ireland. It would mean that she'd lied to Tilly when she'd told her that her father wasn't aware of her existence.

But hold on – maybe they were mistaken, maybe they were jumping to the wrong conclusion here. Diane might have known she was expecting a child, but maybe she hadn't told him. Maybe she'd known what he'd say, and had decided to leave rather than hear it.

But that wasn't what they needed to talk about now. Laura searched Susan's face. 'What are you going to do?'

Susan shook her head slowly. 'I have no idea,' she replied, 'but I know what I'm *not* going to do.'

Forty years old, and pregnant for the first time. How could he? How could he ask her to do that horrible thing, that unspeakable act? It was sickening. The man was a monster.

They sat while their drinks cooled and the conversations went on around them. At length Susan drained her glass. 'Come on,' she said. 'I'm dying to meet the lads – and very curious to see my new stepdaughter.'

Laura got to her feet, fishing her purse from her bag. 'On the house,' Lelia said, passing them with a loaded tray. 'A thank-you for the party the other night.'

The party, which now seemed like it had happened a decade ago. She thanked Lelia and held the door open for Susan to pass through. She linked her arm with her stepmother's and they walked down the village street in silence together.

Laura wondered what the next few months would bring, for Susan and all of them. No more dramas would be nice, she thought. No more surprises, at least for a while, would be just lovely.

Little guessing, as they reached the car and got in, as she stuck her key in the ignition and turned for home, that the next drama was almost upon them.

❄❄❄

Gavin slid the casserole onto the oven shelf and closed the door. 'Four years ago we both came on holidays to Roone,' he said. 'We each rented out Nell's house in July. I took it for the first two weeks, and Laura and the boys came straight after.'

'But you didn't meet here.'

'No – I'd gone before they arrived. I left a book behind in the house, and Laura found it.'

'How did she know it was yours?'

'It had a Dublin Zoo bookmark in it – I worked there at the time. She showed it to Nell, and Nell said it had to be mine, so when they got home Laura and the boys paid a visit to the zoo and found me.'

'And you'd both grown up in Dublin.'

'Yeah, about a mile from one another. You should see her family home though – mine would fit into it three times.'

'Does our father still live there?'

'He does.' A beat passed. 'I presume Laura's told you a bit about him.' A careful tone to the words now, a more cautious expression on his face.

'She told me his name,' Tilly replied, 'and that he's a famous artist.' Now it was her turn to hesitate. 'She said … they weren't close.' Not sure how much she should repeat, not wanting him to think she was gossiping.

He didn't appear bothered. 'They're not,' he said, 'not close at all. As far as I can gather, they never were. Laura moved out as soon as she could, and they've seen very little of one another since then.'

'He doesn't know about me,' Tilly said. 'My mother didn't tell him.'

He made no reply – what was there to say? – but his expression was kind.

'What's he like?' she asked.

He lifted his shoulders. 'To be honest, I hardly know. I haven't met him often enough, or for long enough. Whenever we're in Dublin Laura goes to see him, and sometimes she'll bring the boys, but I rarely go with her. He came to our wedding, which was here on the island, but he left early the next day.' He shrugged again. 'I must say he's always perfectly civil when we meet, but … you sort of get the feeling he's only putting up with you until you leave.'

He's not child-friendly, Laura had said. Or adult-friendly, by the sound of it. Maybe he was different when he was among other artists – maybe he opened up then, maybe he relaxed in the company of people who thought like him, who lived in his world.

'*Fwog!*' Evie exclaimed suddenly.

She and Marian sat across from Tilly and Gavin, poking and pulling at lumps of multi-coloured Plasticine. The table around them was littered with scraps of the stuff; more of it was stuck to the sleeves and fronts of their Christmas dresses, which they'd insisted on changing into for Susan's arrival. A blue blob had attached itself to one of Evie's curls. Charlie hovered by their chairs, snapping up any bits that came his way. Tilly wondered if there was anything he didn't eat.

Gavin peered closely at Evie's endeavour. 'Well, that's just about the best frog I ever saw. Bet you can't make a snake.'

'Yeth, I *can*.'

'Go on so.'

Tilly looked at Marian, still busily prodding at her Plasticine. 'What are you making?'

'Fwog.'

'Inherited their grandfather's artistic ability, obviously,' Gavin murmured.

Tilly smiled. 'And what's Susan like?' She was curious to meet her father's second wife. She wanted to compare her with Diane, see if she could pick out any characteristics in common.

'Susan is delightful,' Gavin told her. 'The lads are mad about her – she comes to visit quite often.'

He was easy to talk to, generous with his information. What else could he tell her? 'Did you ever meet our mother?'

'No. The last time she was in Ireland, I didn't know Laura.'

So Diane hadn't seen the girls, had never been to Roone.

Gavin picked a scrap of Plasticine from the table and rolled it between his fingers. 'Can I ask what you thought, when you met her?'

Tilly watched Marian's little fingers as they kneaded and pulled. 'I had no idea what to expect. I knew nothing about her, apart from the fact that she came from Ireland, and she'd given me up right after I was born.'

She thought back to the thin, anxious face in the café. 'When we met, I got the impression she wasn't happy. Not at ease with herself. And we didn't really … connect. We didn't make any arrangement to meet again – she didn't suggest it.'

'It must have been difficult for you,' he said quietly.

'Yes, it upset me.'

'You'd wonder,' he said, his eyes on the girls, 'what would make a mother abandon her children.'

'You would …'

A short silence fell between them.

'Can you tell me,' she said then, 'who the man in the painting is?' He might be able to clear up the mystery.

'The painting?'

'In the hall. The old man.'

'Oh – that's Walter. James painted him, Nell's husband.'

'Walter? Is he a relative?'

'No – he owned this house before us. He was living here while we were renting Nell's house. We both met him.'

'Ah.'

'He was a nice old soul,' Gavin went on. 'A real gentleman, you know? Terribly polite and old school. I often wonder what he'd think of us living in his house. We've tried to preserve the feel of it, but obviously we had to make a lot of changes when we turned it into a B&B.'

The previous owner didn't know they lived here? That made no sense to Tilly. 'Didn't you buy the house from him?'

He gave a faint smile. 'Hardly.' He lowered his voice, glancing again at the girls, who were paying them no attention. 'Walter died.'

'He *died*?' Quietly too, darting a look across the table.

'The night before Laura and the boys were due to leave the island. She didn't know about it till Nell told her in an email a few days later – poor man wasn't found till after they left. And I'd probably never have heard if Laura hadn't tracked me down to give me back the book.'

The man was dead, so Tilly couldn't have seen him. A brother then maybe, some other family member. It didn't matter.

It had thrown Laura though, when Tilly had claimed to have seen him. It had been disconcerting for her, knowing he was dead. It explained her silence.

'I thought I saw him yesterday. It must have been someone else.'

'Must have. It was actually Andy who found him – have you met Andy?'

'Um, yes.' Reaching for her own scrap of Plasticine, giving herself a reason to drop her gaze. The sudden mention of his name causing a rearrangement of her entire insides. 'Where did it happen?'

'Right here in the house, upstairs on the landing. Andy was doing work for him at the time, I think. Clearing out the attic, or something.'

Four years ago Andy would have been in his mid-teens. Already having endured the loss of his mother, then having the misfortune to stumble on a dead body.

Just then the front door clicked open. 'Susan's here,' Gavin told the girls – and straight away Evie and Marian abandoned the Plasticine and scrambled down from their chairs, and collided with Laura as she entered the room.

'Steady on, you two,' she said, but they ignored her – 'Thuthan! Thuthan!' – in their haste to reach the woman behind her, who stooped to wrap her arms around both of them.

'My princesses!' she cried, planting noisy kisses on each cheek in turn before reaching up to pull off her hat. '*Look* at your beautiful dresses! I've missed you *so* much!' A tumble of richly coloured auburn hair, an attractive huskiness to her voice.

It was clear the girls adored her. They clung to her as she entered the kitchen – and now here came the boys through the back door, football under Ben's arm, eager to be around her too. Grinning as she ruffled their hair and exclaimed at how tall they were getting. Backing away as she wondered aloud if they'd like a hug.

'And this is Tilly,' Laura said, when she got the chance, and Susan extended a hand, smiling.

'Laura's told me about you,' she said. 'What a surprise, a new stepdaughter.'

Her speech was less heavily accented than Laura's or Gavin's, less polished than Colette's. Taller than Laura, shorter than Tilly. Brown-eyed, clear-skinned, wide-mouthed. Make-up barely there – or so cleverly applied that it seemed barely there.

Her shoulder-length hair was tousled, some of it caught beneath a deep red scarf that was draped loosely about her neck. A large diamond ring winked in the light as she tucked a strand behind an ear.

She pulled off the scarf and removed her coat to reveal a navy sweater and dark blue jeans. Not thin, and not plump exactly. Solidly built was how you'd describe her, broad-hipped and -shouldered. Maybe not what magazines would deem pretty, but pleasingly large eyes and mouth. A calm wide smile displaying teeth that were perfectly regular. Her smile looked like she meant it.

Different from Diane, as different as Tilly could imagine, was her first impression. More grounded, more sure of herself, none of the jittery, fluttery mannerisms, none of the fragility that had seemed to emanate from Diane.

'Gavin,' she said, opening her arms, 'good to see you.'

'Likewise.' Their hug was genuine, their warmth for one another evident.

'And where's Her Majesty the Queen?' she asked, drawing back, and Poppy was duly taken from her playpen to be kissed and exclaimed over.

'Now,' Susan said, 'presents.'

'Oh, leave that till later,' Laura said – but Susan unzipped the case and produced wrapped packages that were excitedly torn open to reveal DVDs and annuals and bangles and paper dress-up dolls.

'The usual,' she said, handing a box to Laura that turned out to be perfume.

'Something to keep our gardener warm,' she said, and Gavin unwrapped a fur-lined brown leather hat with ear-flaps, which he placed directly on his head, and pronounced to be just what he'd always wanted.

Another hat was produced, this time for Poppy, sky blue with scattered green dots and a giant green pompom. Finally, she turned to Tilly. 'I hate to leave you out,' she said – and even as Tilly was protesting, she was hunting in the case until she unearthed a small box of chocolate-covered almonds. 'Any good?' she asked. 'I brought a few in case we went visiting. Do take them – I'll feel better.'

So Tilly took them, and Gavin announced just then that dinner would be ready in ten minutes, and that everyone should wash hands.

Tilly accompanied Susan upstairs. 'Your usual quarters,' Laura had said, which turned out to be the room Gladys had vacated, and which someone, presumably Laura, had tidied since then. Must have been while Tilly had been out walking.

Out walking. Andy Baker.

'I love this house,' Susan said, leaving her case by the bed and crossing to the window without turning on the light, although by now it was fully dark outside. 'Isn't it wonderful?'

'It is.' Tilly hovered in the doorway, wondering whether to leave or stay. Light from the landing threw a yellow slice into the room.

'Come and look,' Susan said, so Tilly joined her at the window. They stood side by side, taking in a sky that was packed with stars, and an enormous milky disc of a moon that hung low over the horizon, and a sea that dazzled beneath it, millions of tiny pinpricks of light dancing and jumping on its surface.

'You have different stars here,' Tilly said.

'Oh yes – we do, don't we? That must be strange. Can you see them as clearly where you live?'

'Yes – we're out the country, on a farm.'

'Not by the sea?'

'No. A long way from the sea.'

A car passed by on the road, going in the direction of the village. Tilly watched its headlights cutting through the dark. She followed it until it disappeared, and the silence took over again.

Susan pushed the window open a crack. 'Listen,' she murmured – and Tilly listened, and heard the distant low thunder of the water.

'Imagine living here,' Susan went on softly. 'Imagine never having to leave. Imagine if you could have this all the time, every night.'

Something, some tiny catch in her voice, made Tilly glance at her. A silvery tear was snaking slowly down her cheek. Without a sign of embarrassment she reached up and brushed it away.

'Don't mind me,' she said. 'My hormones are all over the place. I assume Laura told you I was pregnant.'

'She did – congratulations.' Tilly let a few seconds pass, wondering if Susan knew that she was too, but no further comment was made. 'When did you and … my father meet?'

Silence. Maybe she shouldn't have asked. Maybe it was too soon for a question like that.

Eventually Susan said, 'It was at an art auction, a fundraiser for the school where I worked.'

'You're a teacher?'

'No – a secretary. I went along to the auction, just to help out. Luke was there. He'd contributed a painting, and agreed to come along and say a few words. It was a big coup for the school: a father of one of our students owned a gallery where Luke exhibited.' She lifted a hand, let it drop. 'We were introduced, we got talking ...' She trailed off.

Tilly waited for more, but no more came. 'Well,' she said, moving off, 'I'd better get ready for dinner.'

'See you downstairs,' Susan replied, not looking around.

At the door Tilly paused. 'Will I put on the light?'

'No,' Susan said, still looking out. 'Not for the moment,' so Tilly left the door ajar.

In her room she took her phone from her pocket and opened her outbox and found the text message she'd been unable to send the day before. *Happy Christmas, love my present, thank you. Miss you all.* She added *Sorry, been having problems with the phone signal, all well now* and pressed *send*. She watched it heading off to Ma. Middle of the night at home, she'd see it first thing in the morning.

While she was putting Susan's chocolates into her suitcase she spotted the present she'd brought for Laura, and forgotten about. She'd give it to her next chance she got.

In the bathroom she brushed her teeth and tidied her hair and put on a fresh slick of lip gloss. She switched off her light and groped through the sudden darkness to the window. A different view from Susan's room but the same stars. The hills were silhouetted against the sky, black against paler black, their outlines already becoming familiar, something comforting about their hulking shapes. She recalled how luminous with snow they'd been at the start of the day, and she wondered how they'd appear the next time she looked out, and the next.

Imagine never having to leave.

Imagine her baby being born here.

She pulled her curtains closed and went downstairs.

❄

SUNDAY
27 DECEMBER

❄

✳✱✳

I t took several seconds, maybe more than that, to make her way out of sleep, her befuddled brain crawling back to consciousness as she forced her head to turn towards the bedside locker, where the noise was coming from.

The noise, which was her phone.

Her eyes were still closed. She slid an arm across the sheet until her hand connected with the locker. She felt about, and sent her tube of hand cream sliding off to land with a flat thump on the floor. She brushed against the clock-radio, and the base of the lamp, and managed not to knock over her water glass. She didn't find what she was looking for.

She unglued her eyelids, blinked them open. 8:47 was the first thing she saw, in bright green winking digits. Sunday morning, not even nine o'clock, and someone, some ignoramus, was ringing her. Someone wasn't going to stop until she answered. A miracle Poppy hadn't woken.

Gavin up and gone, even on Sunday.

The phone rang on. Better be life or death.

She levered herself into a vaguely upright position and spotted the phone sitting on the far side of the radio. She reached across and grabbed it, and slid back down under the duvet.

Gladys's name showed in the display. Her mother-in-law was ringing her at this ungodly hour: she might have known it would be Gladys. Forgot one of her knitting needles, left her reading glasses behind. She debated cutting her off, but decency prevailed. She pressed the answer key.

'Gladys.' A croaky mumble, which was all she deserved.

'Mrs Connolly … Laura.'

She blinked. Not Gladys, a man.

'It's Larry Kawalski,' he said.

Larry Kawalski, this early in the morning. On Gladys's phone. Laura sat up, snapping suddenly into gear. 'Larry,' she said. 'What is it, what's wrong?'

A loud exhalation. 'Listen,' he said, 'I don't know … this is difficult—'

He stopped. Laura waited, prickling with dread. Something had happened to Gladys.

'It's your mother-in-law,' he said. 'It's Mrs Connolly senior. I'm afraid … I have to tell you' – Laura felt her stomach clenching – 'I'm sorry,' he said, 'I have to tell you … that she … she passed away, just a little while ago. She … just … I'm sorry—'

He came to an abrupt halt.

Gladys was dead.

Laura jumped into the silence. 'It's OK, Larry, it's OK. We'll come to Dublin, just as soon as we can—'

Gladys was dead. Gladys was gone.

She scrambled from the bed, hunting for underwear with one hand as he stammered out his account of how he'd got up to use the bathroom an hour or so earlier and found the door locked and silence within, how he'd called and got no response, and gone in search of help, and eventually roused a neighbour.

'He came back with me and broke the lock on the door, and … well, we found her, we found Mrs Connolly.' An out-of-hours doctor had been summoned and Gladys had been pronounced dead. Larry had located her phone, he'd scrolled through her contacts and found both Gavin and Laura's names, and chosen to ring Laura rather than have Gavin hear over the phone that his mother was dead.

Gladys was dead.

'The doctor's just called some guys, some paramedics,' he told

Laura. 'Mrs Connolly's gonna be laid out in her room here until Mr Connolly gets in touch, lets him know what he wants done.'

Gavin had to be told, she had to tell him. She found tracksuit bottoms, a cleanish shirt and a cardigan. As she struggled into them she assured Larry that he was welcome to remain in the house for his final night in Ireland – wondering, even as she said it, where on earth they'd all fit. She took the doctor's number from him, scribbling it on the back of a receipt she found in her bag.

'I'll call you back,' she promised, 'as soon as we're on the road. In the meantime, maybe you should find a hotel and have some breakfast.' Cringing, even as she spoke, at how trite it sounded. Sending him to a hotel for a full Irish, after what he'd just been through. A good stiff brandy was what he needed.

'The Piggotts offered me breakfast,' he told her. Laura had never heard of the Piggotts, but she presumed they were the Good Samaritan neighbours who'd come to his aid. 'They wanted me to stay at their place till you got here, but I didn't like to leave Mrs Connolly alone.'

Poor man, trying to do the right thing. 'Thank you, Larry. Sorry you had to go through this.' As if he hadn't enough sadness to deal with.

'She was a kind lady,' he said, his voice trembling. 'She was kind to me.'

He was talking about Gladys in the past tense. It sounded wrong. It jarred like a radio not quite tuned correctly, like someone singing slightly off-key. But Gladys *had* been kind to Larry, a man in sore need of kindness at this time. Laura recalled her mental sniggering at the thought of the two of them heading off to Dublin together, and felt ashamed. 'Take care of yourself,' she told him. 'Try and get some rest. I'll be in touch soon, I promise. We'll see you this afternoon.'

As she hung up, her bedroom door opened and the girls appeared. She ushered them back to their own room and got them dressed quickly – and as they emerged into the corridor again, Poppy could be heard chattering to Rabbity, so back they all went to change and dress her too, and begin another day.

As Laura peeled off the damp nappy, she recalled everyone assembled at the gate yesterday to say goodbye to Gladys and Larry. 'See you in the spring,' Gladys had called, waving out the car window as Gavin had driven them away. Thank God, Laura had thought, waving back. Thank God she's gone.

And now Laura had to break it to Gavin that his mother, who'd been alive and well this time yesterday, was dead.

But Gladys hadn't been well, had she? They should have acted on that collapse two days ago: they should have insisted on her staying in bed, at least, like Dr Jack had recommended.

And hadn't he written a prescription, something for her blood pressure? Laura had completely forgotten about it till now. They could have called on Dick Flannery, Roone's chemist, to fill it. Dick would have obliged them, she was sure. So careless they'd been, so unthinking.

But Gladys had seemed fine, hadn't she? She'd eaten her meals, hadn't complained of aches or pains. She'd gone off to Dublin with Larry in high spirits. Who could have seen this coming?

In the corridor the boys' bedroom door was wide open, their room deserted. Laura tapped softly on Tilly and Susan's doors in turn and got no response from either. Both still asleep; she'd leave them a little longer, until she had to call at least one of them.

But there they were in the kitchen, not asleep after all. Tilly was at the fridge, Susan was nursing a cup of something at the table and looking tired, although she'd gone to bed directly after dinner the night before.

The boys were eating cereal and reading comics – and Gavin was there too, still wearing his jacket and Susan's leather hat, taking brown eggs from the basket and slotting them into boxes at the worktop.

'Here they come,' he said, 'all the sleepyheads.' Not meeting Laura's eyes. Talking to his daughters, not to her.

'Morning,' Susan said, 'we were just about to phone the guards.' Opening her arms for Poppy, so Laura passed her over.

'I was going to put on sausages,' Tilly said, 'if that's OK.'

'That's fine.' Laura settled the girls at the table. 'You might fill the kettle for Poppy's formula too.'

'Sure.'

'Gavin,' Laura went on lightly, 'can you come outside? I want to show you something.'

'Just a sec,' he said, not pausing in his task.

'Now,' she said. 'Please.'

He glanced up, saw her face.

'Back in a minute,' Laura told the others, throwing a look in Susan's direction – but Susan was murmuring to Poppy, her head bowed.

He walked out ahead of her. As she followed him through the scullery she grabbed her old quilted jacket and pulled it on. The day was breezy and dry, not a trace of yesterday's snow to be seen, a tiny red dot of a cap in the field the only evidence that a snowman had briefly existed there. She led Gavin across to the orchard and found a spot that wasn't overlooked by the house.

She told him, as gently as she could, that his mother was dead.

His face collapsed. His eyes filled.

'It happened quickly,' she said. 'She didn't suffer.' She reached for him but he stepped back, shaking his head.

'Gavin—'

'No,' he said, his hand shielding his face from her as his shoulders began to shake. 'Leave me alone.' His other arm raised to keep her away, not wanting her comfort.

'Gavin, please—'

'*No.*' Throwing her a fierce look. 'Don't pretend you're sorry. You never liked her. Leave me alone, go back inside.'

A coldness in his voice she'd never heard before. She couldn't think what to say that wouldn't sound insincere.

'Leave me alone,' he repeated, but she couldn't go, she couldn't leave him.

'I'll pack,' she told him. 'We'll bring the boys with us and leave the three girls. Susan and Tilly will be here. It might be best to say nothing to the girls – about … Gladys, I mean.'

He ignored her. He turned his back on her, keeping his grief from her.

'You need to ring the doctor,' she said. 'He's waiting for instructions from you. I've got his number.'

They stood apart from one another, a million miles apart.

'I'm sorry,' she said. 'Gavin, I'm truly sorry.'

She waited another few minutes, listening to the sound of his sadness. Eventually she turned away, leaving him like he wanted.

'Send the boys out to me.'

She looked back. He was brushing a sleeve across his face. 'Send them out. I want to tell them.'

'Will you not come in and have something to eat?'

He gave a shuddering sigh. 'Just send out the boys, would you?'

So she left him among the apple trees and returned to the kitchen.

'Everything OK?' Susan asked. The only one who wasn't eating.

'Everything's fine,' Laura replied, knowing her face told a different story. She found a sachet of green tea and dropped it into a mug. 'Will you have breakfast?'

Susan shook her head. 'Can't face food till at least noon – I'll make up for it then.'

The boys were finishing their cereal. 'Your dad needs you outside for a minute,' Laura told them. 'Get your jackets on' – and off they went. The girls attempted to follow, but Laura distracted them with their treasure box of sparkly crayons and glue and scraps of fabric. While they were busy sticking and colouring, she told Tilly and Susan quietly about Gladys.

'We'll go as soon as we can arrange it,' she said. 'We'll take the boys – Gavin's telling them now – but we'll leave the girls.'

'When will you be back?' Tilly asked.

Laura thought. Today was Sunday, tomorrow the removal, Tuesday the funeral. 'We'll try and get back on Tuesday.' Half six the last ferry was in the winter: if they managed to leave Dublin right after lunch, whatever kind of lunch it turned out to be, they'd make it.

Two days was all she and Tilly had had together, less than two days. Barely beginning to get to know one another, and now Laura was leaving, and when she got back to Roone Tilly would be packing for Australia, if she hadn't already left.

Because of course she would go home. After sleeping on it, Laura had seen that there was no question of Tilly staying. She would phone her parents when she felt ready and she would tell them everything, and when she got home they'd deal with it, because that's what parents did.

How could it be otherwise? If Tilly stayed, if she had the baby here, how could things ever be the same with her adoptive parents? She'd do irreparable damage to them, and to their relationship with her. She'd said they were decent people – Laura couldn't help her to hurt them; she couldn't do it.

She and Tilly needed to talk. They needed to sit down and thrash it out – but when? And Susan needed to talk too: this was why she'd come to Roone. It was almost, Laura thought, as if Gladys had chosen the worst possible time to die. Even beyond the grave, she was doing her best to be awkward—

She stopped, appalled with herself. She slapped the thought away. She looked at Evie and Marian, engrossed in their coloured paper and fabric and glitter. 'I've never been without them,' she said, 'except when I was in hospital. I've never spent a single night apart from Poppy.'

'Don't worry,' Susan said. 'Tilly and I will spoil them rotten' – and she had to be content with that.

'What should we tell them?' she wondered aloud, eyeing them again. 'How will we get away?'

'I'll do it,' Susan said. 'Go and pack. I'll think of something while you're upstairs.'

Laura turned to Tilly. 'Will you come and help me?'

They climbed the stairs together, Laura rehearsing what was to be said in her head. Tilly ducked into her room – 'I'll be with you in a second' – so Laura got their biggest suitcase down from the attic. When she entered her room, Tilly stood there.

'This is for you,' she said, holding out a small package wrapped in pink tissue paper. 'I meant to give it to you before. I know this isn't the best time,' the words running into one another, the familiar flush sweeping up her face, 'but you're going away now and … well, it's just something small, I didn't know what to get, you might not even—'

'Stop,' Laura commanded. 'Give it here.' She dropped the shirt she was holding and took the package and unwrapped it. She unfolded the two brightly patterned cushion covers and held them up. She laid them out on the bed, side by side.

'It's Aboriginal art,' Tilly said. 'There's a store in our town.'

'Thank you, they're gorgeous.'

'Really?'

'Really. You didn't have to do that.'

Tilly smiled shyly. 'I wanted to.'

Awkward, in the light of what she had to say. Laura folded the cushion covers and moved them to the top of the dressing table. She turned and looked her sister full in the face.

'Tilly, I've been thinking about what you told me yesterday, and I really think the best thing for you to do is come clean to your parents, tell them everything, and go home on Wednesday.'

She watched the smile sliding off like wet putty, the skin around her eyes getting pink. 'I can't stay here? You're sending me away?'

'It's not that – it's not a question of me sending you anywhere. It just seems like the best thing to do. I'm sure your parents would much prefer if you went home to them. I'm sure they'll come to terms with it, once they have time to get used to—'

'You don't *know* them,' Tilly cried, dashing tears away before they had a chance to fall. 'You have no *idea* what they're like! You can't possibly know how they'd react. You said you'd help, you *said*.'

'Tilly, I *am* trying to help, I'm trying to do what's best—'

Footsteps sounded in the corridor: Tilly immediately wheeled and disappeared. A second later Gavin was at the door with two sombre boys in tow, and Laura had to switch her attention to them.

Their first close brush with death. You couldn't really count Nell's mother Moira, whom they hadn't known that well, or Walter, who'd been in their orbit for such a brief time. This was the real thing; this they could feel.

Laura sat them on the side of the bed and knelt on the floor beside them. 'You're very brave boys,' she said, finding hands to hold. 'Granny would be proud of you.'

'But why did she just *die*?' Ben wanted to know, in a voice that wobbled like Tilly's had. 'She was fine yesterday, she wasn't even sick.'

'It happens that way sometimes, lovey, especially when people get a bit older. The doctor will tell us what happened when we meet him.'

'Could *you*?' Seamus asked, his freckled face twisted with anxiety. 'Could you just die?' Ten years old, a child still. Laura regarded them both, her darling boys. She wanted to take away their troubles, she wanted to keep them far from everything bad.

But she had to tell them the truth. 'I could – but it would be very unusual, at my age.'

'But you were sick,' he said. 'You had cancer, an' Andy's real mum died of cancer.'

Too big a worry for him, much too big. 'A lot of people get better from cancer too,' she told him. 'I got better. I'm fine now.'

Hear that, God? No second doses: you'll make me into a liar.

'Will we have to look at Granny?' Seamus asked.

'Not if you don't want to.'

'I don't.'

'Me neither.'

'That's fine.'

She remembered her first corpse. Grandpa O'Mahony. He'd died less than a year before her mother had taken off for Australia, so Laura would have been about the boys' age, ten or eleven. Say goodbye to your grandfather, Luke had said, and Grandpa's yellow face in the coffin, looking nothing like Laura remembered, had been horrifying. He didn't look asleep, like her mother had said he would: he was like a wax dummy of himself, a macabre joke someone was playing on them.

And then Granny O'Mahony had died too, just a few months later. Another coffin, another unnerving face that Laura could hardly bring herself to look at. The life gone, that was the frightening thing. The spark that had made Granny O'Mahony into a person was missing. She and Grandpa had been extinguished.

Laura wondered suddenly if their deaths had had anything to do with her mother's departure. Might she have simply moved back home to their house in Kildare, rather than halfway around the world, if her parents had still been alive? Had their deaths actually been part of the reason she'd left?

No time to think about that now. It was coming up to half ten: they'd make the eleven o'clock ferry, they'd be in Dublin by late afternoon. She'd ring Larry when they got to the mainland, let him know they were on the way.

'Get your pyjamas,' she told the boys, 'and your toothbrushes.' The essentials, that was all they needed, and a smart set of clothes. 'Did you talk to the doctor?' she asked Gavin, who'd been standing silently by.

'Yes, it's sorted.' Looking at her waistline, or somewhere around there.

'What about your deliveries? Weren't you to start tomorrow?'

He shrugged. 'They'll have to wait.'

'They can't wait – we need the money.' Especially now, with a funeral to pay for. She thought quickly. Hugh had helped out before, when Laura was in hospital, but he and Imelda were going to Mayo this afternoon to visit her sister. 'Leave the order book with Susan – ask her to send Tilly over to Nell's with it later, she'll find someone.'

He nodded, went off without a word. Still keeping her at arm's length.

Finally they were ready to set off. Laura kissed the girls goodbye at the front door – 'I told them you're going to buy new saucepans,' Susan said, and Evie and Marian didn't look as if they minded in the least being excluded from such a boring task.

'We'll talk when I get back,' she promised Susan.

'We will, of course.'

There was no sign of Tilly, another person mad at Laura. 'She must be in her room,' Susan said, 'I'll get her,' but Laura said no need, they'd already said goodbye upstairs. Had Gavin noticed anything, she wondered, when Tilly had rushed past him in the corridor? Probably not: still reeling over the news of Gladys.

They drove to the pier and boarded the ferry, and Laura explained to Leo Considine why they had to leave, knowing that by the time they were halfway to their destination the whole of the island would know.

And somewhere on the long road to Dublin, while the boys read comics in the back seat and Gavin pretended to listen to the radio so he wouldn't have to talk to her, she thought about the task that awaited her, and her heart sank quietly.

❄❄❄

She heard the others leaving as she rummaged in her suitcase and found the boarding pass she'd printed out for her return journey before she'd left Australia, in the unlikely event that she'd need it.

She read the date: Wednesday, 30 December. Three days from

now. She tore it in two and dropped the pieces in the wastepaper basket beside the locker. She splashed enough cold water on her swollen eyes to fill a paddling pool, and then she went downstairs.

'You missed them, they've just left,' Susan said. If she noticed anything she didn't let on. She showed Tilly Gavin's order book and told her it needed to be taken next door and delivered to Nell.

Next door, where Andy lived. If he was there, he'd see her looking like this. She found she didn't care.

'I could take the twins with me,' she said, 'if you like.'

'That'd be great.'

'Shall we go and see if Tommy's at home?' she asked the girls, and they stopped trying to dress Charlie in one of Gavin's vests and allowed themselves to be wrapped in jackets and scarves and hats. Tilly pulled on her own jacket, regretting the loss of the green scarf she'd returned to Colette the day before.

'You need a scarf,' Susan said, and went out to the hall and returned with the red one she'd been wearing on arrival. Tilly wound it around her neck – it was beautifully thick and soft – and tucked Gavin's order book under her arm and off they went to see who was at home.

They walked through the field, the sharp cold of yesterday much diminished, all evidence of snow completely gone. 'Where thnowman?' Evie demanded, and Tilly picked up his red baseball cap and told her he'd gone to the North Pole to be with Santa and all his snowman friends, and they received the news doubtfully, looking at the nose he'd left behind on the ground.

They stood on the neighbouring doorstep and Tilly rang the bell, feeling thoroughly miserable. Nell answered, a pink apron wrapped around her waist. 'Look who's here,' she said. 'Come in, everyone.'

They stepped into the hall, which was filled with the smell of baking.

'Are the others following on?' Nell asked.

'The others?'

'Laura and Susan,' Nell replied – and abruptly Tilly remembered the previous day's invitation to brunch. 'Change of plan,' she said, and Nell peeled off the girls' jackets and sent them to the kitchen to find Tommy, and Tilly told her what had happened.

'Oh, Lord, that's a shock. Poor Gavin. They're gone already?'

'On the eleven o'clock ferry. They took the boys with them.'

'And Susan?'

'She's here, she came yesterday.'

'God, what a thing to happen. Poor old Gladys.' They walked towards the kitchen. 'Colette is gone to Mass, and Andy's still in bed. But James is here – you can meet him.'

Andy's father, Colette's son, in the act of making coffee. Arresting blue eyes, bluer than Andy's. Dark hair peppered with grey, chin shadowed with stubble. Cream sweater, black jeans. An echo of Andy in the face – or should that be the other way around? Their mouths were similar, she decided. Their chins came to the same little point.

'Hi there,' he said. 'Laura's mysterious sister from Australia: your fame has gone before you.'

Nell murmured the news to him. 'Ah,' he said, 'that's too bad. Sorry to hear that.'

'Sit,' Nell said. 'You'll have something, now that you're here,' so Tilly deposited her jacket and scarf on the little couch and sat at the table, trying to look cheerful.

The girls had already settled themselves on the floor, next to Tommy and his train set. The dog Andy had returned with the day before, like Charlie but with a darker face, was dozing under the table. Did every house on Roone have a dog that looked like Charlie?

She thought of the working dogs on the farm at home, the dogs that Pa trained to round up the sheep. They never came into the house, unless they wanted to be chased out again with Ma's broom. Tilly would have liked a pet dog, but pet dogs didn't live on farms at home.

James picked up Gavin's order book. 'They want someone to do the deliveries?'

'Yes, just for the next two mornings. They'll be back on Tuesday.'

James flicked through the book. 'Andy could do it,' he said, looking up at Nell.

'He could. That might work.' Nell began to slice a pie of some kind that was sitting by the cooker. 'He's dying to get in a bit of driving practice,' she explained to Tilly. 'He passed the test last month, but he doesn't have a car yet. And he knows the ropes – he helped out a bit when Gavin was setting up.'

She wiped her hands on her apron. 'Maybe you could go with him, Tilly – see a bit of the island while you're here. I hope you like apple tart, by the way.'

'Yes,' Tilly said. 'I love apple tart.'

She could go with him. She could sit next to him in Gavin's little white van. She could travel around the island with him, for however long it took to do the deliveries. It was like being handed a gift, like someone had said, 'I thought you might like this.' It was just what she needed to hear.

'As long as Susan can do without me.'

'Oh, I'm sure she could – it would only be an hour or so. Cream or ice-cream?'

'Cream, thanks.' An hour or so, tomorrow and the next day. Whatever trauma lay ahead, at least she would have this.

The tart was wonderful. She said so, and Nell told her the secret was her pastry, which she made with boiling water. 'It breaks all the rules of pastry-making, but it's the best.'

There was a painting of a collie dog hanging above the fridge. 'You did that?' she asked James, and he told her he had.

'John Silver,' Nell said. 'He was gorgeous. I sort of inherited him when I bought this house. But he was old, and he died last year.

Captain is Andy's dog, really' – indicating the dog under the table – 'but we all love him.'

'He looks like Charlie.'

'They're brothers.'

'Ah.' Tilly studied the collie again. 'You know my father?' she asked James.

'Met him briefly at Laura and Gavin's wedding. You know he's famous, don't you?'

'Laura said.' She didn't miss the lightning glance that he and Nell exchanged: aware of the way things were, then. She wondered what her father's paintings looked like. Sold for Monopoly money, Laura had said. Must Google him sometime.

'I saw one of your paintings next door too,' she told James. 'It's the man who used to own the house.'

'Ah yes, Walter.'

'I thought I saw him the other day, but Gavin told me he died.'

Nell poured tea. 'He did, four years ago last summer. He was a dear man, I knew him all my life. His family lived on the island for generations, but Walter was the last of the line. They're all gone now. Darling, will you get milk?'

The last of the line – so Tilly hadn't seen a brother, or a cousin, or any relative at all. Strange that whoever it was had borne such a strong resemblance to him. Strange that Tilly had seen him in the field that had once belonged to him, where he must often have been when he was alive.

Strange – and a tiny bit unnerving.

'Have you seen much of Roone yet?' James enquired, and when Tilly said no, he told her about the holy well and the lighthouse and the prehistoric remains. 'Get Andy to show you tomorrow. And there are some lovely beaches – although you'll hardly be looking for a swim.'

'No – but I was on a beach yesterday, just along the road from here.' Right after meeting Andy, her head spinning.

'One of the local men swims every day of the year,' Nell remarked. 'He was seventy-six last birthday.'

Before Tilly could respond the kitchen door opened. 'Morning,' Andy said. Looking bleary with sleep still, despite the damp hair that suggested a shower. His chin stubbled like his father's, rumpled blue sweatshirt, equally rumpled jeans, nothing on his feet but a pair of thick grey socks.

Tilly tried not to stare.

'There you are,' Nell said. 'Tilly dropped in.'

He gave her a smile. She returned it, thinking how awful she must look.

'Fancy a spot of driving?' his father asked.

'You know I would. Where and when?'

They told him about Gladys. They showed him the order book. 'No problem,' he said.

'Check the names,' Nell told him. 'If you don't know where anyone lives, I can tell you.'

'OK.'

'We thought you might bring Tilly along, let her see a bit of the island.'

Tilly chased the last of her apple tart around the plate.

'Sure,' he said. 'Good idea. Say ten in the morning, yeah?'

'Fine,' she said. 'I'll be ready.' Her heart dancing a little jig.

She asked Nell where the bathroom was, and she was directed down the corridor. 'Third door on the right,' Nell said.

The towel that hung on the bathroom rail was damp. She pressed her face into it. When she wiped steam from the mirror she saw how plain she looked. Still, there was always tomorrow.

'Ten in the morning,' she said to her blurry reflection. Forget about what came next, don't think about it.

When she returned to the kitchen she found Nell alone with the three children. 'James had to go to work,' she told Tilly, topping up her tea, 'and Andy has a football match.'

Football. He was sporty. She stored the information away.

'Can I tell you something?' Nell asked her then, slipping into the chair beside her.

'Yes.' What was this? Had she seen how Tilly was with Andy? She felt her face getting hot.

It wasn't about Andy. 'I'm due in late June,' Nell said. 'I haven't made it public yet, but I've been dying to tell someone outside the family.'

Tilly shaped her mouth into a smile. 'Congratulations. I won't tell.'

Nell was pregnant, and clearly delighted about it. Susan was pregnant, and presumably happy too. Tilly was pregnant, and too afraid to tell anyone, apart from Laura.

Maybe she could confide in Nell, ask her to help – but immediately she dismissed the idea. What could Nell possibly do, if Laura was bent on sending Tilly home?

She had to change the subject. 'What's Roone like in the summertime?'

'Very different. Weather can be mixed, although it's a lot milder than now. Very crowded too, we get lots of tourists. Good for the island, of course, plenty of business for everyone here, but I must admit I prefer it in winter, when it's ours again.'

'I'd love to live here.' She hadn't meant to say it. 'I mean, I know I've only just got here, and I've seen so little of it, but I feel a sort of ... pull, or something.'

Nell nodded. 'I know what you mean. I see it with people sometimes – it's like the island claims them. Laura was exactly the same, Gavin too. They both wanted to come back – I think they'd have ended up living here even if they hadn't got together.'

'You've never lived anywhere else?'

'I have – I did my training in Dublin. I was there for a few years, working in a salon, but I never really settled there. I knew I'd come back here as soon as I could. I'm not really a city person.'

She stopped. She studied Tilly's face, her head tipped sideways.

'You know,' she said, 'if you want something badly enough, you'll find a way to make it happen.'

Make it happen: easier said than done. Tearing up a boarding pass had been satisfying, but it didn't change anything. Without Laura's support it would take a miracle to make what she wanted happen.

'Roone is no stranger to miracles,' Nell said.

It was like she'd read Tilly's mind.

'Laura told you about the tree, didn't she?'

'What tree?'

'The one that fell. The one that bore fruit all year round.'

'Oh yes …'

She hadn't believed Laura; she'd thought it couldn't possibly be true. And now here was Nell saying the same.

'The slice of tart you just ate,' Nell went on, 'was made with apples from that tree. Just because something seems impossible doesn't mean it can't happen. We have lots of evidence of that right here on Roone.'

They heard the front door opening just then. Tilly's heart leaped – maybe he'd forgotten something – but a minute later Colette appeared, home from Mass. They told her about Gladys, and more tea was made, and by the time Tilly got up to leave it was almost an hour later.

She dressed the girls in their jackets as Nell wrapped the remains of the apple tart in tinfoil for them to bring home. 'I'm back at work on Tuesday,' she told Tilly, 'in case you feel like dropping in for a trim before you leave. Call it a belated Christmas present.'

Making her way back across the field with the girls, Tilly thought about wanting something badly enough that you found a way to make it happen. All very well for Nell to say, living on Roone and pregnant with her second child, and clearly living the exact life she was meant to live. Not so easy when everything you wanted seemed completely impossible.

Still, she wouldn't give up hope. Nearly three days until her flight was due to leave: enough time for a Roone miracle.

❄❄❄

Once they hit the outskirts, once the traffic began to thicken and the hotels and car showrooms and warehouses started to merge into a continuous line, the city evoked the same mix of feelings it always did when Laura visited it now. She'd grown up in Dublin, she'd fallen in love for the first time here, the boys had been born in a Dublin hospital. So much history, so many good memories. Of course it had a hold over her.

But the bad stuff was here too. The upheavals of her childhood had occurred here. Aaron had died in a Dublin park. She'd endured years of loneliness and struggle in the city. And now Roone was home, and Dublin was where she came to visit, and that was fine by her.

Since their move to Roone, Gavin had taken a trip to Dublin every few months to spend a couple of nights with his mother. Gladys had treasured those solo visits, and the chance to dote undisturbed on her son, and Laura had welcomed them too, ensuring as they did that Gladys would be less inclined to descend on Roone in between. Win-win.

The terraced house where Gavin had grown up hadn't changed since Laura's last sight of it in March. They'd visited for Gladys's birthday, shortly before Laura had got her diagnosis. Same dark blue front door that Gavin repainted every few years, same small square of gravel out the front, same huddle of terracotta pots standing guard to the left of the door. Filled with daffodils last time, as far as Laura remembered. She wondered if there were bulbs waiting in the soil, biding their time until spring. No Gladys around to see them bloom.

As soon as they let themselves in Larry emerged from the kitchen, looking a little rumpled, and sombre greetings were exchanged. 'Folks have been calling all day,' he told them. 'They've been bringing food.' He made it sound like an accusation, as if the offerings had been delivered purely to annoy him. 'They were asking questions – I didn't know what to tell them.'

Every one of them wondering who the mystery man in Gladys's house was. Tongues wagging, no doubt, up and down the road. Larry in the wrong place at the wrong time, this awful responsibility landed on him. His wife's death still so recent, the timing so cruel.

'I'll go up to see her,' Gavin said, starting for the stairs.

Laura fished comics from the single case they'd brought and ushered the boys into the tidy little kitchen. 'Wait here with Larry,' she instructed, finding the sherry Gladys kept for visitors and pouring him a glass without asking if he wanted it.

She climbed the stairs and entered Gladys's room. Gavin, in a chair by the bed, lifted his head briefly. She went to stand beside him, wanting to lay a hand on his shoulder but not daring.

Gladys looked calm. Whatever the manner of her death, she appeared at peace now. She lay on the neatly made bed wearing the blue suit they'd waved her off in the day before. She'd been made up but not garishly: a suggestion of lipstick, a hint of blusher. The cheeks more sunken than in life, the flesh under the chin gathering in loose folds, no Gladys left to raise her head and pull it in.

Laura regarded Gavin's bowed head. Praying for his mother's soul, or maybe just remembering her. An only child, no sibling to mourn with at this time, nobody to share his reminiscences – and there was nothing in the world Laura could do to change that for him.

He gave the best foot massages: they'd been her salvation when she'd been expecting Evie and Marian, and the size of a hippopotamus. He was useless with money – but money had never featured in her list of priorities. He'd proposed twice, and twice Laura had said no – and sometime after her second refusal, shortly after the girls were born, she'd turned the tables and asked him to marry her, because somewhere along the way he'd become important, and walking down an aisle with him seemed to be the most sensible way to show him that.

He couldn't put a proper knot in a tie to save his life.

He grew the best tomatoes she'd ever tasted.

His instinctive love of animals, all animals, used to please her inordinately.

Without prompting, Ben and Seamus had stopped calling him Gavin and switched to Dad.

'I'll put on dinner,' she whispered eventually. He nodded without looking up. She turned and left the room.

In the kitchen the boys were reading and Larry was hovering, cradling his sherry. 'Have you eaten?' Laura asked him, and when he told her he hadn't, she lit Gladys's oven and put in one of the donated casseroles. *Paprika chicken*, she read in green biro on an address label stuck to the lid. *Reheat for fifteen minutes at gas 6.*

'I made a hotel reservation for the night,' Larry told her. 'Figured you folks would need all the space here. Same place I was supposed to stay in, close to the airport. Good for my flight in the morning.'

Laura hid her relief. 'Gavin will drive you there after you've eaten,' she said, and he thanked her and went off to pack up his things.

'We're starving,' Ben said, even though they'd got takeaway chips on the way up, making the car smell of vinegar from Portlaoise to Dublin.

'Dinner won't be long,' Laura told them. She lit a fire in the sitting room and plumped cushions, looking forward to putting her feet up later.

Two empty wine glasses sat on the coffee table, one with Gladys's pink lipstick still on the rim. They'd sat in here last evening, the two of them, Gladys telling him about Dublin, suggesting places for him to see in the morning. Offering to accompany him maybe, unaware that the next time she left the house it would be in a wooden box.

When the casserole was ready she tapped on Gladys's bedroom

door, and the five of them sat in near silence around the table, the boys doing most of the eating. Laura did her best to keep the conversation going, but with little co-operation from either Gavin or Larry she was forced eventually to admit defeat.

Directly afterwards, Larry went off to retrieve his suitcase. Poor man probably couldn't wait to get away. 'Sorry your trip ended like this,' Laura told him on the doorstep.

He managed the faintest of smiles. 'Guess it was never gonna be a happy one,' he said, and she couldn't argue with that.

'There'll always be a bed for you on Roone,' she said, 'a free one.'

He thanked her politely, but she couldn't imagine him ever wanting to come back. She wished him a safe flight and watched as he drove off with Gavin, remembering the day before when she'd stood outside another house and waved him and Gladys off in just this way.

Two minutes after they'd left, as she and the boys were about to start the washing-up, the doorbell rang. She went to answer it.

'Joyce Mulqueen,' the woman said. Navy coat, sensible shoes, pale brown hair coaxed into waves. Carrying something wrapped in tinfoil. 'I was her closest friend,' she said. Eyes swollen from crying, nose reddened at the tip, trembling mouth bare of lipstick. 'I can't believe it.'

Laura brought her into the sitting room and poured more sherry, the only other alcohol she could find in the house a dusty bottle of crème de menthe.

'We were supposed to have Christmas dinner together,' Joyce wept, 'only she missed her ferry home – but of course you know that.' Dabbing at her face with the tissue she'd pulled from her sleeve, the sherry ignored. Maybe Joyce was more a gin woman.

It turned out that she and Gladys had met at bridge – Gladys played bridge? – which Joyce had taken up after the death of her husband, seven years earlier. 'We became friends right away,' she told Laura. 'We have – we had – so much in common.'

Joyce had spent most of the day in the museum where she volunteered twice a week. 'I only heard the news from Dolores Piggott on my way home: such a shock.' Pausing as she welled up again to press the tissue to each eye in turn. 'I was only on the phone with Gladys last evening. We were going to meet for lunch tomorrow, with that American man who was staying with her. She sounded fine, just fine. I still can't believe it.'

Her offering turned out to be a tea brack. 'It's frozen, I hadn't time to make another one – but it will help you out over the next few days. She often talked about you,' she added, and Laura could imagine how *that* conversation had gone.

Within minutes the doorbell sounded for the second time, and again a few minutes after that, and by the time Gavin returned, the front room had filled with neighbours and friends of Gladys, who were only just hearing the news. They made the pilgrimage upstairs in pairs, and teas and coffees became the order of the day, the sherry bottle, like its owner, having come to the end of its days.

Laura sent the boys to the corner shop for more coffee and tea and milk as Joyce, who had rallied at the appearance of the other callers, bustled about, slicing up the various baked goods that arrived, keeping the teapot full and generally making herself very useful indeed.

'I know you've been sick,' she said, cutting a madeira cake into slices. 'Gladys told me. That must have been hard, with little kiddies to look after, and you expecting as well.'

'It was.'

'Gladys was so worried.' Arranging the slices on a plate. 'She had us all doing novenas.'

'Did she?'

'And your little girls. I've seen lots of photos, and of the boys too, such nice polite boys – and the baby, of course. Gladys was so proud of them all, so delighted to be a grandmother.'

'Yes …'

'And she's shown me photos of your beautiful home too. She used to say it was exactly the kind of house she always wanted.'

Gladys had been worried about her.

Gladys had been delighted to be a grandmother; she'd shown Joyce photos of the girls, of all the children.

Gladys had admired their house.

Laura refilled the coffee pot, marvelling at all that had remained unsaid between them.

By nine o'clock the house was theirs again, with Joyce leading the mass exodus and promising to return in the morning to see if they needed a hand. Gavin went for a walk, and in the emptied-out sitting room the boys were working their way through Gladys's many TV channels, a far cry from the handful they had on Roone.

Alone in the kitchen, Laura washed up. The girls would be in bed at this hour, and Poppy should be going up now too. She'd wait another while before she rang.

She hoped Tilly didn't hate her too much.

She lifted a plate from the soapy water and thought about the two busy days that were ahead of them until Gladys was put into the ground and they could go back home.

She dried the dishes, determined not to think about the morning, and what had to be done.

Just get through it. Just get it over.

❋❋❋

Nothing had been organised, no invitations sent out. They simply arrived, shortly after Tilly and Susan had put the twins to bed and restored some sort of order to the kitchen.

None of them came empty-handed. A box of flapjacks from Lelia. A bottle of brandy from Imelda, married to Nell's uncle Hugh. Peppermint tea and vanilla biscuits from Colette and Nell.

They sat in a little group around the fire, talking in low voices about Gladys as Tilly gave Poppy her bedtime feed.

'Only three nights ago, Christmas Eve, we were all here with her,' Lelia said. 'She was sitting right there where you are now, Tilly.'

'She was fine that night,' Imelda said. 'There wasn't a thing wrong with her.'

'Actually,' Susan said, 'maybe there was.'

She told them about Laura finding Gladys on her bedroom floor the following morning. 'She told me they called the doctor, and he wanted to admit Gladys to Tralee Hospital for tests – he said it could be her heart – but she wouldn't hear of it.'

'But that was Christmas Day,' Imelda said. 'No ferries were running, she'd have had no way of getting to the mainland.'

'Tilly and I got to the island on Christmas Day,' Colette pointed out. 'A man from Kilmally brought us across on his boat. If Gladys had agreed to go to hospital, I'm sure something could have been arranged.'

'It could,' Nell said, 'but it mightn't have made any difference.'

'No, that's true …'

They listened to the soft lap of the flames in the fireplace, and the occasional snuffle from Charlie, sprawled on the hearth rug by Tilly's feet. Poppy's eyes began to close; her sucking became sporadic as sleep came to claim her. Tilly nudged her gently awake until the bottle was empty.

'How old was Gladys?' Imelda enquired.

'In her seventies, I think.' Susan looked to Tilly for confirmation, but Tilly shook her head. She'd known virtually nothing about Gavin's mother, but she'd observed a sort of muted antipathy between her and Laura, a not-quite-meeting of the eyes whenever they addressed one another.

She eased the bottle teat from Poppy's mouth and lifted the baby to rest against her shoulder, rubbing small circles into her back, like

Ma had taught her. When the wind was duly evacuated, she got to her feet. 'I'll put her up.'

'Want me to come with you?' Susan asked.

'No need, I'm fine.'

She felt their eyes on her as she left the room, and guessed Gladys would stop being the topic of conversation as soon as she was out of earshot. She didn't mind: they were bound to be curious about her, turning up the way she had. Colette would probably tell them how she and Tilly had met, and they'd ask Susan how much she knew about the whole thing.

She climbed the stairs, Poppy warm and heavy in her arms. Imagine what they'd say if they knew about her pregnancy, or how she felt about Nell's stepson: they'd have something to talk about then.

She tucked Poppy into her cot and placed the brown rabbit next to her. She gazed at her tiny sleeping niece. August, Gavin said she'd been born. By the time her first birthday came around Tilly's baby would have arrived; he or she would be a few weeks old, if Tilly's calculations were right, and if it came when it was expected.

It. Her baby. Seven or eight weeks gone. No queasiness on waking any more, or not as bad as it had been. No other symptoms apart from an aversion to coffee. No change in her shape yet, too soon for that.

She crossed to the windows, drew the curtains closed. When would she start to show, when would people know by looking at her? Where would she be in a week's time, in a month's time? Where could she go? Who could she turn to for help?

She left the room and made her way downstairs. Susan stood in the hall, speaking softly on the phone. Tilly went to walk past, but Susan reached for her arm.

'She's here now,' she said. 'Look after yourself, talk tomorrow.'

She passed the receiver to Tilly. 'Laura,' she said, and vanished into the sitting room.

Laura. Tilly looked at the phone. After a few seconds she put it to her ear. 'Hello.'

'Tilly – all well?'

'Everything's fine.'

'Good … and tell me, did Nell get someone to do the deliveries?'

'Andy's doing them.'

'Andy – of course. He'd be perfect – he's done it before with Gavin. I never even thought of him.'

A beat passed.

'We've had lots of callers this evening,' Laura said. 'Friends of Gladys, all coming to pay their respects. The Irish are good around death.'

Good around death: what an odd thing to say.

'Tilly.'

'Yes.'

'You're still mad at me, after what I said this morning. I can hear it.'

She didn't contradict her.

'Tilly, I don't want us to fall out. It's the last thing I want.'

She stopped. Again Tilly remained silent. What was there to say?

'It was … quite amazing to discover that I had a sister. I'm very glad you came, I really am – and I hope we keep in touch.' A small laugh. 'God knows, this family hasn't exactly a good track record in that regard.'

Keep in touch. A letter once in a while, she meant. A card at Christmas. Just as long as Tilly kept to her side of the world.

'Well,' Laura said, 'I'd better let you go. Goodnight lovey, we'll talk tomorrow.'

'Goodnight.'

She replaced the receiver and stood for a minute in the hall, hearing a soft burst of laughter from the sitting room. She looked at the jumble of stuff hanging on the hallstand, at the girls' little jackets, and Poppy's minuscule hat that Susan had brought, and Laura's dark green oilskin.

Her family lived here.

She eased the front door open as quietly as she could. She leaned against the jamb and tilted her head up to the stars, and listened to the distant wash of the sea.

Lovey. Laura had called her lovey, without even thinking about it.

I'm very glad you came, she'd said.

When the cold began to bite she closed the door softly and re-entered the sitting room, where the talk had turned to someone called Annie Byrnes, whose bones, it would appear, had the power to predict the weather.

Nothing, Tilly decided, resuming her seat by the fire, would surprise her about Roone.

❅

MONDAY
28 DECEMBER

❅

'**I**'ll be off so,' she said, checking her bag for purse, tissues, phone.

They were in the hall. It was just after nine, and she'd been awake for what felt like hours, watching the furniture in Gladys's twin room slowly materialising as the dawn seeped through the curtains. The other bed was empty: Gavin had sat up all night beside his mother's body, keeping her company before she left the house for the last time. The boys had been shoehorned into the single bed in the smallest room, Ben's head at Seamus's feet.

'Will you not have something to eat?' Gavin asked, his face drawn and grey, his eyes bloodshot after his solitary vigil. At least he was talking to her.

'I don't feel like anything.' Her appetite had deserted her, as she had known it would. She'd make up for it later. 'I'd rather get going.'

She'd have welcomed a lift, but he didn't offer. Her destination lay a mile to the east, she was groggy from not enough sleep, and the day was dull and grey. But he must be exhausted, and in no state to sit behind the wheel of a car.

'You should grab some sleep now while you can,' she said. The undertaker was due at noon. 'The boys are well able to get their own breakfasts, and I'll call you in plenty of time.'

'Maybe.'

He wouldn't. She knew he wouldn't. 'See you soon then,' she said and let herself out, closing the door quietly behind her.

It wasn't as cold here as on Roone, but it was far from warm. She walked quickly, past landmarks that were familiar: the petrol station where she'd worked behind the till for a few teenage summers, the park where she'd played with friends after school, the cinema where she'd had her first date with Aaron.

The film titles displayed on a board over the door meant little to her. With no cinema on Roone she was hopelessly out of touch. There had been talk of a mobile cinema being set up last summer, visiting the island every so often like the mobile library, but nothing had come of it. Pity: she used to love going to the movies.

A group of youths loitered on a corner, shoulders hunched against the cold: they barely looked at her as she walked by. Too old at thirty, much too old to be of any interest to them.

As she walked on, the flavour of the neighbourhood changed. Delis and pet parlours and art galleries replaced the chippers and off licences and betting shops. She eventually reached her road and turned in.

The Whelans, the O'Briens, the Cassidys, the O'Donnells. The same families there for years, their houses architect-designed and detached, most of them surrounded by high walls and locked wrought-iron gates, with boxes for the mail and intercoms fixed to the garden walls. Do not disturb, if you can possibly avoid it.

The polar opposite of Roone, where nobody locked a door, and where garden walls were mostly waist-high arrangements of stones piled on stones with nothing to hold them together but the skill of the workmen, designed more to keep little children in than to keep anyone out. Roone, where everyone disturbed everyone else all day long.

Behind the O'Donnells' wall a dog barked, sounding heartbreakingly like Charlie. A tall woman strode rapidly along the path on the far side of the road, head and shoulders swathed in a deep purple scarf, black bag dangling from a gloved hand. She didn't even glance in Laura's direction.

And suddenly there it was. Her father's house.

Big gates, check. Immaculate lawn, check. Place she'd run away from as soon as she could, check.

She tapped buttons on the keypad attached to the wall. Seconds later the mechanism whirred into life and the gates swept slowly open. She walked up the paved drive and stood on the doorstep and dialled his number on her phone. When the ringing tone stopped she waited for the voicemail beep, and then she said, 'It's Laura. I'm outside,' and hung up.

He never answered his phone. He let it ring and then he listened to the message if one was left, and he chose which deserved a response. He didn't hear the doorbell from his studio at the rear. The great artist was an expert when it came to avoiding the common people.

The seconds turned into minutes. There was no sound from within, no movement to be detected at any of the windows, or behind the glass panels on either side of the front door. Had she made the journey in vain?

He'd always been an early riser; it was highly unlikely that he was still in bed at twenty past nine. And he generally didn't go to his studio before eleven, not until he'd read his two newspapers from end to end and attended to his correspondence. He must be out. What now?

She was about to admit defeat when she heard the familiar slop-slop of his leather slippers across the parquet floor. He never wore shoes unless he was going out; his slippers were replaced more often than any other footwear.

There was a rattling fumble of the security chain being slid across and released, and finally the door was opened. He wore a baggy bottle green pullover and loose grey sweat pants. He was unshaven, the stubble white against his sallow complexion. The greenish pockets of flesh under his eyes seemed to have grown larger in the months since her last visit in March. A pink spot flared, high up on his left cheek. He had an undernourished look about him.

'What are you doing here?' he asked, frowning. 'Isn't Susan on Roone?' His stale breath floated out to her.

'My mother-in-law died yesterday,' Laura told him.

A tiny rise of an eyebrow, otherwise no change. 'Was she sick?' He'd met Gladys exactly once, at Laura and Gavin's wedding.

'No – heart attack, we think.'

He shuffled back to admit her, and she stepped inside. It was colder in the house than out. She smelt polish and woodsmoke and turpentine and coffee, all the smells she associated with here.

'So Susan is still on Roone,' he said. Didn't they talk? Hadn't he phoned her since yesterday morning?

'Yes. We left the girls with her …' but he was already walking away so she walked after him, past the pair of white spindly-legged chairs by the wall with their maroon-and-gold-striped padded seats, and the bronze bust of Gauguin on its mahogany pedestal that had terrified her as a youngster. Past the various paintings by Luke's contemporaries, and the drawing-room and dining-room doors with their faceted glass knobs that Laura had thought for years were enormous diamonds.

As she followed him across the black-and-white-tiled floor she regarded his rear view. In the slight roundness of his back, in the way he held his arms out a fraction from his body, in the suggestion of a rolling waddle in his hips, she could see for the first time the old man he was becoming. Sixty-what? For the first time, she couldn't remember his age.

She wondered, as she had often wondered, what Susan – bright, warm, big-hearted Susan – could possibly have seen in this dour, shambling, ageing creature. It remained a complete mystery to Laura: but then, wasn't that the way of love, wasn't it an inexplicable phenomenon most of the time? Who could say what brought two people together, what drew them closer, what made them choose one another over anyone else?

And every love story was different, every one unique. Look how she'd known, within minutes of meeting him, that Aaron was going to be significant, was going to change her life. With Gavin it had been different. She'd liked him from the start, but it had taken quite a bit longer for the affection she'd felt to develop into something stronger.

Look at Nell, engaged first to one Baker brother, married now to the other. Look at Nell's father, walking away from thirty-something years of marriage, deserting his wife for love.

The kitchen was only marginally warmer than the hall. Didn't he feel the cold, or was it miserliness that stopped him turning on the radiators? Even his minor paintings were commanding five-figure sums, for Christ's sake. She drew her jacket more closely about her, resisted the urge to rub heat into her arms.

'Have you eaten?' he asked, lifting the lid of the bread bin and peering inside. 'I could do you some toast.'

She'd forgotten his total indifference to food. If he wasn't presented with a hot meal in the evening he simply did without, or ate sweetcorn or tuna or the like straight from their cans. He probably hadn't boiled an egg since Susan's departure.

'Nothing for me, thanks,' she told him, her appetite still absent.

'Coffee?' Indicating the bubbling percolator on the worktop.

'I don't drink it any more.'

He raised his eyebrows. 'Since when?'

'Since I got cancer,' she answered lightly. Not once had he come to see her, not one single time.

'Ah.' He nodded slowly, his eyes travelling over her face. 'You're well now though. You're better now.'

'I am. Yes.'

Don't go into the ongoing monitoring, and the ache that she sometimes felt in the breast that was no longer there, and the terror that refused to go away. Don't bother, he doesn't want to know.

'I'll have tea,' she said, 'if you have any.' Warm her up if nothing else. She rubbed her hands together.

He glanced at them. 'Are you cold?'

'A bit. Don't you feel it cold in here?'

'Not really. Hold on.' He went back out to the hall. She heard him opening the door of the cupboard under the stairs.

She looked around. The kitchen was pretty much as she remembered it, same stainless-steel everything, same powder-blue-tiled floor, same cream paint on the walls. A single glass tumbler sat in the sink, the only evidence that the kitchen was used.

He reappeared with a fan heater and plugged it in, positioning it to face the breakfast bar. 'Sit,' he said, so she sat on one of the two leather-and-chrome high stools, still wearing her jacket, and watched as he opened a cupboard.

'Peppermint,' he said. 'Camomile. Green. Berry. Decaffeinated black.'

'Green,' she said, and he took down a box.

'So,' he said, setting two china mugs on the counter, 'anything else to report from your island?'

'Actually, I have some news,' she said.

His back was to her, filling the kettle from a filter jug. He plugged it in and turned to face her again, his expression a bit guarded now. He folded his arms unhurriedly. 'Yes?'

'You have another child.' She watched him. 'Another daughter. She's seventeen, she was born in Australia.' She stopped and waited to see if he had known of Tilly's existence.

For a few seconds there was silence. He held her gaze calmly as the kettle hummed softly. There was a smell of burning coming from the fan heater, but it was taking the chill from the air.

Eventually he spoke. 'I wondered about that,' he said mildly.

'You knew,' Laura said. 'You knew she was pregnant.'

'I did, yes.' Watching her as keenly as she watched him. Trying to gauge the effect his words were having on her. Interested in a detached way, as if this was an experiment he was conducting. As if he'd just pulled the wings off a butterfly and was waiting to see what it did next.

Laura let the information settle. All the time he'd known he had another child. He'd known while Laura was going through her teens that she had a brother or a sister, and he hadn't opened his mouth. He hadn't told her.

'What did you know about her?' she asked.

He let his arms fall open and turned to switch off the percolator and fill his mug with coffee. He put a bowl of brown sugar on the counter. He scalded the yellow polka-dot teapot Laura had given Susan a few Christmases ago, and spooned loose tea into it. Was he simply going to ignore her question?

No, he wasn't. 'What did you know?' Laura repeated. 'Did you even know if it was a boy or a girl?'

He set down the teapot and planted his palms on the counter. 'Laura, at that point, things had broken down completely between your mother and me. She wanted us to—'

'Did you even try to find out?' she asked loudly, cutting him off. 'Did you even care about your child?'

A beat passed. The kettle began to change its tune, the hum becoming more businesslike. 'This is not something you need to concern yourself with,' he said tightly.

'She's my *sister*. How does that not concern me?' Her skin prickled with anger. She could hear the blood pounding in her ears. She wanted to hit him, she wanted to hurt him. 'She's here,' she said. 'She's in Ireland. She came all the way from Australia on her own.'

'This is between your mother and—'

'Tilly,' she said. 'Her name is Tilly. She has your eyes.'

'Laura, I'm asking you to leave it—'

Again she broke in. 'She was adopted,' she said. 'Did you know that? No, of course you didn't. She only discovered this year that she had a father and a sister living in Ireland. She's on Roone. She came to find me – she came halfway around the world to find me. She knew nothing about you. Our mother had told her nothing except that you were still alive.'

She looked at his closed face. She saw the utter coldness in the eyes that Tilly had inherited. Tilly's weren't cold, though.

'Your name isn't on her birth cert,' she said, watching him. 'It says "father unknown". She couldn't bring herself to put your name on it.'

Not a flicker. Not a sign he gave a damn.

'Don't worry,' she said, 'she won't be bothering you. I just thought it was something you should know.'

More silence. She let her gaze drift down to his hands, still flat on the counter. The hands that had brought into being so many marvellous works of art, the hands that were revered by so many. The skin loose and sagging now, the veins rising up starkly, the knuckles more pronounced than she remembered.

Old, he was fast becoming old.

Didn't mean she had to go easy on him. She let her eyes travel back up to his face. 'You shouldn't have done it,' she said. 'You should never have had children. It wasn't fair to us.'

His eyes narrowed. 'You need to stop talking now, Laura.'

'I may as well have grown up with no real parents, like she did.'

'I was here for you,' he said angrily. 'Your mother was the one who walked out: I didn't go anywhere.'

'You packed me off to boarding school the minute she was gone. You couldn't wait to get rid of me.'

'I had a career, I had commitments, it wasn't—'

'Yes,' she said, her heart racing, her words pouring out, 'your precious career left no room for anything else, did it? It was all you ever wanted, wasn't it, to be Luke Potter the artist? Luke Potter the husband and Luke Potter the father didn't come into it.'

'I took you in,' he said, 'when your husband died. I let you stay as long as you needed.'

'Susan took us in,' she shot back. 'Susan looked after me and the boys. You did nothing to make us feel welcome. You couldn't bear it when they made any noise. You wanted us to stay out of your sight. You didn't even bother trying to tell them apart.'

The kettle clicked off. They both ignored it.

'I set you up in that house,' he said. 'I paid your rent until you found your feet. I gave you an allowance.'

'Yes,' she said, 'you gave me money. That was all I ever got from you.'

He'd given Diane the same ultimatum he'd given Susan. He'd told her to get rid of the baby, not wanting any more children, not wanting another Laura – and instead Diane had gone as far away from him as she could.

Why hadn't she taken Laura? Why had she left her with a man who didn't want her?

No more. She couldn't stand any more of it. She slid off the stool.

'Forget the tea,' she said.

She left the room, aware that he was following her. Shuffle, shuffle behind her. At the front door she stopped, turned back.

'Congratulations, by the way,' she said. 'I hear you're going to be a father again. You must be thrilled.'

He didn't react. He said nothing at all in reply. She might as well not have spoken. She looked at him. She looked at the man who had brought her into being, and she realised that all she felt for him was pity.

'You're going to end up alone,' she said. 'You're pushing Susan away, like you pushed away my mother. You're going to die alone.'

He reached past her and opened the door. She got a whiff of turpentine.

She walked from the house and didn't look back. Before she reached the gate she heard the door closing.

That's that, she thought. That's the end of it.

✳✳✳

It didn't take an hour or so, it took two hours.

First there was Nell.

'Take it easy on the road,' she said. 'Watch the bad bend at

Tiernan's – and make sure you put on the handbrake in Leo's driveway, that hill is very steep. And slow down at the crossroads by the lighthouse, it's a tricky one.'

'Maybe you should come along,' Andy said, 'to keep an eye on me.' Loading the last of the orders into the little white van that had *Walter's Place Fresh Produce* in orange lettering on its side, above a cartoon drawing of a basket holding carrots, onions and lettuce. 'You could sit in the back,' he said, 'on top of the cabbages.'

'Don't be so smart, young man – I'm just making sure you bring Tilly home in one piece, or we'll all be in trouble. Tilly, will you be warm enough? That jacket looks very light.'

'I'll be fine.'

'I could give you a loan of my padded one – it's like a blanket. Wouldn't take a minute to get it.'

'Honestly, this one is warm enough. I have two sweaters under it.'

'Well, if you're sure … Andy, that front tyre looks a small bit flat to me. Should you go by the village before you start, and check the pressure?'

'I think,' Andy said, 'Tommy is looking a bit cold' – which finally sent both of them back home across the field.

Then there was Lelia in the café, their first delivery.

'What's the news from Dublin? … And how are you and Susan coping with the little ones? You seem well used to babies, Tilly – did you say you have younger brothers or sisters? … Now, I want to give you some honey to bring back home with you. It's great for sore throats or head colds – are you allowed to take it in your suitcase? Make sure you wrap it up well – put it in a plastic bag: you'd have an awful mess if it spilled … I used to get all my honey from Walter when he was alive, beautiful stuff it was, lavender and hawthorn mostly, everyone was mad for it … Here, Andy, drop these few scones up to Cathy Considine, would you? She's got Julie and the Frenchman home for Christmas, and God knows poor Cathy's scones would break a window if you didn't have a stone to hand. You needn't tell her I said that.'

And after that there was Maisie Kiely, in the third cottage past the turn for the lighthouse.

'Who's this now? Oh, you're the girl from Australia – weren't you very brave altogether to come all that way on your own? I was on a plane once. I went to the Isle of Man for a holiday with Jane Corbett. We got free peanuts on the way but I couldn't eat them at all, far too salty, so Jane had mine. It rained non-stop on the Isle of Man, and we never saw a single cat, with or without a tail, so I didn't bother going away again, I can get all the rain I want right here ... How long did it take you to get to Roone, and were you not exhausted from all that flying, and could you sleep on the plane? ... And what did you think of our snow? We were all flabbergasted to see it, we never get it normally. I couldn't go for my walk on the beach – there's a few of us who try to get out every day, winter and summer, but we couldn't chance it that day, although we did get out the day of the storm, just home before it got bad ... Andy, would you ever tell Nell I want a perm next week, whenever she can fit me in? And it's seven potatoes I get, not eight, Damien doesn't eat them at all, so I'll give that one back to you, or it would only go to waste ... And I hear Gavin's apple tree that was knocked in the storm was the year-round one – isn't that an awful shame? What'll we do for our winter juice now, I wonder?'

And wherever they went, it was the same. Everyone wanting to talk, everyone asking Tilly about Australia and Andy about college. And when they'd covered all the houses on the east of the island they took the link road to the other side and called to the Considine house, and met Cathy.

'I heard the news about Gavin's mother, the poor woman. What's this happened to her again? ... I heard Dr Jack was sent for on Christmas morning. You'd think he'd have sent her straight to the hospital, wouldn't you? I mean, the poor woman must have been on the way out, mustn't she? Surely to God that was a warning ... And what's this your name is again, dear? ... I'll take a few more carrots if you have them, Andy, we have a full house here – they all came home for Christmas. Julie, our youngest, married a Frenchman in August, René his name is, sounds like a girl's name to me but of course I wouldn't say it, and Val and Patricia came too ... This was the old schoolhouse – we bought it when they got the new one built, eighteen years ago next April. Julie was only five at the time. We had to do quite a bit with it, of course ... What's Lelia sending me scones for? She knows I'm well able to bake my own, she's often had one here.'

And then there was Father William's little house, tucked into the side of a hill, and Josie Jordan, his housekeeper.

'When were those parsnips dug up? Father likes his vegetables as fresh as possible. And the potatoes are Golden Wonder, aren't they? We got the Records one time and Father didn't care for them ... My son Cathal is in Australia, Melbourne he's in. Would that be far from you? He's a teacher – he was living in Dingle but he couldn't get a job, only a day here and a day there, sure what good is that to anyone? He's working in a big school now, doing very well, loves it, although he got a bad sunburn when he went first. He met a girl from Tipperary – she's a nurse over there. We do the Skype once a week ... he taught me how to do it last time he was home. He's always on at me to go for a holiday, but what would Father do without me? Sure the man wouldn't manage at all. Oliver, my late husband, used to say a man is no good in a kitchen, and I'm inclined to agree with him. Not a man's job really, is it, cooking a dinner?'

They liked to talk, the people of Roone. And even when it was just the two of them trundling along the island roads, Andy turned out to have plenty to say too.

'When we came here first I was miserable. I hated my dad for making me move. I still missed Mum all the time, and I missed my friends from Dublin too.' Not looking at her as he spoke, keeping his eyes on the road. Maybe that made it easier. 'I was a nightmare to live with for the first few years. I practically shut him out – I'd hardly talk to him. I feel bad when I think of it now – I mean, he missed her too, and I didn't make it easy ... Nell was originally engaged to my uncle Tim, Dad's younger brother. Dad was the one who introduced them when Tim came on holidays. They were all set to get married, they had a big wedding planned, here on the island – and then they had some kind of a row and they called it off, and now she's married to Dad. Weird, isn't it? Tim is married now too – they live in Dublin, they've got two kids ... Nell had a crash here, right at this spot, a couple of years ago. That's why she's nervous of me driving. I was in the car with her – we were going to our old house, the one Dad bought when we moved here. It wasn't Nell's fault. An Italian tourist came around a bend on the wrong side of the road and went straight into us. We were a bit bashed up – it's where I got this scar – but nothing too serious. Nell's car was a write-off, though ... That's where we lived, in that cul-de-sac. We were there for about three years, until Dad married Nell. On their wedding day a little girl was kidnapped here. She was on holidays with her family – they were renting a house just four doors down from us. You might even have heard about it – it made news all around the world. She was found after a few weeks on the mainland and she was fine ... I got a job at Mr Thompson's house, the summer he died. He's the man who used to own the house you're staying in. Nell told me he wanted someone to clear out his attic. Looking back, I'd say she thought it might help me or something, I don't know. Anyway, I liked the sound of making a bit of pocket money so I called to the house and said I was interested. I'd hardly spoken to him before that, I didn't really talk to anyone here if I could avoid it, but he took me on, and there was just something about that attic – I mean, it was a real mess, cluttered with all sorts of ancient stuff, everything covered in dust – but I liked the feel of the place. It was so quiet, you couldn't hear a sound from outside. I looked forward to going up there every day ... I was the one who found him – Mr Thompson. I called around there, I was going to give a fresh coat of paint to his henhouse. I'd finished the attic, and I just wanted to do something for him, I suppose, in return for his kindness to me. He was a very kind man – and … I found him.'

He stopped talking then, and the silence went on a while.

'That must have been tough,' she said.

'Yup.'

He drove carefully, taking no chances. Not showing off like he might have done with a girl sitting in the passenger seat. His fingers were broad, the nails short. He wore the same brown jacket, but no woolly hat today. Tilly presumed Nell cut his hair.

He showed her things along the way. The road sign on the cliff pointing out to sea, telling them that the Statue of Liberty was three thousand miles away. A joke, Tilly assumed, to amuse the tourists – but he told her that nobody had erected it, that it had simply appeared one day. 'That's what they say, anyway.'

As they drove past the cemetery he slowed down and asked, 'What do you smell?' When she said chocolate, he smiled. 'With me it's oranges. Everyone smells one or the other here, but there are no plants anywhere on the island that have those scents, and the nearest chocolate factory is on the mainland.'

Roone definitely seemed a bit different. 'You don't think the island is … enchanted or something, do you?'

He threw her a look. 'Nah. But sometimes it's hard to explain stuff that happens here.'

She wanted to hear about more things that couldn't be explained, but they'd reached the next customer's house, and the subject was dropped.

It was approaching noon when he turned the white van into the field beside Walter's Place. Rain that had begun a little earlier was spattering the windscreen. He switched off the wipers, cut the engine. 'You're easy to talk to,' he said. 'You're a good listener. You were probably wishing I'd shut up.'

She hadn't been wishing he'd shut up. She'd been wishing they could stay in the van for about a week. She couldn't imagine ever getting tired of listening to him. He'd made her forget her troubles for two hours.

Rain drummed on the roof of the van. She looked out at the blurry field with the henhouse at the top. She'd collected the eggs earlier, filled the basket with twenty-two big brown ones as the hens pattered and squawked around her.

'I saw a man,' she said. 'Up by the henhouse, the day I arrived.'

Out of the corner of her eye she saw him turning towards her.

'He was oldish, around seventy, I'd say. He wore a hat, a kind of a flat hat. He was just … standing there. He saw me – I was looking out my bedroom window – and he smiled and lifted his hat.'

'Mr Thompson used to do that.'

Rain, beating a tattoo on the roof.

'But he died,' she said, 'so it wasn't him.'

'No … Must have been one of the locals.'

Must it, though? Didn't strange things happen here? Couldn't she have seen someone who was dead but who hadn't left?

'I saw the painting your dad did of him,' she said. 'The one that's in the hall. He looked—'

She stopped. She shook her head. He'd think she was daft.

The rain was lightening off. She reached for the door handle. 'Thanks,' she said, 'for showing me the island.'

'Thanks for your help,' he replied, getting out too. 'It couldn't have been Mr Thompson,' he said. 'It was someone who looked a bit like him, that's all.'

'Sure, I know that.' She glanced towards the house. 'I'd better go in. I've left Susan on her own long enough.'

'Same time tomorrow,' he said, zipping up his jacket as he turned away, slipping the van keys into his pocket.

'Drop by later,' she said, 'if you're at a loose end. The girls would love to see Tommy.'

Two days left. She had nothing to lose.

❄❄❄

She took her time walking home, got there by half ten. The boys were still in pyjamas, watching cartoons and eating biscuits in the sitting room. Gavin was reading the paper in the kitchen.

'Did you sleep?'

'I did, a bit.' She didn't know whether to believe him.

'Joyce dropped by,' he said. 'She left her number in case you need anything.'

'OK.'

'How was your father?'

Laura unzipped her jacket. 'He was the way he always is.' And nothing more was said on the subject, by either of them.

At ten past noon a hearse drew up outside the house. Two men dressed in black suits and dazzling white shirts shook Laura's hand and told her they were sorry for her loss. She joined the boys in the sitting room while Gavin brought the men upstairs, and a few minutes later his mother was taken away in the oak coffin he'd selected for her. Laura looked out the window and saw a small knot of people gathered on the path. They blessed themselves as the coffin was slid into the hearse.

'Wait here,' she said, when she heard the front door close.

Gavin stood silently in the hall. She couldn't read his face.

'What time did they say for the removal?'

'Half five to half seven.'

'Maybe you should lie down. It could be a long night, we might get people visiting again.'

'I don't want to lie down,' he said. 'I might take the boys somewhere.'

The boys, not her.

'Where were you thinking?'

'I was thinking the zoo.' He looked at her, daring her to tell him he shouldn't.

The zoo. It was the place they'd met, when she'd returned his book. The African Savannah, to be precise. I'm looking for Gavin Connolly, she'd said. You've found him, he'd said. It was as good a place as any to put down a few hours.

'Is it open today?' she asked.

'It's open.'

'Would you mind if I came too?'

'Suit yourself.'

So they took the bus, and were there soon after one. The day remained overcast and chilly but the rain stayed away. They took in the Reptile House and the Flamingo Lagoon and the Kaziranga Forest Trail. They did the Gorilla Rainforest and the Chimpanzee Island and the Elephant House and the African Savannah.

'This is where we met,' she said, watching a giraffe yanking leaves from a tree – but Gavin was talking to Seamus and didn't hear.

Along the way they encountered a few of his old colleagues, most of whom hadn't read about Gladys's death in the paper that morning – or if they had, they made no mention of it. After a late lunch in one of the zoo's cafés, with desserts on the house from Annie behind the counter, it was time to go back and get ready.

Laura sent the boys and Gavin off to change while she stripped and remade Gladys's bed. She wondered what they'd do with the house, which was now Gavin's. Sell it, she supposed, give them a bit more financial security. Put some of the money away for the children's education, invest in a new three-piece suite for the sitting room. Buy a few decent decorations for next Christmas, a new crib to replace the one that she'd failed to find.

The funeral home was a challenge. Two hours of standing beside Gavin as people who were mostly strangers to her trickled in and shook her hand and told her they were sorry for her trouble. Gladys lying in state a few feet from them, surrounded by candles and flowers, while the boys in their good grey trousers and navy blazers sat as far away as they could get from the coffin and tried to look as if they had nothing at all to do with the proceedings.

Afterwards there was the church, which mercifully was just across the road, and more hand-shaking and small-talking. Gladys, after all, had got to know quite a few people in her seventy-one years on earth.

When they finally emerged it was to the rain that had been threatening all day. It was falling in sheets, thundering down on the tarmac. Gavin was despatched to get the car, and became soaked in the process. They crawled home with the wipers slashing water from the windscreen.

They raced through the deluge to the house, the boys whooping at the drama of it, their departed grandmother temporarily forgotten.

The others went to the kitchen in search of something to eat while Laura shook off her shoes and shrugged herself out of her damp jacket. The only advantage of the rain was that it might put people off calling to the house for tea and cake, which they'd felt obliged to offer at the church.

She must dry their things for the funeral tomorrow – she'd put them on the clothes horse, leave them in front of the fire tonight and hope for the best.

She didn't see the envelope until she bent to pick up her shoes. There was a Ben or Seamus-sized footprint stamped onto it. She picked it up and turned it over, and saw her name.

In his writing.

'You want tea?'

She looked up. Gavin, at the kitchen door.

'This came,' she said. 'It's from my father.'

He waited.

She opened it.

Ten thousand euro, the cheque said. Made out to nobody, the space left blank, but of course it was for Tilly. He was being a father in the only way he knew how.

She held it out. Gavin stepped forward and looked at it.

'For Tilly,' she said, folding it and slipping it into her bag.

'I'll fix dinner,' she said. 'Would you light the sitting-room fire?'

She walked to the kitchen, brushing drops from her hair.

✳✳✳

At twenty past twelve Janet McHugh dropped by with a Mass card and half a dozen scones, and stayed for tea and the last of Nell's apple tart.

At one o'clock, after seeing Janet off the premises, they had a picnic lunch of banana sandwiches and ice-cream on a spread-out blanket on the sitting-room floor.

At half past one the girls watched a DVD while Tilly cleared up and Susan walked the kitchen floor with a fretful Poppy, and Cathy Considine dropped by with a Mass card and a loaf of caraway-seed bread.

At a quarter to two Nell phoned to invite them to dinner. 'I asked Andy to say it to Tilly this morning when they were doing the deliveries, but I've just discovered that he forgot. Will you come?'

At ten to two Henry Manning dropped by with a Mass card and a bottle of whiskey, and a report on the state of the hotel – roof repairs ongoing, estimated time the work would take, three weeks minimum.

'When you come to see us again we'll be flying it. You can drop by for complimentary afternoon tea,' he told Tilly, and she could have hugged him for the 'when'.

At five past two Poppy stopped crying and fell asleep, and was promptly brought upstairs by Susan, who grabbed the chance to lie down too.

At twenty to three Maisie Kiely's son Damien dropped by with a Mass card and a jar of lemon curd from his mother, and he told Tilly by way of introduction that he'd built the shed that had been demolished by the tree.

At three o'clock Tilly and the girls baked raisin cookies.

At half past three the doorbell rang again.

'I'm Eve,' the girl said.

Tilly's height, more or less. Tilly's age, more or less. Long, perfectly straight dark red hair, pale greenish eyes. A smattering of freckles. Short red coat, grey scarf. Blue jeans tucked into ankle boots.

'I called to see if you need any help,' she said. 'I give Laura a hand with the B&B when it's open. I was away for Christmas, I only just got back. I heard the news about Gavin's mum.'

'I think we're good, thanks,' Tilly replied. 'Susan's here, Laura's stepmother—'

'I know who Susan is. And you're Laura's sister.'

'That's right ...' Was she going to have to tell her story all over again?

No, she wasn't. 'Did Laura tell you they named Evie after me?'

'No.'

'I was there when she and Marian were born. I'm Evie's godmother.'

'Oh.' She must know them well. 'You want to come in and say hello? They're in the kitchen.'

'OK.' She walked ahead of Tilly and pushed open the kitchen door. 'Hey there,' she said, and the girls rushed to her like they'd rushed to Susan. She crouched and hugged them, and asked what Santa had brought as Tilly took the cookies from the oven and transferred them to a wire rack.

'Where's Poppy?'

'Having a nap, and Susan's lying down too ... you want some tea?' She felt obliged to ask, although she was weary from talking to strangers.

'No thanks,' the girl said, getting to her feet. 'If you need help, give a shout – Susan knows where to find me. See you later, alligators,' she said to the twins who followed her to the front door.

And then she was gone, striding down the path and hopping onto the bike that Tilly hadn't noticed. Lifting a hand to the three of them as she cycled off.

Ten minutes later Poppy and Susan reappeared, and everyone apart from Poppy dunked warm cookies into milk.

At four o'clock Dougie Fennessy dropped by in his taxi with a Mass card and a salmon quiche from his wife Ita, and stayed for coffee and the last of the cookies.

At half past four Tilly and the girls made Plasticine snakes and played dress-up dolls and drew pictures while Susan mopped the kitchen floor and sang to Poppy.

At six o'clock everyone walked next door to Nell's to eat roast chicken, and afterwards James, who had finished work early, drew cartoon animals for the girls.

At a quarter past seven they came home, and Susan put the twins into a bath while Tilly walked the kitchen floor with a grizzling Poppy, who they had decided wasn't sickening for anything, but simply getting a few new teeth, and maybe pining for her mother.

By half past eight all three children were asleep. Tilly and Susan sat side by side with mugs of berry tea on the larger of the sitting-room couches, in front of the coal fire that Susan had lit earlier. Charlie lay in his usual evening spot on the mat by the fire.

'When is your baby due?' Tilly asked.

'June the fourth.'

She waited, but no further comment was made. For the first time Tilly wondered if Susan was entirely happy about the pregnancy. What did she know about her? She was forty years old, according to Laura, and over twenty years younger than her husband, the man Tilly hadn't heard her mention since her arrival on Roone, except in response to Tilly's question about how they'd met.

Bit strange, wasn't it, when they were having their first child together? Bit odd that he hadn't come up once in conversation, the man that wasn't child-friendly – and yet here he was on his third child. Three accidents – or had he and Tilly's mother simply been a wrong combination, and had he got it right with Susan?

But Susan didn't look like Nell had when she'd revealed her

pregnancy to Tilly. Instead, there seemed to be a muted sadness about her.

'I want a girl,' she said. 'I'll call her Emily, after my grandmother.'

'I'll', not 'we'll'. Maybe he'd given her free rein with the name.

'Enough about me,' she said. 'Tell me about your family in Australia', so Tilly told her about Ma and Pa and Robbie and Jemima, and the farm outside town where she'd grown up.

'Do you have a boyfriend back home?'

'No.'

Turning her head to look into the fire that had blue in it, right at the heart.

'I nearly married someone once,' Susan said. 'I was in my early twenties, working in a beauty salon. I was the receptionist, and he was a rep for a cosmetics company. He'd call every so often with a delivery, and we'd chat for a few minutes. One day he asked me to go to the cinema, completely out of the blue, and I said yes. We dated for over a year, and I met his parents and he met my mother, and then he asked me to marry him.'

She stopped. A coal tumbled sideways in the fire, sending out a small sprinkling of sparks.

'And you said no,' Tilly said, her gaze still on the flames.

'Actually, I said yes. We went ahead and made all the arrangements. He got me a ring and I bought a dress and we booked the church and the hotel, and then ... on the morning of the wedding I stood him up.'

Silence. The fire flickered. A car horn sounded faintly on the road.

'I left him standing at the altar,' Susan said. 'He was a good, decent man, and I did that to him. My mother was so angry ... I handed in my notice at the salon, couldn't risk meeting him again. I did a secretarial course and got a job in the school, and for a long time after that I avoided men – I ran a mile if someone showed any interest in me. I felt I didn't deserve to be happy, after what I'd done.' She took a sip of tea. 'And then,' she said, 'about five years later I met Luke Potter, and he wouldn't take no for an answer, so I married him.'

She'd met him in her late twenties, and she'd waited till now to have his baby. Maybe they hadn't had a choice, and it simply hadn't happened. Or maybe they'd agreed not to have children, and this had been a mistake.

But Susan wanted a baby. She wanted a girl she could name Emily, after her grandmother.

'What stage are you at?' Susan asked. 'At school, I mean.'

'I have one year to go in high school.'

'And then?'

Tilly turned to face her.

'What do you want to do, after you leave school?'

'I'm … not sure.' What could she possibly say, without telling her everything?

'Time enough,' Susan replied.

'Yes … A girl called this afternoon,' she said, suddenly remembering. 'She said her name was Eve.'

'Oh yes, I know Eve. Nice girl. She went out with Andy next door.'

Tilly's heart tripped. 'Did she?'

'Yes, for quite a long time. Over a year, maybe two years.'

She had long dark red hair and she was pretty, and she'd gone out with him for quite a long time. She helped Laura in the B&B, which was right next door to where he lived.

Which of them had finished it, and how long ago? Whose heart had been broken? And what did any of it matter anyway, with a return air ticket and a baby standing between them, and a miracle, let's face it, probably not on the cards?

It was looking inevitable, her return to Australia. Nell was wrong: you couldn't make something happen, no matter how badly you wanted it. Tilly would just have to face the music when she got home, deal with the consequences. The thought was unconscionable, but she could see no other option.

They switched on the television, and found a channel with a group of musicians playing the kind of music Tilly had heard in Bernard and Cormac's pub on Christmas Eve. In between the tunes a man with a beard spoke in a language that sounded like nothing Tilly had ever heard. Susan told her it was Irish, and Tilly remembered Breda on the bus to Dingle talking about Irish having been beaten into her at school.

The phone rang in the hall. Tilly got to her feet.

'It's probably Laura,' Susan said.

It *was* Laura. Gladys had been brought to the church; people had called to the house afterwards. The weather was bad in Dublin, the rain very heavy. They'd visited the zoo earlier, which sounded strange to Tilly.

'So how was your day?' Laura asked.

'Lots of people called with Mass cards and food. We had dinner at Nell's.'

A small pause, then Laura spoke again. 'Tilly, I have something to tell you. I called to see our father this morning.'

Their *father*? Laura had made no mention of going to see him before she'd left Roone.

'I told him about you. I hope you don't mind, I thought he should know.'

'... What did he say?'

Another pause. 'Well, he was surprised, of course. He had no idea about you.'

'Did he want to meet me?'

Maybe this was the miracle. Maybe he'd take her in, give her baby a home.

'Tilly, I told you what he's like, didn't I? He was never going to welcome you with open arms. That was never going to happen.'

She was surprised how much it hurt. It tied in totally with what she'd been told, by Laura and her mother, but still it made her eyes hot. She couldn't speak.

350

'Listen,' Laura said, 'don't feel bad. It's the way he is, he can't help it. He's the very same with me. It's got nothing to do with you, nothing.'

What if Tilly just turned up on his doorstep though? What if she did the same as she'd done here on Roone? That had worked out OK, hadn't it? They'd taken her in, they'd let her stay. Oh, it might be a lot harder to get him to accept her, but she could try, couldn't she? She could take a bus to Dublin on Wednesday, instead of to the airport.

'Tilly, there's something else … He gave me a cheque for you.' She said the amount.

Tilly looked at the painting of Walter, ten thousand euro echoing in her head. Well over ten thousand Australian dollars.

'That's all he can do for his children,' Laura said. 'It's all he's capable of.'

Ten thousand euro. Enough, surely, to set herself up here in Ireland, enough not to need Laura's help.

'Are you still there?'

'Yes.'

'Are you OK?'

Her thoughts raced. She could rent a place somewhere – Dingle, maybe. By the sea anyway. She'd have enough to live on until the baby was born. And then she could get a job.

'Tilly?'

'I'm here, I'm OK.'

'Good … Look, I know it's a lot to take in. Try not to let it upset you. Think of how the money will make life easier for you, with the baby coming. It will make a big difference.'

Ten thousand euro. Rent couldn't be that high, surely? They'd only need a small place, a one-bed flat. Even just a room in someone's house.

'Tilly, will you put Susan on for a minute? I'll see you tomorrow, OK?'

'OK.'

She laid down the receiver and called Susan, and then she brought the coal scuttle out for a refill, her head still full of all she'd just been told. The miracle had happened after all: she'd got her wish to stay in Ireland, if not on Roone.

As she passed through the kitchen a flash of pink caught her eye in Charlie's basket beside the stove. She paused to investigate, thinking it to be one of the children's hats – but as soon as she reached for it she saw that it was a cloth doll, lying face down. She picked it up and turned it over. She took in the face, the hair, the dress.

Ah, Betsy. It looked so like her. She'd had precisely the same features. And the dress was just like the one Ma had knitted when Betsy's original one got torn, except this one was pink, not red.

And it was stitched to her body, at the shoulders and the waist, in just the same way Ma had done. So you won't lose it, she'd said, although Tilly had wanted to be able to take it off at night when Betsy went to bed, like she'd done with the old one.

And the hair, ragged at the ends just like Betsy's had been, after Tilly had snipped off her braids, and immediately afterwards regretted it. Really, the similarities were amazing.

She lifted the dress, which was stained with doggy saliva, and grubby from being tossed and dragged about. The little bloomers, yes, exactly the same; these ones not very white, though. She pushed up the left elasticated leg, hardly aware that she was holding her breath – and there it was.

TW.

Tilly Walker. She clamped a hand to her mouth.

Sewn onto the thigh in the strong black thread Ma had used to stitch Tilly's initials into the necks of all her jackets when she was growing up.

TW. Yes, yes, the final leg of the W higher than the other two, she remembered how that used to annoy her.

It wasn't a doll like Betsy. It *was* Betsy.

Oh my God.

Betsy.

It was Betsy, there was no doubt. It was definitely her Betsy. The red dress faded to pink, but otherwise the same Betsy she remembered. They'd been reunited, on Roone of all places. It was unbelievable. It was amazing.

But how was it possible? How could her lost doll have turned up here, of all places? It made no sense. How could she have travelled from Australia to Roone?

And then she thought: She got here the same way as I did. She came on a plane, on the lap or in the luggage of some little girl who'd found her in Queensland and claimed her. A girl, maybe, whose parents had emigrated from Ireland like so many others, and who travelled back here every few years to see the ones they'd left behind.

And somewhere along the way, Betsy had come into the possession of Gavin and Laura. Maybe she'd been lost again by her new owner, and found by one of the children, and commandeered eventually by Charlie, or donated to him.

Or maybe Charlie himself had come across her, lying on a roadside or in a ditch, and dragged her home with him.

It was possible. In theory, it could happen. But the coincidence of Betsy finding her way to the same tiny island, actually materialising in the same house as Tilly, was pretty hard to swallow. It was nothing short of miraculous.

Roone is no stranger to miracles, Nell had said.

Sometimes it's hard to explain stuff that happens here, Andy had said.

But if you poked around them for long enough, surely you'd find a logical reason for every quirky thing on Roone. The apple tree was a special extra-fertile species; the smell of chocolate at the cemetery was being blown across from the factory on the mainland. The road sign at the cliffs was an islander's idea of a joke. Tilly didn't believe in strange phenomena, or magic, or whatever you wanted to call it. She didn't believe in miracles.

Lien believed. Lien would have a field day on Roone. 'We're not the only universe,' Lien would say. 'There's another dimension out there, maybe several others. They're all around us, and sometimes they allow us glimpses.'

When she talked like this, Tilly would smile and tell her to lay off the weed, and Lien would say Tilly was in denial, and they'd eventually drop it, and Tilly would go on believing that there was a rational explanation for everything that happened.

And yet …

There was Laura renting Nell's house directly after Gavin, and finding the book he'd left behind.

There was the pull Tilly experienced for the island, the feeling she'd been here before.

And there was Betsy. Suddenly, after a decade, there was Betsy. *Here* was Betsy. Here was proof, right in her hands, that something completely remarkable had taken place.

She filled a basin with hot water. She plunged Betsy in and scrubbed her with soap until she was clean, and then she rinsed the soap away, and squeezed as much of the water out as she could, and sat her on top of the still-warm stove. She'd be dry by morning, and Charlie would find a new toy.

As she picked up the scuttle and went out to the coal bunker she felt a sudden sharp cramp in her abdomen. She dropped the scuttle and leaned against the jamb of the open back door, and bent forward to ease it.

And then there was a gush of something between her legs, a warm dampness in her jeans. Another gush, no control over it, and another, each wave contracting her abdominal muscles, making her groan with pain, forcing her into a deeper bend. Her jeans stained darkly, black spatters on the ground.

Susan, she called – but no sound came.

❄✳❄

'Long day,' she said.

'Sure was.'

The few callers had left, the boys were in bed. Larry was presumably halfway to Cincinnati – or maybe the whole way by this time. Could be climbing gratefully into his own bed right now. Vowing, maybe, never to turn his back on it again.

Laura and Gavin sat side by side on Gladys's couch. While she was washing cups he'd gone to the off-licence down the road and come back with a bottle of red wine. Come in and sit down, he'd said, and here they were. The television was on – a chat show, people in their Sunday best sitting on a curved red couch. The sound was muted.

'The zoo was good,' she said, 'wasn't it?'

'Mm.'

'Ever miss it?'

'… Sometimes.'

The chat show host was among the audience now, aiming a microphone at a woman who was saying something that made the people around her laugh silently.

'Remember,' he said, his eyes still on the screen, 'a few days ago, you accused me of having an affair with Bernie Flannery?'

She looked at him. 'What?' It had come out of nowhere.

'Do you remember?'

'… Yes, but I didn't really—'

'Well, I wasn't, I'm not – but I did think about it. I did consider it.'

The words slapped her in the face. Bernie Flannery, early twenties, daughter of widowed Dick the chemist, with whom she still lived. Bernie, who taught the boys basketball after school, who could often be seen out walking her two beagles along the coast road, or giving a hand behind the counter of her aunt Lelia's café.

Bernie Flannery. Big hearty laugh, long-legged, game for anything. Doing a correspondence course in business studies, always at home when Gavin called with his vegetables. Presented him with a bottle of

Baileys for Christmas on his last visit. He'd produced it when he got home, prompting Laura's accusation.

'I thought about it,' he said, 'for all of five seconds. And then I realised I was only thinking about it because you didn't want me any more.'

She opened her mouth, but he kept going.

'The thing is,' he said, 'I still love you as much as I ever did. More, probably, since you got sick. The other thing is, it wasn't my fault you got cancer, but I seem to be getting the blame.'

'*What?*'

'You haven't talked to me in months, unless you have to. I don't seem to be able to do anything right these days. You can't bear me near you – sometimes I feel you don't even want to be in the same room as me. You didn't mention the present I got you, you haven't worn it. And I can't for the life of me think of anything I've done to make you treat me like this. So I can only conclude that you don't love me any more.'

'Gavin—'

'So I think the best plan is for us to separate, for a while anyway. I can come here … I can live here. I'm fairly sure I could get my old job back. We could give it a few months, say until the summer, see how we both feel after that. We'd have to work out some arrangement about the kids.'

'Gavin,' she said again, then didn't know how to go on. Didn't know how to start.

He gave her a few seconds. 'So you're agreed then? That's what we'll do?'

'No,' she said, 'I'm not agreed. I don't want you to go.'

She didn't. The future without him was simply too bleak to countenance. He was *Gavin*, for Christ's sake: what would she do if he left?

'Listen,' she said. She stopped, took a breath, started again. 'It was my first time to have cancer,' she said. 'I wasn't very good at it. And even now, when I'm being told I'm clear I'm still terrified out of my wits in case it comes back. I can fight it, I *will* fight it, if it does come back, but I can't be sure I'll win. I'm more scared than I've ever been, and that makes me angry, and you got the brunt because if I shouted at you and snapped at you it meant I mightn't do it to the kids.'

She stopped. Her eyes were swimming. His face was blurred.

'It's not much of an explanation, but it's all I have. You're my punching bag, you're what stops me going out of my mind. And I'm sorry that it's hard on you, and I'll try to go easier, but you married me for better or worse, so you need to suck it up right now, and wait for things to get better.'

'And what if they don't?'

'They will,' she said, because they both needed to hear that. 'I'll calm down after a bit, if they keep telling me I'm clear, and if you stick around for me to abuse. And by the way, I love my present. I just kept forgetting to say it to you – in case you haven't noticed, there's been quite a lot going on since you gave it to me. And I was nervous about wearing it in case Poppy pulled the chain and broke it.'

She blinked, and he came back into focus.

He reached up and thumbed away the tears that the blink had sent running down her face. 'You should have told me all this,' he said. 'How you felt.'

'You should have known.'

'Hey,' he said, 'I've got lots of super-powers, but mind-reading isn't one of them.'

'I still love you,' she said. 'I do. I just – it got pushed aside.'

'That's good to know.'

'They cut off my breast,' she said. 'I don't feel sexy any more. I didn't think you'd be interested.'

'I think it would take a hell of a lot more than that to put me off you.'

'So you'll stay with us? You'll put up with a harridan wife for another while?'

He sighed. 'I'd be a fool to turn down an offer like that.'

'I might need your help,' she said. 'I might not be able to do it without you.'

He smiled then, so tenderly it nearly killed her, 'About time,' he said. 'About time you looked for my help.'

She stood, leaving the rest of her wine. 'Let's go to bed.'

They locked up. They switched off the lights and went upstairs. In their room they undressed, and she set aside the insecurities that surgery had left behind, and got into his twin bed, and began the business of repairing her marriage.

❆❆❆

'You've had a miscarriage,' he said. 'I'm so sorry.'

He was about Pa's age. He wore a suit and he smelt of soap, and his eyes were gentle behind steel-rimmed glasses. He arrived at Walter's Place about ten minutes after Susan phoned him. He questioned Tilly and told her she'd more than likely miscarried, but that he needed to examine her further.

He waited while Nell was summoned to babysit. He brought Tilly and Susan in his own car to a building that looked too small to be a health clinic, and there he laid Tilly on a trolley and did an ultrasound.

'Everything is gone,' he said. 'There's nothing else that has to be done. You just need to take it easy for a day or two.'

He drove them back to Walter's Place and Nell went home, and Susan ran a bath for Tilly and put her to bed afterwards with a cup of tea and two paracetamol.

'You never said a word.' Touching the back of her hand to Tilly's forehead.

'I told Laura. She knew.'

It wasn't yet midnight, the day not quite over. 'Stay in bed tomorrow. I'll tell Andy you're not feeling well.'

'OK.'

'It's good you're not travelling until Wednesday. Hopefully you'll be ready by then.'

'Yes.'

'Anything I can get you, anything you feel like?'

'No thanks … Sorry.'

Susan brushed away the tear that rolled down Tilly's face. 'Silly girl, you've nothing to be sorry for. Try to get some sleep, and I'll look in in the morning.'

The door closed softly, and she was alone.

She wasn't pregnant any more. She wasn't pregnant. She was filled with relief that the baby she and John Smith had made had decided, after all, not to be born. She was dizzy with relief – she was light-headed with it.

So why was she crying? Why were tears flooding out of her, running down the sides of her face and soaking her pillow? Why, side by side with the relief, was there such a feeling of devastation, of unutterable sadness? Why did it feel like her heart was torn in two?

After a long time – half an hour, more than that – she ran out of tears. She turned on her bedside lamp and saw that it was almost one o'clock in the morning. She padded into the bathroom and blew her nose on toilet paper, avoiding the mirror, not wanting to see what the last few hours had done to her face.

One o'clock plus ten made eleven o'clock.

She took her phone from her bag and climbed back into bed. Her mouth felt dry: she drank from the glass of water Susan had left on the locker. She placed the call and listened to the ringing, picturing the dresser where the phone always sat. She imagined Ma crossing the room to answer it, wiping her hands on her apron.

There was a click. Her heart jumped. A few seconds of fumbling, someone breathing heavily.

'Hello?' Too loud.

She swallowed. 'Ma, it's Tilly,' she said. Her voice felt rusty.

'Tilly.' More breathing. 'You OK?'

'I'm fine, I can hear you fine, you don't need to … Um, how are you, Ma?'

'We're OK, we're good.'

'That's good.'

Pause.

'And Pa? And the kids?'

'They're good. Jemima's right here with me, Robbie's gone to Markus's.'

'You had a good Christmas?'

'It was fine. We missed you, though. And how's Bali? You like it?'

She closed her eyes, swallowed back the urge to cry again. 'Ma,' she said, 'I got something to tell you. It's not bad, it's just … something you should know.'

'What's up?' Ma's voice tighter. 'Something happen?'

Tilly shook her head, with nobody at all to see it. 'Ma, I'm not in Bali. I didn't go to Bali.'

Dead silence. Even the breathing stopped.

'Ma, it's OK, it's not bad, honest. I didn't tell you because—'

'Where *are* you?'

'I'm in Ireland, Ma. I flew to Ireland, not Bali.'

'Ireland?' She said it like it was a word she'd never heard, like it was in a language she didn't understand. She made it sound like a food she wasn't sure she liked the taste of. 'You're in *Ireland*?'

'I thought you might not be happy about me going so far,' Tilly said. 'I thought you might worry, so I didn't tell you. But it's—'

'How did you even *get* there?' she asked, her voice full of bewilderment. 'Is someone with you? Did Lien go with you?'

'No, I came on my own. It's OK, Ma, I got here fine.' No mention of Heathrow and what had happened there. No talk of that ever, with her and Pa.

'Ma,' she said, 'I have a sister here. My mother told me when I met her. I came to find her, and I did, and she's great, she's really ...'

She trailed off. Ma breathed some more. Thousands of miles away, and Tilly could hear her breathing.

'You got a *sister* in Ireland?'

'Yeah, her name is Laura. She's married with five—'

'You got a sister,' Ma repeated. 'How'd you find her?'

'My mother told me where she lived. Ma, you should see—'

'She know you were coming? You planned all of this?'

'No, Ma, she didn't know. Nobody knew I was coming.' She'd leave Lien out of it, no point in involving her. 'I just came. I did it myself. Just me. Nobody else was involved.'

'You didn't get in touch with her beforehand, let her know you were coming?'

'No, I ... just went. I thought I'd just ... find her.' She could hear how implausible it sounded. She couldn't tell Ma why she'd done it like that. She couldn't tell her that she hadn't stopped to think, so scared she'd been of what had lain ahead. What she'd thought had lain ahead.

'She coulda been gone,' Ma said. 'She coulda been someplace else.'

'I know, but everything—'

'Tilly, you shoulda told us. You had no right to go making up that story about Bali.'

'I know, Ma, I'm sorry, I'm real sorry – but it's OK, honest it is. I had to find her, I just had to, and I thought you mightn't let me go if I asked.'

Another pause. She could see Ma leaning against the dresser as she struggled to take it all in. She could see her as clearly as if she was standing in the kitchen watching her.

'You got more family there?'

She hesitated. 'My father's in Ireland too, but—'

'Your *father*? You mean she knew who it was?'

'He was her husband, Ma. They were married. It was all – but he didn't know, she didn't tell him about me. They fell out, and now they're divorced, and he – well, I won't get to meet him, he's in another part of the country.'

Another few seconds of silence. She waited.

'Tilly,' Ma said then, 'you coming back to us?'

Instantly her throat felt thick with unshed tears. 'Of *course* I am,' she said, pressing the heel of her hand into each eye socket in turn. 'Of *course* I'm coming back. I'll be home early on Friday, just like I said.'

'OK then.' Pause. 'You're sure you're OK, Tilly? There's nothing more you ain't telling me?'

'I'm fine, Ma. I'm sorry I didn't tell you, I just thought I couldn't.'

'That's OK ... You look after yourself, OK?'

'I will. I'll see you soon, Ma.' Her voice wobbled, more tears treacherously close. 'You'll tell Pa where I am?'

A beat passed. 'I'll tell him. You want him to come get you at the airport?'

'No – I can get a bus, it's OK.'

'Well, maybe he'll come pick you up anyway,' she said. 'Long trip, you'll be tired.'

'No, Ma – there's no need, honest. I'll call from the bus and he can come get me at the station in town.'

'OK,' she said, 'he'll do that. He'll pick you up at the bus station. You let me know the time, you send me a text.'

'I will ... thanks, Ma.'

'I'll say goodbye then,' she said. 'You look after yourself, Tilly. You be real careful now.'

'Bye, Ma.'

A click, and she was gone.

You be real careful now. Tilly pressed the sheet to her eyes. She'd see them soon. She'd be home on New Year's Day, at the tail end of a year she'd be glad to put behind her.

She set her phone on the locker and lay down. She'd tell them about Roone, and the second family she'd met there. She'd describe the island, and the snow, and the house where she'd stayed. She'd show them all the photos she'd taken.

Laura had been right. Staying in Ireland would have been madness, would have hurt Ma and Pa terribly. She was ashamed that she'd even considered it, ashamed that it had taken losing the baby to bring her to her senses.

She saw things so clearly now. She'd have to report John Smith: Laura had been right about that too. He had to be stopped before he did it again. She wouldn't press charges; she'd tell Mrs Harvey, the English teacher he'd replaced. She'd tell her everything, and Mrs Harvey would know what to do. Hopefully it wouldn't come to a court case – but if it did, she'd cope.

She pushed John Smith away and replaced him with Andy. She wouldn't tell anyone about Andy, not even Lien. She'd go back to Australia and get on with her life, and in time she'd forget him. Right now it didn't seem at all likely, or even possible, that she'd ever be able to forget him, but people did, didn't they? Life kept going, people moved on.

Just as well she wouldn't be doing the rounds with him in the morning. Just as well she had no photo of him either.

She wondered what Nell thought of her, knowing now what she did. And Colette, she'd surely hear what had happened. She hoped they wouldn't think too badly of her.

And some day, maybe in five years' time, maybe in ten, she might pay a return visit to Roone, just to see how everyone was getting on. She'd like to meet Poppy when she could talk, and see the changes in her and the other children as they grew up.

After a minute she slipped from the bed and went out into the corridor and tiptoed downstairs, feeling her way in the dark. Her insides ached when she walked. Betsy was where she'd left her a few hours earlier, sitting on the stove. Still a bit damp, but she took her anyway. She brought her back to bed and turned off the light and eventually fell asleep, Betsy lying in the crook of her arm.

❄

TUESDAY
29 DECEMBER

❄

T he misty rain that had been falling relentlessly since they'd got up finally petered out as they left the car and walked into the cemetery, just before noon. A slanted beam of weak sunshine slid from behind the clouds as they took their positions with the rest of the mourners at the graveside.

The wooden box that held what remained of Gladys lay on two planks above the hole it was destined for, a mound of earth piled up neatly beyond it. The gravediggers stood a discreet distance away, leaning on their spades and waiting for the short ceremony to be over.

Laura stood between the boys as the priest worked his way through the funeral prayers. Another couple of hours before they could hit the road. She hungered for Roone, she felt its absence acutely.

She wondered how Tilly would be when they got back. Would she have come around to Laura's way of thinking, or would she still resent being told that her best option was to go home? Poor naive Tilly, falling for the charms and lies of a philanderer, like many a young innocent woman before her. Poor foolish Tilly, having to live with the consequences of her actions.

Was Laura right, though, in urging her to go back to her parents, and maybe endure months of their condemnation? Should she stand by her sister and offer to let her stay on Roone? Should she talk to the parents herself, try to convince a couple she'd never met that she'd look after Tilly and the baby they hadn't known she was having? They'd hit the roof, they'd be bound to, and who could blame them?

And Susan. What was to be done about Susan?

I might leave him, she'd said quietly to Laura on the phone the night before. I might have to leave him. I might come to Roone, she'd said. Could I come to Roone, just for a while, until I figure out what to do? And Laura had said yes, of course she'd said yes, but it wasn't good: it wasn't what Susan wanted. Despite everything, despite Luke having issued her that terrible ultimatum, Susan loved him.

The prayers came to an end. The sun came and went as they watched the coffin being lowered into the grave, as Gavin stepped forward and threw a handful of earth onto it. Gladys making her exit, Susan and Tilly's babies waiting in the wings – and Nell's too, if Laura wasn't mistaken.

The carousel going on, the births and marriages and deaths continuing to roll around. The heartbreaks and the joys, the disasters and the miracles featuring as regularly as the next sunrise, the next high tide.

Gavin stepped back. Laura reached across and found his hand, and held on to it tightly as the sun broke through once more. They'd started last night to repair the damage that the last several months had caused. They had a long way to go – *she* had a long way to go – but they'd made a start.

She'd try to find Walter when they got home, now that she knew he was still about. She'd nag him until he revealed himself to her again. She'd confide in him like before: she'd list her fears aloud to him and he'd shunt them gently away. He'd help her to mend.

They led the way to the pub that had been Gavin's local since his first pint at seventeen and a half. They ate the soup and sandwiches they'd ordered, surrounded by faces that had become familiar to Laura over the last couple of days. Afterwards Gavin settled the bill and they bade everyone goodbye and piled into the car, their luggage already in the boot.

'Keep in touch,' Joyce said, 'pop by next time you're up,' and Laura promised she would, and knew she probably wouldn't. Nothing to bring them back to Dublin any more, with Gladys dead and Laura's father as good as dead to her. No reason to make the long trek east after this, unless Gavin wanted to put flowers on his mother's grave.

They hit the motorway and Laura dozed, and didn't wake until Gavin slid down his window to pay at the toll booth, fifty miles outside the capital. When he drove off again she took out her phone and rang Susan.

'We're on the way,' she said. 'We'll see you in a few hours. All OK?'

'Girls are all fine, but there is a bit of news,' Susan replied, and Laura listened to an account of Tilly's miscarriage.

'How is she?'

'She got up around noon. I wanted her to stay in bed but she says she feels OK.'

Tilly, not pregnant any more, nothing now to fear from going home. But a miscarriage, whatever the circumstances, was still a cause for sadness. A hard lesson learned, and she hadn't yet turned eighteen.

'Tell her we'll see her soon,' Laura said. After hanging up she checked her watch, and decided there was time. She turned to Gavin. 'Can we do a quick stop somewhere? I'd like to get Tilly a goodbye gift' – so they left the motorway at the next town, and she found a small boutique whose after-Christmas sale was in full swing, and in less than five minutes she bought a ring with a little blue stone that she figured would have to fit one of Tilly's fingers.

'Home,' she said, getting back into the car, and Gavin turned it in the direction of Roone, and home they went.

❄❄❄

'Want to talk about it?' Susan asked. 'I'm a good listener.'

The girls were colouring at the far end of the table, Charlie hovering nearby. Poppy was perched on Susan's lap, gnawing on her rubber rattle. Tilly and Susan sat side by side, Tilly in Laura's dressing gown, eating the toast Susan had coaxed her to have.

'I don't mind,' she said. 'It's all over now anyway' – and she told Susan, in as few sentences as she could, about the disaster that had been her and John Smith. 'What happened last night was for the best,' she said, 'I know that …' She trailed off, still feeling unaccountably forlorn, still feeling that a cross look or a sharp word would undo her.

'Tilly,' Susan said gently, 'you lost a baby. It's bound to hurt, no matter what.'

Tilly nodded, deciding to leave the last bit of toast. Deciding she didn't really want to talk about it after all.

'What did you tell Andy?'

'I told him you'd caught a cold, and I wasn't allowing you outside.'

A cold didn't sound like much of a reason not to join him. He probably thought she couldn't be bothered; he probably assumed she'd been bored the day before. If he only knew how much she'd loved it, how much she'd looked forward to going with him again today.

She needed to change the subject, so she told Susan about finding Betsy. Susan listened with growing disbelief.

'It couldn't possibly be your doll, Tilly. It must be one that just looks like it.'

'That's what I thought,' Tilly said. 'Hang on.' She went upstairs and brought down Betsy, almost fully dry by now, and showed Susan the initials beneath the bloomer leg.

'That's incredible, even for Roone. How on earth could it have ended up here? We must ask the others when they arrive, find out where they got it.'

They left Betsy by the stove to finish drying and made welcome-home cards for the travellers. They played Snakes and Ladders while Poppy was having her nap. They sat on the window seat and watched raindrops racing one another down the glass. The day wore on, and as the light began to fade, Tilly thought about her imminent departure.

Her flight to London was at two in the afternoon, which meant she needed to be at the airport sometime after twelve, which meant getting the eleven o'clock ferry off the island.

She was dreading it. Although she was eager to see Ma and Pa and the others again, she hated saying goodbye to Roone and the people she'd met here, hated the thought of being so far away from them that her day would be their night.

She hated the prospect, despite her resolve to forget him, of not living next door to Andy any more. Ridiculous, when they'd met for the first time three days ago, and a handful of times since then.

Stop. No more of that. She went upstairs and had a bath and got dressed. She took the torn pieces of her boarding pass from the waste paper basket. Could she stick it together, would it be accepted? She left the pieces on the dressing table and went down to help Susan with the dinner.

At three minutes to seven precisely, as Tilly was setting the table and Susan was taking Ita Fennessy's reheated salmon quiche from the oven, they heard the front door opening – and there the others were, home from their trip.

'OK?' Laura's hug was brief; she drew back to search Tilly's face. 'Are you alright?' They stood slightly apart from the others in the hall.

'I'm OK ... I rang home last night. I told them where I was.'

'Good. I'm glad you did that. Did they hit the roof?'

'It was Ma, she wasn't too bad – and I've decided to do what you said, and report him.'

'Good for you.'

'And,' she said, 'there's something else. My boarding pass ... er, it got torn.'

'Got torn.' Laura's face unreadable. She knew though, she must know.

'Yes – I wonder if I could print another, if there's anyplace ...' She trailed off, feeling foolish.

Laura smiled. 'Finally, a problem we can easily solve. Gavin has a printer, he'll do it for you after dinner.' She drew a small box from her pocket. 'This is just a little something. A souvenir of your trip.'

Tilly opened it. She pulled out the ring and slid it onto a few fingers until she found the right fit. 'It's gorgeous, thank you. You didn't have to do that.'

'I know.'

Nobody had ever given her a ring before. She'd bought herself one with birthday money a few years ago, but lost it two weeks later.

'You'll come back to visit,' Laura said. It wasn't a question. 'Now that you know where we are. Now that you have the funds.'

'I will,' Tilly replied, hope jumping in and swimming around with the sadness.

***

'I went to see Luke,' she said.

She outlined her visit to her father, trying to make it sound like it had gone a lot more pleasantly. 'I told him about Tilly.'

'Ah,' Susan said. 'And how did he take it?'

Laura hesitated, not wishing to cast him in too poor a light to his wife. 'He … didn't seem too surprised.'

'He knew.'

'It would appear so – but he did try to make amends.' She told Susan about the cheque that had been dropped into Gladys's house later in the day, when they were at the removal.

'Yes,' Susan said thoughtfully. 'That would be him. He likes to work in mysterious ways.'

It was late, Laura wasn't sure how late. Heading for midnight, probably. They lay in Susan's bed, side by side. The light was off but the curtains were open, allowing pale light to pick out the wardrobe, the chest of drawers, the armchair. It was easy in the dimness. It was comfortable.

'He rang,' Susan said. 'This morning.'

'Who did – Luke?'

'Yes. He told me he was sorry. He says he wants to try and be a good father to our child.'

A short silence followed. Laura tried to picture him with a baby in his arms, a small child on his lap. Had he ever once held her when she was small? She had no memory of it; there were no photos of such a scene that she was aware of. And of course he'd never held Tilly. But he wanted to try now, and maybe it wasn't too late for his next child.

You're going to lose Susan, she'd told him. You're going to end up alone. You're going to die alone. Had it made a difference? She'd probably never know.

'So you'll stay with him.'

'For the moment. I'll see how it goes.'

She was giving him another chance. Maybe Laura should too. A new year looming: maybe it would bring better times for all of them.

'Gavin and I,' she said carefully, 'have been having our own difficulties.'

She heard the small sound of Susan's head shifting on the pillow to face her. 'You have. I've hated seeing it.'

Of course she'd noticed.

'We'll be OK,' Laura said.

'I know you will. It's been a tough year.'

'Sure has.'

Another silence.

'Can you believe the doll?' Susan asked.

'You know, I can. Maybe I've lived on Roone too long. But it is pretty amazing. I nearly threw it out when Gavin produced it, but something stopped me.'

'Incredible. Is Tilly going to bring it home?'

'She is. She'll probably pass it on to her little sister.'

Another silence.

'Tilly,' Laura said. Just that.

'I know,' Susan replied. Just that.

Outside, the moon slid silently across the sky as Tuesday night became Wednesday morning.

❄

WEDNESDAY
30 DECEMBER

❄

✱✱✱

Just after eight, thin fingers of light beginning to spread across the sky outside, shapes still grey and dim and fuzzy-edged. Lots of time before the ferry.

She left her room, Betsy dangling from her hand, an old newspaper from the scullery tucked under her arm. She padded in stockinged feet to the end of the corridor and turned the handle of the white door, the one with a flight of narrow uncarpeted wooden steps leading up from it. She'd opened the door the day before, thinking it to be the linen cupboard, when Susan had sent her upstairs for a clean towel. She hadn't climbed the steps then, but she figured they must lead to the attic.

The higher she went, the colder it became. At the top she found herself in a pitch-black, icy space. She hugged Betsy to her chest and felt gingerly along the rough cement wall for a light switch – and found not a switch but a cord that she tugged.

The resulting feeble glow, from a single bare bulb, did little more than cast shadows – a small window set into the sloping roof wasn't much help – but as her eyes became accustomed to the gloom she began to distinguish shapes, and to see more clearly what was around her.

Cardboard boxes of varying sizes, piled in haphazard heaps. A jumble of suitcases and rucksacks. Half a dozen plastic carrier bags slumped against one another, miniature shoes spilling from one. Tottery columns of thick books, or photo albums.

A metal tank on concrete blocks, presumably for water. A vacuum cleaner missing its hose, a huddle of plastic toys in various states of disrepair. A tall structure with protruding limbs, whose function was uncertain: a coat rack, part of a shelving unit?

The silence was immense, like the place had been wrapped in cotton wool. She remembered Andy saying he liked the peace of it. A few inches to her left was a thick wooden beam, one of several that spanned the room from floor to ceiling. She looked up and saw a network of rafters that sloped down to meet them.

As she made her way towards what looked like the most shadowy corner of the attic, she almost stumbled over something on the floor, half hidden behind one of the beams. She bent to investigate and found a little wooden doll's house with its front wall missing. No, not a doll's house, just a rectangular structure, like a single room, with a pitched roof. Inside, nestling in tissue, she found little plaster figurines of a kneeling woman, a man with a shepherd's crook, a baby in some kind of a cradle. A sheep, an angel, a donkey, a cow. Nativity figures, she realised; it was the makings of a Christmas crib. She wondered why they hadn't brought it downstairs and displayed it.

She kept going, shivering now. Moving cautiously, fearful of disturbing any creature that might be lurking. She reached the corner beam and felt in the near-darkness until she located the angle where it connected with a rafter. She bundled Betsy into the newspaper as neatly as she could and tucked the package into the angle, and wedged it in. She took a few steps back: nothing to see.

Here her old doll would stay, waiting quietly in her dark corner as the weeks and the months and the years passed by, until Tilly returned to Roone.

Leaving a doll behind: she was well aware of how foolish it would seem to anyone observing her. Leaving anything behind, as if it could possibly make a difference. But it could, it could. Betsy would be her link: she would be at the end of the thread that Tilly would unravel as she made her way over land and sea back to Australia. Betsy would be her most tangible connection to Roone.

She closed the attic door quietly behind her and returned to her room. She showered quickly and dressed, piling on the usual layers, and made her way downstairs. She took her jacket from the hallstand and wrapped Susan's red scarf around her neck. As soon as she opened the kitchen door Charlie's head popped up from his basket.

'Come on,' she whispered. 'No noise, they're all asleep' – and out he hopped, and followed her through the scullery, tail flapping.

She stood for a moment outside the back door, drawing in big breaths of the air, thinking how impossible it would be to remember the pure taste of it when she was back in Queensland and surrounded by soggy summer heat.

The day was brightening, the sky more white than grey now. Charlie trotted ahead as she walked through the yard, past the coal bunker and Gavin's collection of garden tools propped against the wall. She turned right when she reached the field, and made her way to the little orchard.

Blocks of wood, presumably from the tree that had fallen in the storm, were heaped against the low wall that surrounded the orchard. The bricks from the shed it had crushed were gone, carted by Gavin to the far side of the field. The crater it had left behind was still there; maybe they were planning to plant a new one in it.

She looked upwards at the tree closest to her – and saw what looked like a pair of pale green globes, no bigger than blueberries, clinging to the end of an otherwise bare branch. And there was another pair at the end of the neighbouring branch, and another.

And everywhere she looked, she saw more. The tree, she realised, was covered with them. She reached for the lowest branch and drew it down towards her, and peered closely.

They were apples. They were tiny apples, and there were dozens of them. The tree was growing apples in the middle of winter. In a few months, March or April maybe, they'd be ready to harvest. She walked among the other trees, examining them carefully, and found no signs of new growth on any of them. It was like one had been chosen to take over, after the first had been destroyed.

And, for some reason, it didn't strike her as odd at all.

She looked up the field towards the henhouse and saw dark smudges of hens bobbing about. No sign of a man there now, no figure of any kind. Maybe, after all, she'd imagined him. She'd been tired and overwrought, and upset by Laura's response to her arrival. Her mind might well have played a trick on her, presented her with a kindly face as a comfort.

She looked back at the house and saw all the windows, including her own, still curtained. She whistled softly for Charlie and he came haring across from the opposite side of the field. 'Come on,' she whispered, turning for the gate.

Next door was quiet too: no need for anyone to be up at this hour. She crossed the road and strode along with the sea on her left, heading away from the village. Charlie trotted ahead of her, nose almost touching the ground, stopping to cock a leg briefly on the grassy verge every few steps. After less than five minutes she reached the little lane that led to the sea. Tilly whistled again and Charlie loped back, and together they headed down the lane that widened and became sandier with each step.

And after fifty yards or so, there they were on the beach, a wide strip of sand and pebbles that stretched for what looked like half a mile to her right. She walked down to the shore, her shoes sinking into the damp sand as she neared the water's edge. She bent for a fistful of pebbles and flung them as far as she could: they made a chorus of soft splashes when they landed, causing Charlie to give a single bark before racing off across the sand.

She looked out to sea, at the great body of water stretching away from her to the horizon. She listened to the music it made, the beautiful murmuring orchestra of it. She felt like she was opening up, like everything in her was unfurling and reaching out to the sea, and being nourished by it. She thought this must be what people meant when they talked about something touching their souls.

She watched a seagull as it crossed the sky, followed its course as it swooped and climbed. She knew with certainty that one day she would live by the sea. It might not be this sea, it might be miles from here, but the time would come when she could stand on a shore again and look out to sea in precisely this way, every single day if she wanted. The thought heartened her. It lessened the loneliness she'd woken up with.

A drop of water touched her face, and another. She thought at first it was ocean spray, carried on the breeze, but it soon became apparent that it was beginning to rain. She called for Charlie and they made their way back to the house, turning in at the gate while the shower stopped as suddenly and as quietly as it had started.

She wondered, pushing open the back door, if Andy was up yet. She would have liked to say goodbye to him and the others, but she hadn't seen any of them yesterday.

'I thought you were still in bed,' Susan said. She sat by the kitchen window, cradling a mug. Charlie made straight for his water bowl and lapped loudly.

'I went down to the sea,' Tilly told her, rubbing drops from her hair with the little towel that hung on a hook by the sink. 'It started to rain. I borrowed your scarf, I hope you don't mind.'

'Not at all. It must have been chilly. Are you all packed up?'

'Pretty much.'

The kitchen clock said five past nine – had she spent that long on the beach? It hadn't felt like it. It had felt like a few minutes. She rubbed her cold hands together.

The stove was lighting. 'Now that you're here,' Susan said, 'I want to run something by you.'

Tilly plugged in the kettle. 'Yes?'

'I hope I'm not being insensitive, after what happened – but I was wondering if you would be at all interested in becoming my baby's godmother.'

Tilly turned to look at her in astonishment.

'If you'd rather not, that's perfectly fine. I thought it might be something that would appeal to you.' She paused. 'I thought you might be looking for a reason to come back.'

Laura was right. She was lovely.

'I would, I mean I am – but I have no idea what a godmother does. I'm Presbyterian and we don't have them.'

'Oh, I don't think that would matter; it certainly wouldn't to me. All you'd have to do is come to the christening – I'd like to have it here on the island – and say yes to any questions the priest asks, and that's about it.'

Lots of things hopped into Tilly's head, in no particular order.

Susan's baby was due in early June.

School closed for two weeks around the end of June.

She'd have an excuse to come back to Roone.

She'd meet her father: he'd have to be there.

It would be summer on Roone.

She'd see Andy again. In six months she'd see him again.

'I'd love it,' she said. 'Thank you so much.'

'Oh good, I'm glad. You think your parents will be alright with you coming again?'

'They will.' They would, she was sure of it. Ma and Pa had always wanted what was best for her. They'd always wanted her to be happy.

A beat passed. 'Tilly, Laura told me she'd been to see your father in Dublin. She told me about the money he gave her for you.'

'Yes.'

Susan hesitated. 'I can't explain,' she said. 'I can't make excuses for him. I didn't know a lot of things about him when we married – I think you can't know someone properly until you live with them, and we didn't live together beforehand. But I've stayed with him, and we've made a life together, and quite a lot of the time we're happy. And now we're having a child, and I'm hoping he'll be a better father this time round.'

'You think he'll mind me being godmother?'

'I think,' Susan replied, 'he has nearly six months to get used to the idea.'

Tilly wouldn't be a shock to him, like she'd been to Laura. He'd be well prepared to meet her. After her disappointment with her mother, and after all she'd heard about him, she wouldn't be expecting a momentous encounter, an emotional coming together. And who knew? Maybe they'd both be pleasantly surprised.

Maybe that was why this invitation had been issued: maybe it was Susan's way of bringing him and Tilly together. Or maybe it had nothing to do with that at all. But still, it looked like they were going to meet.

'Of course,' Susan said, 'I'll expect you to visit Ireland fairly regularly in the future. Just to keep track of your godchild.'

Tilly smiled. 'I'll see what I can do.'

❋❋❋

When she came downstairs with Poppy and the girls the clouds were parting to let the blue sky through, and Tilly and Susan were already up. While she fed Poppy on the bench Tilly filled bowls with cereal for the girls and tied dribblers around their necks and mopped up milk spills and made green tea for Laura and Susan.

'Have you met my au pair?' Laura asked Susan. 'I'll miss her when she's gone.'

'She's coming back,' Susan told her, and Laura pretended to be surprised as Susan told her about the godmother plan they'd devised the night before.

'Excellent idea,' she said, 'and yes, I think Roone is the only possible venue for the christening. You'll have holidays in June, Tilly?'

'I'll have two weeks, starting around the end.'

'Perfect. Go out to the hall and bring in the phone pad.'

Tilly did as she was told.

'Write this down,' Laura instructed, and dictated her email

address. 'Email me your bank details when you get home. And take this phone number too, and leave us yours, and your home address as well, just in case. There'll be a bit of organising to do for June.'

As Tilly was writing, there was a tap at the back door and Colette appeared. 'I came to say goodbye,' she said. 'Nell has gone to work, but she sent a few pieces of gingerbread for the journey.' She handed Tilly a tinfoil-wrapped package. 'And Andy was wondering,' she said, 'if you need a lift to the ferry.'

'Oh – um, I think Gavin …' Tilly looked at Laura – and Laura saw, in the blush that was starting to creep up her face, in the eyes that were mirror images of their father's, what she hadn't spotted up to this.

Andy.

'That would be great,' Laura said quickly. 'Gavin was going to do it, but it would suit him if he didn't have to, with the deliveries. I was going to phone for Dougie's taxi, but if Andy was free, that would be so much better.'

The vegetable deliveries could have waited a bit, nobody would have minded – but who was Laura to stand in the way of a younger, more fanciable chauffeur?

Andy, who was presumably doing his best to forget Eve. Tilly, who'd been used and abused by the man she'd fancied herself in love with.

Sounded like the perfect match to Laura.

❄❄❄

On the doorstep she took a few final photos of everyone before dropping to her knees and hugging the girls.

'I'll miss you,' she said. 'Will you remember Auntie Tilly?'

They nodded, but they wouldn't. She'd have to keep reminding them by turning up every so often.

'Really lovely to meet you,' Susan murmured, pressing her cheek to Tilly's. 'You'll be back before you know it.'

'Hope all goes well,' Tilly replied. 'I'll be waiting for news.'

Her new half-brother or -sister – and now godchild as well. She really must find out what godmothers were actually for – they must have *some* function beyond attending the child's christening. She'd bone up on it when she got home.

Gavin had said goodbye earlier. I believe we'll see you soon again, he'd said. No getting rid of you now.

I'm afraid not ... but I'll do my best to make myself useful.

Damn right you will – I'll have a list of jobs ready. C'mere, he'd said, wrapping his arms around her. Look after yourself. Bring me a boomerang next time.

He was the one who'd found Betsy. She washed up on the beach, he'd told her, just a few days before you arrived. I thought Poppy might like her, but she only has eyes for the rabbit, so we passed her on to Charlie. I can't believe she's yours.

They all thought she'd packed Betsy into her case. She let them go on thinking that.

The boys hung back behind their sisters, no doubt praying she wouldn't attempt to hug them, so she didn't.

'Write me a letter sometime,' she told them – did children write letters any more? 'Your mum has my address.'

'Don't hold your breath,' their mum told her, 'but they might surprise you.' She handed Tilly an envelope. 'This is for your folks,' she said, 'just introducing us to them, and telling them that we were delighted to meet you. It might make them feel easier about you coming back.'

Tilly smiled. 'You think of everything.'

'I do – it's one of my many talents. And this,' she said, pressing something into Tilly's hand, 'is for the trip, just in case.'

Tilly opened her hand and found a fifty-euro note. 'No, I can't take this—'

'You can and you will,' Laura told her. 'You might fall asleep and be robbed again, or miss another flight and have to wait hours for the next. If it makes you feel better, you can send it back to me when you get home.'

'I will, as soon as I get there.' She pressed Laura's hand. 'Thank you,' she said, 'for everything. I was so scared coming here.'

Laura smiled. 'We did alright, didn't we? After our shaky start.'

'We did.'

'I think we need to get going,' Andy said.

They turned. He stood by the gate, Tilly's case already loaded into the boot of his father's car. 'It's ten to,' he said.

'OK.' Tilly turned back to Laura. 'Thanks,' she whispered again. She pressed a kiss on her sister's cheek before giving a final wave to everyone and hurrying down the path.

They drove off in a flurry of goodbyes. Tilly sat back when they were out of view, determined not to cry. Resolved to enjoy these last few minutes with him.

'What route are you taking?'

'London and Singapore.'

'And when do you get home?'

'Early on New Year's Day.'

'Australian time?'

'Yes ... we're ten hours ahead right now.'

Don't talk about that. Tell me you'll miss me, tell me you want me to come back.

'I'm coming back,' she said, and he took his eyes off the road briefly to look at her.

'Yeah?'

'In June. Susan asked me—' She broke off. Maybe Susan's pregnancy wasn't official yet. 'Susan asked me to come back.'

'To Dublin?'

'No – to Roone. She'll be coming to Roone ... for part of the summer. I'll have holidays in June, two weeks.'

He made no response. It didn't matter to him: it made no difference whether she came back or not.

The pier came into view. The ferry was approaching. She regarded it miserably.

'I was thinking,' he said, 'we might keep in touch.'

His profile was impossible to read.

'Email,' he said, throwing her another quick glance. 'If you want to.'

'Sure,' she said. 'I'd like that.'

They pulled in opposite the pier. The few cars that had been brought across began to move off. Andy took out his phone.

'Tell me yours,' he said. 'I'll email you mine,' so she recited her email address and he tapped it in. 'I'll email you tonight,' he said, his eyes still on the screen. 'It'll be waiting when you get home.'

He looked up.

They exchanged smiles. Tilly's heart turned a cartwheel.

'Better make a move,' he said, and got out. He wheeled her case across the road, where a short line of cars was waiting to embark.

There was no sign of any other foot passengers. A drop fell on her uncovered head, and another: the rain was never far away in Ireland. Hopefully it was drier in the summer. Hopefully she'd be able to wear her blue linen top.

They walked down the roped-off pedestrian gangplank.

'That's Leo,' Andy said, and Tilly looked at the man who was guiding the cars into their slots. Stocky and weather-beaten, dark bushy beard that reminded her of Bernard in the pub across the water. Worn leather bag slung over his oilskin coat, navy corduroy pants tucked into wellingtons.

When the cars were all parked he walked across. 'You're Laura's sister,' he said, taking her hand. 'You're the talk of the island. And since this is your maiden voyage, it's on the house.'

He walked away as she was thanking him. She watched as he moved from car to car, taking money and issuing tickets.

'Well,' Andy said, 'I'd better be on my way.' Not going on his way, not moving. 'Not sure how this goes,' he said.

'We should probably hug,' she said, before she could think about it and decide against saying it.

He took his hands out of his pockets and they hugged as the rain fell. They were almost the same height. His hair smelt of the sea. She closed her eyes and forbade herself to cry.

They drew apart. 'Goodbye,' he said. 'Safe trip.'

'Goodbye,' she said, the feel of him still with her. She watched him retrace his steps up the gangplank. When he reached the car he looked back and waved, and she waved back, being careful to keep her smile in place. She turned then, unable to watch him driving off.

She saw a little covered structure near the far end of the ferry, presumably where foot passengers went in inclement weather, but she ignored it. She wheeled her case to the ferry's rail while the rain continued to fall. Nobody joined her, nobody got out of a car. The rail was ice-cold but she held on tightly with both hands and looked out to sea as the ramp was winched up and the ferry pulled slowly away from the pier, and she felt again the dip and roll beneath her feet as they settled into the rhythm of the water. Less obvious here than on Kieran's little boat, the ferry big and steady on its course, but still there was the feeling that she'd left solid ground behind.

She thought of Betsy, tucked away in the attic. She thought about the weeks and months ahead, when the notion of her old doll waiting for her in Ireland would occur, and make her smile. She thought of the people she'd encountered since her arrival, and the kindness she'd been shown, and the family she'd found on Roone.

She thought of Andy Baker who'd tilted her sideways, and the email that would be waiting for her when she got home, and the umpteen responses she'd type before settling on one that was fit to send back to Ireland.

She thought of the money that would soon be hers. When it arrived she'd get presents for everyone in Walter's Place, and for Nell and James and Andy and Tommy. She'd get something for Paddy and

Breda in Dingle too – she'd ring them and ask for their address. And Bernard and Cormac and Ursula in the pub, and Colette and Susan. She'd find everyone's address – she'd track them all down.

She'd write a thank-you letter to her father for the money he'd given her. It would only be polite. She'd put her address in the top corner of the envelope.

The rain fell solidly as she was carried away from Roone. She turned at last to look back at the island, at the houses and the beaches and the hills and the fields that gradually became smaller and smaller. She looked until the entire place was nothing more than a series of dark rises and falls along the horizon.

Six months, she told herself, her face wet with tears and Irish rain, her heart overflowing. Six months.

Acknowledgements

Many thanks to my editor Ciara Doorley and all at Hachette Books Ireland for seeing book number twelve safely from my head to the bookshop shelf, ably assisted along the way by copy-editor Hazel Orme and proofreader Aonghus Meaney.

Thanks also to my agent Sallyanne Sweeney at Mulcahy Associates, London, for taking care of the official stuff along the way.

Big thanks to Geraldine Exton and Cameron Wilkie for making sure I got the Australian stuff right (any blunders are mine, not theirs: they're true blue Aussies).

Lots of thanks to Sharon Noonan, Thomas Bibby, Verette O'Sullivan, Patrick Mercie, Siobhan Moloney and Rosanne Fitzgerald for providing all the other advice/encouragement/chai lattes I needed along the way, and to Noelene Hofman in Tasmania whose chance remark brought two miniature goats into being. (All will be explained.)

Sincere thanks to Mary Clerkin and all at The Tyrone Guthrie Centre at Annaghmakerrig for opening the door anytime I come knocking, and for dishing out the haute cuisine along with the uninterrupted writing time.

Most of all, thanks a million to you, dear reader, for having enough faith in me to choose this book. Whether you picked it up in a shop, found it in your local library, or swiped it from a friend's bookshelf, the fact that you're willing to read it means far more to me than the sum you spent or didn't spend on it. I do hope you enjoy it. xx

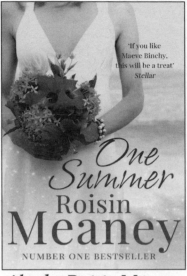

'If you like Maeve Binchy, this will be a treat'
Stellar

One Summer
Roisin
Meaney
NUMBER ONE BESTSELLER

Also by Roisin Meaney

ONE SUMMER

This summer on the island, anything is possible…

Nell Mulcahy grew up on the island – playing in the shallows and fishing with her father in his old red boat in the harbour. So when the stone cottage by the edge of the sea comes up for sale, the decision to move back from Dublin is easy. And where better to hold her upcoming wedding to Tim than on the island, surrounded by family and friends?

But when Nell decides to rent out her cottage for the summer to help finance the wedding, she sets in motion an unexpected series of events.

As deeply buried feelings rise to the surface, Nell's carefully laid plans for her wedding start to go awry and she is forced to make some tough decisions.

One thing's for sure, it's a summer on the island that nobody will ever forget.

Available now in print and ebook

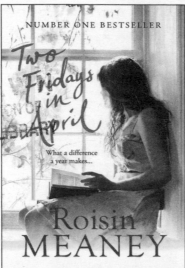

Also by Roisin Meaney

TWO FRIDAYS IN APRIL

What a difference a year makes …

It's Una Darling's seventeenth birthday, but nobody feels much like celebrating. It's been exactly a year since the tragic death of her father Finn, and the people he left behind have been doing their best to get on with things. But it hasn't been easy.

Daphne is tired of sadness, of mourning the long life she and her husband were meant to share, but doesn't quite know how to get past it. And she can't seem to get through to her stepdaughter – they barely speak any more, so Daphne knows nothing of the unexpected solace Una has found, or of the risk she's about to take.

When Una fails to appear for birthday tea with her family, Daphne suddenly realises how large the distance between them has grown. Will she be given the chance to make things right?

Available now in print and ebook